pivotal

nikki vallance

Hashtag PRESS

Published in Great Britain by Hashtag Press 2019

A CIP catalogue for this book is available from the British Library.

ISBN 978-1-9993006-7-8

Typeset in Garamond Classic 11.25/14 by Blaze Typesetting

Printed and bound in Great Britain by Clays Ltd, Elcograf S.p.A.

Hashtag PRESS

HASHTAG PRESS BOOKS
Hashtag Press Ltd
Kent, England, United Kingdom
Email: info@hashtagpress.co.uk
Website: www.hashtagpress.co.uk
Twitter: @hashtag_press

acknowledgements

So many people have helped me realise my dream of Pivotal reaching the bookshelves, I am at risk here of either missing someone out or bumbling along ad infinitum, like one of those award ceremony acceptance speeches everyone wishes would end. Even in writing this opening I've just remembered two more!

In an attempt to strike the right balance and still express my gratitude to everyone without writing a whole extra book's worth of thank yous, I have tried to group my acknowledgements into some kind of logical structure. For anyone who doesn't get an individual mention please know it is only a matter of space and that all my friends and family, and many others who have supported me throughout my life, have contributed to the successful publication of this novel.

Pivotal began as a heart-flutteringly exciting goal, to reintroduce creativity to my life. For this I thank my very brilliant and talented coach, Rachel Bamber. As a coach myself I knew I wasn't reaching my potential. Within a week, after a flash of inspiration, my goal changed from 'get more creative' to 'write a book' to 'publish a novel.' On three further occasions during the nine years it took to complete the novel, I sought out coaching support to help me find a way to prioritise my writing. Additional thanks go to Nadia Finer, Leigh Howes and Julia Bickerstaff for their ability to bring out the best in me.

Books need readers. From the beginning, I began testing my writing on friends, those who I knew were avid readers and could be trusted to give honest and constructive feedback.

Mostly I shared short stories which were competition entries. Thanks to Debs, Tricia, Stephanie, Carolyn and Melanie for taking the time to read these and comment. As early readers of my novel, I am eternally grateful to Debbie and Caroline, for your kind and generous feedback, often at short notice and on a tight deadline and to Alexia for your insight, unwavering encouragement over the years and input from the outset. Pivotal is all the richer for your involvement.

Writers need writers. Once I had tentatively given myself permission to call myself a writer, I realised I knew nothing about the publishing process or how to finish my book. I sought out other writers through my network, at author events and festivals. Their advice and support have been invaluable. Thanks in particular to Marisa Garreffa, Toula Mavridou-Messer, Jenny Ford, David Jenkins, Becky Alexander, Phoebe Morgan and Kathryn Hitchins for sharing their knowledge and experience with me and to Winnie M Li, Ruth Hogan and Freya North for articulating their writing lives in such a relatable way. You helped me feel like a proper writer. A special thanks to RM Fernfield, my writing buddy, who kept me accountable in the latter stages to complete my first draft. A posthumous thank you to Daphne Du Maurier for writing such compelling stories and to Mary Wesley for her brilliant novels, full of guts, individuality and the use of one perfect word where others would use ten.

Being a late adopter of social media and having resisted it for years, I would never have realised it would enable me to feel part of so many communities. Thank you to all my friends, both on and off-line for supporting me through my challenges and helping to celebrate my successes. To Barrie

Johnston, Helen and my other Fluxus friends for keeping me fit and sane. To Julia and the 100daygoalers for providing, structure, inspiration and support from first draft to published book and to Sarah and the Warrior Mums for always being there. To all my writer friends in the Bloomsbury Writers and to Margie, Anita, Karen, Jo and Gill from the Writers' Pod for your support and encouragement. Thank you lovely Liz for introducing me to the real Dulcie Braybrooke at your wedding and to Dulcie for letting me use your name for your purely fictitious alter-ego.

Keeping the plates of parenthood spinning, whilst running my coaching business, looking after my own wellbeing and generally just living life, has at times been enough of a challenge before throwing my writing into the mix. I feel extremely fortunate to have such a wonderful support network to share in the ups and downs along the way. Adam, Kylie, Maggie & Mike, Dave & Sue, Abby, Holly, Jess, Debbie & Andrew, Steve & Trish, Deepak & Sushmita, Steve & Sharon I'll be forever grateful.

During the research phase of the book I was lucky enough to learn from experts in various professions/locations, who helped me scatter facts amongst the fiction. Thank you to: the staff at Gloucester Cathedral, the Tourist Information Centre, the Painswick Rococo Garden and various other cafés and bars for lending me your local knowledge. To Ben Stewart for being my initial Sydney location consultant. To my friend, actress Jane Stanton for infecting me with her love of Tango, to Kim and David Benitez at Tango Movement in London for our private lesson and to Gwen at Gwen Hallam Dance for reigniting my passion for ballet, the bedrock of all dance discipline. A special thanks goes to several hypnotherapists. To Ayse Banbridge for the opportunity to experience hypnotherapy for myself. To Ursula James as inspiration for the central character of Dr Kath O'Hannon, and for putting me in touch with Juli Arthurs; thank you for your generosity in answering my many questions.

Converting a manuscript into a published book requires a lot of determination, professional input and a talented team behind you. Thank you to: Juliet Mushens, Kate Barker, Tanera Simons and Juliet Pickering, agents who gave me great advice at events and one-to-ones. To Joe, Aki and Pippa at TLC for your frank and constructive feedback. To Anna Ganley from the Society of Authors, whose path crosses mine at regular intervals, for your kind and insightful signposting. To Sarah Stiffin my online tech guru. To Helen and the team at Literally PR for your expertise and professionalism. To my amazing editor, Anna Hoggarty for seeing Pivotal for what it could become and helping me get it there. To Helen Braid for a fabulous cover, the whole team at Hashtag Press for turning out a book we can all be proud of and especially to Abiola and Helen for believing in me and in Pivotal, almost from the moment we first met.

Pivotal asks the question: Do we have power over who we become based on the decisions we make? I truly believe we do, and that people can overcome challenges and strive to be the best versions of themselves. But it is also true that the way you learn to respond to opportunities as they arise and the love and support of those around you can make all the difference. In this, I am blessed with the most wonderful family. An army of fans spread around the world, from France to

Australia, Gibraltar to the UK, thank you all for your faith and patience!

I feel blessed to be surrounded by the most generous, loving and supportive family, who had absolute belief in me and my ability to finish the book, even when I doubted it myself. To Bernard and Janine for being the best brother and sister. To Hayley, Liam and Lachie for your love and acceptance. To Cameron for inspiring me every day with your strength and determination. To Jasmine for being so kind and caring, with wisdom beyond your years. To Mum and Dad, for everything you do, everything you are and for teaching me that anything is possible. To each of you, one sentence is not enough to express my gratitude and love for you. And finally, to Alan, my husband, my superfan. Thank you for sharing your life with me. Then. Now. Always.

To Mum and Dad, for everything.

Tis strange how the heart can create
Or colour from itself its fate,
We make ourselves our own distress,
We are ourselves our happiness.

- LETITIA ELIZABETH LANDON -
The Troubadour (1825) Title poem, Canto IV.

prologue

He put down the pen, an anniversary present from his second love. The letter finished, finally, except for the valediction. This, the last letter he would write, had been the hardest. He had chosen to write it by hand, despite the weakness he felt throughout his body. It had needed to be personal and the word-processed version just wouldn't do. Besides, he'd always preferred the flourish of pen and ink.

Strong and steady, the words had flowed, emotion lifting him from his weary state and choreographing his thoughts into perfect phrases. From heart to hand.

In life he had kept his promise and never told but now he dithered. *How should I leave it? She'll be reeling by the last paragraph. How can I tell her she means everything to me and yet we'll never meet? How can I bring everything she's ever known into question and still claim to have her best interests at heart? If I had known. If only I had known before.*

He shook his head, pushing the pointless debate away. This letter was his chance. His one chance to convey his heart-wrenching, all-consuming, unconditional love for a daughter, whose life he would not, could not share. He picked up the pen again and wrote his last words.

Your ever-loving Papa

part one

the letter

July 2007

Dulcie

Dulcie waited for her harbour-side exhibition to open. Dwarfed by one of the gallery's pillars, she sneaked a peek outside. Set against the backdrop of the Opera House across the water, considerable numbers had already gathered, with others flocking to join the queue. Who would have thought her pottery would have drawn such a crowd? She might even make some money this time.

Help pay for the London trip at least, she thought.

A fun trip tagged on the beginning of another she felt obliged to make. She hadn't been back home for many years. She didn't have the funds or desire to return to England.

The letter, half hanging out of their rusty mailbox ten days ago, had changed everything. Bruce Anderson, her agent, flounced into her personal space.

"There you are Dulcie darling. You're looking stunning this evening and I love your new hair! It is so important to make the right impression. Are you feeling nervous? Have you had a glass of bubbles yet? And where is Peter? He really should be by your side you know–men, eh?" He flicked his fringe and placed a hand on his hip to punctuate his point.

"Oh, shush Bruce. I just want to breathe in the atmosphere

before everything gets too frenetic." Dulcie scraped her fingers through her hair, repeatedly failing to tuck it behind her ears. "Have you seen the queue? All those people are here for me?"

"Honestly, you shouldn't be flying solo. Poor darling. Don't worry. I'm here and I'll look after you," he said, putting a protective arm around her shoulders. "Stick with me. I'll make sure you meet only the right people. It's not the quantity, it's the quality, you know. Mind you, I have clearly done rather well on the PR, haven't I?" Bruce tweaked his cravat in that self-congratulatory way, his theatrics reminiscent of a certain Mr Hardy.

Dulcie laughed and allowed him to steer her away to fetch her first glass of Yarra Burn. He was in his element. She really wasn't too fussed about the showy side of the art world. She had never been seeking success. In fact, her drive to create was much more deeply embedded than any ambition for materiality. Her modest income from her ceramics was a bonus. It was a basic need to feed her soul that made her rise at five a.m. most mornings, when the world around her was still and peaceful.

As for Bruce's red and black theme, she wasn't convinced. A smart, black, fitted suit, with a kick-pleated pencil skirt and a red, silk blouse may fit the part, but she was far more at home in scruffy jeans and a T-shirt. But the hair! What was she thinking? A blonde bob? Her big hair had been her trademark since the Eighties. Halfway down her back, frizzy and unkempt, it had suited her round face and rounder figure. Squeezed into the suit with support underwear galore, she could pass for a voluptuous size sixteen, but an uncomfortable one at that.

Elizabeth

All dressed down and nowhere to go, Elizabeth stood in front of the grand fireplace staring at herself in the mirror. Nina Simone's 'The Other Woman' played through her Bose speakers on the integrated entertainment system she had bought herself for a birthday present last year, when she was feeling particularly extravagant.

It was the last piece of the jigsaw in her renovation of the Grade II listed Chelsea townhouse. The whole project had been completed in record time with very few hitches, thanks, mostly, to her superb architect and project manager, Morgan Carter. Her instruction to 'spend what it takes' had no doubt sealed the success of the project.

A smug reflection stared back at her tanned, elegant form, draped in La Perla black silk, edged in turquoise lace. Her smugness increased as she noted the curve of her left breast. It had been partially revealed, as the robe had inched open, when she had bent to admire the fresh pink lilies delivered this and every Saturday morning. The blooms, expertly arranged by her housekeeper Idita, were her consolation; Nina Simone's song was her anthem.

The lyrics perfectly portrayed her life. Snatched moments

of pure passion and delicious intimacy followed by days, sometimes weeks, of a landscape barren of emotion.

Snap out of it she told herself. *You chose this. How else could you have thrown yourself wholeheartedly into your career and made such a success of it?*

The track permeated her consciousness. True it was melancholic, but she loved to revel in being single. Something she certainly wouldn't be doing if she were Andrew's wife.

There was no time to be self-pitying. Elizabeth inhaled the floral scent, wafted by the swish of her robe, as she turned to survey the rest of Idita's handiwork. Yes, the room was ready for her visitor. She couldn't remember the last time her stomach had fluttered so with excitement. Andrew had been to the flat before but never on a Saturday evening and never to stay for the whole night.

Maybe this is a sign he might be ready to devote himself to me? Finally.

She clicked through the impressive hallway, a showcase for her exquisite taste in fine arts and antiques, into the kitchen. Another triumph! The sleek cherry wood in contrast with the pale flagstones and the aqua cracked-glaze work surfaces.

The Winterhalder and Hofmeier bracket clock showed a quarter to eight. Time to put the goat's cheese and caramelised onion tartlets into the oven. Funny, unaccustomed as she was to cooking in her flawless kitchen, this morning's preparations for dinner had been surprisingly enjoyable. It was such a long time since she had done anything more than heat up Idita's pre-prepared food, she had forgotten how therapeutic culinary creation could be. It helped that for several years her room-for-one vacations had been Italian cookery courses on the Amalfi coast. Exorbitant in price but definitely worth the expenditure, if only to distract her from the long, lonely days of summer whilst Andrew was away with his wife and brats in their St Tropez villa.

Enough! Time to focus on herself again and the finishing touches.

As she drifted through the hallway to her bedroom suite, the opened envelope on the console table caught her eye–an invitation for the August bank holiday weekend. An RSVP was requested, something she had yet to attend to. No decision needed to be made. She'd be there. No need to check the diary as there was rarely anything in it except work.

Standing in front of the dressing-room mirrors, she admired her reflection once again. Was she narcissistic? Who cared? Why shouldn't she celebrate the toned and sensuous body she had perfected over the years through sheer determination? Recognising early on that a curvy size ten was not her natural state, Elizabeth had invested in her health and fitness with the same drive and discipline she'd applied to her career–failure was never an option!

Liza

"Oi luv, get me a drink, would ya? A fella could die of thirst in 'ere. 'Specially with such a hot show, if ya know wha' I mean, eh?"

Liza briefly raised her eyes to the ceiling before leaving them in a steady gaze directly in his. Leaning forward to give him a clear view of her cleavage, her words spoke what her grey-blue eyes had already told him; if he had been capable of reading them.

"Oi mate. I'm not your love, nor am I your hostess. Ask that leggy blonde tart over there."

She knew she could get into trouble for displaying her belligerence, so she shifted her expression from distain to feigned desire, instantly confusing the punter. Her words stayed in the air as she pivoted on her patent, black, peep-toe shoes.

With an almost imperceptible sway of her hips, she enticed his attention right back down to her faux-leather-clad curves. She leaned forward, pretending to adjust her hold-ups, just to make doubly sure he forgot the sting in her response.

The balding, sweaty banker, straining his blue pinstriped shirt from years of overindulgent business lunches, sat open mouthed and displayed a definite stirring in his crotch.

Across the dingy club, Gino surveyed the exchange through his scotch. Not quite sure of what had taken place, he would check with Liza later. She always told him the truth, eventually. As she wove through the cramped tables, he congratulated himself once again, on ensnaring such an agile and sexy dancer.

"It's an investment," he had told himself when he had set up his eponymous lap joint–Gino's Girls.

There had been loads of wannabies and has-beens floating around the scene but most of the skilful dancers were taken, locked into more notorious establishments; their managers having far more than a mere financial interest in the juiciest talent in their clubs.

Liza had been working at Stringfellows at the time, regularly making twenty to thirty percent more than any of the other girls. He had been content to have won his prize. She was the most sought-after dancer in the trade. Sure, she had been sexy, cute and well-preserved for a thirty three year old but, to Gino, her most attractive feature was the prospective pound signs he could see on her forehead. She certainly stood out. Men were round her like bees to a honey pot, and her face had that look of a naughty secret, which made you feel compelled to discover it.

Her feistiness was the only issue. He soon had that quashed; made sure she knew her place. He had reeled her in, wooing her, lavishing her with gifts and flowers, treating her to his full attention. He had known it would be tough persuading her to leave the security she had, but once his mind was set, he always got what he wanted and he had wanted her.

Finally, shuffling her left cheek onto the purple leather and chrome stool beside him, Liza caressed his thigh, just the way he liked it.

"Baby, would you get me a *Virgin* please?" she asked in her best Marilyn.

They sniggered at their in-joke. Any barman worth his shaker would immediately mix a tomato juice with Worcester sauce and a dash of Tabasco to make a Virgin Mary. This was Liza's favoured drink ever since he had known her. Funny. Most of his other dancers got through their evenings on several glasses of something more potent. Liza didn't drink alcohol at all. He still needed to fathom that one out, after all these years. He'd get to the bottom of it one day.

Liza's stock reply to anyone who asked was, "My choice of drink reflects me–passionate, full blooded and tasty, with a fiery kick, which comes out of nowhere. Oh, and a virgin, of course!"

She downed her glass and slid off the stool. "I'm going to make a move babe. I've got to get out of this stinking costume and take a shower."

"Mmm." He leant in close, sniffing her, pupils dilating. "I'd like to watch that."

Saliva pooled under her tongue. She swallowed as surreptitiously as she could, willing herself to say the right thing. "Aw, do you mind if I take a rain check? I'm really knackered and Angelo has his hospital appointment tomorrow morning."

He removed her hand with his thumb and forefinger and dropped it as if it were a snotty tissue.

"Sure. You can go. This time. But you owe me, yes?" Gino said. He did not expect an answer.

*

The entrance hall to the flat was dark and depressing, what with the ceiling lamp broken and the street light outside obscured by an unkempt laurel bush. It had been originally planted with good intentions by the landlord to hide the wheelie bins.

Liza nearly missed the blue envelope, propped on the veneered sideboard. It pretended to be a stylish piece of furniture and failed miserably, due to the water stains left by the vases of yesteryear and the claw marks from the downstairs neighbour's cats.

Negotiating her way round the bicycles propped against the banister, desperately trying not to snag her stockings on the pedals, she leant to retrieve it along with her other post. The Gloucester postmark fleetingly registered in her mind, before the local church clock chimed the quarter hour, jolting her back to reality.

Climbing the communal staircase as quietly as she could, Liza eased open the front door to the flat.

"Hello," she whispered.

Silence.

Her friend, who'd been babysitting, had fallen asleep on the sofa in the lounge. Liza tiptoed to her son's bedroom. He was out, *sparko*. Her heart welled with pride and unconditional love. His handsome face peaceful and his dark eyelashes resting against his pale skin. She closed his door, resolving, for the umpteenth time, that he would have everything he needed in life, whether or not she had to compromise to give it to him.

At 3.30 a.m. there was little movement in the street outside. Liza watched as the odd car passed, whilst she made a large mug of tea. One of the neon lamps flickered annoyingly, as the drizzle started to fall. In less than three hours she would be getting Angelo's breakfast ready. She really ought to sleep. Like many other nights, for as long as she could remember, sleep would elude her.

Quietly, she undressed, dropping her clothes to the floor, and crossed the landing to the small pink and grey bathroom. She let the shower wash away her sweat, sex and the voyeuristic eyes and hands of the punters, whose virtual groping touched her far deeper than skin on skin.

Her long, wavy hair wrapped in a towel, she moisturised her body, taking care to mind the bruises. Amazingly, Gino knew exactly how to avoid places that would show in the skimpiest of outfits.

Dressing in faded skinny jeans and a baby-pink roll-neck jumper, she sat cross legged in the threadbare, chintzy armchair in the corner of her bedroom.

I guess I've made my bed and ought to lie in it. What else can I do?

Cradling the remains of her lukewarm tea, Liza stayed in the chair and waited for the day to begin.

Annie

Annie drove the last leg of their return journey into the sunset of a beautiful August evening. Despite the weariness of a long-distance traveller, she harnessed the last rays of holiday contentment. Provence had been wonderful, the miles back up through France worth every, "Are we nearly there yet?" and "Why can't we listen to *my* music now? It's not fair!"

Thankfully, Thomas had been sleeping since Dover and Beth had given her approval to the final cassette of *The Witches*, having dismissed it north of Paris as, "Way too babyish."

When Simon Callow narrated the final sentence, Annie gave a sorrowful sigh. "Such a good story and so well read," she said, expecting a response. "Beth? Colin?"

Nothing. Everyone had nodded off. Not even her husband had been able to keep his eyes open.

A few more miles of country lanes and they would arrive in Swallows Green, back to their home nestling in the Hertfordshire/Bedfordshire borders. Whenever she approached the terrace of chocolate-box cottages, just beyond the converted school house the property developers had fought over, she had to pinch herself and remember to be grateful that Clematis Cottage, with its smart red door, was theirs.

As she pulled onto the gravel–the front garden sadly ousted to provide off-road parking by the previous owners–the crunching tyres caused her family to stir from their slumbers. Colin stretched and yawned, before sleepily unbuckling and lifting Thomas from the back seat.

Annie delved into her bottomless pit of a handbag, searching for the house keys on their separate keyring. Turning the key with one hand and pushing hard on the door with the other–necessary for successful entry due to the age of the house–a recognisable, stale, musty air reached her nostrils.

As with every return from holiday, she wondered whether the smells were always there and only noticed by visitors unaccustomed to the house and its foibles. This time though, something else also lingered in the air. Something Annie sensed but couldn't quite identify; a flat grey fug threatening to dampen her mood.

Maybe the sensation in the pit of her stomach was the stirrings of excitement at being home and not the precursor to an anxiety attack. At the end of term she'd experienced a few moments when waves of panic had swelled to within an inch of her collarbone. She had hoped it would dissipate but maybe it was back.

She made a date with herself to investigate getting some support and dismissed the sensation with her usual practicality. Many tasks lay between now and the day she'd welcome thirty new children into her classroom.

Colin squeezed past, manoeuvring his dozy toddler onto the futon in the snug. "Bless," he whispered as he passed Annie again. "Poor little fella's out for the count. Best let him sleep, eh? Leaves you free to do your thing."

Colin thought he was helping and it suited Annie to let him continue to believe it. Part of her wanted to snap at him and ask which of the post holiday tasks did he think were his responsibility. She didn't have the energy.

Piles of post and free newspapers lay on the bottom stair. Jenny, the next door neighbour at number twenty-eight, had kindly agreed to feed the chickens and water the garden whilst they were away. Evidently, she'd also gathered the two weeks' worth of correspondence.

Annie bent to bundle everything into her arms before plonking it on the kitchen table without a second glance. Her first job was to unlock the back door and fling open the windows to let the summer evening into the room.

Scents of hot, dry grass mingled with the honeysuckle that clambered wildly over the back porch. She could faintly make out the village clock chiming the half hour underneath several lawnmowers competing for prominence; a male-voice choir with too many aspiring soloists and no cohesion. Her second, but no less important, task was to filter the water, for that first, mandatory cup of tea.

"Mum, can I knock next door for Jules?" Beth asked, barely audible over the hissing of the kettle.

"No darling, I need you to help unload the car. Maybe you can pop round tomorrow morning instead?"

She had really wanted to bark at her daughter, "Don't be so selfish," but caught herself just in time.

Beth didn't need to say anything. Her body language alone answered Annie's question. Assuming the obligatory, "Oh you are so unfair!" slouch, she reluctantly stomped her way back to the car, her grumpy face hidden by the open tailgate. She was only eight! What was it going to be like when the hormones kicked in? Annie would need to remember to bite her tongue or count to ten in future or else they'd be bound to clash soon.

Colin continued to empty the boot with enthusiasm, somehow missing his daughter's strop. Annie marvelled at his ability to single-task; she wished she had the same luxury, as she sorted the dirty washing into piles, finished making the tea and worked her way through the stack of mail. She cursed the day her mother had taught her to be super-organised, encouraging amongst many things, her obsessions for neatly-folded towels in the airing cupboard and a strict shoe-polishing regime on a Friday night. Whether it was learnt behaviour or a natural talent, today being super-organised felt more noose than blessing.

It was some hours before she turned her attention again to the solicitor's letter and its contents. She racked her brains to understand what it all meant. Itching to contact her family to know if they too had received a similar blue envelope, she turned it over to look for any further clues. The franking stamp showed a posting date a few days before they had left for France.

She was glad it had been delayed in the post. She suspected it would have played on her mind for the whole holiday if she had known about it before they had left.

Most peculiar was the fact it had been sent to her maiden name. She would have to wait and wonder for the rest of the month, whilst keeping it to herself. Not easy, knowing her next and final task before bed was to call her mother to update her on the holiday news. Annie was rubbish at keeping secrets; from her mother most of all.

Elizabeth

Having spent the rest of the afternoon preparing herself with the same care as she had the three-course meal, Elizabeth waited the short minutes after pressing the intercom, to release the imposing, glossy front doors. She could hear him walking to the penthouse.

Tingling, she held her breath, unable to quite believe she was about to receive her lover for the night. It was bizarre. She had fantasised about this moment many times over the last four years, but this was so much more intoxicating than she had pictured. Closing her eyes, hugging her pillow to her body, imagining him close and gently cradling her face in his hands.

She met Andrew's eyes, coquettish, through her smooth bob. His presence filled the hallway as he stepped through the door and leant back against it gently. It closed with a satisfying clunk of solidity.

Elizabeth looked stunning. Elegantly draped in a red jersey dress cut to flatter all the right places. He immediately visualised the body beneath. How could she be wearing anything else? The dress fitted her like a second skin. Longing to pull her to him to explore, but also wanting to prolong the speculation, he focused on her face. She was radiant, her eyes warm and expressive, her red lips parted, invitingly.

"I hope you're hungry?" she asked.

"Well, something smells delicious!"

Deliberately, Andrew avoided the double meaning in her question and parried it with a double meaning of his own. Giggling, she took his hand and led him through to the lounge.

This girl had style! He had been captivated on his fleeting visits to the flat during its renovation, but the finished article blew him away. The seductive touches were not lost on him either: sandalwood-scented candles; gentle jazz standards at just the perfect volume; the Billecart-Salmon Rosé on ice, its distinctive coral label reflecting in the silver Champagne cooler. His senses were assaulted from every direction, none more so than by the vision of loveliness standing in front of him.

"Actually, I'm ravenous my gorgeous darling. Please tell me you're on the menu for dessert?"

"We'll have to see. That depends on how good you are, doesn't it?"

"Oh, I'm good. I'm always good but you know that. I'm an angel." His choir-boy impression always raised a smile on her lips.

"Come on, let's eat," she said.

Andrew trailed his hand around her waist and traced the curve of her hip, whilst she swished past him, with the same confident authority as her command. Quite how he was meant to keep his hands off her and partake of a feast he wasn't sure. He dutifully followed her to the dining table, laden with stylish modern cutlery and understatedly expensive cut glass crystal.

*

"You are one talented woman," Andrew said, as he savoured the last spoonful of the *Cœur à la Crème* with raspberry coulis, which had flirted with his taste buds for the last fifteen minutes of the meal. "What on earth are you doing recruiting arrogant, ungrateful traders, when you could be creating such orgasmic food? Think of the pleasure you'd be giving us poor, lowly peasants, who can only manage to heat up a ready meal in the microwave or scramble eggs with freshly chopped parsley and be self-satisfied with our meagre achievements?"

Accustomed to receiving praise from her clients, candidates and work colleagues, not to mention her personal trainer, hairdresser, beautician and image stylist, all of whom constantly fawned over her with over enthusiastic compliments, Elizabeth let the corners of her mouth lift into a gracious acknowledgement of Andrew's words.

She wasn't so comfortable with the exhilaration his comments had caused, seemingly reaching every nerve ending and whooshing back to her heart and groin. Whatever the sensation was, she knew it was dangerous and ought to be kept firmly at bay. Though she desperately wanted to let go, her head always calculated the risk in doing so. She had learnt the hard way that self-preservation was only possible if she ring-fenced her emotions from intruders.

Admittedly, there were times with Andrew when she wanted to give him the key code and password to that precious isolated part of her. Her instinct told her, far from leading to an ecstatic existence, it would take her down to a very difficult place. Elizabeth knew she ought not go there, not even for Andrew.

"My darling, it makes me happier than words can say to know you appreciate my cooking," she said, chuckling to herself. "Do you know, I thoroughly enjoyed myself today? Popping out to the local deli to buy cheese; choosing the best organic meat from the butchers recommended by my neighbour, who, by the way, is *very* charming and almost swept me off my feet with his sexy French accent. I had no idea I lived next door to such an attractive and attentive diplomat."

Elizabeth successfully managed to portray what easily passed for effortless sparkle and Andrew was entranced, hanging on her every word, drinking in every fluid movement of her body, as she transferred the used crockery to the kitchen.

He matched her mood, their conversation dancing round the flat, bouncing and dipping and weaving, as naturally as swallows courting in the warm air of spring. Neither wanted to break the spell for fear that the wildly anticipated night of passion might disappoint, after such a wonderfully intimate evening.

Andrew followed Elizabeth into the kitchen carrying two newly-refilled flutes from the second bottle of *Billy* champagne–a favourite they had discovered together attending a wine tasting at the Park Lane hotel several years before.

"Oh, I was just putting the coffee on. You could have stayed comfortable where you were," she said.

"No, I couldn't. I'm here tonight to be with you. Why on earth would I want to sit and contemplate the world on my own? Let me propose a toast," he said, lifting his glass. "Here's to a delicious meal, a triumphant renovation and my glorious lover, for whom my passion never dies. It's almost five years since you seduced me and I've never gotten over it!"

Andrew's generous gushings turned into shallow sentences through her filter of self-doubt and cynicism. He was endearing though, when drunk and unguarded, perhaps she should at least try to believe he was being genuine.

"I seduced you?" Elizabeth raised her eyebrows. "I think you'll find it was the other way round, you big flirt!"

Lifted again now and floating through on a haze of Champagne, she let down her defences and led Andrew back to the lounge. She fancied something cheesy and romantic to listen to and selected Chris de Burgh's 'Into the Light', immediately evoking an atmosphere of the Eighties and the social bubble they had both once been part of.

"I wish we'd been an item then," she whispered, swaying to the apt lyrics of 'The Lady in Red'. "Maybe things would've been different."

She nursed her brandy, poured by the oh-so-considerate Andrew, who seemed to know what she wanted without asking, and closed her eyes.

Either a lifetime, or fleetingly later, she couldn't tell which, he enveloped her in his arms. His body moulding into her back and synchronising with her sway. Opening her eyes, she just made out their shadowy image in the mirror above the fireplace. She wasn't sure why she had been anxious. The metre of distance between them at the table had kept her wary. He had been far enough away to allow her control. Now, she was lost.

The diminished space melted her resolve like a bowl of quality ice cream cupped in warm hands. Slowly, everything but the sensuousness of the moment became irrelevant. Their usual frantic fumbling, driven by pent-up desire and practical time constraints, was replaced by languid, sensitive touch and a heightened awareness of each other's needs. With complete security, she knew for the next few hours, before they succumbed to a post-alcohol, post-coital slumber, Andrew was hers and she was part of an *Us*.

Dulcie

Bruce was never far from Dulcie's side, helping her to work the gallery's split-level rooms separated by chrome, glass and opaque white Perspex partitioning. Expertly placed spots reflected light off the many surfaces giving the space an almost jewel-like quality.

The cleverest lighting displayed her voluptuous vases to perfection, luring the observer towards them, sirens to the sailor, captivating and deadly—no price too great once the heart was won. Large heavy plates with bold Aboriginal colours were grouped aesthetically, suspended vertically against the Perspex, as if floating above one another, solid yet vulnerable.

After three hours, politely networking with media, TV stars and countless others asking the same questions about inspiration for her designs, future projects in development, and the odd requests for commissions, Dulcie was ready to escape.

She could see Peter with James and Mikey, their two eldest children, hovering by the door to the kitchen, commandeering the trays of pricey canapés whilst checking out the young waitresses. They seemed to be having great fun and she loved sharing her new world with them.

Secretly though, she'd prefer to be back in her workshop on the small-holding, overalls and hands splattered after an early-morning session, being summoned by James hollering from the back porch. He was a great kid, well, man now she supposed. *Twenty years old! Where did all the time go?*

Bruce touched her elbow gently. "You okay? Looks like you're flagging a little. Shall I get you another glass of bubbles to pep you up?"

"No thanks. I'm done in I think. I was heading for Peter and the boys when you caught me. Would it be terribly poor launch-party etiquette if I were to sneak off home?"

"No worries. Most guests will start drifting away soon anyway, now we're down to the final hour. I can be the face of Dulcie Braybrooke for you darling. Actually, it's a very good idea to make a move earlier, leave your adoring fans wanting more!" He stopped and took her hands in his. "You should be proud. There's a real buzz in the air. Honestly, I heard mention of comparisons with Claris Cliff several times over!"

"Now, you're just teasing me. Don't be unkind!" Dulcie, unaccustomed to playing the lead, felt as if she had had an amazing first night but wasn't entirely sure whether she could replicate the performance.

"Your trick now is to disappear for a while. Use your overseas trip to get everyone speculating about what's coming next. Be a bit of a diva, darling. I know I would if I had half your talent!"

"Aren't we forgetting that elevation to the status of diva requires me to at least make some committed sales?"

"True. I suppose I was getting a little carried away by my

own spin, if I do say it myself!" Bruce's bravado almost masked the creeping question marks of his self-doubt.

"Oh, don't get all needy on me now. It's your job to look after *me* you know. You did promise you would earlier remember?"

The warmth in Dulcie's voice and softness of her touch reassured him everything would come good and that his instincts to go big, bright and brash for the launch, with a New York loft theme, were right on the money.

Bruce nodded towards a large vase nearby. "Talking of sales, I've marked up the under-offer pieces with some sparkly stickers. No harm in encouraging a little healthy competition."

"Uh-huh. Look, there's Peter signalling to me now. We will try and sneak away and have our own little celebration with all four kids together. Ben's babysitting Libby at home and I promised we'd let them know how things had gone."

"Ben. Now there's your budding protégé, showing some real artistic talent." He winked and added, "Dreamer too, just like his mum, eh?"

"They were so disappointed not to be able to be here. Especially Libby. I do believe she is the most precocious seven year old I have ever known! I pity Ben. She's more than likely been babysitting him!"

Bruce laughed in acknowledgement of Dulcie's description of her youngest child and only daughter. "Ah, she's a sweetie really!"

His words trailed behind her as she snaked through the room, trying to avoid eye contact with anyone other than Peter, who waited patiently by the banana palm. It had been strategically placed beside the entrance to partially obscure the view into the gallery, creating an air of intrigue for visitors.

"Darling, you look wrecked." Peter reached out, pulling her in for a hug. "I'm really sorry I was late. One of our land deals started to look a little rocky right before close. Luckily, we managed to smooth things over and it looks like it will finalise tomorrow."

Funny, how that term of endearment could sound so special when uttered by someone close, Dulcie thought. *They were good now, weren't they? That sodding business.*

"Take us home to the babes, Pete." Dulcie linked her arm through his. "I can't wait for all six of us to celebrate together."

"Ah," Peter said, tipping his head towards the boys who were still chatting up the waitresses. "Dragging the boys home before midnight might be tricky. Not sure they're ready to leave quite yet. I could get you a taxi if you want to go now. I can stay and keep an eye on them and hold the fort with Bruce. It looks like there's loads of interest in your work and we should pump it for all it's worth."

"Well, if you're sure?" Dulcie unlinked her arm and exaggerated her smile at Peter's suggestion of separate departures.

She had hoped the journey would be a chance for them to bond a bit. They'd spent so little time together recently; she wasn't sure if they were on the same wavelength and suspected their taxi chat would have been superficial and banal. Admittedly, if she went home alone her mind and body would be hers, free to wander through her library of fantasies built up over many years.

With reluctance and uncertainty at the consequences of

these thoughts, Dulcie agreed Peter should stay on with the boys, whilst she returned to their home on the outskirts of the city.

*

There was still plenty of life in the evening for many. The bright lights of the bars and clubs bounced off the taxi's windows and shone like spotlights into the rare puddles of Sydney's late-July streets. The traffic swooshed through the standing water, a noise reminiscent of her other favourite city. In fact, you could almost define London by that sound.

Dulcie was reminded again of her impending trip, less than a month away. She was a little suspicious of the unusual invitation to her home town of Gloucester. It was odd, a meeting of that nature being called for a weekend, especially a bank holiday in the UK.

The blue letter had explained the arrangements had been made, to some degree, on her behalf, due to her living in the southern hemisphere; they allowed her 'to travel comfortably and arrive punctually.' This seemed to be of the utmost importance.

Whilst the invitation was intriguing and piqued her interest, she couldn't think of a reason for her presence to be required. Instead it had planted a kernel of an idea, which now seemed to have grown like Sleeping Beauty's hundred-year hedge and enveloped the genuine and original purpose for a trip to England. Either way, the travel arrangements were set. Departure on 14th August 2007, direct from Sydney, Mascot to London, Heathrow and she would arrive the following day. This gave her almost two clear weeks to rediscover London, familiar to her from twenty years ago yet, no doubt, much changed.

The taxi pulled up to the solid wooden gates at the end of a modest track. Most of their neighbours in the town had opted for ostentatious driveways with formal planting and Hollywood-style security gates. Dulcie and Peter's only concession to modernity outside was the accent lighting, serving to demarcate the route to the house, whilst highlighting several abstract garden sculptures, expertly placed to draw the eye away from the unkempt outbuildings.

Dismissing the taxi-driver's offer to deliver her direct to her door, she settled the fare and took the shorter, terraced footpath in her bare feet. Gel inserts can help but for someone more inclined to pad around in flats, one hour of heels would have crippled, let alone the five hours she had just endured.

She stepped though the fly-screen porch door, with faded and flaking federation-yellow paint, as inviting to her as if it had been sleek and glossy, into their chaotic home. The house was asleep. Simultaneously placing her shoes near the mat and shrugging off her jacket, she submerged herself in the serenity. They could celebrate tomorrow.

Deciding not to disturb her babies, she carefully tiptoed around the pile of shoes, runners, and other footwear she had just added to and up the open-tread pine staircase. Truth be told they weren't babies any more, but her maternal instincts would transcend any attempts for her children to fly the nest. No matter that the growing pains had already started.

Creeping past their bedrooms, Dulcie sighed. At least her younger two had a few years to go before they stopped calling her Mummy or started whining to stay out later.

Still a little bewildered by all the attention, she sought solace in the haven of her bedroom. Throwing off the remains of her new public image, she grabbed her comfy pyjamas and fluffy Egyptian cotton towel, tension dropping away at the thought of a much-anticipated long soak in her roll-top bath.

Lying back, hair in a butterfly clip, strands escaping already due to the novel shortness of her new cut, she felt at peace with the world—her world, her wonderful family, her home and the fabulous view in front of her.

When Peter's in-house interior designer had suggested the open plan bedroom/en-suite, with views out across their property, she had been dubious. It probably worked for his wealthy clients' houses, but theirs? The room was large, the view entirely uninterrupted and certainly not overlooked by anyone; in some ways the ideal situation for windows large enough to allow the outside in.

She had supposed it had been her prudish upbringing that made her reserved about displaying all. She had found it difficult enough getting used to the idea of the open-plan lay out. *A bath in the bedroom? How kooky? Surely it would feel exposed and impersonal?*

Once everything was finished, Dulcie had revelled in it. She found that zoning the space between the two functions gave it more intimacy, and the opportunity to relax, virtually within nature, provided an unimaginable sense of freedom. She loved it!

Luxuriating in the bubbles, Dulcie felt utterly free to contemplate the scandalous fantasies she had created during her seventy-minute journey out of the city to her home on the edge of the Blue Mountains. It was one of the reasons she'd forgiven Peter and the boys for not leaving with her; she rarely had the opportunity nowadays to sit and dream.

Before Peter's business had gone bonkers and her launch preparations had taken over, she had enjoyed many a frugal month, happily eking out the family's limited funds to make a warm and loving home for them. Whilst they may have been fiscally on the line when the kids were young, their lives had been wealthy in many other ways; hers enriched by several hours of solitude, working quietly in her studio sketching, moulding, designing and making all kinds of outlandish precursors to her current successful collection of desirable ceramics.

During her studio time, she always let her mind wander, allowing herself what-if dreams, often taking herself back to those perfect days. There was always that one special relationship, before Peter. He was always there, maybe pushed to the back of her mind, instinctively hidden away, but regularly nurtured by a wistful reverie of what might have been. Recent events with Peter had stirred up these thoughts and why not, they were harmless enough, weren't they?

Her bathwater almost cold now, suppressing several yawns, Dulcie recognised it was time to give in. Wrapping herself in the huge, mushroom-coloured bath towel, she tottered off the couple of metres to her bed, deciding not to bother with dressing into nightclothes. Damp skinned and just a little frustrated with her own lack of staying power, she got under the covers. Sleep won priority over sexual fulfilment on this occasion.

Liza

The heavy rain crashed against the bedroom window. Her semi-consciousness becoming more alarming, as her reality reasserted itself. Sleep, if you could call it that, had arrived an hour or so before her alarm. Still sitting in the chintzy armchair, she was at least grateful she had managed to catch forty minutes during the hours since she had finished her tea.

With time to kill before breakfast, she turned her attention to the forgotten post. Working through the junk mail first, with the ridiculously tempting offers of credit, guaranteed to cripple all but the most careful households; then the brown-enveloped bills, expected but nevertheless unwelcome. She avoided the Gloucester post-marked blue envelope until it remained the only unopened item.

For several minutes she was reluctant to break the seal. There was nothing to give cause for concern per se, but she knew the contents would affect her. Whilst still sealed, her life remained what it was; her self-reliance and determination creating a bubble of an existence, shielded by an almost impenetrable force field.

For many years it had been her only way of getting through,

of surviving on her own. It was a long time since she had thought about her family. Some things were better left buried.

There it was. Her name beautifully inscribed in black ink on the pale-blue envelope, the return address a small gold sticker on the back.

Currie, Hampton and Stephens LLP
Hampton House
32 Clarence Street
Gloucester
England

"Oh, fuck it! What's the worst that can happen? I'll still be alive after I've opened it!" she declared to the empty room.

Before she could change her mind, she tore at the corner where the adhesive had not stuck. Her pragmatism returned as she removed the letter, this time typed, on matching blue Conqueror. Pluckiness or no, she sensed a real possibility the lid may now be off her Pandora's Box.

Dear Ms Braybrooke,

Messrs Currie, Hampton & Stephens have been instructed to request your presence at our offices on 25th August 2007. Your appointment is scheduled for 10 a.m.

The full purpose of the meeting will be disclosed at this time. This information is given in the strictest confidence and must not be disclosed to any other family member. We apologise for the vagueness of the instruction, which is at the wishes of our client. Should you incur expenses, including any necessary to cover travel and accommodation, costs will be reimbursed in full on presentation of receipts.

Attendance is not compulsory but may have a bearing on the outcome of the meeting and in the resulting benefit to those attending.

Yours, Samuel Hampton (Senior Associate)

Liza had been right to suspect the letter was related to family issues but re-reading it several times, she was no wiser to its meaning. On the one hand she was curious, on the other, there was a get-out, 'Attendance is not compulsory.' This was not the time to decide. Her alarm had rung, Angelo was stirring and breakfast was a bigger concern than trying to fathom fancy legal invitations.

Leaving the debris of her post-opening strewn on the bed, the blue envelope and its contents took on less significance still, as she headed for the kitchen to make a fresh mug of tea.

Sheena, her closest friend, the busty redhead who used to work a double act with Liza for some of the greedier punters, had beaten her to it.

"Hiya babe."

The women hugged with genuine affection. They didn't see as much of each other as they would like, mostly because Sheena was no longer working at the club. It didn't seem to matter though. They always picked up again as if one of them had just popped to the loo during the adverts.

To Liza, Sheena was one of very few people who really knew her; accepted her without judgement for who she was. She was also one of a very few who could be called on to help out with a childcare crisis. Last night had been a nightmare. Her normal arrangements for Angelo had fallen apart because her childminder's kids had some bug or other and she might be contagious.

The jovial exchange still rang in Liza's ears as they greeted each other.

"Don't worry hon, no probs. I can help out. Ray's away at the moment on a long-haul job to Italy, won't be back till Friday night. I'm at a loose end anyway. My plans were a bottle of vino, a Domino's pizza and back-to-back episodes of 'The West Wing'. Ray can't stand it. Says it's too clever. I always catch up when he's away. That Rob Lowe, he's gorgeous, isn't he? Hey, look, I can watch it just as easily at yours. What time do you need me over?" Sheena had said without taking a breath.

"Whoa Sheena babe! Slow down! Nine o'clock would be great, if that's alright with you? Angelo will be asleep and you shouldn't have much to do. Thanks for getting me out of a hole. . . again."

Liza pulled out of their hug the next morning. "You are a lifesaver babe. I just don't know what I would do without you sometimes. I look at the mums at Angelo's school and I just know from their faces they think I shouldn't be there."

"Really? Why?"

"They're a stuck up middle-class clique who wouldn't know a true friendship if it walked around with an A-board saying, 'True friends will always be there for you.' They'd probably be wondering which catchment of senior school it lived in and whether it was on the church fundraising committee or not, before deciding whether to exchange pleasantries!"

"You're hilarious babe," Sheena said laughing. "But don't let's gas for too long. You don't wanna be late for the hospital."

"Gotta be there on time. Even if we have to wait for ages to be seen."

"You worried about the little man?"

"Nah. We've been down there loads of times before and this is just a check-up. It'll be fine." Hearing Angelo making his way from the bedroom, Liza kept her answer light in case he overheard.

A bleary-eyed, bed-haired, six-year-old stood in the kitchen doorway. Baggy superhero pyjamas two sizes too big drooped over his skinny frame. He was adorable! Though she knew she was biased, Liza suspected he would be breaking hearts in not so many years.

"Morning my angel. Come give Mummy a cuddle."

"Aw Mummy. Don't call me angel! You know I don't like it and it's not my name!"

"Okay, okay I'm sorry. It's just you *are* such an angel. You've never given me any trouble. I'm so lucky."

He skidded across the two metres between them, gave her legs a hug and demanded cornflakes and apple juice because he was "so hungry!"

Sheena left them to it. Off home for a quick nap before her shift started at the local petrol station. Turning to wave back at them, as they looked down from the balcony window, it tickled her to think of such a happy family who really had every reason not to be. Time in their company always boosted morale.

Liza was on her wavelength smiling down at her friend, whilst counting her own blessings. The struggles she had been through to bring up her son were not to be made light of but she couldn't be happier with her family. Angelo was her family; she his.

When the blue line had appeared seven years ago, strong and clear, there had been no indecision. Liza was having this baby. From that moment, the bond with her son had been unshakeable. No matter what life threw at her she had known only good would come of his existence. It was her chance for happiness. Her chance to finally belong to someone and have someone belong to her.

She watched lovingly as Angelo finished his cereal with gusto. He was a dream to look after. She knew he would be off to brush his teeth and get changed without prompting. She bent to kiss his forehead, ruffled his thick, dark hair and left him to it whilst she prepared a rucksack with everything they might need for their trip into central London.

Packed, coat on and almost ready to leave, she was helping him put on his shoes when she remembered to fetch the appointment letter from the stack of papers on top of her chest of drawers.

Thankfully she spotted the Great Ormond Street Hospital letterhead immediately, poking out from under a leaflet on carbon-monoxide detectors, yet another 'to-do' on her list.

Concerned not to be late, she hastily turned back to leave the room, her black rain mac flaring as she span, scattering the papers she'd left on the bed. Annoyed at her clumsiness, she gathered up everything, junk-mail and all, intending to deal with it later. The distinctive pale blue paper called out to her again. It wouldn't go away. It might as well have been a red, glossy poster with her name in size seventy-two font.

Doubly annoyed she had let it niggle, Liza snatched up the unassuming document, with its potent content, and swept out of the flat. Angelo was behind her, uncertain as to what had happened to his mum between shoes and slamming the front door shut.

Elizabeth

The inevitable morning after the night before arrived. The subtle shift of power predictably followed. Or was she imagining it? Andrew, putty in her hands from the previous evening until just a few hours ago, when they had fallen asleep, sweat mingling and limbs entwined, was now almost fully dressed in his golfing gear. He pulled his aqua and yellow Lyle & Scott Argyle sweater over his head. It lit up his face and set off his carefully cultivated tan.

God you're handsome, Elizabeth thought.

All her confidence from the night before had dissipated. Careful not to say or do anything too heavy that might push him away, she casually remarked on how the colours suited him. His unexpected response, that his wife had given it to him for his fortieth birthday, brought Elizabeth back to reality.

Despite the dappled sunlight filtering through the shutters, softened by the ivory voile drapes, what should have been a perfect lazy summer Sunday morning seemed to her, cheap and shabby; not a comment on the bedroom décor, more the atmosphere between them.

Last night was different, wasn't it? I'm sure it was. He's just being practical this morning. She could hear herself beginning to justify Andrews's lack of emotion or demonstration of feeling.

He was busy on a golfing weekend with some corporate clients–his excuse for not being at home–and he ought to at least put in an appearance. He had multiple commitments in his life: wife, kids, properties, career, it was entirely understandable he had no space left to commit to her. He had never promised anything other than spending a Saturday night together.

She should be grateful. It was a big thing for him. He was probably feeling a little awkward, out of his comfort zone. They were in her territory for the first time and no doubt it made all the difference to Andrew; she knew it would for her.

Elizabeth smiled at Andrew in the full-length wardrobe mirrors. Practiced at hiding her emotions, there wasn't an ounce of her vulnerability on show.

"Pass me my La Perla darling," she said, moulding the sheet to her body with one arm across her breasts to remind him of her nakedness underneath.

Just enough modesty mixed with a hint of come hither and the grace of a Debutante, graduating from finishing school, enabled her to achieve her desired effect.

Semi-clad in her robe, standing behind him, arms around his waist, her manicured fingers expertly inched down-wards.

They both followed the image of her hands making their tantalising journey. As they stopped short of their destination, she caught his questioning, almost disapproving look. She gave her answer by breaking away to let him go. She had deferred in a battle she had known was un-winnable but had left Andrew wondering quite who had the upper hand.

*

"I've booked a taxi for ten-thirty. Does that suit you, gorgeous?" Andrew called over the noisy cascade of her shower.

"Yes, should be fine. I'm nearly done in here. Put some coffee on would you. It's the cupboard above the machine. Should find everything you need."

Confidence fully restored and provocatively clad in her robe, which clung to her damp skin, Elizabeth padded through to the kitchen following the enticing aroma of Fortnum and Mason's finest, medium-roast, Columbian blend. There was nothing quite like the smell of freshly brewing coffee. It could possibly only be topped by its precursors released during roasting and grinding.

Memories always came flooding back of her childhood trips with her father, never her mother for some reason, visiting a 'proper' coffee shop. Not an American café chain, selling insipid, tasteless, hot milk masquerading as a cappuccino, more a coffee emporium trading its wares with knowledge and pride in an old-fashioned arcade, squashed between a barbers and a shoe menders.

Freshly ground coffee instantly evoked the same delight as on those special occasions, when she and her father had walked hand in hand through the arcade, nostrils assailed several hundred yards away from Giovanni's, long before the slim frontage came into view.

As they opened the door and its bell rang to announce their

presence, they were always hit by a sensory overload. Elizabeth would stand in awe, her pocket-sized perspective making it impossible for her to see over the solid walnut counter. What she could see were the rows upon rows of containers of almost a hundred different coffee beans, like jars in a sweet shop. They were neatly labelled purely for the benefit of the customer, distinguished by roast, origin and flavour, as Giovanni and his staff had no need of such methods of identification.

The constant whirring of the grinding machine; the chatter of the customers and staff; the clattering of the beans against metal as they were poured into the weighing pan; the intensity of her recall was matched only by the intensity of the aroma and of the feeling that being alone with him was a treat.

Elizabeth guessed, as she reached for the espresso being handed to her by Andrew, this must be why in adulthood she had become an ardent fan of the real thing and couldn't abide the instant stuff.

Maybe things were already heading in the wrong direction with mother, even then, Elizabeth thought.

"Hey lover," Andrew said, gently waving his hand up and down in front of her face. "You seem a long way off."

"Oh I was remembering happy times with my father when I was a young girl."

"You don't often talk about your childhood, your family, your mother. How come?"

She took a long, deliberate breath. "It's just not relevant. I grew up, moved on and away. That's it. End. Of. Story," she said, pursing her lips closed.

Andrew, wary of potentially exhuming traumas long laid to rest, decided he best leave it alone. As his wife repeatedly reminded him, empathy was not his strong suit; besides he had just got a text saying his taxi had just pulled up. He drew her to him for a gentle kiss, hoping she would forget he'd even asked. Far from upsetting her, he wanted to keep things just as they were.

He headed to the door and down the stairs before he stopped and shouted, "I'll call you, my lover." He craned his neck to catch one last glimpse of her as she looked down on him.

She knew he would call. Balance was restored again. She could forget about the past and focus on their future. Why she put herself through those ridiculous teenage anxieties, yo-yoing from high to low, God only knows!

Moving to the lounge to observe his departure, her body rippled with pleasure as it remembered his words and actions of the previous fourteen hours. It should keep her going for a while, replaying the memory as a fantasy until the imprint of their sex faded away.

With renewed vigour, she set about straightening the flat from their exploits, singing along to every track on her *Lazy Sunday* playlist. Nora Jones's 'Turn Me On' was providing the perfect amount of mellowness when her Blackberry pierced through; the business-like ring tone jarring literally and metaphorically with the sweet melody. Unknown number. She hated that. *Always puts you on the back foot.*

"Hello?" Her tone indicated the caller only had seconds to grab her attention before she would ring off.

"Is that Ms Braybrooke?"

Annie

"Mum, you know we'll be there. We never miss Dad's barbeque. The kids love it. Mixing with their cousins and messing about in the woods and Colin and I can't wait to get away from London and into the real countryside."

"But you live in the countryside Annie. You have a lovely little house with a sweet garden. There are many people with far less. You should count your blessings a bit more often darling."

There it was again, the disapproving tone. Annie could easily have made a sarcastic comment but held back, mouthing a silent 'Aargh' down the phone.

How did her mother always manage to bring her back to that small, eager to please, guilt ridden ten year old, preparing for her first confession? Her mind drifted, remembering the terror as she had waited her turn to step inside the booth. What on earth could she confess about? Such a happy-go-lucky, loving, obedient child; as far as she knew there was nothing she had done wrong.

Opening the heavy wooden door concealed in a wall of modern panelling, her heart pounding in her ears so loudly the priest must surely hear it, she had followed the process diligently, right up until the point when she had knowingly committed a sin. Completely stumped for a genuine reason to ask for forgiveness, she had lied. She had made something up, an argument with one of her sisters or some such plausible event. The guilt had welled up inside her and to this day had never subsided.

Still eager to please and knowing she would always fall short of expectation, she accepted her lot and turned back to her mother's niggling.

"I just wasn't sure you'd all be coming over, what with the *invitation* being the same weekend. It's clearly something important. Would it be wise to have the children and Colin around distracting you from any decisions you may need to make?"

"There you go again. We're not meant to be talking about it," Annie snapped. "You're not even supposed to know I have a meeting with them that weekend. I only told you to stop you wondering where I was on the day and making a fuss. Please don't say anything to anyone. Colin doesn't know what it's all about either and he's happy to leave me to it. Can we drop it now? Please?"

"Oh, all right. I'm only trying to help," Mum sniffed.

"Sorry. I think it's best we stop talking about it now. If there's anything I can tell you going forward, I will, okay?" Annie said, scrunching her eyes closed.

Unable to leave it alone, her mum continued, "I mean. It's a bit short notice isn't it? And you said it was addressed to you as Ms Braybrooke? How odd is that?"

"Look I don't know," Annie said through gritted teeth. "Maybe they assumed I'd kept the family name like you did, with us being all girls again in my generation?"

"Maybe. It's just strange you were contacted and not me. I'm fascinated and if I'm honest, a little put out. Anyway, we'd love to have you all to stay."

"Thanks Mum. Honestly, I've really got to go now. We're meeting friends for a picnic at Knebworth Park and I've not even started on the salads yet. You don't want to make me late now do you?" Annie teased, a knot immediately twisting in her belly. In a softer tone she finished with, "Love you. Call you Wednesday."

They were going out soon, but not so soon that Annie had to get ready straight away. Colin had popped to the supermarket with the children for some essentials, including items demanded to keep up the family-picnic tradition. Beth always insisted on her favourite sandwich filling of homemade egg and cress. Eggs they had in abundance, five freshly laid that morning and proudly collected by Thomas in her ancient chicken-shaped basket: a present from Miss Doris, two doors down, when they had moved in ten years prior. She had insisted Annie keep it as a house-warming present, suggesting that, as soon as she could, Annie ought to build a henhouse of her own.

Miss Doris had been an avid keeper of chickens, so lovingly tended, her Victoria sponge always won first prize in the village show–she claimed it was "All down to the quality of my girls' eggs!"

When she had moved away from the village six months ago, Annie had taken them on, pledging to keep up the sponge-baking tradition. She had grown very fond of Miss Doris and was sad to see her leave. One less colourful character in Swallows Green, one more cottage ripe for updating, lifting it to a price bracket beyond the means of most of the locals.

Thankfully, it had been bought by an equally enchanting individual. A Dr Kath O'Hannon, a genuinely supportive neighbour, who, whilst she did commute to her London practice, also made time to mix with the community.

Kath was a welcome addition, unlike the city types who had come and gone, leaving no trace of their existence on the place, barring a demand-led property boom and over-inflated profits for the landlord of the Crow and Bucket, as they disposed of their disposable income. Annie wouldn't say Kath was a friend, more a friendly face, but she definitely had potential. Instinctively, Annie was calmed and reassured by her arrival in the village.

She heard the car's gravely prelude to her family's voices, punctuated by doors slamming, and experienced a blip of panic; time really had disappeared since they had left, and being late for the picnic was now a definite possibility.

Whilst Tony and Sam, their oldest friends, were often tardy, it was somehow acceptable to make allowances for them. They were so laid back and disorganised, their lateness almost defined them.

Annie and Colin on the other hand had set themselves up as perfect role models in social etiquette: always choosing the ideal wine for dinner parties by thoughtfully checking with the host prior to arrival. Leaving just at the right moment, before the party mood dipped and those remaining sensed they had outstayed their welcome and arriving ten to fifteen minutes late, although invariably still the first in any case.

"Hi honey, we're home!" Colin shouted from the hallway. "How are you getting on? Nearly done?"

"Nowhere near ready," she snapped. "Mum called. I'm way

behind and we're going to be late now and you know how I hate being late."

Annie hated being grumpy almost as much as she hated being late.

"Don't worry. I can help," Colin said, wrapping his arms around her.

"Yes Mum, Daddy saves the day. He's a superhero you know!" Thomas piped up, tunnelling through both sets of their legs and holding onto her ankles.

Cute though he was, she did wonder where he got his ideas from. Hadn't he noticed the save-the-day role normally fell to her, not his dad? Ah well, at least she had some extra pairs of hands to help. All she needed now was to find a way to escape them and get back to mashing the hard-boiled eggs.

Elizabeth

She knew she should keep negative thoughts to a minimum as they wouldn't make for a successful meeting at the solicitors. Trying to stay focused and wishing she hadn't turned into quite such a snob like her mother, Elizabeth approached Gloucester city centre in her steel blue Audi TT.

Having not been back for twenty years, enough time had passed for urban improvement, but by her recollection the city was typical of many places regenerated in the late Seventies–mostly a concrete eyesore. Pulling into one of myriad multi-storey car parks on the ring road, poor Gloucester could do no more than match Elizabeth's lowest expectations, as she made a note of the car park's clumsy design, claustrophobic ceilings and poor layout.

Just as I thought, nothing changes. Still, what do I care? I'm not planning to return to my roots anytime soon. I bet mother would love that. No chance. Now what road am I heading for?

She knew a rough route to the Legal Quarter. Hardly as glamorous as the description made it sound, just an area covering a few streets where the solicitors' offices had congregated due to internal specialisation; this possibly being the only fact she had retained from her geography studies at school.

It amused her to recognise the clusters of outlets of the same nature, hoping to benefit from the cross fertilisation of customers. If you were in the footfall of the right competitor, it could significantly enhance your opportunities for trade. Perhaps this was the reason she had remembered the fact, priding herself, as she did, on her commerciality.

She noticed there were indeed some changes as she strutted down Northgate Street. Most of the main shopping areas seemed to have been pedestrianised and some of the usual high-street brands were present. Coffee shops spilled out onto the streets, attempting but not quite achieving, the continental-style cafe culture she was used to in London.

Elizabeth had noted significant investment had been pumped into the docks area and decided once her meeting was over she would make time to explore, before heading to her hotel on the outskirts of the city.

The Visit Gloucester brochure her P.A. had downloaded included details of local attractions and the antiques warehouse in the docks appealed; she'd love to pick up a special piece tucked away amongst the tat. Whenever she could she spent some of her rare free time browsing for antiques in the Portobello Road arcades, hoping to outdo the dealers with her expertise, and often walked away with the smug superiority of success.

She rounded the corner into Clarence Street and spotted the Georgian cream stone frontage, several buildings along, on the right-hand side. Hating to be late or lost, she had phoned in advance to get directions and landmarks. She doubled back to a local café, passed during her reconnaissance. With half an hour to kill, it looked like a passable alternative to the branded chains and preferable to appearing keen by arriving too early.

The last impression she wanted to give was one of eagerness, always an error, she found, in any formal meeting.

Void of any meaningful information, the letter had conjured up all sorts of possibilities. Some good. Some not. The sprawling Braybrooke family tree had been known to deliver pockets of wealth to distant cousins in the past. Perhaps a spinster great aunt had keeled over and decided to favour Elizabeth.

Intrigued though she may be, not a soul at the offices of Currie, Hampton and Stephens would be aware of her curiosity, doused with scepticism, as she stepped over the threshold.

Dulcie

Touching down at Heathrow, adrenaline overriding any symptoms of jet lag, Dulcie was up and out of her seat as soon as the seat belts sign allowed. Memories of her early life came flooding back. Guiltily, she encouraged them out of their hiding place. She couldn't quite believe she had done it!

Once Bruce, her indefatigable agent, had booked her flight, she hadn't been able to leave the thought alone. On several occasions, not least of which the taxi ride home from the launch, the idea had pushed its way into her mind, with all the persistence of the perennial dandelion.

Dulcie couldn't make up her mind whether it was fortune or misfortune that she should be required to attend her Gloucester meeting.

The potent recall of their chemistry and the minute amount of discontent long buried beneath her peaceful family existence, had synchronously combined to guide her fingers to dial Matty's number. It hadn't taken long to find his details on Friends Reunited; to be truthful Bruce had researched it for her. Though she was capable of such things, she had no real interest in becoming sucked into the past. With this one exception, there were no ghosts begging resurrection.

Impatiently queuing past the superficially friendly cabin crew, she was only a few hours away from seeing his face again. If curiosity had proverbially killed the cat, what would it do to the ceramicist? Why did she go and suggest meeting Matty again? She was rapidly concluding her settled life had been in large part due to the lack of his unsettling presence.

Trying to ignore her compulsion to revisit memories of their past, she told herself it would be fine. That was another time. Life had taken them in different directions and now they were just two old friends reconnecting. Dulcie decided to quit worrying and look forward to their meeting later that afternoon. This doubled as a practical decision as she had reached passport control and ought to be concentrating on getting out of the airport.

*

She couldn't believe her eyes! Was that really Matty standing by the pillar in the arrivals hall of Heathrow's Terminal Three? He stared straight at her, his characteristic, cheeky grin spreading across his face.

"Hi there!" His simple two word greeting full of warmth.

"What are you doing here? We said five-thirty at my hotel? I thought you were working on that thing? I really wasn't expecting you to meet me here."

"Really?" Matty raised his left eyebrow. "I'm sorry, I couldn't wait till later. Surely you're not surprised?"

"Yes, really!" Dulcie leant on her trolley to steady herself.

"Twenty-three years! Incredible! And you're still just as gorgeous as ever Dulcie."

She scrabbled around in her box of pre-prepared sentences. Nothing there for this scenario. Should she respond naturally and risk gushing and gabbling to hide her nervousness? Regardless, would her pupils, which had involuntarily opened to maximum aperture, give away the unspoken fizz his words had sent careening through her body?

"Let's go and get a coffee," she eventually suggested, trying to prevent the long pause from morphing into an awkward silence.

"Sounds like a plan," he said.

Heading for the nearest coffee shop, packed with anticipatory relatives and weary travellers, Dulcie spotted a table for two at the back, overlooking the drop-off point. The waiter followed her gaze and indicated to one of his team to clear the table for them, as they weaved their way towards the window. Having gallantly deposited her suitcase in the corner, Matty turned to head back to the counter.

"What would you like?" he asked.

Pausing to ponder his potential double meaning, Dulcie politely requested, "An Americano with cold milk, please."

It seemed an age, in reality seven minutes, until he sat down again. Dulcie couldn't be sure but she suspected Matty had deliberately brushed her hand as he passed her the chunky white mug. Intentional or not, it sent a pin-ball thrill whizzing around her insides. She focused her attention on opening the sachet of brown sugar and pouring it into the hot, dark liquid.

"Penny for them?"

Matty's words lifted her face, their eyes meeting. Uh-oh, another whizzing pin-ball collecting bonuses in every erogenous zone as it went! She had imagined their reunion often since they had spoken a few weeks ago. Dulcie had expected to feel fondness and affection; she also understood there was a part of her hoping for more.

Matty had been ambiguous in his emails, encouraging yet cool, flirty yet friendly. Undeniably her body was telling her a fundamental truth; from her side at least, there was a compelling need to feel his touch, again. It was as if no time had passed at all and they were sitting on that same bench, on the verge of adulthood, where he had first held her hand.

"So, go on then, whatcha thinking about?"

Dulcie smiled. "S'funny. I had so many things to say, to ask, to share. But actually now, right now, I'm just enjoying being here. . . with you."

Their eyes locked again. Their shared silence filled with the unspoken words that passed between them. Now she knew. It was there for him too. *Blimey!* Were they really about to go there?

Matty looked away first, picking up his spoon and collecting the chocolate-sprinkled froth from the sides of his cappuccino. Dulcie mouthed a thank you to his bent head, remembering how thoughtful he had always been.

"How about I tell you more about my Gloucester summons?" she said, hoping to diffuse the tension still further.

She told him as much as she could of the mysterious request to return and meet her family's solicitor. "It's all a little bizarre. That small blue envelope landing in the mailbox all the way from England one day. I mean, it's rare to receive anything in the post these days–the occasional postcard maybe. It took me back to my student days when everyone hovered round the pigeonholes, waiting to collect letters from school mates. I remember I used to write lots. I even kept a few of yours."

There. She was straying back into risky territory.

"I kept all of yours," said Matty, in the softest of voices.

"Ah." She didn't know what else to say.

"What are your plans for the rest of the day?" he asked.

"I guess I need to head into central London and check into my hotel. Maybe grab a bite to eat and do a little window-shopping. I've gotta find something to keep me busy, so's I can beat the jet-lag and stay awake for as long as possible. You? I'm sure you said you had a deadline or something?"

"Oh, I managed to rearrange things. The presentation got put back by the client."

"That's lucky!"

"Not sure it was luck. I'm officially working from home today," he said, making air quotes with his fingers. "But I won't tell anyone if you don't." He winked at her, grinning again. "Would you like some company? A friend to keep guard on that exhaustion, which could ambush you at any moment?"

"That would be very kind but I feel at a real disadvantage here. Everything seems to be about me. You must have somewhere else to be? Something else you could be doing?" Curling the fingers of both hands around the mug, Dulcie took a slurp of her coffee.

"I lead a pretty boring life, compared to you and your jet-setting."

"Hardly," she said, gesturing towards the airport concourse. "This is a recent development and you still haven't answered my question."

"Seriously, there's not much to tell. I have a house near Mum's–she moved up to Hertfordshire you know. I cycle to the station, commute into work. It's alright but work is work.

Long hours, you know? Actually, I wish I'd done a *Dulcie* and followed my passion. You were always so great at art. I'm glad it came good in the end."

"I must admit I was surprised when you told me you were a market analyst. I could've sworn you'd end up on stage. You were stunningly good as Tony. That sixth-form production–what happened?"

"Life I guess. Maybe if you'd been my Maria? Perhaps I should have fought harder?" Matty shook his head. "No point in dwelling on what might have been. We're here now aren't we? Go on. Let's spend the day together." He scraped back his chair and offered her his hand.

"Alright. You've twisted my arm. As long as you–"

"Great! Let's get going. I'm glad I decided to surprise you. We're going to have fun!"

She had been going to say, "As long as you remind me to phone home." She wouldn't forget, would she? Pete and the kids meant everything. Dulcie pushed away her mother's warning from years ago. It had been hovering behind the scenes ever since she had landed.

"Love can lead to pain just as easily as to joy. Be sure of the path you choose.'"

She took Matty's hand and let events unfold, choosing not to choose her path, just yet.

part two

the meeting

August 2007

Liza

"Ms Braybrooke, you may go through now." The kindly receptionist indicated the large cream door on the left with a nod of her head.

Liza wasn't sure but thought she detected a look of affection in her crinkled, lived-in face. Maybe it was the rosy cheeks or the wispy hair escaping the knot at the nape of her neck? Whichever, it summoned similar feelings of warmth and approval to when her ballet teacher had praised her early efforts.

Another welcoming reception greeted her in the office the other side of the door. Liza couldn't believe things were now going so smoothly. Her protracted train journey from London, the route riddled with bank-holiday-weekend engineering works, had seemed like torture. Her anxiousness had reached a crescendo by the time she finally stood outside the solicitors' offices.

She had anticipated a grumpy old man, scary, officious and full of contempt and judgement of her appearance. She had tried her best to choose an outfit suitable for the occasion, failing at every attempt.

Her previous interactions with the legal system had not

included invitations to smart Georgian-fronted offices with racing-green front doors. This coupled with her wardrobe full of work costumes, had led her to the conclusion she had nothing suitable to wear. Eventually, she had dug out an old black pencil skirt and a greying white blouse, forgotten and stuffed at the back of the cupboard, presumably originally worn to a Jobcentre Restart interview.

The young man sitting behind the desk, who stood to greet her with a confident handshake and a beaming smile, couldn't have been further from her imagined encounter. He put her at her ease immediately, indicating she should sit before he returned to his position in the heavy studded-leather chair behind the desk.

*

Currie, Hampton and Stephens LLP, tucked away in a Gloucester side road close to the pedestrianised section of the city centre, specialised in family law and probate. Most of the time Samuel Hampton, their Senior Associate, was unable to use his impressive prize-winning knowledge gained during his degree and articles. He believed he was destined for better things, often imagining he was a partner in a magic-circle law firm in London, Carter Clifton perhaps?

Even though he was often underwhelmed by the contents of his in-tray, Samuel always worked diligently, completing his tasks with dedicated proficiency. Few were aware of his ambition, especially his father Nicholas Hampton, the youngest and most commercially minded of the partners.

Quentin Currie had long since ceased to be anything but

a sleeping partner, having had health and marriage problems since a car accident had left him unable to function adequately in the real world. His eccentricities had begun to impact on clients. All had agreed, at a meeting called by the loyal hardworking backbone of the practice, Jonathan Stephens, it might be best if Quentin took a back seat for a short while. That was four years ago.

Without taking the credit, Jonathan had narrowly avoided the dissolution of the partnership. This had given Samuel the step into his father's firm, as Nicholas had always planned and here he was, administering the Braybrooke family affairs which for once held his interest.

Family trusts always provided stimulating work. The undercurrents and enigma surrounding the 'blood is thicker than water' premise often proved things not to be quite so clear cut. Many a family feud found its origins in this very office. Strong emotions could result in standard lamps toppling and vases breaking; a metaphor for the sometimes irreversible damage to relationships once the details had been revealed.

His current case had the capacity to develop into one such volatile drama. He had been eager for the bank-holiday meetings. His part had been defined; to follow the instructions prescribed by the client; to communicate effectively with the beneficiaries and under no circumstances to attempt to influence or persuade any one of them towards a final decision.

Samuel had conscientiously obeyed, initially thinking the task relatively easy to execute. Any other family and this may have been true. He had a vague awareness, from his father's dealings with the Braybrookes, proceedings were unlikely to be simple once the meetings had begun.

*

He studied Liza. She looked uncomfortable in her chair, in her clothes and with the setting.

"All the control is yours Liza," he said, hoping to put her at ease. "Both at the meeting and in any subsequent decisions you will need to make as a result of our discussion today. I'm just here to ensure you are fully informed of your options and to give any impartial advice as to the legal aspects of the trust. It is not for me to judge or in any way dictate the course of action you should take."

Liza visibly relaxed into her chair. "I'm sorry Mr Hampton. I'm not normally as introverted. It's just that... well... this is all so weird. First, the cryptic letter, then the return to Gloucester, which in itself is something very out of the ordinary for me. I'm taking several giant leaps outside of my comfort zone and I'm not entirely sure why?"

"Please, call me Samuel. Honestly, I prefer it. The law to me is not about stuffy traditions. It's about helping people like you, Ms Braybrooke, make informed choices."

"Likewise, call me Liza. That's what everyone calls me nowadays," she said, a grin emerging from the corners of her eyes and mouth.

Samuel took this as his cue. He removed the Trust documents from a black box file sitting in front of him on the green-leather-inlayed, reproduction Edwardian desk.

Samuel spent the next fifteen minutes relaying the contents

of the Trust documents, occasionally pausing for Liza to question him on anything requiring further explanation. He passed the papers across the desk for her to look over and waited in silence.

"This. . . no really? Are you sure this is correct? A house and land worth nine-hundred-and-fifty thousand pounds and one-point-nine million in cash?" Liza stared at the documents, as if somehow keeping her eyes glued to them would bring them into sharper focus.

"Oh yes, I'm completely sure." Samuel lingered before adding, "Of course, there are the other conditions to be met but yes, the total estate is just under three million pounds. I suspect you will need plenty of time to think things through. Very few people in your situation are able to absorb this kind of information without thorough contemplation."

"Samuel?" Liza asked, dipping her head to one side and twiddling a section of hair. "Would you be able to help me think things through? Me being a dumb lap dancer and all? It's all those big words you know!"

"Sorry Liza, I didn't mean to imply." Samuel blushed.

"Don't worry." She giggled, and added, "I'm only joshing! I do get it a lot you know. Especially when I'm wearing my blond wig, like today."

She was both letting him off the hook and letting him know he should take care not to make assumptions based on her appearance.

"Thanks, I'm relieved I haven't offended you. It would be more than my job's worth! Besides it wouldn't be a very good start to this day of meetings."

"Can I call on your support with the legal jargon later? I'm heading back to London today and I'd like to use the train journey to go over things again."

Liza stood, smoothing her skirt and looking about for something to use to carry the documents. Foolishly, she had only brought a small, black handbag, just large enough to carry her phone, purse and lipstick.

Samuel stepped in. "No problem, call me any time." As he spoke he handed her his card and a zipped, black-leather documents folder.

"Are you sure? I mean this is yours, isn't it?"

"Absolutely sure. You can return it next time I see you."

His kind eyes caught hers for, perhaps, just a moment longer than they should, as he stood before showing her to the door.

Elizabeth

Continuing to be unimpressed by the parochial nature of all things Gloucester, Elizabeth sat, impatient, in the tatty outer office of the solicitors.

This could be such an impressive corporate advertisement for the firm, she thought.

She couldn't help but notice the drips of gloss paint on the skirting and internal doors, the small patches of worn carpet beneath the carefully positioned coffee table.

Surely this should be where the entire interior decoration budget is spent. After all, first impressions really do count! If I ever decide to give up my lucrative career, I'll have to remind myself I have an eye for these things and see if I can't become the next Jocasta Innes. In fact, didn't Morgan say as much during the renovation? As a highly sought-after architect of the highest repute, he should know. Her self-satisfied musing was finally interrupted, a full five minutes after she had dismissed the black faux-leather sofa as an obvious Florence Knoll replica.

"Ms Braybrooke. Mr Hampton will see you now." The frumpy receptionist said, catching her eye over the top of her glasses, and pointing to the door of the inner office on the left.

"Thank you."

It was important not to let her standards drop, however backward a place she was visiting. Smiling graciously at the older lady, she noticed her properly for the first time.

*

"Tell me, what's this about Mr Hampton? May I call you Samuel? I do hope the meeting won't take too long. I have a spa appointment back at my hotel at three." She sat without permission, deciding this was appropriate, since she was the client and the solicitor was just a solicitor.

"Ms Braybrooke. Thank you for arriving promptly today." Samuel turned on just enough charm and adapted his approach to Elizabeth, as with all his clients, in his usual chameleonic way. "In answer to your question please be assured all will be clarified shortly. I have no issue with you calling me Samuel. Proceedings should take approximately thirty minutes, although you may take as much time as you like. There's plenty of time until my next meeting today. I'm all yours, so to speak."

Samuel carefully mirrored Elizabeth's language and pace, displaying superb listening skills and creating an immediate sense of trust. He gave her the floor. "Would you like me to explain your entitlements in detail or would you prefer to read through the papers yourself, before asking questions?"

He's good. Elizabeth was impressed with his customer-relationship skills. *Mind you, they're all common techniques any business-services professional must master to have a hope of success.*

Mindful Samuel was waiting for a response, she decided to give him an easy time and let him do what he was probably paid a very good wage to do.

"Naturally, you must lead me through the process. I guess I may have appeared a little forthright. I suppose I am guilty of high expectations when it comes to my business interactions."

"No need to apologise Ms Braybrooke. You are in charge." Since they were both aware Elizabeth had not apologised, Samuel's statement brought them back to a level playing field.

"As you will have deduced from your invitation to this meeting and your subsequent decision to attend, details will be revealed to you which otherwise may not have been. Firstly, however, I must ask whether you have complied with the instruction to refrain from discussing the impending meeting with other members of your family?"

Samuel paused to allow Elizabeth to answer. He noticed her grey-blue eyes turning a little greyer before she spoke in a cold, dispassionate voice.

"I have no reason to speak to any members of my family at any time. That instruction was so facile I had quite forgotten it until you mentioned it now."

Samuel made a mental note to ask his father to remind him about the history behind the remark. His professional training belied none of his thinking as he removed the original Trust documents from his file, along with a signed copy for Elizabeth, which he passed across the desk.

'You, amongst others, are a possible beneficiary of a Hidden Trust, to be administered through this office on behalf of an anonymous benefactor and trustees. I say possible because the bequest is dependent on two conditions: first, you must agree to undertake the venture as prescribed in paragraph one point two, a business plan for which is detailed in appendix A. Do note the monies are to be reinvested in the restoration of the estate in the first instance, with any remaining cash earmarked for start-up fees, running costs etc. Second, you must agree to unconditional acceptance of any other beneficiaries who so agree as business partners."

Samuel looked up from his notes, checking to ensure his client was with him. Satisfied Elizabeth was fully engaged, he continued. "I will let you read through the full documents in your own time but would like to draw your attention to clause eleven point two, which allows you six weeks for your deliberations to 8th October and requires written confirmation of your acceptance of the terms within seven days of this date.

"Also, to clause eleven point three, which requires your decision to be independent of any of your co-beneficiaries and hence requires you to refrain from discussing either the Trust or your decision, with any family members. The full fiscal entitlement, which will be equally divided amongst those who have agreed to participate, is stated in Schedule A, Trust Property. I think that covers the salient points. Do you have any queries at this point?" he asked.

"No, that all seems clear." Elizabeth's low-key response was typical of her reaction to any transaction. She never revealed her opinion and remained as poker-faced as ever.

Samuel couldn't find any sign of enthusiasm or excitement. Certainly no shock or avarice at the sizeable estate she could soon be sharing.

"Very good Mr Hampton." She stood decisively. "Thank you for your help today. I will be taking up your offer of support during the coming weeks. Can I ask, are your fees covered by the Trust or would any correspondence between us be chargeable?"

"Everything is inclusive. Although you should be aware, I have a week's leave in mid-September. If you have any queries during this time, please do call the office and Mrs Rathbone will be able to direct you accordingly."

Elizabeth shook his hand, picked up her Tanner Kroll, peacock-blue, attaché case, with the documents safely contained within, and her matching handbag. She swept elegantly through the door to the outer office and smiled magnanimously at the receptionist, Mrs Rathbone, whose name plate she noted for the first time.

She also noticed the gentle rain on the multiple panes of glass in the Georgian sash windows. Once again, her elegance was in evidence as she stylishly manoeuvred into her Burberry mac without any apparent effort. This, noticed by both Samuel and Mrs Rathbone.

"Quite a classy lady," Samuel remarked once the entrance door closed behind her.

"Yes."

Samuel could hear admiration and disapproval all wrapped up in Mrs Rathbone's single-word response.

On the other side of the door Elizabeth allowed herself to relax the corners of her mouth, and with a gentle sway of her hips, as she took the three steps down to the pavement, her mind was already focusing on the connotations of her newly acquired knowledge. On automatic pilot, she somehow negotiated her way back to the concrete car park. Oblivious to everything around her as the drizzly rain still fell, her head was full of wonderful projections of the future. She and Andrew could now become a permanent *Us*.

Dulcie

Distracted, excited, inquisitive, anxious, guilty? Dulcie wasn't quite sure how she felt, or how she wanted to feel. Her stomach had been churning for days. Much had transpired since her launch party four weeks ago.

When she had first read the letter, she had guessed it must be something to do with the eccentric Braybrooke branch of the family tree but had been far too preoccupied making arrangements at home to give it much more thought. The meeting, the original reason for her return to the UK, now upon her, added an extra intensity to her gurgling. *What on earth could it be about?*

In the end, because she was running late, Dulcie decided to ask the hotel's concierge to book her a taxi to the door of Currie, Hampton and Stephens. She was staying a few miles out, in Upton St Leonards, not far from her parents in Painswick.

She was tired, having been up late chatting online with her eldest sons and committing herself to a trip to the cathedral. James and Michael were insisting on photographic evidence of all the Hogwarts locations, as huge Harry Potter fans. Being away from them all meant long periods of the day when she couldn't talk to them.

Libby had begged to speak every day and had been struggling to sleep in case she missed her call. Dulcie did miss the sound of their voices. Overlapping threads of emails couldn't make up for her need to feel connected to her brood. As for her parents, she'd still not decided whether she would pay them a visit.

Perhaps best not to tread on that sleeping dog's tail.

The taxi driver's announcement broke through her thoughts.

"Okay m'dear, this is it, Hampton House, Clarence Street."

She settled the fare and stepped onto the pavement, looking up at the somewhat austere, cream-coloured stone offices, with the heavy door. *Entirely appropriate for a firm of solicitors. Not too ostentatious. Formal, reliable and very typically British.* Dulcie was still fascinated by historical buildings. Many years ago, she had completed one term of an architecture degree and occasionally wondered how things might have turned out had she pursued the academic route her parents had wished for.

Having pressed the buzzer beside the brass plaque to the left-hand side of the door, Dulcie waited, noticing the spits of rain giving a measles-like appearance to her new, tan-leather boots. She had been indecisive that morning after checking the weather forecast and had hoped for a perfect late-summer day. It had showed potential; a bright, crisp start reminiscent of those back-to-school days of her childhood, where the almost autumnal air, coupled with the smell of new leather shoes, held the promise of a fresh start.

Dulcie had taken the risk with her footwear choice to complete her smart-casual look; the mid-blue bootleg jeans, the matching tan belt and a crisp white cotton blouse. She was hoping to portray effortless individuality, with hints of creativity and business success.

Until very recently, Dulcie had hardly cared for her own appearance but some of Bruce's panache had rubbed off on her. Enjoying her new-found image awareness, she realised she was rekindling a love of retail therapy, which had been left behind with the rest of her UK life. Peter had encouraged her to spend a little extra on herself as his way of saying sorry and she had taken him at his word, even if it did feel extravagant.

Thankfully, for both practical and aesthetic purposes, she had settled on a heather-and-turquoise flared mac with a wide buckled belt as 'rain insurance' after spotting it in a department-store window, during her time in London.

"Please push the door," a friendly female voice instructed from the intercom. The door-release buzzed and she pushed the large brass handle with a little effort. "Good afternoon Ms Braybrooke. Shall I take your coat? Mr Hampton is expecting you. Please do take a seat."

Dulcie smiled gratefully as she passed her coat to the receptionist. "Thank you, Mrs Rathbone. Great to meet you in person at last and thank you for your help with my accommodation. It is a lovely hotel, comfortable and quiet. Perfect after such a whirlwind of activity back home and then in London."

"I know what you mean, dear. Mind you these bank-holiday meetings are hectic enough for me!" Mrs Rathbone said. "Can't wait until I can put my feet up for a piece of Lardy cake and a nice cup of tea."

"I guess the timings are a little out of the ordinary. Hopefully you've not got too long to go?"

"It's okay. Mr Hampton only has one more meeting today. Oh look, here he is." Samuel poked his head round the door to his office. "Mr Hampton, are you ready for Ms Braybrooke now?"

"Certainly Mrs Rathbone and thank you for all your hard work today."

Mrs Rathbone giggled. "Such a charming young man you are Mr Hampton."

This should be fun, Dulcie thought to herself, as she followed Samuel through and took a seat in the comfortable chair opposite his desk.

"Ms Braybrooke, I trust my letter was clear and easy to follow?" Samuel asked. Mrs Rathbone had kept him updated on her communications with Dulcie over the past couple of weeks but he wanted to confirm she had followed his instructions accurately.

"Sure, Mr Hampton. No worries." Australia made it impossible for her not to have picked up the odd phrase and a slight twang.

"You must call me Samuel," he said.

"You too–I mean Dulcie not Samuel. That would be silly!" she said, detecting a flustered girlishness in her own reply and sensing the sparkle in her blue-grey eyes ramping up a couple of notches.

The next quarter of an hour flew by; detailed dissemination of the Trust papers, interspersed with flashes of harmless flirtation. Dulcie was thoroughly enjoying herself. Blown away at the gift, yet full of how and who and why, she found it simpler to focus on the explanations Samuel gave her and the lightness of their interactions.

She was also bemused. How had she existed for such a long time without paying any attention to her own femininity?

Whether it was her recent success, her return to London stirring her recollection of a different era, her rekindling of old and dangerously thrilling friendships; whichever, she was behaving differently and why not?

"So, what are you saying? Is this is a decision I need to make for myself, by myself?"

"More or less, although I'll help all I can." Samuel beamed.

"I'm sure you will. I'm just not sure I will be able to make the most of your expert assistance." Dulcie laughed at her own innuendo. Samuel joined in. A more pleasurable client meeting he couldn't remember.

As they shook hands to say goodbye, he hoped Dulcie would decide to jump into the venture with both feet. Forgiving himself the pun, he dutifully kept his thoughts to himself, not wishing to compromise his professional obligation to remain impartial.

He tracked her progress from his window, her blond bob lifted by the eddies around the entrance steps, which always deposited a red and gold collection of fallen leaves from the Virginia creeper on the building opposite. She had declined his offer of a taxi in spite of the rain. He watched Dulcie walk away towards the docks until she turned the corner into Eastgate Street.

Annie

Annie was running late. Again. As she rushed along in the drizzle, she kicked herself for expecting to find parking close to the solicitors. The road works on the B4073 from her parents' house in Painswick; the Saturday shoppers circling the ring road like worker bees queuing to re-enter the hive, disappearing excruciatingly slowly one by one into the multi-storeys.

Annie had made a judgement call; she would park down by the docks and walk back. Big mistake! More road works, one-way systems and inoperable ticket machines added further delay.

She had been permanently preoccupied since receiving the blue envelope. That innocuous-looking piece of post had already imposed a hugely disruptive influence on her psyche. She felt out of kilter. Being late was the worst way to arrive at a meeting, which threatened ominously to tip her into the unknown. Hoping she would have time to compose herself before she was called to see Mr Hampton, Annie gratefully pushed open the heavy green door, glad at least to be out of the rain.

Mrs Rathbone smiled welcomingly, Miss Marple-style, over the top of her reading glasses.

"Hello, Annie dear. How are you?"

Annie was relieved to see a friendly face. "Mrs Rathbone. Thank goodness it's you! I feel all dishevelled and out of sorts. It's such a strange situation and I wanted to make the right first impression."

"Oh, don't you worry about that dear, Mr Hampton is a polite young gentleman and would never have passed comment. Anyhow, you have plenty of time. The meetings have been running over a smidge. You can pop and get yourself sorted if you like. The cloakroom is just through there on the right."

Mrs Rathbone pointed to a large panelled door to the right of the desk with a silver plaque, marked Cloakroom, just legible despite its worn, over-polished appearance.

"Thank you. I'll neaten myself up and perhaps we can have a minute or two to exchange news? A catch up is long overdue and there's plenty to tell!"

Annie's fluster diminished, the familiarity of their old next-door neighbour taking the edge off an otherwise alien situation. Pushing through to the generous cloakroom, she instantly picked up on the feminine touches of Mrs Rathbone's influence; the Marks & Spencer rose hand wash and cream; the fluffy, pink hand towel; the single magenta carnation in a tall William Morris vase.

Now feeling much more with-it, she appraised her reflection in the antique bevelled mirror above the sink. She was unsure of her choice of outfit, a classic black trouser suit with a soft chiffon blouse. The suit was a-typical for Annie, who usually chose the casual side of smart-casual. Being a teacher, she had paid little attention to her style over the last ten years. She rarely had the need to dress any other way.

She had enjoyed selecting her new suit. Spending time and money on herself was a novelty. Secretly, she had taken the most pleasure from treating herself to some beautifully feminine sheer cream underwear with fine lace edging. No-one else bar Colin would see it and whilst she was sure he wouldn't notice; something made this decadent purchase compulsive.

Damn it! When do I ever do something for me?

Something was changing for her. Perhaps prompted by the mysterious nature of the meeting she was about to attend? A risk-taking, bolder Annie was surfacing. Looking up, the blond sleek hair framed her face, as her grey-blue eyes stared back. She grinned at the memory of her mother's reaction to her radical change of hairstyle. True it was very different; true it was not-Annie! She did acknowledge it would be a shock to all who knew her. To be fair, it was a shock to her too.

A few days on from the final scissor-snip, every time she caught her image reflected on any surface, her brain would question, *Who's that?* for a few fleeting seconds before the reality of her boldness returned and she recognised her new self.

Still smiling, she picked up her mac, her beret and soft Italian leather attaché case and returned to reception, to gossip with dear Mrs Rathbone.

*

"Much is the same here, my dear. You know how they've tried over the years to update and upgrade the place. You'll have noticed the docks development no doubt?"

"Actually, I've not had much time to explore this weekend.

Life seems to go at an alarming pace. No time to stop and ponder. Mum mentioned there had been some *post-Potter* investment. I guess it didn't hurt the city when the cathedral was selected for those corridor and courtyard scenes?"

"Ah Annie, I wouldn't really know. I'm the wrong generation. I 'spect it's your Beth who's been eagled-eyed trying to spot our very own historical landmark woven into the magical stories?"

"Yes she's definitely a Harry Potter fan and is insisting we do the tour tomorrow. I'm not sure if it runs on Sundays though. A conflict perhaps due to the true purpose of the building as a place of worship?"

Mrs Rathbone laughed. "I don't think I'm the right person to ask, since I am neither a fan of the films nor religion."

They were interrupted by Mr Hampton. His cheerful smile greeted them both.

"Hello Ms Braybrooke, through you come." He gestured for Annie to join him in the inner office.

Every bit the gentleman Mrs Rathbone had described, he stood holding the door for Annie as she passed through, closing it carefully as she sat on the client-side of the desk.

"Is it an ancestral portrait?" Annie asked, commenting on the heavy, gilt-framed painting of a portly gentleman behind the desk. He was suitably officiously attired in a green velvet waistcoat, his beady eyes and pinched nose emanating Dickensian pomposity.

Samuel laughed. "It's funny you should ask. You're not the first client to do so. In fact no-one is quite sure who he is. My mother spotted it at an auction some years ago when the building was last refurbished and thought it would add an air of authority to the office. I like to think of him as a secret proprietor, ensuring we give the proper level of service at all times."

Warming to his sense of humour, Annie put any fears of formality to one side, ready to let the mystery of the meeting unfold.

They spent the next thirty minutes discussing the terms of the Trust and the implications of its various conditions. Considering the extreme nature of its potential impact, Annie would have expected to feel worried. Instead, as she chatted with Samuel, it was as if she had foreseen this crossroads; as if her decision would be a simple left or right which would take her down the correct path.

Odd. Usually change made her wary. Always cautious, always thinking of others and evaluating the effect it might have on their lives. Annie couldn't work out why she was at ease with this uneasy situation.

Certainly, Samuel's calm manner played a part in mitigating her concerns. He was a charming, emotionally intelligent man, facilitating her tentative steps towards understanding her options, if not quite the necessary acceptance that a decision must follow.

"I really mustn't sway you in any way but if it helps I would gladly be a paying customer of the venture. Perhaps I'm not the right demographic for your ideal target client, but I do think it is an amazing idea." His smile lingered encouragingly as he spoke.

"Oh I know. There is a revival of all things ballroom, which has been growing for several years now. Many of my colleagues and some friends have caught the bug. I have several major reservations though; the location for example. Has the trend reached the Cotswolds? In any case it's very prescriptive, the business model, I mean." Annie slowed herself down so she could think more clearly. "Are you sure it specifically says, 'creation of a School of Tango?' And there's my complete lack of business expertise. I've no dance training, unless you count my grade-one ballet of many, many years ago! Loving dance and being a professional dancer are not the same thing."

"Yes, it is both specific and prescriptive, I'll admit. Clause five point one states: '. . . *creation of a residential school of Argentine Tango, to be jointly run by all the beneficiaries who have accepted the terms of the trust by 8th October.*' However to clarify, I have checked several times and there is no obligation for you to be able to teach or dance the Tango, merely for you to be involved in the formation of the school and its administration. It is this last point which will trigger your inheritance."

Looking up from her notes, Annie asked, "Is it okay for me to read my scribbles back to you? I'd like to be sure I've got everything down, in simple terms, if you know what I mean?"

"Of course," he said, easing himself back into his chair. "Fire away."

"So," Annie began. "I have potentially inherited an old house and a substantial amount of money. Someone, who wants to remain anonymous, has died and would like me and some others to renovate the house and set up a Tango school. What else?" She stopped, searching her pages for a particularly peculiar aspect, which she had noted, underlined and finished with several question marks. "Oh yes. We, and I don't even know who *we* might be, must decide to run this business together, before we meet or else we forfeit the whole lot?"

"That is an excellent summary. In *real* English." Samuel winked.

"I'm glad you think so. It's such a strange request. I just wanted to be sure."

Annie imagined she might thrive on such an opportunity or if not, she may regret not giving it a try. This foolhardy enterprise could be the key to opening her next chapter. A step away from the dutiful person she had become. Could she allow herself to shake off the dependable, risk-averse Annie and rediscover the creative, carefree soul kept hidden inside?

Pia

Pia sat in her hired silver hatchback. She monitored the racing-green door in the Georgian façade through the drizzle of the English summer. Her eyes cycled from the door to the digital clock display–14:17–to the street and back again.

She wasn't supposed to be here; had told herself it made no difference how they looked. After several weeks of vacillation, she had succumbed to her burgeoning curiosity. Moving back to her mum's, albeit temporarily, had brought out a rebelliousness she'd forgotten about.

"What good will it do, Pia? You should stay away, if you ask me," Mum had said.

Pia's efforts to remind her mum that she was a grown, independent woman in her forties and could do what she liked, had come out more belligerent adolescent than account director with a twenty-five-year career under her belt. Maybe it was being back home in the cottage? Or could it be the news she herself had received the previous month in the very same building that made her come here? Whichever, Pia had chosen to ignore her mum's advice.

Finally, Ms Braybrooke emerged from the office with a dazed expression on her face. Her blond bob gave Pia no clues to their relationship. Could she be her new business partner? Could she be her sister? In six weeks she would have her answer.

*

Pia had inherited her father's Latin skin and thick dark hair. The contrast with her pale blue-grey eyes made heads turn. Especially when she had been growing up and out and about with her adopted mum, Helena, whose pale skin and mousey blond curls immediately gave rise to suspicion.

She often joked about her lineage with her London friends, many of whom teased that she must be the milkman's daughter.

"Who's that?" they would ask, winking, picking up the photos of the two of them from the bookcase in her dining room.

"Yes, I know. I look more like my cats than I do my mum."

They would all agree her cats bore a strong resemblance.

Raised as an only child of a single mother in the Sixties, she'd had her fair share of standing out. During her earlier years, her mum had been on the receiving end of prejudice and abuse on a daily basis from their middle-class neighbourhood. Not once had Pia seen her rise to the bait. The taunts of 'slag' and 'whore' appeared to bounce off her thick skin, causing little or no visible reaction.

Pia had found it harder to maintain the same stoic dignity. Recounting stories of her father in her head, holding her mum's love and devotion close to her, she had developed the same thick skin over time. All her life, Helena had been the only family she had known. It had always been just the two of them. Even when she had travelled to New York, Boston or Singapore with her job, she had never missed their weekly chat.

Now, sitting with Helena in Samuel Hampton's office, Pia can't quite take in the words. The letter she holds asks more questions than it answers. She reads her father's handwriting for the first time. The blue ink, smudged on the faded almost parchment-like paper, had been written some months earlier. The envelope had been addressed to Pia, to be opened on the event of his death.

My darling beautiful daughter,

I made a decision years ago to stay away, out of your life. Our history is complicated and it would have served no purpose to stir up the past. With Helena's help, I have watched you become a beautiful and accomplished woman. To you, I know I am a stranger but you must know two things.

First, that as soon as I found out about you, I loved you with all of my heart, always wanting the best for you. Second, that I utterly adored your mother. She was the love of my life.

Please take my gift and share it with your half-brother, PJ. He is loving and loyal and very much looking forward to meeting you. I know this is a lot to absorb all at once but there is one more thing I need to tell you. I believe you also have a younger sister.

She has been invited to take up her inheritance and share the gift with the two of you. As yet she will not know of her connection to either of us. You could say whilst you have been in a darkened room, in which I have just switched on the lamp, she has been living in an alternate universe ignorant of our very existence.

I will leave it to you and PJ to decide how much of our story to tell. Do not be sad. You have many years ahead of you. I only hope your dancing will bring you all as much joy in your lives as it did mine.

Your ever-loving Papa,
Pablo x

"Mum! What's this all about? I thought I knew everything about my mother and father?"

"Darling, I know," Helena said, furrowing her brow, as she turned to face Pia sitting beside her. "It came as a shock to me too. When your father first got in touch he was actually looking for your sister."

"Sister? What sister?" Pia shouted, fury rising inside her and spewing out into the room. Pacing the floor, Pia continued with a flushed face and animated gestures, "Look, I'm sorry but this is just too much to take in! The inheritance; my father in touch with you but you don't let me see him; he's now dead! I knew I had a half-brother although I'd never met him but a sister too? A sister, not a half-sister? How's that possible? What on earth are you all on about?"

"May I offer a suggestion?" Samuel interrupted. His warm tone and kind eyes were directed at Pia.

Pia stopped still and shoved her hands in her pockets to calm the shaking, reminded by his question that she was in his office and not alone with her mum.

"Please do," she replied as steadily as she could.

After all it wasn't his fault her world was turning upside down. One of her mother's favourite phrases tapped her on the shoulder. *Don't shoot the messenger, he's only doing his job.*

She waited for him to speak, noticing for the first time how sharply dressed he was in his crisp white shirt, plain silver cufflinks and classic navy and red tie. If she was not mistaken there was his pedigree right there; never mind the stuffy portrait of the pompous old geezer hanging on the wall behind him, the Christ Church College, Oxford colours spoke volumes.

"I appreciate there is more than enough revelation in the Trust documents and accompanying correspondence from your father to knock you sideways. Perhaps we should take a break for some fresh air and a cup of tea? Maybe resume the discussion at say eleven o'clock?"

"Yes, yes. What a great idea," Helena gushed.

Relieved to be given an opportunity for the dust to settle, she wondered whether Pia would want some time apart or to sit together and let her explain.

Pia stayed by the sash window looking out onto the street. Grey skies loomed with hostile clouds full of rain yet to fall. Motionless she spoke, her voice controlled now and level. "Mum. It's a typical English summer's day out there. Let's stay here and have a nice cup of tea."

Helena nodded.

"Right then," Samuel said. "I shall ask Mrs Rathbone to make us a brew. Earl Grey alright with you two?"

Pia crooked her head towards him and nodded in response. He smiled back, eyes earnest and twinkling, before strolling through to the outer office to request their refreshments.

"He's a very charming young man isn't he?" Helena asked, spying the blush on Pia's cheeks. "I've always thought a younger man would suit you. And now you've stopped all that gadding about, maybe you could–"

"Oi, he's not that much younger Mum." Pia wagged her finger. "Tut, tut and there you go again. Always trying to match make. We don't even know if he's single and in any case I'm not sure now is quite the time for a new relationship, eh? Sometimes, I think you forget I had a whole other grown-up life before I came back. I love you Mum, but honestly, I don't need mothering."

"Sorry darling. Once a mother, always a mother. Come and sit back down with me," said Helena, grateful Pia had taken her comments in the light-hearted way she had intended.

Pia sat once again in the chair she had recently vacated, almost ready to hear her Mum's version of the story.

"You know I'd never willingly keep secrets from you, don't you?" Helena said.

"I guess," Pia mumbled.

"Well, let me say these recent months have been some of the most difficult of my life. I had no option but to stay silent and before I explain, I want you to trust I would have told you everything if I'd had the choice."

The wait before Pia spoke seemed endless. The silence itself noisy. She scrutinised the grey clouds for a second time, trying to convince herself these new developments in her life were not as ominous as the skies she was tracking.

"Pablo." Pia heard her own wobbly voice speak his name. "Pablo. Yes, of course his name would be Pablo. Do you have any photos Mum, of him when he was young, I mean?"

Her mind was not on the future; the inheritance; the complexities of the legal arrangements. Instead, she had a burning need to understand everything about who she was and where she came from. It was a familiar feeling, woven through her adult life, rising to the surface more prominently at times but always there at the back of her mind.

She had accepted she would never know her father, deciding it should stay an unsolved mystery; it would only hold her back unless she let it go. That was in the past. Now the impact of his letter, seeing his handwriting, his words, brought the desire right to fore with a crushing force. She hugged herself, arriving right back at the moment she had first discovered she was adopted.

"My Pia. Yes, I do," Helena replied softly. "Would it be better if I took you home and told you everything I know before we do the legal thing?"

She smiled. "You know what, I'd like that Mum. Thanks. Sorry for acting like a spoilt brat. It's just–"

"I know. I'll go and tell Mr Hampton and arrange a return appointment. I'm sure he won't have a problem with that. He seems such a nice young man."

"Too young Mum!" Pia feigned an exaggerated frown. "There you go again. How many times?"

"Perhaps she doth protest too much?"

They both laughed. Helena had not had time to seek out Samuel, before he re-entered the office carrying the tea-laden tray, the same twinkly-eyed smile on his face.

Pia exchanged a questioning look with her mum. Had they been caught out? Had he overheard their last sentences? As a precaution, Pia collected herself and politely accepted hers with milk, no sugar. She remained seated, quietly sipping the cuppa; so comfortingly British and used as a soothing solution to any crisis.

She zoned out of the discussion between her mum and

Samuel: future dates being optioned; some importance attached to a deadline prior to the bank holiday at the end of the summer. Their words a backdrop to her tumbling thoughts, her questions acrobats simultaneously spinning and somersaulting inside. Relieved at last to be departing, Pia shook hands with Samuel, as Helena thanked Mrs Rathbone for the tea.

Samuel stood steadying the heavy front door against the wind. "I hope the rain holds off for you."

"Thanks. Come on! Let's get going Mum. See if we can get to the car before the heavens open."

*

Back in Helena's comfy, if a little cluttered, cottage, which for many years had provided Pia with a bolthole too, they sheltered from the storm. Hail pounded the roof, wild and thunderous so there was no mistaking the silence beneath.

Pia usually found its country-side tranquillity a welcome contrast to her hectic city life and her on-off significant others. She'd never quite found the right someone, and a retreat over its threshold felt like a nurturing embrace; the three of them, a family: she, the cottage and Helena.

Today, an awkwardness had set in on the journey back and stalked them through the front door. Neither wanted to speak first. Helena was scared to upset Pia, whilst Pia sensed she was owed something first, much as a child when she'd felt unfairly reprimanded for an act of disobedience and ordered to say sorry.

Staring at the un-lit wood-burning stove, a recent addition

to the fireplace, Helena sighed and spoke in a wistful tone, "From when you were a baby and as you were growing up, I told you everything about your mother and father, or at least everything I knew. She was a young woman who fell in love with a dashing young man who was travelling through."

"Yes, I know Mum. And he had left the country before she knew she was pregnant with me." Pia sounded flat, almost bored with the familiar tale. "She couldn't keep me because her Catholic family wouldn't allow it."

"Well, that was that. For most of our lives since, I have loved you as my daughter. It has been you and me. We just got on with it. Part of the adoption agreement was that we were barred from contact with your mother and her family. As for your father, I only knew his first name and that he had returned to Argentina. My limited contact with him has been photos exchanged via a PO Box, and that's it, I promise."

"You're not telling me anything I don't already know. What's been going on in recent months? Why didn't you tell me Mum?" Pia's hurt crackled in the air.

"Look, I know you've heard all of this before, I'm just saying you've always known as much as me. It only changed when I got an email from Pablo in May. Please let me explain?"

"But May was two months ago!" Pia snapped

"I know darling, I don't know if I got it right, maybe I should have told you about him sooner?" Helena frowned. Oh I don't know. What a mess I've made. Can you forgive me?"

"Pia reached across and took Helena's hand. "There's just too much to take in. I need a bit of time to work it through, you know?"

"Of course you do."

Pia added her other hand to the pile of fingers, creating a hand sandwich.

"Mum, why don't you start slowly and I'll let you know if it gets too much?"

"It's a deal."

Elizabeth

She sat in the dark, watching the shadow of the tree outside her flat. Verdant, elegant, invisible during the day, so in keeping with its brothers and sisters lining the wide avenue, even the rustling of its leaves in a stiff morning breeze would fail to catch her attention. Dusk onwards though and its spirit awakened, the smallest of movements playing upon the walls of her home; ghoulish, exaggerated monsters threatening to capture her if she came too close.

It had been several hours since Andrew had left; her eyes red and swollen had no more tears to cry. Her usual routine, disrupted by trauma, was trying to reassert itself.

Why are those curtains open? I hate the shadows. The whole point of the heavy-duty damask had been to cocoon the space in claret womb-like comfort.

Sitting on the Persian rug by the dead embers of the open fire, Elizabeth shivered. Her chin on her knees, arms cradling her slim, well-defined legs, she wasn't sure how long she had been there. Her body broken; at least her reliable ego had reappeared. An automaton, she selected the self-preservation module from her library of lifetime experiences and pressed return.

Despite feeling mentally battered and bruised she was too strong-minded to allow the events of the previous twelve hours to be anything other than a minor setback. Something would turn things around. She, Elizabeth Braybrooke, dogged in her pursuit of perfection, decided this was a just small blip to overcome.

Over? What did it mean anyway? The word had been spoken so many times, it no longer held any potency. All she needed was time to gather her thoughts, lick her wounds and develop the right strategy to get her back on track. There was no way Andrew had meant it. *Over! What rubbish!*

Her vision had been clear; his expected answer obvious. With his business brain, her sales savvy and their shared passion, this opportunity would be the making of them. Hadn't he frequently mentioned feeling shackled by his marriage in all their conversations from car to bar to hotel pillow? No way he would refuse her; sales person supremo; voted best business developer for the last three years running in their internal Movers & Shakers Awards. There was no-one in the business with greater influencing skills.

Elizabeth remained certain in her belief she could lure Andrew with this dream scenario and land the catch. She never failed at anything. Not since her twenties anyhow. She could see all the merits of this new venture: the resurgent popularity of dance, the ready-made venue and modest seed capital, her recent property development success. It didn't take a genius though, to determine her brilliant career in the city alone would not be enough to pull this off.

At the outset, the house renovation would eat up eighty percent of the inherited cash and the business would require significant further investment for its operations. But this was not about the money, this was about her future with Andrew.

A few hours ago, his involvement had seemed an impossibility. He had flatly refused to buy-in to the dream and leave London or his wife. Elizabeth knew she had to turn it round somehow or risk losing him. If he wasn't motivated by the idyllic country life à deux she had portrayed, she would offer equity, build a great business case and put all her recruitment guile into securing his agreement to becoming her Chief Finance Officer instead.

Her meeting at the family solicitors had sparked a frisson of excitement. This was the opportunity she had been waiting for. She could become his one and only; she could finally allow him to help her recover from that other time, to trust again.

As the door of number thirty-two Clarence Road closed behind her, she had allowed herself a vision of the future; there she was spinning and gliding elegantly in his arms; at last a couple meant for each other with nothing to hide.

The charity ball in October would be the perfect occasion. Her firm, Howard Barnard, one of the most prestigious executive search firms in the Square Mile, was hosting the event this year at The Mayfair, Radisson Edwardian Hotel.

Andrew, being the managing partner and public face of Bonner and Tuce, big four accountancy firm, had been invited to host the evening. Elizabeth had been asked to be Tess Daly to his Bruce Forsyth. Her trip to Gloucester had also provided her with the ideal outfit with which to ensnare him. Tucked away at the back of a vintage boutique in the Emporium, she'd spied the perfect evening dress—a Fifties classic in red taffeta.

The strapless number would give her an air of vulnerability; the cinched-in waist and full skirts complimenting her curves.

She may just have to purchase a pair of stilettos and a new clutch bag. Whilst she had a whole wall of her walk-in wardrobe dedicated to footwear and accessories, she was unable to recall the last time the choice of shoes was as crucial. In any case, if a girl couldn't treat herself to a new pair of shoes for a special occasion, when could she?

The newly refurbished Burlington Arcade and Beatrix Ong were calling. Feeling a little guilty for not calling her personal stylist first, she sneaked out of the apartment to avoid bumping into any of her tenants. Attempting to travel incognito, with her on-trend black mac and large sunglasses, to conceal any last remnants of her earlier emotions, she still cut a very noticeable figure as she hailed a cab to Bond Street.

Liza

What a weekend! Liza, dazed by the comings and goings of the previous forty-eight hours, sat in the shabby-chic tearooms. With its eclectic collection of bone china; dainty floral cups nestled on mismatched saucers; local artists' urban prints galleried on its pastel-painted walls and sturdy old school desks along one side, heavily laden with mouth-watering home-made cakes, it was one of her favourite places.

Her table beside the steamy windows gave her a full view of the café, the staff flitting backwards and forwards attended to the cosmopolitan blend of customers. Relatively off the beaten track and yet permanently packed with regulars, each of whom believed it was their best-kept secret, it was a little countryside haven. Slap bang in the middle of North London.

Liza guessed there might be numerous *little havens* to be discovered in the Cotswolds. She also suspected her chances of paying any of them a visit were remote.

Surely there were too many barricades to bring down; too much entanglement to disentangle, and there was her biggest hurdle—Gino. She shuddered at the thought of him discovering her plans. She tried not to dwell on him, hoping her intuition would take her down the right path this time.

Ideas, thoughts and problems tumbling over each other; T-shirts, jumpers and jeans in an endless wash cycle all jumbled and indistinguishable from each other. It was clear after two cups of camomile tea and the same number of hours' deliberation, Liza would not be coming to a conclusion any time soon. Every time she dismissed the venture as an unachievable pipe dream, her soaring joy, when Samuel had explained the gift to her, returned, convincing her Tango was her ticket out!

The journey back from Gloucester to London had been uneventful but even those uninterrupted hours reading through the Trust papers, coupled with this morning's time spent picking over them again, hadn't helped.

A jolly peel of laughter from a couple of friendly-looking mums in the corner by the cakes triggered an epiphany. Sheena was the solution! Her lovely, positive, warm, gorgeous friend. She'd help her find a way through.

Having realised she had to talk to someone, her other friend Candy from work too closely connected to Gino, Sheena was the obvious candidate. Galvanised into action, Liza packed up her papers and shimmied towards the counter to settle the bill. She resolved to pop by to see Sheena on the way home. She must just double check the confidentiality clause; fairly certain she was only barred from speaking to her family, as if that would ever cross her mind.

With a jittery excitement she left the café and headed up to the Clock Tower, crossing the road, passing fashion boutiques, shiny wine-bars and her favourite independent bookshop. Waiting patiently at the bus-stop for the W3, she looked around relishing the Crouch End bustle she loved. Would she miss it if she left London? Would she care about it anyway if she was free to build a new future? How great it would be for Angelo and how much happier they would be. There were numerous reasons to go for it. Could she make it work?

Liza spotted the double-decker bus coming round the corner, stopping at the queue of traffic held by the red light. Whilst it would take her towards Finsbury Park and near home, she would hop off a couple of stops before and call in on Sheena. Fingers crossed she'd be home for the bank-holiday weekend. If not, Liza wasn't sure what she would do with her spare day.

Remembering she'd forgotten her travel card, she fished about in her purse for the exact change. The driver hardly noticed her nondescript figure, as she deposited the coins in the chute. She felt invisible today. Grateful to be out in the ordinary world and away from the club, and Gino, she still felt jittery. Gino had insisted on taking Angelo to London Zoo. Reluctantly, Liza had agreed.

Most of the time she tried to forget there was any connection between her beautiful boy and that man. Her unconditional love for her angel was so far away from her feelings for his father, it seemed inconceivable Angelo's gentle soul had been spawned by such an ogre. There had been Gino's charm, at the beginning and, he could still be lovely, when he chose to be. Choices, those were always Gino's to make.

As the bus reached her chosen stop both she and it juddered, the vibrations of its engine resonating through the rubberised yellow handle.

*

The black wrought-iron gate squeaked as she opened and

closed it behind her. She walked the few steps of the original Edwardian-tiled patchwork path to the recessed porch. Long since converted to flats, she pressed the doorbell for 17a, the ground-floor garden flat occupied by her best friend.

Relief flooded through her as Sheena's recognisable form appeared, a shadow behind the stained-glass panels.

"Babe! What a lovely surprise!" Sheena spread her arms wide for a big hug.

Liza stepped inside the hallway and lost herself in the warm friendly embrace. "Is it okay to stay for a while? I'm not interrupting your plans am I?"

"No probs doll! Come through, come through. I'm just in the garden. Gotta make the most of the sun now it has finally decided to make an appearance. Not that I ever get a tan though. Look at all these freckles."

Heading along the dark, never-ending corridor, through the Tardis of a flat, Liza followed her cheerful companion towards the large, patio doors at the back.

The tiny courtyard garden was mostly paved and although a little overgrown, the established shrubs threw welcome shade over the chunky wooden bench table. Sheena's crazy creativeness gave the space a colourful Caribbean feel.

"Oh, I love these cushions! You made them, right?" Liza asked.

The felt appliqué animal shapes in orange and lime green contrasted the geometric turquoise and shocking-pink fabric; planters in the same summery tones were gathered in gaggles towards the far wall and close to the back door, little families clustered, full of tumbling lobelia and bright marigolds.

"Yeah, a little bit of making is always good for the soul.

Talking of which, would you like a glass of homemade lemonade? It's a new recipe. Just tried it today. I love it. Really quenches the thirst, you know?"

"Yes please. Sounds great! It's surprisingly warm now considering how the clouds were threatening a downpour earlier! So, where's Ray? I half thought you'd both be out and about making the most of the bank holiday."

"He had a last minute triple-time job called in yesterday, and we're gonna take a bit of time off together in a couple of weeks instead. Too much of a good rate to pass up. In any case I'm happy here kicking back with no-one else to please but myself today." Sheena hesitated, unsure quite how to broach the subject of Liza's rare excursion out of London. "You know I wasn't expecting you back so soon babe?"

Liza had been elusive on the details, keeping most things about the trip to herself. She must have had her reasons. Sheena wouldn't ever push, knowing Liza would talk if she wanted to. Still, it was unusual, as they had shared the most intimate details of each other's lives for years.

They fell into a comfortable silence whilst Liza picked over her thoughts wondering where to start.

"I think I may just have found a way out." Her statement full of precious hope.

Sheena clapped her hands together. "Really? How? That's amazing!"

The next few hours were filled with laughter and sparkle enjoyed between two old friends. Liza's excitement was infectious. She tucked away her doubts and fed Sheena with all the vital information about her possible new future, Sheena fed the two of them with toasted pitta and hummus, olives, delicious feta parcels from the local Greek deli and a fresh tomato and mint salad, picked from the abundant hanging baskets on brackets above the kitchen window.

"When I first got the letter I was reluctant to open it, you know? I mean the Gloucester postmark alone freaked me out," Liza said.

"You sure you're alright to talk about it? We don't really discuss your family and your past."

"Yeah I know. It was shit but that's not the biggest problem." She broke off, her eyes darting, searching for an answer. "This is an amazing opportunity but how am I going to make it happen? I shouldn't be thinking twice but I feel like I can't do it. It's too risky, surely? I mean, Gino explodes if I forget to buy skimmed-milk for his coffee, even though he hardly ever visits us. It kinda makes sense. I am a forgetful cow sometimes. I mean it's fair enough. It is his flat. Oh God!" She clamped her hand to her mouth. "What happens if he finds out I'm planning to leave? He'll stop me one way or another. Even if I get away, how can I be sure he won't follow me? I need to put Angelo first. I need to protect him. Maybe it's best to stay. It's probably a bad idea isn't it? Things are fine here. I've got you at least haven't I?"

"Enough! Stop. Talking. Crap. You have to make it happen babe!"

Sheena had never judged her friend, had always been there to pick up the pieces after every abuse. Neither had she truly spoken her mind before, knowing Liza had to come to her own conclusion. She had stood by her, until she was ready to see his poisonous, destructive ways for herself. Liza was quiet. Lost in her internal launderette again.

Sheena waited until she looked up. Taking Liza's hand, holding it tight, she spoke more gently, "Don't doubt yourself. You don't believe it now but I know you'll make the right decision. You can get away. I will help you. Together we will find you all the support you need to grab this thing by the balls. We can even sign up to some Tango lessons at the YMCA together." She gave Liza's hand an extra squeeze. "All those reasons to stay are not reasons to stay and I know, deep down, you know that too."

Dulcie

Dulcie rubbed her shin. Bumbling around hoping to work off her excess energy, packing and repacking things, she had thwacked it against the coffee table. She sat down to inspect her injury; the pattern of broken skin resembling the sequence of a stone skimmed on water.

No blood at least. I'll have a bruise later no doubt. What an idiot.

She should have been more careful, but her childhood clumsiness only ever resurfaced when she tried to do too much at once. Her mum had perpetually reminded her to "Pick her feet up" and "Look where you're going" whenever she had been distracted. Oddly enough lack of coordination had never surfaced in her dance classes as a child. Somehow they were different. Some Tango research was in order soon.

The news at the solicitors had been disorienting. It filled her body with uncomfortable levels of anxiety and excitement. How could she decide quickly when there were heaps of considerations? If she could just reach Peter and talk it through but he would be sleeping and it would be hours before they might speak.

Up until today, everything had seemed like an exciting

adventure. Leaving Samuel's offices she had been full of optimism and enthusiasm, believing as she most often did, things happened for a reason, and the choices she had to make would reveal themselves to her without too much introspection.

It became clear, after several hours of dithering, she would not be concluding anything tonight. Except, she didn't want to be alone with her thoughts. She dialled reception and made a reservation for seven-thirty that evening in the acclaimed Orchard restaurant.

She avoided her phone, leaving it charging by the mirror instead of checking for messages. There would be several from home once her family woke, full of questions about the meeting. There would be calls from Matty too, who had well-meaningly pledged to keep in touch. Dulcie did feel in need of human contact yet also in need of anonymity.

Her hair had turned frizzy in the drizzle, with little curls framing her face. Not wanting to go through the rigmarole of washing and blow-drying it straight again, she grabbed some of its bulk and secured it with a clip at the back. She checked her reflection and was pleased to feel more her Dulcie-like self. With a quick misting of perfume, she patted her pocket for the key-card and strode through the door, hoping to leave the see-saw of indecision behind her.

Taking the grand sweeping staircase to the main reception, she followed the signs to the restaurant with an impressive vaulted ceiling. A large, round bay window at the far side looked inviting as the late sunshine filled the panes with a golden glow.

Surprisingly for a Saturday, very few tables were already occupied when the maître d' appeared with a swish and a swagger.

"Good evening Madam. Do you have a reservation?" It seemed such a pointless question.

"Yes, seven-thirty. It's a table for one, Ms Braybrooke. You do have my name down, don't you?" she replied as politely as she could. Never easy with a giggle brewing in your throat.

"Ah yes, certainly. Here you are." He consulted the schedule, highlighting and ticking against her name. Looking up again, he surveyed the empty room, as if searching for a spot to allocate her was a skilful operation. With a triumphant smile, he led her to a small table by the very window she had been drawn to.

The sun was now setting behind the tall poplar trees, projecting a spectacular array of warm hues onto the feathery cirrus clouds high in the sky.

"What a beautiful spot. Thank you," she said, delighted in his selection.

It hit her that she couldn't recall the last time she had dined alone in a proper restaurant, if ever. It made her think of Peter.

Bloody time difference. I wish we could talk right now. But what on earth would I say?

Behind her, diners were starting to fill up the tables. Trying to push away her internal conversation, she immersed herself in the role of anonymous tourist, and dove into other people's chatter. Fond of people-watching, this people-listening seemed like fun too.

Dulcie shifted in her seat, head tilted to her right, as an excuse to take a closer look at her neighbours. Mrs Window seemed miserable. Mr Window was a measly man, several inches shorter than his wife, with a mean face and a whiney, flat intonation.

"Excuse me," he called to the waitress with assumed

superiority. "I've been discussing an issue with my wife . "We're not able to reach the balsamic vinegar beneath the oil. Could you ask the chef how he proposes we eat it? Is there a method of dipping the bread he can suggest?"

Was this guy for real?

He didn't stop there. Three more times he sent the waitress back to the kitchen to insist the chef explain how they should dip their bread. *What a parochial idiot!* If he was representative of the local clientele she couldn't imagine the Tango school taking off.

The pace of change in Gloucester had always been a little sedentary. It had played a part in her decision to leave twenty-plus years ago. Having chosen not to stay in contact with her family, she did wonder about the lifetime of events she had forfeited, and how sheltered her own life might have been.

During the rest of her meal, her thoughts kept racing backwards and forwards between home and here, Peter and Matty, Tango and her pottery. What a muddle.

Dulcie patted her napkin around her mouth. The delicious food and the buzzy atmosphere had delivered some distraction but her plan to push away her indecision had failed. Time to head for bed and hope sleep would allow her brain to unscramble her confusion. Today had been a big day. Who knew what tomorrow would bring.

Annie

"Look Mum, I told you, it's not anything of any consequence. I'm just not able to talk about it yet!"

Annie's discomfort was obvious to everyone on kitchen duty at the family party, except to her mother, Betty.

Annie had been all too aware of the questions mounting in her mother's mind since returning from the Gloucester meeting yesterday. She accepted Betty was trying her best to hold them back, at the same time knowing an eruption of her own volcano was imminent. Undoubtedly, she needed to talk the whole thing through with someone. Being cooped up with the very people she was unable to confide in made the elephant in the room loom larger.

Those family members and friends roped in to help with barbeque preparation filled the awkward atmosphere with overenthusiastic suggestions for marinades and salads hoping to steer the discussion away from the forbidden topic. To some extent they succeeded.

"How about a herb mill? Do you have one Betty? I could do some halloumi kebabs, if you like, with mint and coriander?"

"Gosh, that pork tenderloin looks delicious. I need hoisin sauce and soy right?"

Soon, Betty was distracted and in her element. The chatter became an excited buzz, as the chef and sous chefs succumbed to the odd glass of G&T, chilled rosé or Colin's notoriously potent Pimm's. Somehow, the memory of its propensity to induce a hang-over nine times out of ten, had always faded by the time the annual celebration came around again. Much like the pain of childbirth, the pain and suffering of the intoxication never quite seemed enough to overcome its fruity moreishness, prompting most to accept the proffered tumbler with a reborn naivety.

Annie was relieved of her duties by a conspiratorial nod from one of the kitchen cohort, who had noticed Thomas struggling to get down from the treehouse ladder. He'd been calling for his mum, the final step just too big a leap to the ground. There were plenty of other adults in the garden, including his dad, Colin. Sometimes nobody else but Mum will do.

"Thanks Irene." She smiled gratefully at the kindly neighbour, another familiar face she'd grown up with.

Everything around her was familiar: the large higgledy-piggledy house with solid furniture; sideboards dressed with carefully placed photographs, a biography of the significant moments in her life; the faded paintings on the walls, purchased years ago, becoming permanent fixtures once placed in the very positions they occupied today.

She took a short-cut through the library, her favourite room, with its floor-to-ceiling books and her father's courtly but comfortable, high-backed reading chair.

The double French doors were open to the garden. Scents of the impeccable borders, mingling with those of the newly lit charcoal, wafted invitingly into the space. Yes, it was all familiar, yet somehow Annie was seeing it all as if it was a documentary on television. Despite being a regular annual tradition, begun before she had grown and left home, her view of it had changed.

No matter what she decided to do, this bank holiday weekend would now be associated with the revelations disclosed at the Currie, Hampton and Stephens offices yesterday. Unnerving wasn't the word. The whole thing–the gift, the terms of the trust, the necessary upheaval should she decide to accept was overwhelming! She would talk to Colin again.

Last night they had whispered into the small hours. He had been as supportive as he could, but ultimately, legally, the yes or no was down to her. Absentmindedly, she had reached the treehouse, ducking under the trailing branches of the adjacent weeping willow. Thomas had been waiting patiently, as Annie had worked her way down the nettled path towards him.

"Mum!" Thomas berated her with a disapproving frown and an unspoken reprimand in the single word.

"Sorry darling! Gosh, you look just like your daddy when he's not happy."

"Daddy's always happy. I love Daddy he's silly. He makes me laugh."

Inside Annie was hurt, the sharp pang of jealousy a pain in her solar plexus. She knew she was the sensible parent (someone had to be), but she wished she could be more fun. Perpetually burdened with a sense of responsibility and duty since her children had been born, she'd lost the fun-loving Annie who used to climb the very same treehouse. It wasn't Colin's fault. He'd always been there for her.

He reminded her again last night. "We're a great team when we pull together. If you want to do it, let's do it."

She wasn't at all sure she would ever reach a decision. The terms of the Trust required her to go into business with potential strangers, return to Gloucestershire permanently, uproot her family and give up her job (even if she hated it at the moment, it at least provided her with a secure income). It would also impose a career change for Colin, and all because an unknown benefactor had determined she may be worthy of this inheritance.

That was another thing, where did it come from? And why to Annie? It was madness, wasn't it? Annie the owner of a dance school? The thought made her tummy pirouette. Perhaps this was her chance to act on her wistful Saturday evening dream of being on *Strictly Come Dancing* one day. She shook her head.

Annie wasn't a business woman, she was a teacher and a good one. What would be gained by changing direction now? And a partnership with strangers, how would that work? Who in their right mind would go for that? It was certainly a flawed idea, regardless of her lack of business acumen, even she could recognise that!

Whilst Colin was upbeat about a move to the West Country, probably brought on by his not-so-secret desire to become a cheese-maker, it was ludicrous to think they could both start new enterprises synchronously and there was the renovation. Last night Colin had done some quick calculations. They would need to invest at least one and a half million in the dilapidated property.

"We could make it work but that would be eighty percent gone before we even start thinking about running costs, never mind sharing it. Then again, it's not really about the money, hon. It's whether you'll be happier," he had said.

Colin was right. Annie's biggest concern wasn't the money. It was the move, putting them right on her mother's doorstep. Colin had no issue on this front. As mother-in-laws went, he enjoyed an easy relationship with Betty, in whose eyes he couldn't put a foot wrong; the son she never had.

When Annie had first brought him home from university to meet her parents, Annie had been miffed at the attention her mum had paid him. Betty had become giggly around him, flirty almost, insisting he dance with her to The Shadows, every time they came on the jukebox at The Yew Trees Inn. She would do that cringy thing after one too many drinks and compliment him on his muscles and his moves, declaring she wished she were twenty years younger. Colin had always laughed it off as harmless fun.

"I know you find it annoying hon. She's only letting off steam just like you do in the clubs and you know your Dad's got two left feet, so you can't blame her really," he would say.

Annie had put up with it for Colin's sake. He had made her feel loved and safe and special, especially when they were driving away, back up the M5 to Warwick.

"Love to Colin. Now that is one thing you got right at least." Her mother's recurring comment, yet another criticism masquerading as a compliment, would always surface in her weekly calls home from university.

Thomas would love it, without a doubt. He was young enough to adapt to a new environment. There would be more time to go fishing with his dad, to be read The Gruffalo on his granddad's lap, to be spoilt rotten with cupcakes by Nana Betty.

Beth was another story. She was firmly settled into school with especially close friendships. There was her dance teacher. She'd idolised her since beginning lessons at the age of three. Annie could only imagine the preadolescent stubborn resistance with which Beth would respond, "No Mum. I am not leaving! Don't you care what I need or want?"

Annie did care. Beth appeared to be showing signs of having a real talent, maybe even being good enough to take her dancing very seriously. How could Annie deprive her of an opportunity, she herself, would have loved and never had?

With everything pointing to a no, she couldn't work out why her deliberations were feeling drawn-out and difficult. Sitting on the bottom of the ladder, long since vacated by Thomas, Annie was the picture of weighty contemplation.

Her older sister, June, held court by the barbeque, delivering both the funniest jokes and the first batch of meat to her father for cooking.

"What's up with Annie?" Her father and June looked towards the ash tree within whose branches the treehouse was securely nestling.

"Oh, I don't know. She's doing her 'weight of the world is on my shoulders' thing again." June said, mimicking her sister and crossing her arms.

"Now, now darling. Don't be unkind. You know how caring and sensible she is. Maybe it's the thought of the new term just round the corner?"

"If you say so, Dad. If you ask me she needs some therapy to get those mood swings sorted out. Might put her in touch with someone. Friend of mine is a stress specialist. Started out in HR and now working with high-flying executives, who really do have something to be stressed about!"

"Honestly June, you should listen to yourself! You have a solution for everything. Sometimes you should realise you can't fix the entire world. I'm sure Annie will find her own way to resolve whatever's troubling her," Dad said.

Michael knew as little as his wife, Betty, about what was going on, yet evidently far more than his eldest daughter. Where his view differed from both of theirs was in respecting Annie's reasons for keeping the meeting with the family solicitors private. His only concern was to see her happy, something which increasingly seemed not to be the case. He decided he would make the time to encourage her to find someone with whom she would be able to talk things through. He sensed June was at least accurate in her assessment–Annie was in need of professional support.

*

As they packed up the car the following morning, aiming to get away by ten to avoid the worst of the holiday traffic, Betty supervised from inside. When they were finished Annie's dad gave her a big hug.

"If there is anything you need. You know. . ." He took a step back to look at her face and hold her shoulders, just as he used to when she was younger. "I can always pop up for a visit even if your mother is busy with her church things."

"I'll be fine Dad," she said, pulling her face into a fixed smile. "It's just a bit of the post-holiday blues. And what do you mean if? Good one."

Michael's eyes twinkled. "She's on all the committees bar one nowadays. She's never in. Sometimes I wonder whether I should come out of retirement and re-join the faculty just to feel useful!"

"I'm sure your students would love that. Maybe get back to your fishing or take up Tai chi or something?"

"What are you two gossiping about? We ought to get going, honey," Colin said, leaning out of the window, crooking his neck to see a proper grin on Annie's face, and Betty almost losing a slipper, as she rushed out of house with Giraffey in her hand.

"Oh thanks Mum!" Annie said. "You're a life saver! We would have been in real trouble with Thomas if we'd left Giraffey behind!"

"No problem darling. Now, off you go, you don't want to get caught in traffic and ring me when you get there and any time if you want to chat. Love you."

part three

the therapy

September 2007

Liza

Liza sat patiently in the narrow hallway on one of the two mismatching chairs. The slim console table between them held several leaflets in neat piles offering advice on a range of support services. A cork notice board hung on the opposite wall, with overlapping information sheets crammed full of further advice. Its neighbour was a poster. In large bold hand-written letters it read:

PHYSICAL AND VERBAL ABUSE OF OUR STAFF OR OTHER MEMBERS OF THE PUBLIC WILL NOT BE TOLERATED. ANY ABUSE WILL BE REPORTED TO THE POLICE AND YOU MAY BE PROSECUTED.

Looking back towards the table and the vase of dusty silk roses, which were fooling no-one, Liza wondered how many others had sat in this seat thinking the same thoughts, as they nervously anticipated the unknown. She also wondered if she was making a habit of sitting in waiting rooms; this very similar to her anxious wait at the solicitors. There were differences: this one was much closer to home in North London; this was a meeting with someone she hoped would help reset the applecart.

Sheena had kept her promise to help her find support and had come up trumps or at least Sheena thought so. Excitedly, she had gabbled down the phone.

"Hey babe, I've got it! This is it, the answer or at least the right person to get you through the tough stuff to get to the answer."

"Hold on a minute Sheena! What are you talking about?"

"Sorry. I forgot you're behind the game. Let me fill you in. First, are you able to talk? I should have checked. No Angelo in earshot? No git nearby?" Sheena asked.

Whilst Liza knew there was no love lost between Gino and her friend she rarely called him names. Maybe it was prompted by the hope of Liza's imminent escape from his oppression.

"Yeah, I'm on my own for a bit. Angelo's on a play date with one of his school mates. No sign of Gino for a few days, thank God. Only really seen him at the club. He's got his eyes on, and probably his cock in, one of the new girls. Gives me a bit of respite anyway. Timing's perfect. If he was in one of his obsessive phases he would have instantly spotted something was going on."

"You know we were talking about you needing some professional help to make your decision?" Sheena took a deep breath. "I was talking to a friend of mine, Suzy. She said she knows this amazing hypnotherapist. By all accounts she has helped loads of women through difficult times. Suzy knows her through the charity she works for. Seems to think she's the mutt's nuts and perfect for you."

"Well, I suppose it might be worth a try. The only thing is, I bet it costs a bomb. I am completely strapped at the mo. I'm not sure." Liza couldn't quite bring herself to share her dear friend's enthusiasm.

"Well, that's just it!" Sheena had babbled on, splicing her words together as she had reached her punchline. "She volunteers once a week at this women's refuge on Holloway Road and there's no charge. It's free!"

And so, a week later, here Liza was, about to make the first tentative step towards unchartered territory.

A couple of mums were arriving back with babes in buggies. They negotiated the double doors of the tiny porch with familiar ease; happy, relaxed and laughing together. Liza sensed the soul of this shabby building was warm and welcoming in contrast with its appearance.

"You alright there?" One of the mums asked.

"Yes I'm fine." Liza replied. "I have an appointment with Dr O'Hannon. I'm waiting for her." She twisted the strap of her bag round her fingers. "That's probably obvious, huh? Do you live here then?"

"Just at the moment. For a little while, till I find my feet. Oh you mean Dr Kath? You'll have fun, she's great!"

"This your first session?" the other mum asked, whilst untangling herself from the easy-to-assemble buggy, which was impossible to disassemble.

"Yep. Due in soon." Liza shuffled in her seat and almost drew blood biting her lip.

"Honestly, don't worry," the first mum said. "It'll be cool."

Liza watched them move through the security door at the end of the corridor, toddlers in tow. She had told a teeny-weeny white lie. She wasn't due in for another half an hour. She had arrived in plenty of time to make sure she wasn't late and she'd met Suzy outside earlier.

"Would you like to come and meet some of the mums?"

Suzy had offered. "Or you could sit in my office if you don't mind being surrounded by the stacks of papers. Keep meaning to de-clutter, but it never seems to be the top priority. I've gotta pop out to collect a generous donation from a lady who kept all her six-year-old son's clothes and shoes, only to find her long-awaited second child was a girl!"

"It's alright. I'm happy to wait in the waiting room, if there is one?" Liza had looked about her for a reception and couldn't see anything obvious.

"Ah, I'm afraid all we have are the chairs in the hallway. Not ideal but space is at a premium and we have very few visitors, if you get my meaning, so a dedicated waiting area would be a bit of a waste."

"Oh, don't worry. I'll be happy enough here. I'll read through a few leaflets or I could just sit and take the time to chill. It's rare to have any time to myself."

"Okay lovely, as you wish,'" Suzy said.

Suzy's caring manner had given Liza some comfort. She had trusted Sheena, based on years of friendship, to know she would be in safe hands. Having only met Suzy a couple of times before today, she had no doubt she was well-meaning. Still, it had been a leap of faith that Suzy could know what was right for her, when they barely knew each other. Today's face-to-face contact had reassured her. Suzy was one of the world's givers, with a genuine interest in other people's happiness.

She heard movement from the landing above: a door opening; an exchange of closing greetings; followed by footsteps down the stairs behind her. She held still until the young woman to whom they belonged had turned into the corridor past her again, heading towards the entrance to the refuge.

"Liza? Is that you down there?" a voice called from the landing. "Come on up. I hope you haven't been waiting in that awful reception too long?"

She stood, eagerly taking the first three steps, then doglegged up the stairs, their steep nature necessitating caution and a slower pace. A smiling face awaited her as she reached the top.

"Hello Liza," Dr Kath said, shaking her hand. "It's lovely to meet you. Do come through and take a seat."

Elizabeth

Her project-management skills were being tested. Using every ounce of her sexual capital, Elizabeth was finding it impossible to pin Andrew down. He had been elusive at worst, distant at best, since she had told him of her opportunity to run the Tango school near Gloucester. It was proving hard work to convince him of its viability.

One thing she had got right–she had backed off the relationship, focussing instead on the investment potential and wealth creation that might persuade him to join her. She had figured that once his head was involved as an equity partner, she could ensnare his heart over the many hours they would spend together during its set-up, especially if she could persuade him to learn such a romantic dance with her.

This morning's task was to find some support for herself. It was proving an incredibly tortuous time for her emotionally. Ordinarily, her composure and self-restraint didn't allow room for feelings. She had long ago suppressed the need for emotional connections, years before she had opted to be the 'other woman' in Andrew's life. Now though, the meeting revealing her inheritance had stirred the sensitive, passionate woman within.

She couldn't imagine life without some element of Andrew, but she could quite effortlessly imagine a significantly more rewarding life; taking flight in this hot-air-balloon of a crazy idea to run a Tango school would be life changing. Mistakenly, she had let her guard down, permitting herself to visualise the two of them flying high together. Now she was torn. Whilst his lack of interest in her venture had been clear, she had not been expecting the news to be a catalyst for him to end their affair.

Elizabeth's head was in chaos. As a result, in a highly uncharacteristic way, she recognised the need to seek advice. Outwardly, she did not display the tiniest hint of her inner churning. She remained as cool and direct as ever with her colleagues; as sparkling and engaging as ever with her clients. However, increasingly, it was becoming a harder act to perform. Her complexion was suffering, she was sleeping terribly and as she closed the door to her flat each night, the façade fell away and floods of tears would roll down her face.

Picking up her phone she dialled the number from the website: The O'Hannon Hypnotherapy Clinic, Harley Street. The referral to this establishment had come from a meeting with one of her clients, the CEO of an exciting new online retailer. An appealing distraction from her customary investment bankers, Chloe Williams also was one of the few female executives amongst Elizabeth's portfolio.

Elizabeth was surprised Chloe had requested her. Howard Barnard had a whole retail division, jam-packed with executive search consultants all of whom had an extensive network in the sector. They'd hit it off immediately, with common interests in high fashion, five-star travel and fine dining. She recalled the meeting fondly.

"I'm interested, what made you ask for me? I wouldn't say I'd be your regular choice of consultant, as I have little or no exposure to your industry," Elizabeth asked.

"Do you know what it was? I firmly believe people buy people," Chloe said. "My husband heard of your reputation through his accountants at Bonner and Tuce. To me, a good recruitment partner is like gold dust. In my experience, once you both agree on what good looks like, they can recruit any role for you."

Elizabeth laughed. "That's true. Although most of my profession survive on their existing network and can't see beyond."

"Well, I need someone I can trust to get it right and I've heard that's you!"

"Thank you. Tell me, how do you juggle your long hours, your family, hobbies and still look so amazing?" Elizabeth sat forward, eager to hear Chloe's secret.

"Well, you don't look so bad yourself. I gather you are always out wining and dining. Goodness knows how you keep so trim?"

"Blood, sweat and sheer determination. At the moment, I'm permanently exhausted. Work gets the best of me, with very little left at the end of the day. Hence my original question," Elizabeth said.

"You've observed quite correctly that my life is full on. It would be very easy to drop the ball on any one aspect. It may look like a Cirque du Soleil performance to you; in reality I often struggle to get the balance right. Most often I find it's me I neglect. I think that's true of most mums, who invariably put everyone else first."

"I'm not one. . . yet. . . but I've heard that said before. What do you do? How do you rebalance things?" Elizabeth leaned closer.

"About a year ago I took a long hard look at myself and realised I was heading for my last performance unless I changed something," Chloe said. "Completely by accident, I was reading an article in the *Sunday Times*, the lifestyle section I think. It was all about executive stress management and ways to become more effective by being less busy. So, I made a note of the columnist, a Dr Kath O'Hannon. You may have seen her TV show, *Talk to Dr Kath*?"

"No, not something I have time for I'm afraid," Elizabeth admitted. "Occasionally I get obsessed with a boxset that's been raved about. Otherwise, I keep in touch with what's happening via Radio Four and skimming the *FT*. That's about the sum of my media exposure."

"She reportedly had lots of success working with women in all walks of life who are either dissatisfied or disillusioned with their lot," Chloe explained. "The TV series was all about relationship therapy. She's written several self-help books, including the one on executive stress and has endorsements from politicians to top female celebrities." Chloe paused as the waiter refreshed their glasses with a bone-dry and aromatic Sancerre.

"So, you went to see her?"

Chloe smiled. "Something about her rang true for me. I picked up the phone first thing the following Monday morning and within a week I had started a series of hypnotherapy sessions with her. I haven't looked back."

The terrace bar with its views over the Thames was full of

young professionals, cash flowing as easily as the wines being poured into elegant glasses. Elizabeth, scarcely aware of her surroundings, let a little more of herself spill out.

"Can I share something with you? Something personal I mean. In general I don't make a habit of discussing my private life. Professionalism runs through my veins and there are some boundaries that should remain uncrossed."

"Don't be silly, share away!" Chloe said. "The better we understand each other, the better our working relationship will become. I firmly believe that."

"If you're sure? It's just you've already given me lots of your precious time and I don't want to impose."

"Go for it," Chloe said, taking a sip of her drink.

"I may have an opportunity to be involved in an exciting new business. My instinct is telling me to go for it. My head is telling me it would be foolish. I vacillate between yes and no on a daily basis. Something is stopping me from coming to a conclusion. Do you think your hypnotherapist could help?" As Elizabeth heard herself speaking she realised she already knew the answer to the now-redundant question.

Whilst still uncertain of her future, a wave of relief spread through her at the thought of being expertly guided through her deliberations. An eminent specialist providing her with safe passage through the choppy waters she had been experiencing.

*

The ringing tone was followed by a polite and friendly greeting.

"The O'Hannon Clinic, Trudy speaking. How may I help you?"

There. She had done it! Appointment booked with Dr Kath. Elizabeth would begin unravelling the knots of her indecisiveness. Tuesday morning. Seven-thirty.

Pia

News of her father's bequest was gradually sinking in, settling somewhere between her normal world and the surreal. Now it was a known fact she couldn't un-know it. For the first few days she had been in denial; her daily routines giving her the comfort only a ritual can. Her morning jog; her healthy muesli; her not-so-healthy cup of strong black coffee; her hot shower with body scrub reviving her senses, leaving her mind and body tingling.

It wasn't the same as being back in her own house, with her own space. Her Tuesday night training runs with the Highbury Harriers; her Thursday-is-the-new-Friday meet-ups with colleagues at the Pig and Whistle. But it would have to do.

Today she was meeting PJ at the house. The thoughts she had suppressed resurfaced uninvited, as she let the water fall over her face. What would her half-brother be like in person? Would they feel as close offline as they did online? Their connection was instantaneous and their communication was frenetic and compulsive, since he had shared that first photograph in that first email.

Plus there was the house. Her memories of it from childhood walks returned, fuzzy, except for the trespass signs. They had often encountered these at junctions where the bridle paths butted up against the high chain-link fences. She remembered glimpses of an imposing estate between the wooded borders, overgrown with ferns and brambles. She felt a frisson of excitement.

Pia took the same care over her choice of clothing as she would for a first date: low, comfortable shoes with a small heel, so as not to feel ungainly, and a figure-hugging, floral dress with a flattering swish. She wanted to make the right impression. It seemed important. After a series of jokey texts, PJ's last text with the arrangements had been both succinct and cryptic:

Meet me at the house at eleven o'clock ready to dance.

Pia hoped she'd chosen well. With an intensifying tingle of expectancy, she applied a modest amount of make-up and trotted down the wooden staircase of her mum's cottage. The sounds of her descent brought Helena to meet her in the hallway. She had been keeping out of the way, baking ginger-nut biscuits in the kitchen.

"You all set? You look lovely."

"Thanks Mum. Yep, ready to meet my long-lost brother for the first time. Mind you, with all the emails we've been exchanging, I feel like I've known him forever," Pia said.

"Wonderful, darling. I'd give you a hug but I'm covered in flour. I don't want to spoil your beautiful dress." Helena was not joking; the blue of her classic blue-and-white striped apron was hardly visible; a heavy dusting of the white powder had settled in her hair and smudges of the stuff appeared as random splodges on her face.

"Mum! What have you been doing? Is there any flour left for you to bake with?"

"Ah, yes. I had a little fight with the plastic container in the larder. The advantages of keeping it airtight may be outweighed by the fact the thing is impossible to open without Vesuvius erupting everywhere."

Pia giggled at the image. "Oh Mum, you are funny! I'd better get my skates on. Don't want to be late and leave him hanging around in that rambling place on his own."

"Enjoy yourself. I'll get on with my biscuits. Bring him back if you like. It'd be nice to meet him at last," Helena said.

"We'll see. Maybe one Braybrooke at a time might be best, eh?"

Pia hopped in her car, waving to her mum, as she reversed off the drive. She knew Helena would stand in the open doorway, waving back until her hatchback disappeared down the lane.

Pia drove the few short miles to Painswick, wondering if she should have offered to bring her along. She was feeling guilty for being so self-absorbed lately. After her initial anger had subsided, she realised she ought to be saying sorry to her mum who had been put in a difficult position. Helena must have been tempted to confide in her, so rare was it for anything to come between them.

Since the day of the storm, a few weeks ago, they had both avoided discussions about her father, preferring to keep the mood light and airy. Pia knew she needed to broach the subject again soon but for now she was content to enjoy the adventure with her new brother without too much meaningful contemplation. Besides she'd be moving out again, once the house was habitable, and she didn't want her time with her mum dominated by negativity.

Deliberately choosing the lanes through the Cotswold

countryside, she navigated her way to the Big House, as it was colloquially known. Finally, she took the left turn off the B-road down the long and overgrown driveway.

The wet spring followed by a half decent summer had generously supported an abundance of plant growth. Most avid gardeners, like her mum, had been delighted with the mass of cottage annuals and the vigorous conquering of their borders. Her garden had been a riot of summer colour, set against a lush green backdrop, with little need for the weeding required by a formal scheme. The story here was different. Without the employ of the groundsmen, who had long since given notice when the old man died, nature had been allowed a free run of the place.

Crawling along at a few miles per hour, to prevent the brambles from scratching her paintwork, Pia came to a stop by the towering wrought-iron gates. She pulled up alongside a rather fetching, pale-blue Hillman Imp. The stylish vintage car, complete with chrome bumpers, was in immaculate condition. No PJ to be seen.

Pia noticed the gates were ajar, the heavy-duty padlock looped back through one side. Goodness, she felt like the second Mrs de Winter about to stumble across the moonlit Manderley in her dream. Her heartbeat quickened. Pushing the gate open a foot more, she followed the path, almost totally obscured at this point by nature's legacy. Fallen branches from previous winters littered the woods either side. Mushrooms, lichen and moss had claimed the dead wood, bringing new life to old. Saplings of ash, oak and hazel were beginning to colonise the undergrowth. It was their final push of the year before the leaves began to fall.

Nearing the house now, there was evidence of human intervention. Attempts to curtail the boundless march of greenery could be seen in the piles of prunings by the wayside. Pia paused to review her progress. It dawned on her the track had widened substantially, that in fact it was a lane intended for vehicles; a continuation of the driveway along which she had approached.

Still no sign of PJ; she was perplexed. Doubting herself, she checked her watch to make sure she had arrived at the agreed time. She had foolishly assumed the jazzy car outside the gates was his. She had assumed, equally as foolishly, he would have waited somewhere a little more obvious. Was this how it was going to be? A magical mystery? A game of hide and seek? Where was he? She really hoped he wouldn't jump out at her and shout, "Boo!"

With all this solitary exploration, her nerves were beginning to jangle. She took a deep breath, told herself to pull it together and emerged out from the tunnel of trees into the sunshine.

There it was. The grandiose residence. It had the look of a retired, ageing captain; proud and dependable, upright and of good character. A smidgeon less dapper than in his heyday, but no less impressive. Immersed in its withering beauty, Pia stood absorbing the reality. She was now a guardian of this marvellous building.

Not more than a minute or two later she heard her name being called in a distinctive Latin accent.

"Pia! Pia you are here! I was inside exploring and spotted you from the upstairs balcony. I am sorry I didn't wait for you. I was just too curious. What a beautiful place she is, no? And now I have you to share her with!" PJ stood on the steps, sweeping his arms out wide ready for a grand embrace. "I am so glad to see you. Come here. Let me give you an Alverez *abrazo.*"

"You are exactly as I had imagined," Pia said after she had extricated herself from his hold.

"Really? How do you mean?"

"It's all good. Don't worry." Pia linked her arm in his.

He was indeed exactly as she had imagined. Poised and charismatic with a dash of Pan-like mischievousness. Just as in every one of his three hundred and ninety six emails over the last three weeks. Yes, she had been counting.

Dulcie

"Hey there!" Matty called out as he sauntered towards her.

They had agreed to meet outside Topshop on Oxford Circus. It was the first landmark Dulcie could think of, the selection of which she had instantly regretted on her arrival: too many people, too many doorways, too many directions to keep look-out for Matty's arrival.

She knew she needn't be anxious. He would spot her first; for some reason he always did. Sure enough, whilst she was watching the hoard of tourists jockeying for position at the crossing, he approached rounding the corner from Regent Street.

Her heart skipped with the instant connection, which sparked whenever she saw him. She had convinced herself a meeting with Matty would help her work through the dilemma she was facing regarding her inheritance.

"Hello you." Her greeting was deliberately simple.

They kissed continentally, on both cheeks, laughing nervously as neither was sure how many kisses were appropriate. A discussion ensued with tales of embarrassing situations, with various acquaintances from Switzerland to Hungary, Provence to Paris, of not quite knowing the correct etiquette and almost always getting it wrong.

"What's the Sydney protocol then?" Matty continued, as he gently guided her, negotiating their way through the crowds, narrowly missing a collision with a kamikaze cyclist.

In opting to maintain momentum, as the lights changed to red, he failed to spot the bike as he stepped off the pavement. A thrill raced through Dulcie's body; the effect, a combination of the incident and Matty's tender touch when he caught her waist to protect her from harm.

"Where are we headed?" Dulcie had moved on from their previous topic, now completely under Matty's spell.

"Not sure really. Thought we might have a wander down to Carnaby Street. It used to be one of your favourites right?"

"You have an incredible memory! I can't have mentioned it more than once or twice."

"I remember everything about you." In so few words he said so much.

"Carnaby Street sounds fine," Dulcie responded, tucking her hair behind her ears, brushing over his comment. "I love wandering round rediscovering London. I didn't expect to enjoy it this much."

"It's good when you take the time to enjoy it. Problem is most of us Poms just take it for granted."

*

The transformation of her favourite quirky shopping street took Dulcie by surprise. Gone were the shops full of tourist tat of her Eighties recall. It still had a great atmosphere but was now crammed full of flagship stores of some of the world's best-known fashion brands, interspersed with the odd independent boutique. Dulcie didn't mind, after all, she was the tourist now, here to breathe it all in and have fun.

After a couple of hours browsing and chatting about their families, Matty fascinated at how Dulcie managed her four kids and her business, Dulcie saddened by stories of Matty's divorce and his father's Alzheimer's, they headed to a trendy whole-food cafe for a well-earned cuppa and a slice of carrot cake.

"So, tell me all about it," Matty said.

He had been waiting for Dulcie to download all the details of her Gloucester escapade. She had mentioned it in their text exchange prior to meeting up and not since. There had been no rush. He was content to wait until she was ready. Now she regaled him with the full account of her weekend: the city, the solicitors, Samuel, the inheritance, the hotel and all. Her fluid, funny storytelling held him captive and was only interspersed with, "Ooh, aah and no way, really?" He let her finish before flooding her with questions.

"Wow! That's some revelation! Remember you said, 'Oh I'm sure it'll be fine' before you headed off on your adventure? How are you feeling now? If it was me I'd be wary of such a gift out of the blue. No such thing as a free lunch and all that. Do you know anything about where this came from? Or, who the others might be?"

"I am feeling totally mixed up if I'm honest," Dulcie confessed. "I can't think straight. Unsurprisingly, I feel torn. This whole return to the UK thing has untold implications."

"Go on."

"I guess my biggest dilemma is the question of making a

permanent return. It's so enormous I don't think I can make up my mind that quickly. To the deadline, I mean," Dulcie explained.

"That's understandable but what about the other questions of why it's happened and who you would be partnering with? Getting clear on those might help you make up your mind, don't you think?" Matty asked.

Her head buzzing, Dulcie took a couple of sips of her Earl Grey before replying, "Maybe."

"Do you have any idea who the others might be? You've not said as much, but you must have some idea?"

"Putting two and two together, the location of the meeting, the wording of the instructions, it's gotta have a family connection," Dulcie said.

"You weren't tempted to contact them? Your mum and dad, the other members of your family?"

"Nope."

Matty wondered whether she would elaborate.

"Bloody Braybrookes. I'm not interested in digging up the past. In any case the letter implied I would lose the right to participate in the inheritance if I did. End of story. Can we talk about something else please? Your next cycle race? Your mother? Anything," Dulcie begged.

The last thing Matty wanted was to push her away. He didn't want to force the matter.

"No worries, as you would say. Let's settle up and go for a walk and talk along the South Bank," he suggested. "We can hop on the Bakerloo line to Waterloo and I can show you the delights of more regeneration. I suspect it's changed quite a bit since you were there last."

Dulcie grinned. "Sounds good."

As Matty went off to pay, again, Dulcie couldn't help wishing they could talk through how they felt about each other, never mind how she did about her family. A jumble of uncertainty and bewilderment, she really had no direction.

Too many demons, temptations and heartache.

But how indulgent it would be to spend more time with this wonderful man. I can't make a choice about this on my own. I can't talk to Matty. I definitely can't talk to Peter–yet. I need to be clearer in my own mind first. What a mess.

"Anybody in there?" Matty was by her side again.

"Sorry I was miles away. I'm thinking it's just all too much for me to sort out. Maybe I should just go home and back to my family. All these years of working for the love of my art and now I can make it work for me there. You know, earn a proper living. What do I want with emigration, Tango schools, throwing my family into disarray? And there's Peter. What about Peter and the kids?"

"What about me?" His question was out before he could stop himself. Matty put his hand up to his mouth. "I'm sorry. I'm trying to be patient but it's difficult–for both of us."

"I'm sorry too. I'm a mess right now. You on the other hand. You are, and always were, altogether too gorgeous for me!" Dulcie dipped her head, her hair covering the blush on her cheeks.

"Hey that's not true, and you know it. Truce?" Matty said.

"Truce."

Before long they were wandering past the street performers entertaining the crowds queuing for the London Eye. The sights and sounds of a busy tourist attraction provided the perfect diversion for them both. The bustling promenade full of happy relaxed faces; the late-summer sun shimmering on the river, regularly disrupted by the wake of boats negotiating the invisible lanes of the water highway; the bars and restaurants whose patrons were spilling out onto the streets.

Old and new buildings happily co-existed. Sleek concrete steps flowed into dark cobbled alleyways and back out again into contemporary landscaping, where groups gathered to watch pavement artists chalking accurate yet idiosyncratic representations of the London skyline.

"Do you fancy stopping for something to eat?" Matty asked.

"Yes please, after heaps of hours sightseeing I'm done in! Starting to get museum feet, if ya know what I mean?" Dulcie's Australian accent showed through, as it always did when she was tired.

Matty spied an intimate table for two, outside on the terrace of a chic tapas bar. Whilst strolling, they had been entirely focused on reminiscence. They had regurgitated all sorts of stories of their time together: the moment they'd met at the sixth-form West Side Story auditions, where Matty had been cast in the lead role; the paint pot Dulcie had kicked over, watching his fight scene rehearsal instead of her feet, whilst painting one of her backdrops; the theatre trip to Romeo and Juliet where they had spent the coach journey home snogging on the back seat, before they were told off for "inappropriate behaviour" by the drama teacher.

As they were shown to the table, Matty fell quiet, revelling in their togetherness. In the lull before their sangrias were delivered, they sat side by side watching more of London go by. Having been distracted by the fun of the afternoon, the weight of Dulcie's worry now returned. Being brave and taking advantage of the fact Matty couldn't see her face, she spoke, calmly and openly.

"There is something between us which is compelling. There always was. We both know that. Now we have reconnected, I cannot imagine a life without you in it. I have no idea where this will lead us, but right now, I have to focus on the reason why I came back here in the first place. Will you let me do that?"

"Was it the whole reason?" he asked.

The letter had been the initial draw, yes, but Dulcie wanted him, of that he was sure. She would have known, as he did, any rendezvous would be likely to lead her to a crossroads from which she couldn't turn back.

"Not the whole reason but it is a big thing you must admit? Meeting up with you again just makes it more complex. It's impossible for me to see a way through the maze really."

"If you need to put me to one side for a while I understand. Make sure you do what's right for you and your family," Matty said.

"That's easier said than done," Dulcie confessed. "If you cut me through the middle, I think you'd find the word selfish running through me and what about you? I hate to think of you alone."

"Rubbish, I'm fine. It's three years now since my divorce." Matty sighed. "It was tough but I realised she wasn't the one, you know. . ." He broke off, clearing his throat. "Besides we've stayed in touch and it's all good. Maybe this single life suits me?" His crow's feet crinkled into a smile. "Maybe. . . I'm the selfish one?"

"You? Selfish? Nah. Not buying that!"

They both laughed, easing the atmosphere a little.

Their jug of fruity red sangria clinked and fizzed pleasingly as the waiter placed it on the bistro table with two glasses.

"Have you decided yet madam?" The waiter nodded towards the specials board a few feet away from them on the wall, pad and pen at the ready.

"Now there's the question, eh Dulcie?" Matty winked.

"Oi cheeky," she said to Matty. She turned to the waiter. "Why don't you bring us a selection of the best small plates you have? We'll go with your recommendation. Let's live dangerously."

"Certainly madam, my pleasure."

They giggled conspiratorially, as he scuttled off to the kitchen to place their order, efficiently clearing the neighbouring table along the way.

"You are naughty Matty! The poor thing didn't know where to look."

To Dulcie's surprise, Matty sounded serious, "Listen, I've been thinking. Have you thought about a therapist? Or something to help you get un-stuck? It's a bit of a long shot, I know, but my mum knows this hypnotherapist. She's meant to be really good. If you can squeeze in several sessions with her whilst you are here it might make a difference? You know, accelerate your decision making? Help you see the wood for the trees?" Taking a gulp of his sangria, he added before Dulcie could reply, "Look I'm not saying this because I want you to stay, although obviously I do. It's really just my way of trying to offer support and you've not said anything yet and now I think I may have overstepped the line!"

"You haven't. I know you're thinking of me, which is

wonderful." Dulcie squeezed his left hand with her right. "And I appreciate it. . . To be honest, and I know I keep saying this, I'm open to all ideas at this point. The only thing is, if she knows your mum, isn't it a bit too close to home? I mean, I might need to talk about you?"

"I'm pretty certain everything you discussed would be treated as confidential." Matty turned to face Dulcie and took her other hand in his. "You have my permission to talk to her or anyone else you choose about me. I would tell the world about you if I could."

Annie

That afternoon everything seemed to be conspiring against her. Whilst she normally prided herself on her instinct, Annie wished she had not a single ounce of intuition in her body. Those blasted premonitions, which seemed to be occurring more and more often recently, for reasons she couldn't fathom, on this occasion had led to the most expensive packet of chewy mints she had ever purchased.

Sometimes she wondered whether fate was dictating her life and so, on this trip to the petrol station, her thinking followed this course: *I'm running late to pick up the children from school. I really shouldn't stop to fill up, but, if I don't fill up I may not get to school. Right, I'll just take half a tank. This station is always more expensive, really only for emergencies and I should save the pennies. I wonder if I might get a passionate kiss at some point this evening, maybe when Colin gets home. Whilst I am waiting to pay I'll just check out the mints. Mind you if I choose those, the chewy ones with the harder outer layer, I bet I'll crack a tooth.*

And so it was, three minutes and forty-one seconds into her onward journey, having had several of the sweets, originally meant for an entirely different breath-freshening purpose, she experienced a strange sensation. Not painful but sharp, as if a shard of the sweet's outer casing had wedged itself between the tooth and the gum. She spent the rest of the school run planning how to dislodge the offending foreign object.

Not until sometime later, once the children were safely home and causing a riot over the remote control, did Annie realise her premonition had become a reality. With the realisation came a dull ache, not of tooth pain but of the likely impact on her bank balance; she just knew this was going to hurt. An emergency appointment, an X-ray and a ceramic crown a few weeks later, her instinct on that occasion had unfortunately proved spot on.

Now back into the term-time routine, the expected relief, once the familiar weekly pattern had been re-established, had not kicked in. The events of the last week of the holidays had completely thrown her. Clearing up the remnants of her family's hastily scoffed Saturday sandwiches, Annie tried to think things through.

In a way she wasn't at all surprised about the tooth incident. They say bad luck always comes in threes. Her mum and sister had cornered her, once most of the guests had departed the barbeque, piling on the pressure.

Back at school, her headteacher had questioned her involvement in the Christmas production, suggesting her focus should be on more academic endeavours, since she had now taken on the year-two class. Something had to give.

Dad is right. I should get some help. I'm gonna end up imploding soon if I don't. Annie wondered if she might be going a little crazy. Spending too much time in her head was counter-productive. It was her normal way of being. The constant self-chatter, usually a comfort to her, keeping her motivated and moving forward, was overwhelming. An asynchronous din. Good indistinguishable from bad; right unidentifiable from wrong.

In an attempt to quash the internal debate, Annie decided to pop out to the Village Store for some matches. She had planned a relaxing candlelit bath after Beth and Thomas had gone to bed. Colin would be out at a committee meeting, likely followed by a few pints at the local. A little bit of pampering should help.

She checked the large kitchen clock, emptying the soapy water from the washing-up bowl. Just enough time to walk down and back before she was on duty as Taxi-Mum, collecting Thomas from a birthday party and Beth from her singing lesson.

She strolled down the road to the shop with a slightly improved demeanour. Taking things at a slower pace never failed to lighten her load. The air was ozone fresh; the autumn sun low, diffused by a hazy sky, the clouds clinging to the horizon in preparation for their role in the sunset encore, before the dusk curtains fell. It made Annie smile at the memory of cooler evenings. She looked forward to the log fires and chunky home-knit jumpers soon to follow.

She did love her surroundings: the gentle arable hills, the comradely village community. Passing the eclectic huddle of houses, grand Edwardian villas interspersed with clusters of workers cottages, she agreed with herself it wasn't as majestic as her mother's view over the Cotswolds. No matter, it was reassuringly hers.

Of course, she did have happy memories of her childhood there too. It was just that she'd always been the back-stop in the games of cricket, leaving her sisters to have the bowler/ batter glory. She was always the one who'd re-set the monopoly board after Emma had stropped it over and the first to put her bike away without being asked. Her mum had always praised her for her dependability, she would have loved more of that.

She and Emma would meet in London occasionally for a glass of wine and surprise each other with wildly differing recollections of the same events.

"You were Mum's favourite," Emma would say.

"Rubbish," Annie would reply. "She was so impressed with your Dorothy in the school Wizard of Oz, she gave you Milo as a reward."

"Don't be daft. He was your puppy. She got him to cheer you up after you'd broken your ankle falling off the stage and I made such a fuss she let me name him to keep me quiet."

Funny how memory distorts things. Crossing the road just before the Farmers Arms, she resolved to catch up with her mum and talk things through. She would undoubtedly have some pearls of wisdom to share. Some may even be of use.

The bell chimed, announcing her arrival in the shop. Maureen Hunter stood up from behind the counter, where she had been replacing the stock of paper bags. Ironically, they had never made the move to the plastic variety. It was entirely coincidental her stubborn traditionalism had now given her a competitive edge on the global giants, whose superstores had long been breathing down her neck.

"Morning Annie dear. Oh it's afternoon now. Silly me! Afternoon."

"Afternoon Mo, how's tricks?" Annie replied, immediately at ease in such friendly company.

Maureen and her husband George had run the shop for many years before Annie's arrival in Swallows Green. They were part of the old guard, their own children long since flown the nest. Likely past retirement age, although Annie was too polite to ask, she and most of the neighbouring families had adopted Mr and Mrs Hunter as Nana and Gramps. They followed the progression of youngsters, keeping a keen interest on them as they grew from babe to teen. Surrogate grandparents with watchful eyes.

"Oh, not bad, and you? How's that elegant young lady of yours, Beth? And my favourite pocket-sized choirboy-in-the-making, Thomas?" she asked.

"They're fine. All golden and relaxed after their holiday. More than I can say for us. Seems we are only just back and life hits us like a train. No time to stop and reflect on the sunny memories. Even up-loading the holiday photos from the camera is another to-do on the long list of chores, which seems to never end."

"Hey now, that's not like you to be flat. Surely it's not that bad?"

"No, I suppose not. Everything seems to come all at once though and I don't seem to be able to make decisions about things any more. This morning it took me ten minutes dilly-dallying to choose between eggs and porridge for breakfast!"

"It'll be better soon, you'll see. Sounds like you need to give yourself permission to take some time for yourself. Now what can I get you? Maybe a slice of homemade apple-and-cinnamon loaf perhaps? That'd definitely cheer you up!" Mo smiled.

"Thank you. It does sound delicious but I am trying to

be good after all the *pain et fromage* and *tarte aux pommes* on holiday. Not to mention the *vin de table*, which was way too nice and way too cheap to resist. I'll just take a box of matches if I may please."

"Okay dear, but don't be too strict with yourself. A small treat now and then won't hurt eh?" Mo winked as she spoke, words wise as ever.

"I know and thanks for the offer. Next time perhaps?"

The till clinked shut, coins safely deposited in their correct slots.

"How did the barbeque go? And your mum and dad, are they well?" Mo asked. "We always have a giggle when they're up here visiting. Last time they were in I heard all about their trip to Amsterdam. You know, when Michael got directions for a 'decent coffee shop' and it wasn't quite what he was looking for." Her face crinkling at the memory. "Oh and your mum had to save him from falling in a canal when a cyclist sent him flying."

Annie chuckled. "They do seem to be having an adventurous retirement. They're fine, thanks. I'll let Mum know you were asking."

"Yes do, dear. Have a good weekend."

Annie turned to leave as the jangle of the bell announced a new customer. Mo would want to focus on their needs. She held the door open, saying hi to Dr Kath before gesturing her to enter.

Striding back up the street, Annie was struck by the aptness of their encounter. Funny how solutions came out of nowhere when you were not actively looking for them. Mo had done her best to lift Annie's spirits but she couldn't ignore her post-holiday pledge to get to the bottom of the grey fug and seek help. With the inheritance decision piled on top, she had all the more reason to organise an appointment. Her dad's words resurfaced too.

Everything was pointing to Dr Kath. She supposed June's recommendation of a stress expert had been well-meaning, if a little judgemental, but her dad's suggestion to investigate her own support had been a gentle nudge in the right direction.

Now to her next move. No more prevarication. Her determination to act propelled her home in double quick time. Without hesitation, in case she persuaded herself out of the idea, she reached for the business card lying on the window ledge in the hall. Before she had even closed the front door, she dialled the mobile number, nervously waiting for her call to be answered.

Liza

"Do sit down, make yourself comfortable. Thank you for being prompt. I'm sorry to keep you waiting. I've been running behind all day!"

Dr Kath indicated Liza should sit in a large chair with a matching foot stool. The chair itself sat by the window of the room with its neutral, some would say bland, décor. Dusty wood-effect blinds, although closed, let in a small amount of light between the slats, creating a pattern of shadowed stripes on the carpet.

Liza sat as instructed, nervously anticipating the unknown. She was eager to get started, get it over with actually. Formal stuff, meetings, were not her scene. This was just as awkward, perhaps more so, as the meeting at the solicitors.

With hindsight, she shouldn't have arrived early. She'd given herself too much time to get nervy. In the absence of knowledge, she had filled the vacuum in her head with all sorts of ideas about mind control, being forced to spill secrets or to act in undignified ways. Her mouth parched from her anxiety; she croaked a request for a drink of water.

Dr Kath filled a plastic cup from a jug on her desk and handed it to Liza with a sympathetic smile. Knowing most of her clients found their first time daunting, she took her through a description of the process by way of giving reassurance.

"Whilst you're sipping your water, I'll explain a little bit about what's going to happen today. This first session is a bit different from the rest in a couple of ways. First of all there is a questionnaire. You will be pleased to know you won't be required to complete a form; I can do that for you as we work through the questions. It's there to help me get to know you, and for you to make the most of the process. When we start the hypnotherapy, I will kick off with a one-off technique at the beginning to get your thoughts flowing.

"From session two onwards I'll take you through the same format each time: we take some time to update on how you are, what's been happening, any issues you want to cover; we follow with the hypnosis, creating a trance state; then the therapy under trance and finally once you are back, fully alert we'll go through feedback on the session. Now, I'm sure you have plenty of questions before we start so please feel free to ask."

For sure Liza had questions buzzing round her head. *What happens if there's something I don't want to discuss? Can you make me do things while I'm hypnotised? Are you in control? How is it different to us just talking things over? What if I can't go under? How many others have you seen in my situation? How long does it take? How does it work? Does it work?*

Rather than release her river of concerns into the room, afraid of showing her ignorance, Liza chose to begin with the most basic of questions.

"How long will it take?"

"This first session? About an hour and a half."

For a few seconds, with no further questions forthcoming, the outside filled the room: a siren, kids in the garden, an argument at the bus stop. Liza was holding back. Dr Kath suggested she should explain how things worked in a little more detail. Liza agreed, relieved to be out of the spotlight for a while longer.

"Once we have discussed your reasons for being here and I have understood your objectives, I will take you into a trance state in order to try and resolve the issues we have discussed. Many people believe the urban myth that they will be forced to give up their secrets involuntarily during the trance state. Often my clients are fearful of the blatant exhibitionism brought out by celebrity hypnotists on television. In these cases the subjects are extroverts up for entertaining and selected for this reason. I must stress, this will not happen. In any case the professional code of ethics I follow ensures my commitment to not use my skills for entertainment purposes."

Dr Kath took Liza's gentle sigh at this point as a sign she was feeling more reassured. "Everything we speak about is in confidence. During the trance you have free will. You may choose to speak out loud, although you may also find yourself internalising ideas. Either is fine. You may be wondering why we should bother with the hypnosis at all?"

"Funnily enough, I was just thinking that."

"I don't want to assume your level of knowledge, explaining things you may have already researched and understood. What do you know about the subconscious and conscious parts of the brain?" Dr Kath asked.

"Not much really." Liza shrugged. "Sometimes it feels like

there's a battle going on up there and I can come to conclusions without ever knowing where the ideas came from."

"That's when your subconscious is at work, finding solutions based on past experience, on long-held beliefs or values which may, or may not, be valid today. Sometimes it can be difficult to hear the dialogue within. The process of hypnosis heightens the focus on the subconscious mind, putting it at the fore. It can create a freer flowing imagination and sometimes, like dreams, produces metaphors which can be explored to better understand the issues."

"Hmm. A bit like when you are drifting off to sleep, or just waking up it seems easier to see things more clearly?"

"A little like that, yes. The hypnosis brings the subconscious mind to the front, pushing the conscious mind away. Sometimes, what I would call hard-core analytical people, find it harder to let this happen as it doesn't come as naturally to them."

"Do you think I will struggle?" Liza asked.

"I think you will be fine. If you feel as if you are finding it difficult, don't worry. Everyone is different. Another urban myth: I don't put you in a trance. It will happen naturally for you. Everyone's process is individual," Dr Kath explained. "Are you okay for me to begin working through the questionnaire?"

"I think so," Liza said.

It was not uncommon for Dr Kath's clients to feel reluctant to start. Most came to her after they had exhausted all other possibilities. When they had reached a crunch point. Most had not shared their innermost thoughts with anyone yet. For her sessions to be of use Liza had to be ready to let go. She had to want it badly enough.

"Try to relax," Dr Kath said. "Remember everything you say here is confidential. I am here to help you. I understand you will feel out of your comfort zone. In my training I had to go through exactly the same process, to be hypnotised and resolve my issues. I've sat in your seat, so to speak. Don't worry, you may find it odd at first but it gets easier. Once it is familiar you should be able to trust I will not be asking you to eat an onion, pretending it's an apple!"

They laughed at the image they had both seen on a TV programme years ago.

"I already trust you won't be asking that!" Liza said.

"Good. Perhaps start by telling me some of the basics. Where do you live? Where do you work? Any family? That kind of thing."

Listening to the window rumble, resonating with the engine of a stationary bus at the nearby junction, Liza replied. "I'm a sorta-single mum, living in North London with my gorgeous son, Angelo. I work at Gino's club, sometimes dancing but mostly now just organising the girls."

Dr Kath made notes of Liza's responses, listening out for further questions raised by what was not being said. She would come back to *sorta* later.

"So, what about other family? Close friends?"

"There's Candy at work," Liza said. "I see my good friend Sheena loads. She's the one who referred me to you. She's always there for me, especially if I am caught short with Angelo."

"That's great. Your son sounds like the centre of your world and good friends are precious, aren't they? Now, how about we talk a bit about what you need from me. What brought you here to see me?" Dr Kath asked.

"Do you know what? It's difficult to know what to say really. I'm not sure what I need."

"Don't worry if your thoughts wander all over the place. As I'm keeping notes we can make sense of it all at the end. Sometimes it's like trying to unravel a tangled kite string. At first you can't see where the end is, you just loosen little sections until you can follow a thread. Eventually the knots become more obvious. We can work on those together. How does that sound?" Dr Kath asked.

"Worth a try I suppose." Liza looked down and picked at a dried yoghurt stain on her skirt. "Until a few weeks ago, life was pretty predictable. I was in my routine, getting by, doing my best to give Angelo everything he needs. Surviving, I guess. Then, to cut a long story short, out of nowhere I was summoned to see a solicitor back where I grew up. When I get there, he tells me I might inherit loads of money, a country house and must use the money to set up a Tango school! It gets even weirder when he tells me I'm not the only one involved and I'm to make my decision before meeting with any of the others. It sounds amazing but I'm wary. I mean it could be legit but then again. . . you know?" Hearing herself say it aloud, Liza realised how implausible the whole thing sounded. "Besides it's not as simple as that. I can't just drop everything, even if I want to. . . can I?"

Liza searched her face for a reaction but Dr Kath's expression remained neutral.

"I can see why that would throw you. Do you have a time limit?" Dr Kath asked.

"I have a deadline. October 8th." Liza sighed.

Dr Kath made a note. "How can I be of help to you at this stage?"

"Suzy, you know, the manager here and Sheena, the friend I mentioned earlier, both suggested you might be able to help un-fog my fog. . . If you know what I mean? Help me work out what to do. I'm not sure I deserve it but I'd like to maybe see if I can make it work. I have to be careful not to make things worse."

"I'd be delighted to work with you to make sense of things," Dr Kath said. "I need to be clear though, the timescales are a tad tricky. There is no guarantee you will have resolved everything by then. Only you can know what is right for you. I can however guarantee my complete commitment to an impartial and confidential service. I do believe hypnotherapy could give you an accelerated pathway towards your conclusion."

Dr Kath noticed Liza's shoulders loosen and her hands becoming still in her lap. To further put her at ease she asked more questions about Angelo. Liza lit up. Her eyes smiling, her face animated as she gabbled on about her "Angel."

Her answers increasingly full and open, Dr Kath steered her through the remainder of the questionnaire, skipping from parents to partners, from money to hopes and fears.

Liza was one of those clients to whom structure was unfamiliar. Not wishing to constrain her with a rigid process, she let her traipse down tangential tracks, which often looped back on themselves. Pleased to have gleaned some nuggets of information, she may have missed taking a more direct route, Dr Kath was done. It was good to see Liza's genuine desire to reach an outcome from the therapy. Her determination would be essential in the search for a solution.

Dr Kath needed commitment from Liza. Dealing with whatever was locked inside her subconscious wouldn't be easy for her. From what she could see, Liza seemed tough enough and motivated enough to stick with it. Her paying clients had the added incentive of committing their hard-earned cash to the process. For her pro-bono clients it would be all too easy for them to stop coming to sessions, at the most crucial point, without that drive.

"We are going to start the hypnosis shortly, now we have gone through the preliminary questions," Dr Kath explained. "But before we do, can I just ask, have you had any more thoughts on what you hope to gain from the therapy?"

"Yes. You know I mentioned Angelo's father. Things aren't that great at all. I could use some help there."

"In what way? What do you want to happen?"

"I need to be sure I can do it. I think—God knows how, but I think I need to leave Gino."

Dulcie

Today, leaving her hotel, Dulcie opted for a longer walk along the river, before hooking a right past Kings College and up through Theatreland and Fitzrovia. The tube might have been a move obvious choice, but for now she was experiencing the dual benefits of exercise and the London buzz–anything to take her mind off things.

For someone known for her agreeable disposition, Dulcie was feeling anything but carefree. The morning sunlight reflected on the Thames, already busy with water-traffic, as she recalled Matty's suggestion. She did need to talk to someone, preferably impartial, who could get her through the next few weeks. The confluence of events since her return had eroded the very essence of Dulcie. She sure was riding the rapids and hoped the appointment she had booked would bring her some calm. At least she felt reassured, when Dr Kath had introduced herself as such on the phone, that they would get on.

Forty-five minutes of brisk walking in the crisp September air had brought her to the immaculate offices of The O'Hannon Clinic. She sank into the exquisitely soft Italian leather couch, cleverly selected to make the clients feel simultaneously important and relaxed with that one piece of furniture.

"How are you finding London? A little cooler than home I expect?" Dr Kath suggested.

Almost without exception, discussions about the weather were a safe, inoffensive ice-breaker, rarely requiring any meteorological expertise, and mostly giving people time to collect themselves.

Unfortunately, the opposite was true for Dulcie. Too polite to mention the mixed emotions it evoked for her, she replied, "Yes, this is about as cold as I have been for a while. Bit of a contrast."

Dr Kath smiled. "Thanks for coming to see me and thank you for completing the questionnaire online. It will help to speed us along. I gather you are pushed for time at the moment?"

"You could say that! You'll have seen the cut-off for the inheritance question early October and my flight is booked for seventeen days' time."

Dulcie liked Dr Kath. She had a good feeling this was going to work, despite being a hypnotherapy novice, with no real understanding of what to expect. Something about Dr Kath instilled confidence. It may have been her questions, gently probing into areas requiring clarification or her stillness as she listened attentively to Dulcie whilst she spoke. She was calm and unflustered and it was catching.

"I've been babbling on, I'm sorry. I'm sure you don't need to know all about my kids and their hobbies Dr Kath!"

"Don't worry, I'm happy to discuss anything you feel is beneficial. It's your time. Would you like to talk through any concerns with me before we start the trance process?"

Dulcie fumbled around in her head, trying to find a good place to start.

"Here's the thing. I'm utterly baffled by the Tango school, the house and inheritance stuff. All those years of being a mum and my pottery being fulfilling yet making me zilch money. There I was living halfway round the world with my mostly-solid man and my kids. Then, just as I find critical acclaim for my work, an agent, clients, success, this happens. I kinda thought coming away to England would help me put everything into perspective. But oh no! Before I've got used to the concept of my creativity having value, along comes this juggernaut, blasting through my life! I'm feeling extremely resentful of having to choose!"

"We can work through your conflict in the sessions, for sure. It sounds like you feel both the timing and the significance of your choices are unfair?" Dr Kath looked up from her notes.

"Yep, you've got it!" Dulcie said.

"Anything else before we start? As I explained earlier, you will be in control of everything that surfaces whilst your unconscious mind is at work."

"I won't be likely to divulge my innermost secrets?"

"No, not unless you want to do so. Is there something you are particularly concerned about?"

"There is one more thing. . ." Dulcie said, looking down at the floor. "I may have another reason to return to England."

"Would you like to discuss that now or later?" Dr Kath asked.

"I'm not sure. It feels disloyal to my family, my husband, even if things aren't perfect. It's the kinda thing that would go off like a bucket of prawns in the sun, you know?"

They both laughed at the Aussie idiom.

"That's a new one on me but I think I get your gist. It's your call. I'm not here to force you to talk about something if you don't feel comfortable." Dr Kath waited.

With no answer forthcoming, an argument between two builders working on the scaffolding across the street penetrated the room, their kerfuffle over a kebab kicked over the edge by a clumsy boot. Listening to their shouts, liberally strewn with expletives, whilst amusing, would not move Dulcie forward.

"Maybe you could tell me how significant you feel this other reason to return might be?" Kath suggested.

"Well I am sure it is a big thing." Dulcie inspected her fingernails, picking at the cuticle of her left thumb.

"For us to make any kind of sense of your options, do you think you need to share it? Or can you deal with it on your own?"

Again, Dulcie thought carefully, this time oblivious to the heated discussion continuing outside and now involving the site manager. Her reluctance to share was purely a symptom of the depth at which she had buried her emotions. Having not permitted herself to go there; having never admitted to herself it was of any consequence, until she had landed back at Heathrow, it was difficult to speak it out loud.

"Maybe you're right," she said. "This is where I have come to find clarity. I know it might affect the overall outcome. This thing does need to be thrown in with all the others. If I tell you before we start, it might me help work through the issues and I'm guessing help to get more out of the process?"

"Go on. Take your time."

Dulcie took a sip of water from the glass Dr Kath had placed beside her.

"I have a deep connection with Matty, my old friend, you know the one whose mum referred me to you. I am very concerned if I spend any more time with him it will turn my whole world upside down. You see coming to England might end up being a decision of the heart with, literally, world-wide consequences."

Contemplating her response, her face impassive, Dr Kath selected her words with almost the same care as a mother would the name of her new-born. "Thank you for trusting me with your most private thoughts. I am not here to judge you. I am here to help you reach conclusions; the right ones for you. I very much hope you will find the answers you are looking for."

Somewhat unburdened and feeling braver now, Dulcie added, "You see he was my first love."

Elizabeth

Elizabeth started the day by slipping into her work persona. Her suit may have been tailor-made of the finest navy wool weave; her blouse of the palest powder-blue silk; her sling-back court shoes of the softest nubuck but there the illusion of chic femininity ended.

Accustomed to shielding herself from the most brutal arrogance prevalent in the City, Elizabeth had developed a manner which was, in contrast to her outward appearance, as tough as a pair of old leather boots fished from the bottom of a river. Whilst she had known her meeting at the clinic was unlikely to be anywhere near as confrontational as those in her day job, she had wanted to be prepared. Retreating back behind the Elizabeth she displayed to the rest of the world made her feel safe. It was pure survival instinct, honed to perfection.

As she took the lift to the fifth floor of the Harley Street offices, with its marble floor and bevelled mirrors, a tiny blip of insecurity pushed through her defences. The irony of Elizabeth, with her strength of character, seeking the help of a therapist, was irritating. No matter. She had made a commitment. She would see through the first appointment and leave it there, sceptical any further therapy would be of use.

Since her meeting with Chloe Williams she had been crying less and coping far better. She was like one of those toys that wobble but always right themselves. Now more together, feeling perfectly poised, she wondered what had possessed her to make the call. Her barriers were up long before she had stepped into Dr Kath's consulting rooms.

Just over an hour later, noticing the sensations in her body, she came back into the minimally furnished room from her trance. Fully alert and taking in her surroundings, Elizabeth accepted her view on therapy was evolving. Potentially she had judged too soon.

"How are you feeling now Elizabeth?"

"Much calmer, thank you."

Dr Kath nodded.

"Do you know, I was unaware of how tense I was? It's only the before and after comparison that makes me realise it." Eager for Dr Kath's opinion, she fished for recognition, much as a child would from a parent. "You can you see a difference, can't you?"

"I can. Now take your time. Please have some water if you'd like. You may be a little groggy at first."

Elizabeth took a deep breath, expelling the pent-up emotions, which had been whizzing around inside her during the session. After a few minutes her breathing settled into a regular rhythm. Her eyes bright and attentive, her cheeks flushed, she waited, ready to move forward.

"How was that for you?" Dr Kath asked.

"Good I believe. The first part was extreme. All those emotions in quick succession. I feel like I've gone a few rounds in the ring! I do feel more serene now, if a little heavy-limbed. Although I have to say, whilst my body feels satisfyingly weary, my mind is buzzing with ideas."

"That is a common reaction. You are beginning to tap into parts of your subconscious which have been neglected or suppressed. After several sessions you may find themes rising out of the noise. For the time being, try not to spend too much time on analysis or prediction. In the end, the conclusions may not be the obvious ones," Dr Kath explained.

"Okay but out of curiosity, how quickly did I fall into trance?"

"Oh, a few minutes. Five at the most. Not long anyway."

Elizabeth's eyes widened. "I thought I would find it challenging. I was certain I wouldn't be susceptible, if that's the right phrase? I thought I'd be one of your most difficult clients."

"Yes, that's right, susceptibility or sometimes it's called suggestibility. It is a measure of the ease with which people will fall into hypnotic trance. It does vary from person to person but can sometimes be as much to do with circumstance as an inherent ability. Many research studies have devised tests and scales for its measurement. I'm yet to be convinced of their usefulness, since I am treating individuals and believe it is about the quality of their trance and not the speed of reaching the state. Out of interest what made you anticipate difficulty?"

"Being completely honest, when I arrived, I was dubious," Elizabeth confessed. "I brought all my resistance and arrogance into the room. I apologise if I appeared stand-offish. It's my natural defence mechanism whenever I'm in a situation where I feel out of control."

"Don't worry, you weren't problematic. Most people are wary before they start, mainly driven by their fear of the unknown. The way I look at it is this. If someone has made it to the seat in front of me there's a high probability they have tried most other options already and have come to me wanting this to work," Dr Kath said.

"That's a very accurate description of my situation. I was hoping to find answers after an intense couple of weeks spinning out of control."

"Your mention of control has crept in twice in as many sentences," Dr Kath looked down at her notes. "Is your need for control something you have noticed in the past?"

"Completely, for as long as I can remember. I'm not sure where it comes from but I don't see it as a problem. It helps me achieve my ambitions."

"Fascinating. Perhaps we can work on that next session? Along with getting clearer on the pros and cons of a move out of London."

Elizabeth was struck by the insights she had already gained. Her assumptions about hypnosis being of questionable merit had been overturned. Far from being the light and fluffy drivel of her preconceptions, the whole experience had been an eye opener. Her overwhelming feeling was one of wellbeing. She didn't have a complete set of answers yet by all means, but she sensed they would come. Oddly, she felt predisposed to being nice to those less fortunate than herself. Her Elizabethan demeanour, her need to show strength and yield power as a strong woman, defending herself against pretenders, now seemed to be of less importance.

As they wrapped up the meeting Dr Kath suggested

Elizabeth should visit the cloakroom on the way out. Standing in front of the mirrors above the sinks, she was grateful to have been tipped off. Two long black streaks of mascara had dried on her cheeks. Next time she must remind herself pre-session make-up removal was a necessity!

Annie

Opening the door to her beautifully restored Victorian cottage, Dr Kath indicated to Annie she should enter, with a balletic sweep of her free arm.

"Thank you for seeing me out of hours Kath or should it be Dr O'Hannon? I really appreciate it. I have to admit, it would have been really tricky getting to meet you otherwise–officially I mean."

"No problem. My study is set up for just such appointments and I often work here in the evenings. I understand my central London clinic is not convenient for all, especially for those who don't live or work in London. In any case, when you run your own business you are never really off duty. Please call me Dr Kath, most of my clients do. It's kind of a halfway house."

Dr Kath led the way down the corridor, showing Annie into the second room on the left.

Annie immediately spotted the blue-and-mustard art-nouveau fireplace tiles, proudly rescued from behind the MDF box, which had masked their glory. Whilst Dr Kath gathered her notepad and paperwork, Annie sat down and noticed more Victorian detailing, including the antique samplers on the back wall; a period feel without the tendency to clutter.

She was not at all surprised by the sympathetic touches, which paid respect to the character of the cottage. Dr Kath displayed the same care and attention to detail in her home as Annie had witnessed in her immaculately-turned-out appearance. Nothing flashy or showy; a classic elegance.

"You have made this into such a lovely room! The people before did their best to eliminate the soul of the place. I find it such a shame when people do that, don't you?"

Dr Kath acknowledged Annie's complement graciously, at the same time steering the conversation towards the purpose of her visit. Since they had previously discussed Annie's reasons for seeking help on the phone, and Dr Kath had already reviewed Annie's questionnaire, she suggested gently that perhaps chit-chat on home styling could wait.

"Ready?"

Annie crossed and uncrossed her legs several times, eventually settling on a mirror copy of Dr Kath's position. She nodded.

"Excellent. Let's get started then."

Annie did as instructed and sat back in the chair, weight evenly distributed, feet firmly planted on the floor. She made an effort to focus on her own breathing. Her mind still racing, Dr Kath's soft and calming voice was telling her to listen to her breathing; to concentrate on being consciously aware of the rise and fall, the in and out; to close her eyes, allowing her thoughts to come and go.

"Don't fight them. Just let them roll in and out like waves on the sand. They will rush in and fall away. Follow the natural rhythm. You will not lose them. They will be stored away in your subconscious. They may be important. They may not.

If you need to remember them, you will be able to remember them. For now, just keep focussing on your breathing, as I begin to count. . ."

Annie could feel the tension in her body easing. She followed Dr Kath's soothing words, which took her on a journey down a tunnel, heading for a beach. Annie could see the natural light away in the distance. Dr Kath gently counted the steps as they both moved forward towards the exit. Soon, Annie could make out the shape of an archway ahead. Sunlight bounced in, reflecting off the stone walls. A beckoning breeze lifted her hair and warmed her face. Serene and secure, she was aware of only Dr Kath's voice and a warm and fuzzy feeling throughout.

"How are you feeling?"

"I'm feeling. . . floaty," Annie replied, realising the thick, muffled response was her own voice, reverberating purely inside her head as if her ears had been switched off.

"Good. Hold on to the floaty feeling. If you feel at any stage you are too uncomfortable or anxious you can return to this place. Here you are safe."

"I feel safe."

"Great. Now, at this point I want to use the technique I mentioned before called Storm. I will explain again what will happen so you know what to expect. I'll ask you a series of quick-fire questions. With each question I would like you to think of a time when, for example a time when you were most at peace. Memories will come to the surface, often with a strong emotion attached. There is no need to speak these out loud. Just as with your thoughts before, let them come and go. They will tumble and merge, crash and clash; extreme and transient at the same time. You will feel as if you are there, in these moments, your senses alert, experiencing your memories as reality. Remember, you have nothing to fear. You are in control and you are safe."

"Okay. I'm okay," Annie whispered.

Dr Kath fired the questions to Annie. "Think of a time when you felt truly loved. Frightened. Most joyful. Totally alone."

Before long Annie was lost in memory after memory. They did indeed tumble and merge. Loved: her First Holy Communion, feeling like a princess as her father sat her on the sideboard in her white lace dress, a shiny pink bow in her hair.

Scared: sixteen, her period was late after a stupid mistake with a boy she didn't even really fancy, fearing more than anything her mother's disapproval.

Joy: at the sight of Beth's tiny new-born hand clinging to her finger as she cradled her close.

Alone: carrying her loneliness inside because her friends just wouldn't understand and there was literally no-one she could talk to.

Uncontrollable laughter: catching the giggle-bug with Thomas as she tickled him until tears were rolling down their cheeks.

Let down: by her closest colleague Tina, whose side-swiping criticism had inflicted a career body blow, bringing Annie's performance into question.

Jealousy: poking her baby sister in the eye when she thought no-one was looking, for the pain of no longer being the centre of attention.

Happiness: as she and Colin left the church, married and about to start their bright future together.

Dr Kath's prompts came and went as Annie rode the

emotional rollercoaster, soaring to heights before plunging to dark depths. She gradually slowed the ride, bringing Annie back into the room. As the prompts lessened in frequency and her voice became louder, Annie was able to notice other sounds again. A car door closing. Footsteps on the next-door path. A wood pigeon, its cooing amplified down the chimney on which it had landed.

"You will become aware of your breathing and of my voice. I will begin counting to ten. One, two. . . the closer I get the more alert you will feel. Three, four. . . you will notice the sensations in your body. Your feet on the floor; your shoulders against the back of the chair. Five, six. . . taking a deep breath, you will feel your lungs fill and then empty. Seven, eight. . . you might feel like stretching and yawning. Nine, you may open your eyes. Ten, and you are back in the room."

Pia

The static crackled over the melancholic violin intro. Pia took her position in front of PJ, trying to remember all his posture tips whilst running through the eight-step basic sequence in her head. PJ loved this piece. It was one of his father's favourites; a rare recording from the fifties that carried all the hallmarks of treasured yet overplayed vinyl.

"Don't look so frightened Pia. Relax, you've got this."

Pia scrunched up her face. "I'm not so sure."

"Come on, be confident. That last run through, you were great." PJ smiled. "Remember, let me lead you, no. Feel the music and forget about the steps. Just let it happen naturally."

As he transferred his weight backwards, he gave Pia the subtle clues she needed to follow the direction of his movement, not with his hands, but with his body.

"Forward, side, close, *cruzada, cruzada,* back, side, close. That's good." He nodded. "Try to look up Pia, no. That's it," he said as they finished the first sequence of eight and began again.

Heartbeat raised a little, Pia sensed a tiny bit of progress. Her muscles started to agree with the movements her brain was telling her to make. She still needed to concentrate on where she was placing her feet and whether to shift her weight onto the right or the left side but it was getting easier. The more she relaxed, the more fluid her movements became, their bodies gently gliding together across the floor. Their movements were slow and unhurried, the steps contained in a relatively small area of the room.

When it came to the final bars of the haunting melody and they made their final turn, she couldn't remember how many times they had repeated the sequence. They remained on the spot for a few beats as the track faded, foreheads together, neither wanting to break the pose.

"Wow! That was amazing." Pia said, in between great gulps of air. "Can we have a break now please? My heart is pounding."

PJ grinned. "Of course, Bella. No problem. You deserve it."

Complex emotions running through her, simultaneously exhausted and exhilarated, Pia had no more energy left and equally could dance all night. Wearily satisfied, she couldn't stop smiling, despite her aching body and sore feet.

How she had not identified her passion for this previously she wasn't sure, although gradually pieces of the jigsaw were falling into place. Many times she had been asked whether she had trained as a professional dancer, when out in clubs or at parties. Since primary school she had known she had rhythm, her music teacher commented, "A natural talent that should be nurtured."

Somehow her confidence had waned when she turned into a gawky teenager, feeling clumsy and heavy next to her petite peers. Perhaps if her mum could have afforded dance classes, things may have turned out differently much sooner.

Strange this opportunity had presented itself now. She was in between jobs–clients had been cutting back their IT investment, and she'd fallen foul of a particularly aggressive sales target set by an even more aggressive new boss. Already fed-up with living out of a suitcase, Pia had decided to vote with her feet. Voluntary redundancy had seemed like the sensible option. She'd loved London in her thirties but somehow she'd been absent during the exodus of most of her good friends. Whilst she had been clocking up the airmiles into her forties, they had settled into their home-counties townhouses with large leafy gardens and trampolines for the kids.

"Mum, I'm selling up and coming home," she'd announced in their weekly call.

"You know best darling," Helena had responded.

At the time she'd thought her mum's response noncommittal, expecting more debate, but of course Helena had already known what lay around the corner. Ready for a new challenge, Pia had felt the need to justify her decision, protesting the congestion and pollution a little too emphatically.

It seemed her Latin looks may have alluded to her true calling and, intentionally or not, she had arrived at the same destination by an alternative route. It was synchronicity surely. One exciting adventure lay before her and all the unknowns were doors temptingly ajar in an unfamiliar new home, rooms ready to be explored.

Pia towelled her face, cheeks still red with effort, took a swig of water and turned back from her day-dream at the window.

PJ smiled at her. "Are you ready to go again?"

"Must we? Just a few more minutes rest? Please?" she said, still puffing from the exertion. "I am your older sister, remember."

"Sorry, I get caught up in the dance and forget how new all this is to you. Let's break for lunch and we can take a wander round the grounds. You can catch your breath, no?"

"I do run, you know. Well, I did until recently, before I moved back. I've even done a couple of half-marathons."

"And that is good. But remember my motto—to dance is to live! You will see."

"But it's not everything. You must want more in your life than just Tango, surely?"

"Of course, you know this. Maybe we make a deal. You show me how to find love and I show you how to fall in love with the dance?"

"PJ, I'm hardly a relationship expert but I'll give it a go."

"Now come."

Wearing his black towel as a halter, taut around his neck as it carried the weight of his arms, he tilted his head, beckoning Pia to follow his lead through the heavy oak doors concealed in the room's panelling.

The autumn sunshine caught the air in beams of spinning dust through the majestic windows. Floor to ceiling, they filled the music room with light to counterbalance the dark wood.

I love it already by the way. To dance is to live. Yep, that's perfect for me, Pia thought.

Breathing a deep sigh of contentment, Pia followed, increasing her pace to keep PJ in her sights as he turned left, right, then left again through a maze of corridors. All covered in faded and fraying carpet, they led out to a small courtyard garden, long overtaken by rampant weeds. Up ahead PJ leant against a solid studded door, bearing most of his weight on his right side.

I thought I saw something in the way he walked. The tiniest imbalance.

As she picked her way along the gravel path, now virtually obscured by years of neglect, she called out, "Are you okay?"

"Never better. Ready for the next surprise?"

"Try me."

"Off you go," he said, depressing the lever on the wrought-iron latch.

Leaving PJ behind and pushing through the exit into a dark, cobbled passageway, Pia was unclear what should have surprised her until, with delight, she reached a view of a beech copse framed by the archway at the end of the passage. It was just beyond the boundary walls; a palate of autumn richness assaulted her: copper-red, raw sienna, yellow ochre, burnt umber.

Seeing the trees in their prime, in her opinion, the phase in the annual cycle where the leaves had turned but not yet fallen, took her back. She was flooded with family memories of many a weekend walk in Frith Wood, a young girl dressed against the chilled air in navy cords, a cream cable-knit sweater and red wellies.

It was cooler in the dappled shade so she walked through to the other side of the copse; hopping over roots, weaving between the trunks, snapping twigs and crunching frazzled ferns underfoot. Moderately breathless from her roaming, she paused to absorb the next treat.

Back towards the mansion, she spied smoke rising gently from a bonfire, somewhere within the walled garden. The smoky smell, mixed with that of damp soil beneath her feet, was evocative of her childhood frolicking through the leaves. How anyone could choose a permanent residence in a hot country and miss the wonderful seasonal contrasts, Pia would never understand. Every year, at every change, she tingled with excited anticipation of the newness, based on years of similar experiences safely stored and triggered by her senses.

"Oh, I've missed this. Autumn in the city just isn't quite the same. I am going to love working here." Spoken aloud, her words floated gently to PJ who had caught up and was quietly standing a few metres away in the shade.

"I'm glad you feel that way, because I'm going to love working with you," he said, joining her. "I think we'll make a great team."

"You are limping. I see it PJ," she said, pursing her lips like a disapproving matron. "Are you sure you're alright?"

"Nothing a steroid injection can't fix. Occupational hazard, I think you'd call it in English. Dancers and knees. . . you know?"

"We've still loads to learn about each other. Your English is great, by the way."

"University and Dad, of course, although his accent was quite strong."

"Here in England?"

"Carlos the third, Madrid. My girlfriend, she was English. So, you ready to eat?"

"Yep." Pia linked arms again in what was becoming their signature move. "Tell me all about Madrid. I've never been. How long were you there? Were you dancing then? What was she like?"

"Time to get back to the house. We can walk and I'll give you my potted history. It's not that exciting. I'm sure yours is more glamorous!"

"Ha. Walk? Hobble you mean?"

Liza

Getting to her second session with Dr Kath was proving tricky. Sheena was already lined up to cover the school run, but Gino had called and asked her to meet him at the club early; at six o'clock. He had something to discuss and insisted she be there. Knowing she had to keep the therapy secret, she couldn't say no for fear of arousing Gino's suspicion; she wasn't quite brave enough yet.

"I'll be there but what's it all about anyway? Why can't we just talk about it on the phone?"

"I told you. You'll be here at six and we will talk," Gino said. "I'm not prepared to discuss it now. It's too important. Be a good girl and do as you're told."

Liza watched the large kitchen clock. The hands ticked round to two-thirty. If she didn't leave soon she'd miss her bus and be cutting it fine for the appointment at three-fifteen. She wished she had been able to rebel, be defiant in the face of his controlling ways. Her sugary sweet, "Sure thing babe" might have sounded too false. She held her breath, wondering if she had shown her hand, skin clammy at the thought of being found out. After what seemed an age he replied.

"Make fucking sure you're on time," Gino ordered.

The dial tone kicked in. Feeling a little braver, Liza mimicked his once charming, now sickening manner.

"Make fucking sure you're on time. Ahhh! That's what I'm trying to do you tosser! But not to your shitty little meeting. I have far more important things to be doing right now!"

She checked her handbag for phone, keys and purse, remembering with a grin when she had asked Angelo to fish around this morning for the pound he needed for the clown workshop at school.

"Darling, you look adorable, but I think you are meant to take it to school and change there," she had said.

He had been standing in her bedroom doorway, still sleepy-eyed, wearing the Pierrot costume they had managed to cobble together the night before.

With the grin still spread across her face, she pulled on her boots, threw on her mac in case the forecasted rain actually arrived and hurried off to the bus stop. She had an unexpected spring in her step. Gino couldn't faze her today. As long as she could get through her next few sessions with Dr Kath she had started to believe she would find the courage to break free. Liza liked this feeling. The prospect of getting her life back was a juicy thought, a tropical fruit full of exotic promise.

Someone was watching over her; she and the bus arrived at the stop together. She jumped on and travelled the few stops to the refuge, considerably calmer than on her previous visit.

Dr Kath had been right. It wasn't easy to open up your thoughts to someone else. Not because you were telling them stuff. No. More because you were telling yourself things that had been hidden away. They had got through lots last time, much of it focused on Gino and the inheritance, how she felt about it and what she wanted to do next.

Standing in the entrance porch, Liza was feeling in high spirits. She pressed the buzzer; expecting the door to be answered as swiftly as it had been before. Three minutes later and still no movement through the glass. She pressed again. After a further two minutes, Liza wondered if she had made a mistake. Maybe Dr Kath wasn't there? But surely Suzy should be?

Suzy had greeted her last time but that had been after she had texted to announce her arrival. She tried texting Suzy again but it didn't deliver. She didn't have Dr Kath's mobile number. She was beginning to feel exposed and concerned she would run out of time for a full session, worse still, that she would miss it altogether. At last she heard someone approaching. It was Dr Kath.

"So sorry to leave you standing there. Suzy is off sick today and I've been helping out at the back. Come through and we'll get ourselves settled upstairs."

"Thanks. I thought for a minute I'd got it wrong. I've been really looking forward to it and didn't want to have to wait another day."

"That's a good sign. If you embrace the whole process with the same positive attitude, you should see lots of benefits. Apologies again for getting you worried." Dr Kath smiled before turning to lead them up the stairs to her room.

Once Liza was safely ensconced in the comfy chair, Dr Kath asked, "How's things since I saw you last?"

"Not too bad. Nothing much happening out of the ordinary. Angelo's thrown himself back into the new school year with gusto. He's a funny little chap. Mostly likes talking with the teachers. Keeps himself to himself. Doesn't seem to have formed any close friendships yet. Spends a lot of his time with his nose in a book, a definite bookworm you know. S'pose it's not a bad thing?"

"No, not at all. Foundation for all learning they say."

"Oh sorry, that reminds me. I just need to text Sheena, do you mind?"

"No problem. Everything alright?"

"Yeah. I just need to ask if she can give Angelo tea. Slight change of plan. It'll be fine." Liza fired off a quick note to her friend and switched her phone to silent. "There, all done."

"Actually, I was just going ask how Gino's been?"

"Oh, predictably domineering and demanding. Moody. I don't seem to be able to please him whatever I do. My tactic is to stay low and try to keep out of his way. Same old, same old." Liza rubbed the back of her neck. "Let's talk about the other stuff."

"If you're sure? Are you any clearer on what you might do?"

"I was, until just before coming out to see you," Liza confessed. "I've been doing a lot of thinking on how to make it happen. Especially at night, once I'm back from work. I find sleep evades me at the best of times. It's hardly worth trying to sleep. Thoughts of the future are engulfing my every waking hour."

"I understand. I can imagine how enticing the idea of a new start must be. You said you were clearer until you set off, though. What was it that changed earlier?"

Liza twisted the strap of her bag tight around her fingers. "I had a call from Gino asking, no, demanding, actually, ordering me to meet him at the club at six this evening."

"And that's unusual?"

"Very. We rarely speak during daylight hours, much less see each other anymore. He moved out long ago. Said I cramped his style but still gets insanely jealous if I even look at another man. Anyway he's been seeing some tart or other these last few months. Younger, fitter. Think he even paid for her to have her tits done."

"So, what's concerning you about his call?" Dr Kath asked.

"I dunno. I don't like it when he's erratic. He's extremely volatile when he's upset. I'm worried maybe he's found something out or maybe he suspects I'm up to something, 'cause I've been more compliant recently. I've been trying not to give him any reason to be angry. Maybe he's noticed? Thing is, it's such a good opportunity, I'm scared he's going to do something to spoil it."

"Yes, that makes sense. Perhaps we can explore some of those fears today?" Dr Kath paused to give Liza time to process her thoughts. "Is there anything else you'd like to share before we start? If we get going now, we should have your session wrapped up for you to get away in plenty of time."

"No. I'm good," Liza said, folding her hands together in her lap.

Liza fell into her trance like an old hand, the release of tension spreading through her body with every breath. Coaxed on by Dr Kath's soothing words, she soon arrived in her safe place. Her mind had taken her to a sumptuous spa hotel suite, with voluminous scarlet silk drapes hanging from the four-poster. The crisp white linen sheets lay pristine on the newly turned-down bed. The sunken bath was already filled to the brim with bubbles. Two Champagne flutes with their own bubbles stood waiting on a recessed shelf designed for that very purpose.

"Tell me, where are you now?" Dr Kath asked, her gentle question floating in without disturbing the dreamy vision.

"Somewhere safe and warm."

"Are you alone?"

"No, I don't think so. At least I must be expecting someone 'cause there's two glasses," Liza said.

"Who might it be?"

"Someone who will treat me like a princess."

"Is it someone you know?" Dr Kath asked.

"I don't think so."

"But you are in need of a prince?"

"Oh yes. Definitely!" Liza exclaimed.

"Gino's not your prince?" Dr Kath asked.

Liza winced. "Gawd no! No way!"

"Tell me about Gino."

"He doesn't treat me right. He used to be my prince. I thought he was the one."

"Can you remember that feeling, when things were good?"

"Yes."

"Why don't you go back there and tell me some more?"

Liza returned to the morning after their first night together...

Was it a cliché or was it true that a woman in a man's clothing, the morning after the night before, was a turn on? With Gino's pale-blue shirt skimming her bottom, his CKs hugging her hips tightly, loose around the waist, Liza certainly felt sexy. Her tousled hair stuck out endearingly in all directions, framing her rosy face.

She stood in the kitchen doorway of his very masculine, usually unsullied, bachelor pad, watching him rustle up eggy-bread on his sleek black stove. Coffee percolated noisily on the side, masking her footsteps. Unwilling to break the spell, she continued her observation with a Cheshire-cat grin.

It seemed this time she'd hit the jackpot. Unusually for her luck, Gino fulfilled all the criteria of the ideal man: tall, dark and handsome, not to mention six-pack fit and successful. Best of all though, he was gentle, kind and treated her like a princess. Yes, he did buck the trend!

Not wanting to question it for too long in case the clock struck midnight and her world became all mice, pumpkins and tattered clothes, Liza let him in. Down came the barriers and you could hear the clanking chains of the portcullis, hauling up the imposing gate to her fortress.

He looked up from the black, steaming coffee he had just poured into the Wedgwood espresso cup, his breath catching at the vivacious vision standing in the doorway. Almost speechless and certainly breathy, he growled his commands.

"Come here babe! Give us a suck on those lips!"

Obligingly, needing no persuasion, Liza padded towards him, her eyes pools of deep blue, her pupils huge, adoring. His sensuous kiss stirring an echo of the previous night's exploits, she was uncaring of his scratchy stubble. He seemed perfect. Any nagging doubts regarding his suitability got pushed to the back of her mind; actually, out of the window.

Flushed at her new-found happiness Liza gushed, nervously chatting about every thought that came into her head. Stories of her past flooded the kitchen with laughter and tears. She wanted him to know her, warts and all. Now she had committed herself, there was no option of holding back.

Gino lapped it up, seemingly in awe of his star catch. He sat mostly silent, attentive yet faintly aloof, giving him a mysterious air. Liza realised she had been rabbiting on through at least three tracks and two travel bulletins, plus who knows how many advert breaks on the radio. She paused for breath, coyly wrapping his shirt more tightly together, hugging herself a little defensively. Now unsure whether she had given too much of herself away too soon, she was about to ask him about his stories, when his mobile resting on the counter buzzed loudly, improbably sounding like a lowing cow.

Suddenly, she felt completely out of place, as he began talking business in earnest. She wondered if he even remembered she was there, let alone any of the heartfelt emotions she had divulged. Liza decided to do what might please him most and took herself off for a shower whilst he finished his call.

As she moved through his flat she visualised all the feminine touches she would add, once he invited her to share his space; that he would, she did not doubt. Yes, everything was far too sparse. His minimalist style meant there was hardly any colour. Her peacock-blue silk dress, lying in a crumpled heap from the night before, added a splash of something different to an otherwise grey-and-black bedroom. The white carpet would have to go as well; not at all practical if they were planning on having kids. He had definitely mentioned making babies last night. Surely there must be some foundation to thinking he could be the one.

Experiencing awkwardness, she dressed back in last night's

outfit, designed to seduce and ensnare, she choose her moment to re-join Gino in the kitchen.

Hovering in the doorway for the second time that morning, it was obvious Gino was still engrossed. It was time to leave, and to think over where things were headed. Blowing him a kiss as he caught her eye, she waved and split. He'd call her anyway, when he was ready to see her and tie up the job. The thrill of a new man her more dominant thought as she waited at the bus stop, hoping he would wave back from the window.

Dr Kath followed Liza's vivid recollection closely, pleased she had unlocked this memory, which had answered some questions. The momentum of the therapy was picking up but it was time to close the session.

Dr Kath watched Liza as she counted her back to full consciousness. She admired this plucky lady. They still had a way to go before she would be ready to face her personal demons, but real progress had been made. Time pressure aside, she was keen to ensure they capitalised on their findings whilst being acutely aware of Liza's pressing commitment.

"We should discuss what has come up for you today. Does that work for you?" Dr Kath asked gently.

"Yes, please give me some feedback." Cheeks rosy, her eyes feverish, there was an urgency in Liza's gabbled words. "I feel like I'm getting somewhere. It's good. I don't want to leave it hanging. I should be alright for a while longer before I need to head off to the club. Tell me, what do you think?"

"Perhaps I should ask you first. What do you think came out for you? Any patterns?"

"I know for sure I've been looking for someone to care for me," Liza hesitated, searching for the right words. "I mean really care for me. Unconditionally and to put me first. The One."

"Yes, your need to be treated like a princess, to belong to someone special. Where do you think it comes from?"

"I dunno. It's a bit odd really. I've always had to look after myself. Been good at it too."

"Yes, I can see that. You come across as a survivor," Dr Kath said. "Someone keeping it together. The question is have you chosen that way of life or is it a coping mechanism, to help you avoid dealing with something else?"

"Hmm. . . that might be true. Where has it come from though?" Liza wanted to get to the bottom of it all.

"Shall we look into it next time?"

"Yes, that would be good. Now, what about Gino? Do you know, I've not thought about that night for years? I can't believe I didn't see the signs!"

"Why do you think that is?"

Liza mulled over the question. Dredging her brain for some clue to her gullible acceptance of his courtship. She spoke quickly, as if to herself. "I wanted to believe it. The whole charade. It was a fairy tale; like I'd finally found the happiness I was searching for. It was that thing–what do they call it? Where you only hear and see what you want to and you filter out the rest."

"It seems like that might have been what happened. You have an unconscious bias driving you towards partners who fulfil a princely role. Once you place them on a pedestal, it takes some doing for them to fall off."

"Hmm." Again to herself Liza muttered, "And even when they behave like shits I still can't see it. I really loved him. He was right up there like Nelson on his column." She looked directly at Dr Kath. He hooked me good and proper, didn't he?"

"Seems so." Conscious of the time, Dr Kath steered them to the arrangements for Liza's next session. "Would you be able to make it next Thursday? Say eleven in the morning?"

"Yes, I can drop Angelo at school and head over afterwards. Are you sure I'm still allowed to see you here? I know it's meant to be a drop-in clinic for the refuge."

"You're fine. It's not a problem. It's convenient for you and I am here anyway. We can stick to the arrangements as long as you are discreet. It's a place, by its very nature, which is meant to be off the radar."

"I know. Only Sheena knows I see you and I've not even told her exactly where we meet. Suzy told me all about how the refuge is run," Liza said.

"Great. I'll see you next week then."

They both stood to say goodbye. Liza lingered at the door, reluctant to head out into her grey reality.

"Thank you again. The world seems full of colourful possibilities when I'm here. . ."

Dr Kath placed a hand on Liza's arm. "I understand how you are feeling, now you have glimpsed a different future. Remember how strong you are. You have already coped with many tough encounters. You are a very determined and resourceful woman. Right?"

Liza wasn't feeling particularly resourceful yet but buoyed by Dr Kath's words she slipped into her rhino skin, heading purposefully down the stairs and out onto the street. Just gone half past four. She was okay. As long as the traffic ran smoothly, she'd be home before five. Time for a quick shower and change into something alluring to soften Gino's mood. Yeah, he was a conniving bastard, but he was still a man, whose cock was most often in charge. He liked to think he could lord it over the girls; that he was superior to his punters. Liza knew better. Sex was his weakness. She knew exactly how to tackle Gino's tackle, leaving him begging for more.

Dulcie

In the days following her first meeting with Dr Kath, Dulcie had laid low. Limiting contact to a few brief emails with Bruce, the kids and Peter, and the odd interaction with room service.

Having time on her hands, seemed to be pulling tighter on her skein of tangled thoughts. In one short session many issues, lurking in the depths of her loch of a mind, had risen to the surface. Additionally, her indecisiveness was fuelled by Matty. Having concluded there was a need to explore her attachment to him further, she'd left the clinic befuddled. Now, back on the leather couch, she twisted her fingers together, unlocking and locking them several times.

"How have you been?" Dr Kath asked. "Any developments on the Matty front?"

"I'm good." Dulcie looked down at her hands, nails bitten and cuticles raw.

She tried to avoid Dr Kath's scrutiny, hoping she wouldn't notice the Matty question had been left hanging. Since they both knew it had gone unanswered, Dr Kath believed Dulcie was yet to dislodge the biggest boulder blocking her path to a decision. Her silence on the subject only served to highlight its significance.

"Are you sure?" Dr Kath asked.

"Honestly? No." Dulcie paused. "I'm not good. You guessed it. I'm stuck and I don't know what to do next. It's all too difficult and I just want to run away! I know I'm hiding from everyone."

"Do you know it's perfectly normal to feel that way? Lots of people struggle to find a way through. Most don't have the complexities of your situation to deal with and still decide to stop therapy, preferring to stay in limbo than deal with their challenges. I can definitely help you, if you want to keep going. If you don't, it's your decision and I will understand."

Dr Kath remained quiet. Having been given a way out, Dulcie would now have to weigh up her options. Stopping the therapy now may give her temporary relief from the chaos in her head. She could delude herself she would be better off heading home. In time though, those unresolved feelings would resurface. Exporting them halfway round the world wouldn't eliminate them. Eventually Matty would re-emerge. Just as many of her previous clients had done, Dulcie would realise these things too.

"I don't really want to run away. I did that before, all those years ago. I told myself it was circumstance, fate if you will." Dulcie broke off mid-flow. Something had clicked for her. "Can we start the therapy please? I'm not ready to go there yet, but could we maybe talk about some of the other stuff?"

"No problem. It's your time. We can look into the other aspects of the situation first if you feel it will help?"

"If we can, I'd really appreciate it. Thanks," Dulcie said.

"Try to relax now and focus on my voice," Dr Kath said gently. "Listen only to your breathing and my words. You will hear other sounds but let them go. Soon you will reach a truly peaceful place."

Dulcie's subconscious took her home, sitting in her studio at the potters' wheel letting the clay take shape in her hands. Her arms were covered, finger-tips to elbows, in a pleasingly mucky way.

"What are you doing now?" Dr Kath asked.

"I'm finishing a large plate in my studio."

"What's made you choose to be there?"

"It's just me and my plate," Dulcie said. "I don't have to think about anything else. In fact, I can't think about anything else. I need all my concentration on the task."

"And why a large plate?"

"It's simple yet difficult to execute."

"Is it for someone specific?" Dr Kath asked.

Dulcie frowned. "I'm not sure. I think it's for someone important. Maybe a commission?"

"Go on."

"Hmm. It's a business transaction, so that's both good and bad."

Dr Kath jotted down Dulcie's answer, followed by the words good and bad, each with a question mark.

"Business represents income, which gives me independence. Choices if you know what I mean?" Dulcie explained further. "But it's bad because my creative freedom is curtailed. I am no longer crafting something for its own sake. I don't want to feel like a sell-out."

"I understand. You're happy moving towards financial self-sufficiency, but you're bothered by your creativity being overshadowed by the subjective value placed on it by others?"

"Yes! Exactly!" Dulcie's eyes darted about behind her lids.

"Why don't we look at the value *you* place on your artistic independence? Given the option, would you prefer to return to a time when your ceramics were unknown, where you had absolute control over the final product?"

Dulcie hesitated. "Maybe."

"How about if you were so successful your clients paid handsome sums for your work, whilst still allowing you artistic licence?" Dr Kath questioned.

"Now that would be ideal."

"And what about giving it all up and changing direction?"

"I can't imagine ever doing that," Dulcie replied, her lips set firm.

"What about location? Are you tied to one creative space?"

"I suppose not. As long as I have a studio with the right tools, materials and atmosphere, I could make my pottery anywhere."

"How about a separate income, unconnected to your art? How would that fit in?"

"It could work," Dulcie said, after a small pause.

"If we look at the inheritance, bearing in mind everything we've just talked about, where does that leave you?"

"A move to England wouldn't prevent me from continuing my art. If the inheritance generated its own income and could cover the set-up of a new workshop, I could carry on designing and creating, without having to work on commission."

"And what information do you need to evaluate that option?"

"I guess to know more about the contract, any restrictions and the projected incomes," Dulcie said.

"Are there any other details of the trust to be looked into at this stage?"

"Not really, apart from learning about Tango maybe. I'm still curious about the connection but it doesn't feel important."

"Any other deciding factors?" Dr Kath asked.

Dulcie swallowed several times before replying, "My family is the big one."

"Who does that include?"

"My four gorgeous kids. . . and Peter, I suppose." Dulcie added as an afterthought.

"What makes you say suppose?"

"It's the word–family. To me it represents the unit, the six of us. Peter and I don't have everything perfect. . . that gets me down sometimes. . . but we do get the family bit right."

It struck Dr Kath they were at a turning point. Where should she take things next? Explore the broader concept of family? Probe the Peter question further or stick with the impact on the children? She allowed Dulcie to dictate the focus. Taking her lead, she stuck to immediate family.

"The unit, how does it fit in to the inheritance question?"

"I'm really not sure. . . I mean we couldn't stay as one unit and I think my *Us* matters most."

"Tell me more about that."

"Mainly it's the older two," Dulcie said. "My sons James and Mikey. They have their education almost behind them. James is at uni and Mikey will follow soon. I'd predict they would want to stay in Sydney. The younger two need to stay with me, wherever I go, but I don't think they'd be keen on a move to England either."

"And Peter?"

"That's a whole other subject. Part of the problem is his business. It's going great guns and he wouldn't be ready to give it up for some whim, even if on paper it looks like heaps of money. He'd think it was risky."

"What do you think?" Dr Kath waited, observing Dulcie closely.

"I respect his views. He's worked very hard, put his heart and soul into it. He was the one drawn to Australia as the place to make something of himself. He doesn't feel England has anything to offer," Dulcie said.

"Even if you decide to come back here?"

"Peter's not prepared to say until I make the call."

"And what do you say?"

Dulcie took her time, as if dredging up her answer from a deeper recess.

"It's like an ultimatum. . . I'm disappointed. It feels like I'm less important to him than I thought. Like. . . I'm not his number-one priority. He's been working such long hours; I think we've been drifting apart. . . recently. . ." Dulcie's shoulders stiffened.

"What is it? Something else?"

"We had a huge row. I accused him of having an affair. He was never home. He said I was crazy and selfish and should be grateful he was working hard for us, for the kids' future."

"And?"

"And it hurts. I'm not selfish," Dulcie said firmly. "I put everything on the line for him when I followed him to Sydney. I kinda think it should be my turn but. . . we've been together a long time. I should have known he'd never do that. We tried to clear the air before the launch. I don't know. More than anything I want to be sure we're alright now."

"What do you need to do next?" Dr Kath asked.

"I know I need to tell him how I feel but it's very difficult. We're just not in synch, mentally or physically. We can't really speak properly until I head back."

"How does that play out in relation to your deadline?"

"I'll be cutting it fine. If I can sort out how I feel and get crystal clear before I return home, at least I can be fully prepared for that heart-to-heart."

"You sound resolved." Dr Kath smiled and Dulcie opened her eyes. "It's good. We're close to wrapping things up soon. Is there anything else you want to discuss today?"

"Yes, actually there is. . ."

"Take your time. What is it?"

Dulcie hesitated, a question forming on her lips, at first with no sound, as if she were debating with herself. "Do you think I should see Matty?"

"Do *you* think you should?"

"I want to. I've been avoiding him. I found my feelings overwhelming the last time we got together. My brain goes fuzzy when he's near. Most of the time it's like no-one else exists when I'm with him. Rational thought is impossible. I am torn between desire and duty. I can't see what's best."

"You seem uneasy about putting yourself in the same position again. What's troubling you?" Dr Kath asked.

"That I might do something I will regret later."

"What are the consequences of *not* seeing him?"

After a very long pause came a sigh full of yearning. Then Dulcie replied, "I might regret that even more."

Annie

"I am with you, as we step out of the tunnel, just as before. Feel the sand beneath your bare feet. Wriggle your toes and listen to the gentle rush of water as the waves lap against the shore and trickle back into the sea. This is tranquillity. A haven to be visited whenever you feel stressed or out of control. Your place."

Allowing Annie the space to settle fully, Dr Kath waited for her to speak.

"It feels good. I like it here," Annie said, unprompted, her body still and breathing even.

"What is it you notice?"

"There is no pressure to do anything in particular. I can just be. I feel relaxed and happy. I am alone but I don't feel lonely. I have the freedom to explore. I need no permission."

"That's right. You're in control. It's not always the case though is it? Sometimes you believe you need external approval to make changes?"

"Sometimes," Annie said.

"Do you need permission from someone in particular?" Dr Kath questioned.

"Yes, from Michael."

"Who is Michael?"

"He's my father," Annie said.

"What do you need permission for?"

"Anything big. Any decisions about my future."

"Is it a recent thing?" Dr Kath asked.

"No." Annie waited a beat. "It's always been there."

"Who created the rule?"

"No-one. He didn't say anything. It's just a look."

"I see. Is it possible you have attributed meaning to that look without actually knowing his intention?"

"It's possible," Annie said, her brows pulling in slightly.

"Have you ever asked him to explain, when you've seen that expression?"

"No."

"What has stopped you?"

"I'm scared to."

"What are you scared of?"

"Being judged. His disapproval. What if I don't meet his expectations?" Annie asked.

"I see." Dr Kath jotted a note on her pad. "May I make a suggestion? Perhaps your fear has more to do with your own perception than your father's true feelings? Maybe it's your need for his approval that drives your thinking?"

"Maybe. How does it help me when I'm trying to make such a difficult decision?"

"Could you try to think of the problem in a different way? Imagine you have already talked to your father and he has effectively approved your decision." Dr Kath suggested.

"I'll try."

"So, now envisage taking up the inheritance. What would it mean to you?"

"Everything would be altered. There would be a seismic shift in my life."

"In a good way?"

"A bit of both. I could leave the job, which has been making me miserable recently," Annie said.

"You mentioned the stress before. Aside from that, do you enjoy being a teacher?" Dr Kath asked.

"I used to love it."

"What's changed?"

"It's partly the paperwork and the targets. You know the league tables and all the focus being on performance or at least it feels like that. The people and the politics. Since Miss Amelia *can-do-no-wrong* Potterton arrived last year, the dynamic has shifted."

"How has it affected you?"

"Well, before, for many years, actually since I first started at the school, I was supported. Trusted by the headteacher, you know? She relied on me as a sounding board, treated me as an equal," Annie explained.

"And that's important to you?"

"Yes, to feel valued and secure. That's how I felt. These days I get the impression I'm being displaced. I try my hardest to please. Whatever I do doesn't feel good enough. I've noticed she's not confiding in me half as much, but it is the sarcastic quips she shares with Amelia which undermine me the most," Annie said.

"Who is making the comments?" Dr Kath asked.

"Erm, I suppose, mostly Amelia." Whenever Annie spoke her colleague's name aloud her voice was full of venom. It was noticeably out of character.

"How would it be if you left it all behind?"

"I'd be relieved, but it still feels unfair! It would be impossible to get another teaching post without a good reference. On top of which I would feel pushed out when I've done nothing wrong!" Annie snatched at her words, red blotches creeping across her face and neck.

"It's normal to be cross, but remember you're safe here. You're in charge and you can determine how you feel. Take a moment to listen to your breathing," Dr Kath coaxed. "Follow the in and the out. Notice my words. You can cope with anything. Your positivity will overwhelm you and protect you from any strong, hurtful emotions. You can make them diminish into insignificance. You're in control."

There was more work to be done to disentangle Annie's issues with her father and her need for fairness. There was a rawness to them which prompted Dr Kath to leave them for today and focus the remaining time on a new area. Experience had taught her the longest-held beliefs were the hardest for her clients to alter; over time as they became more accustomed to the therapy, it was easier for them to confront their insecurities.

Once Annie's breathing had eased and her taut jaw had slackened, Dr Kath moved to Annie's favourite topic. "So, tell me, how about Beth and Thomas? How are they doing?"

"Good, I think. Thomas is a delightful little three-year-old. He's very cute and funny. Not quite as bright as his sister was at his age, but very even-tempered and easy. Beth, on the other hand, is a challenge. She's at that pre-teen age when she wants to be older than she is, starting to push against me already. She's too quick-witted for me and I often struggle to keep up with her. I'm dreading the emotional and hormonal melting pot ahead of us."

"How do you expect a move to affect them?"

"That's a big question!" Annie took her time, as she rifled through her thoughts before she added, "I think the family would be split down the middle. Colin and Thomas would move happily. Beth and I would probably both choose Bedfordshire over Gloucestershire. Tom could settle anywhere. Colin likes the idea, especially with the added support of my parents nearby. Beth–how can I convey it? I'd say she was superglued to her life in Swallows Green."

"You've left someone out," Dr Kath said. "What about you?"

"I don't want to move back."

"Do you know why?"

"It's a retrograde step. I enjoy the independent life we have built here. In the past I used to exist in the shadows. Most people enjoy the protection of the family umbrella. I would rather be out and take my chances in the rain. Away from them, I thrive."

"Them?"

"Mum and my sisters," Annie explained.

"You have misgivings about returning because you believe they will dominate you again?"

"Mum has never stopped trying to dominate me," Annie said matter-of-factly. "June is her mother's daughter and Emma well, she eclipsed me from the day she was born."

"Is there anything you could do to minimise their influence over you?"

"I'd love to be more confident," Annie said wistfully. "I'm fine when I'm away from them. It's like I revert to childhood behaviours as soon as I reach Oxford and the A40. I always try to do the right thing and never quite manage it."

"You can be self-confident," Dr Kath said. "Concentrate on your strengths. You're a dedicated teacher, a wonderful mother. You juggle all the demands on your time without complaint. You have created your own successful life since you left home. You can do it again whenever and wherever you choose."

Dr Kath gave Annie a few moments to absorb the suggestions, planting the seeds and watering them with silence. She knew it had worked when Annie spoke.

"I suppose I might be able to in the right circumstances."

"That's a good place to start. Hold on to that possibility," Dr Kath said. "I'm going to finish on that positive note. Very soon you will be fully alert as I count you back. . ."

The session left Annie feeling disorientated. It was a peculiar sensation. Her debrief with Dr Kath was pleasant and informative. They compared diaries and confirmed the next appointment.

All the while, Annie's subconscious still sitting on her shoulder. Whilst part of her was playing the Annie everyone knew, the other Annie was marvelling at the results of their discussion and voraciously foraging for further meaning. It was like they had been using a metal detector to discover nuggets of self-awareness, which had been mapped and left to be retrieved at a later date. She was convinced Dr Kath would notice this part of her, loitering in the room, long after she had gone.

For the short walk home she was on autopilot. She felt dazed as she approached the house, with no recollection of her route from A to B, she plumped for the side gate to give herself more time to reflect in the garden. She sat under the pergola her dad had helped to build a couple of summers ago, making the most of the shelter from the autumn air. The pearly-pink flowers of her New-Dawn climbing rose had scrambled effortlessly up and over the oak frame. The fragrant scent of the last of the September flowers tickled her nostrils. It would be sad to leave her lovely garden. She would miss tranquil moments like these.

She played back through her memories, like time-lapsed photography; images of the overgrown neglect when they first moved in, through every summer as they had transformed it, into the mature and established place it was today. Annie felt a sense of pride and accomplishment. There was something she was good at.

A renewed optimism fluttered in her stomach. She could do this again. She could build a new home. Her amateur horticultural skills would be useful for the new venture too. With a lightness of step at the possibility of new beginnings, she headed for the backdoor, calling out to announce her arrival.

Elizabeth

The early-morning sky was cheerless; the clammy air clinging to her clothes, seeping through to her skin. She stepped up into the taxi. Her second seven-thirty appointment with Dr Kath in as many days had seemed an excellent idea yesterday. Kath had agreed cautiously. Indicating, without insisting, a longer interval between sessions usually proved more effective. Elizabeth had understood the rationale; downtime might allow the subconscious to better process the insights gleaned.

She, on the other hand, had reasoned there was a clear advantage to riding the momentum; giddily hanging onto the magic carpet and letting it take her to unimagined destinations. Besides, there was an urgency to her situation necessitating a faster than average pace.

Following yesterday's hectic and extended working day she had assumed her exhaustion would lead to a deep refreshing sleep, leaving her ready to start again bright and breezy. Her plan had been thwarted by the red, blinking light on her answerphone, which had greeted her on her return home. Andrew's call had turned the evening on its head. Sleep had come a long way down her list of priorities. She hoped it wouldn't hinder progress today.

They trundled along in the traffic, already heavy in spite of the early hour. The cab was muggy, its heater blasting out warm, moist air, which condensed on the cold glass. Unpleasant. Elizabeth sat forward, peering out of the small gap of the open window. The rush of cooler air, whilst still damp, welcome on her face.

"Best I drop ya 'ere love," the taxi driver said. "Road's closed at the other end of 'arley Street 'cause of road works. Is that okay? Don't wanna get stuck down there. It'll take ages to find a way round it otherwise."

"That's fine. I can easily walk from here."

Handing over her fare and instructing him to keep the change, Elizabeth negotiated her descent to the pavement. If there was an elegant way of exiting a London cab, she had not yet found it. Those little half steps were more of a hindrance than a help. Evidently, they were not designed with high heels or decorum in mind.

The dank air hit her again. It was a real contrast with yesterday's bright crisp September morning. Shame autumn had decided to make an appearance already. Elizabeth dreaded the wind, which lifted her hair and the rain, which converted her neatly coiffured bob into a frizzy mess. On the other hand, Joe, her wonderfully exclusive hairstylist, now Art Director with a swish Knightsbridge salon, relished the seasonal onset. Sparing no expense, Elizabeth would visit him twice as often in an attempt to tame her innately wavy hair.

Arriving early at Dr Kath's building, she took the spare twenty minutes to survey and repair the weather damage. Back in front of the same cloakroom mirrors less than twenty-four hours later, she was pleased to note she'd escaped relatively unscathed. Perhaps it was the new straightening serum Joe had recommended to her? Mind you, at eighty pounds a bottle, it ought to be almost guaranteed.

Smoothing down her kingfisher-blue coat dress, she granted herself a moment of narcissism. Far from looking drained by lack of sleep, she saw herself shining; radiating the confidence of a woman who always got what she wanted. The buzz of the last day was providing all the energy she required right now. Later, she would fall into a crumpled heap. For now she permitted herself to take pleasure from the high.

Practically bouncing through the door to the outer office she greeted the receptionist with an uncharacteristically genial smile.

"I have a seven-thirty appointment. Elizabeth Braybrooke. I'm a little early. Is it okay to wait here?"

"Sure. Please do help yourself to a complimentary tea or coffee."

"Thank you."

Wandering over to the burnished console table, Elizabeth opted for a perky peppermint tea. Whilst coffee was her beverage of choice, she'd often found the quality unpredictable in these types of situations. Many an inferior cup had she drunk, in the interests of politeness, at her clients' offices. At least herbal teas were more reliable. She was in luck. Today's selection was from a recognisably high-end brand.

Slowly sipping the hot invigorating liquid, she flicked through her emails on her phone. Nothing too pressing. After the appointment she might take her time to wander back to the office; use the walk to chew over the findings, from what she imagined would be an enlightening hour with Dr Kath.

"Ms Braybrooke?"

"Yes?" Elizabeth looked up.

"Dr Kath is ready for you now."

Juggling her chic black attaché case, her black handbag with pops of kingfisher-blue detailing and her tea, she made her way to the comfortable sofa.

"Good morning, Dr Kath."

"Good morning, Elizabeth, and how are you this morning?"

"Do you know? I'm feeling quite peppy. Raring to go in fact." Elizabeth smiled.

"Excellent. Shall we get on with it? I expect you have another busy day on the cards?"

"It's not looking too bad at the moment, but I rarely have a day which pans out as expected," Elizabeth said. "It's the nature of headhunting. When your product is people, all sorts of unpredictable things occur. Invariably you are left with the same to-dos at the end of the day as when you started. I can't wait to put it all to one side for a while and nurture myself instead of others."

"Right then. Let's get cracking!"

Elizabeth soon reached a state of extreme relaxation: eyes closed, head resting on the back of the chair, breathing easy. She exhaled a deep satisfied sigh. There it was; she was ready.

"We've arrived in your haven. Where are we?" Dr Kath asked.

"I'm at home in my apartment."

"Tell me about it. What can you see, hear and feel?"

"It is sumptuous," Elizabeth said. "I see fine objects, remembering where and when they were chosen; I feel the deep pile of the carpet yielding beneath my bare feet. I am in my bedroom. The curtains are drawn. There are candles on every possible surface and an abundance of rose petals strewn across the white bed linen. It's clichéd but I don't care. The silk of my gown caresses my skin. Pure romance."

"Who set the scene? Was it you?"

"No, it was my darling Andrew."

"It sounds like this might have happened already?" Dr Kath asked.

"No, but it will. . . I have everything I want in that room. Now I can see it, I will make it happen."

"You are confident?"

"Oh I am." Elizabeth said.

"More than yesterday. What has changed?"

"Andrew." A smug expression spread across Elizabeth's face.

"In what way?"

"He came to see me last night. He told me he loves me and he will follow me wherever I go and support me whatever I choose to do."

"Were you expecting him to react this way?"

"No, not at all!" Elizabeth said. "It came out of the blue. The last time we spoke he was quiet, reserved, closed. On the move to Gloucester, he was adamant he would not follow. He told me in no uncertain terms he would never leave his wife and children."

"And yet he decided to visit you late in the evening yesterday, without any warning, having changed his mind?"

"Uh-huh. Amazing isn't it? I guess he's realised how much I mean to him."

"How long have you been waiting for this?"

"The last few years. At first, when we first started seeing

each other, I used to feel more secure knowing he was married and wouldn't ask for my commitment. I had always preferred my independence. Safer that way. You can't get hurt. But somehow, I was hooked. I couldn't imagine life without him. I can't believe it really. Never let myself think it would happen. It's just wonderful," Elizabeth said, seeing the life she wanted with Andrew unfold in her mind.

"And he knew how you felt before? That you'd wanted more." Elizabeth nodded. "Do you not have any concerns about the sudden nature of his decision?"

Elizabeth shifted uneasily in her seat. "What do you mean?"

"I appreciate this may be difficult to hear, but do you think it is possible he may change his mind again?" Dr Kath turned back a few pages of her note book. "You seemed quite clear he had declined your suggestion of a new life together. You said as much again, just now and now he's saying the complete opposite. Do you see how it might look a little odd?"

"You mean I need to make sure I can trust him? I'm confident he is genuine. He has told his wife."

"You're sure?"

"She was the one who told me," Elizabeth said. "Her message was on the phone when I got home yesterday. So, you see now why things are good?"

"I can see why you would think that, yes. Is there anything else to think through on this?" Dr Kath asked, knowing there was more.

"No, it's all good thanks."

"Okay we'll leave it for now. Shall we talk about the inheritance next?"

"Sure, I'm very confident I can make it work. I've even

indicated to the solicitor I will have my answer to him well before the deadline," Elizabeth said.

"Do you have any worries there?"

"Only the other unknown beneficiaries, but I'll sort them out. I tend to lead; others tend to follow," Elizabeth said confidently.

Dr Kath couldn't help but admire Elizabeth's conviction. "May I share a thought?"

"I suppose so," Elizabeth said almost sulking. She didn't want anyone to ruin her mood.

"Your confidence is impressive; however, I'm just wondering what might happen if things don't quite go to plan. If your vision doesn't come to fruition, do you have a plan B?"

"I'm not fretting about it. I can cope with most eventualities."

"What might you not be able to cope with?"

"I'm not interested in seeing any of my family." Elizabeth's reply was clipped and unfeeling.

Now they were getting somewhere. Dr Kath prodded the emotional wound, ready to assess its severity and triage Elizabeth's reaction.

"Perhaps we should–"

"No," Elizabeth interrupted. The small word was clinical and sharp; a shiny spinning bullet packed full of explosive. As an afterthought, as if feeling the need for justification, she continued, "Like I said, I'm not interested in them in the slightest. It would be a waste of my time to give them another thought."

"I understand. But is it not possible other members of your family could be involved? I think you mentioned there were specific instructions not to consult with them?"

Elizabeth deflated, her shoulders sagging, like a three-day-old balloon. Her mouth dropped open. The confidence, bordering on arrogance, of moments before had dissolved. The virtual blow causing her to contract as if an actual punch had been landed. Dr Kath had exposed the rawest of raw nerves. Elizabeth's physical response had answered her question. Sometimes she would delve deeper, help her clients to reveal, then heal their scars. This wasn't one of those times.

Liza

Gino stood at the back of the darkened club, next to the stage; a sinister silhouette fashioned by the spotlights behind. Liza checked her watch. She was bang on time. It was six o'clock. She tried and failed to assess his mood. It was impossible to read his expression in the shadows.

Empty of clients, the space felt stale: the floor sticky with spilt drinks, the odour from the toilets, a pungent mix of urine and bleach, no longer masked by stale tobacco since the smoking ban. Its potency dominated the air. It made her question how she could contemplate working here any longer. Did she have a choice?

She'd lost count of the number of times she had thought about leaving, only to find that yet again he had turned on his most loving and generous charm. After the worst arguments came his most persuasive pleadings. Every time he would promise to stop. Every time she would believe him and relax. Until she forgot to buy the right milk or tidy Angelo's books out of the way.

She had developed all sorts of techniques and strategies to keep the shells from cracking as she walked across them. From years of coping with Gino and his volatility, Liza approached realising she had been in training for this moment all along.

"Babe, I'm here. I'm keen to know what's happening. Something good I hope?" Liza asked.

Ignoring her question Gino grunted at Liza. Pulling back a chair at the same table, he positioned himself directly opposite her.

Gulping, she told herself to stay calm. Her eyes were drawn to his hands as he fiddled with a beer mat, repeatedly turning it over and over between his fingers. She must hold her nerve. Knowing he detested unnecessary small talk, her best strategy was to let him speak first. He was the one who had called the meeting. He was the Boss.

Candy had arrived early and popped her head round the door. "Oh, hiya babes. Fancy me giving you a mini-pedi later, since you're in already?"

Without turning to see who it was, Gino growled, "Get out! This is your space later, when you get your tits out. Until then I don't want to see you."

"Tosser," Candy mouthed, over the top of his head, leaving the door swinging as she retreated.

Liza could read his mood now. Fuck. It didn't look good. Still she waited. She chose the minimal provocation tactic. Inside she screamed at him to spit it out and get on with it!

The technical team ran through lighting sequences for the night's set. Occasionally, doors banged open and shut backstage. The beginnings of babble emanated from the girls' dressing room. He'd have to make a move soon. Finally, just as the sound check began, he spoke, the single word sending a Pacman monster of dread chomping its way round her body.

"Angelo."

She repeated her son's name in as light a tone as she could manage. "Angelo?"

"He's my son, right?"

"Yeah Gino. You know he is and you can see him whenever you choose," Liza said.

Her skin sticky, her stomach cramped as violently as it had in labour. Where was he going with this? How come he was even mentioning her darling boy? For them to speak about him was rare; for Gino to acknowledge parenthood still more so. At least the *talk* wasn't about her recent trip out of London. It didn't look like she had been rumbled.

Several minutes passed in silence and the sound of Liza's own thumping heartbeat played the role of a ticking countdown. She could not predict the outcome, only that an explosive event was almost upon her. She tried to keep her eyes still, for fear their movement would reveal her feelings.

"From next month he will be living with me." Gino's matter-of-fact statement detonated, ricocheting off every surface.

"You what? I don't think so!"

Clamping her nearest wrist on the table, his grip a vice from which she could not escape, he paid no attention to Liza's outburst. With an arctic tone, he dictated his demands.

"You will begin packing up his toys and clothes. I'll have his room ready for him to move in a week next Saturday. We've chosen a jungle theme. I'll make sure he gets to and from school every day. You won't need to be involved anymore. I'm taking my responsibilities as a father extremely seriously. This is for the best and you will do as I say or you know what will happen." His grip around her wrist tightened further.

"But–I–but–he's my son too! I have the right to keep him with me. I'm his mother for fuck's sake!" Liza screamed.

"There will be no discussion. You have no rights. You are not a proper mother to him. You're a whore, and let's face it, a washed-up one at that. Not exactly the role model a father would want for his son," Gino said glaring at her.

"You bastard! How dare you?" Liza was barely able to function.

Summoning up every ounce of restraint, she battled to regain her composure. Clear thinking was vital, as the rage he had stoked inside threatened to envelop her. Her primal instinct to protect her son took over. Above all else, she must keep him safe.

She sat, mute, her jaw aching with the effort of not speaking. What were Gino's motivations? None of it made sense. He'd never been interested in family before. Was he trying to punish her for some reason? Maybe he had found out she'd been seeing Kath? Maybe he thought she had been disloyal somehow? Maybe it was his poisonous jealousy of her past, which had somehow translated into jealousy of the bond she had with Angelo? How could she get out of this?

Her immediate thought was to acquiesce. At least if he thought she would comply he might let her go and she'd have time to think. Something told her to ask a question.

"You said we've chosen a jungle theme. Who is we? You've not said anything to Angelo yet have you?"

"Do you think I am stupid?" Gino snapped.

"I was just wondering."

"You dumb bitch," Gino snarled. "I won't talk to Angelo until everything is ready. I don't want to disrupt his schooling or fill his clever little head with worry. A clean break is what's best for him."

"Who is we?" Liza pushed, even though she knew she shouldn't. She couldn't help herself.

"Rochelle and me."

Her next word came out as a strangled repetition, resembling the slaughtering of a pig rather than a spoken name. "Rochelle?"

"You heard me."

Liza swallowed down the bile rising from her stomach. "But she's barely older than Angelo! And she's a dancer too! How could she be a better mother to him than me?" She said, desperately trying to control the squeal in her voice.

Had this man gone nuts? Gino was a manipulative womaniser, sure, but he was also a selfish self-centred egotist, with very little time for anyone but himself. It didn't make any sense.

"You are incorrect. Rochelle was a dancer, past tense, and from Saturday she will be my wife and business partner. She has always wanted kids and will make an excellent mother to my son."

He released her from his hold, the action signifying the end of the matter. Rubbing her rubescent wrist, Liza stayed seated. Stunned by the exchange. *What the hell am I going to do?*

Gino leant in close, dismissing her with a menacing hiss. "Remember that night all those years ago, when you first tried to get away? Any funny business and you won't be getting up again this time. Capisce?"

Remember? How could she forget? His threat took her straight back to the pre-Angelo memory of seven years ago.

Every night she relived that day in her dreams. The day when Gino's veneer had vanished.

*

"Look I've told you before you have nothing to be jealous of babe. Obviously, I'm not a virtuous virgin! Why would you expect me to be? I'm a lap dancer for fuck's sake!" Liza said.

Liza tried and failed to convince Gino. Trying to stay calm and soothe his ego, the stirrings of deja-vu crept in. She knew she should stand up for herself. Her courage gave her hope she could turn the situation around. Unfortunately, her hope was short lived and replaced by a baser emotion. Fear welled up, as he backed her into the corner of his grungy office. His face only inches from hers, his smoky, beery breath lingering between them making her nauseous. She stared back at him with fading defiance.

"Who do you belong to?" His whispered question hung in the same rank air.

"You baby, obviously!"

"Why don't I believe you? You slut! I see the way you catch their eyes and it's always the fresh-faced lookers, in for their first time and you make totally sure they'll be back to stuff wedge in your thong!"

"But it's my job baby. You know that," Liza pleaded.

"Don't you baby me!"

She tried again to placate him, his ever-reddening, unshaven face touching hers, his hands pinning her shoulders to the wall. Torn between love and hate, Liza stayed still, her mind hatching a plan to escape his intentions. A wrong move and he would thump her hard.

A shadow passed across the textured glass hatch, which acted as the cash office when the club was open. Liza kicked the rusting metal rubbish bin. It clattered over, scattering ticket stubs, fag ends and used johnnies onto the grubby vinyl floor. It was enough to prompt Sheena to turn the handle of the locked office door.

"You alright in there?" she asked.

"Yep, we're fine," Gino growled. "Just doing the final cashing up for the night."

"I think I left my travel card on top of the lockers in there. Can you let me in so I can check?"

"I can see it!" Liza piped up.

Seizing her opportunity, she ducked under Gino's armpit, as he turned his head to look directly behind him.

She grabbed the pass, unlocking the door with the key fortuitously left in the lock.

"Here you go," she said, handing the plastic wallet to her friend.

Gino shuffled a few papers on the desk. He commanded Liza to go out to his car and wait whilst he finished up. Snatching her mac from the back of the door, she linked arms with Sheena and headed down the long narrow corridor to the club's service entrance. When they reached the dirty white BMW parked at an awkward angle between the chain-link fence and the bins, Sheena slowed to say goodbye. She was thrown by Liza's ballsy stride right past the car and out through the raised barrier.

"You'll be in trouble!" she hissed.

"Fuck it!" Liza whispered with renewed rebelliousness. "He's being unreasonable."

They slowed their pace as they reached the T-junction. A moment of indecision flickered on Liza's face. Sheena would be turning right onto Hornsey Lane past Sid's Scrapyard. She could see the piles of old tyres over the crumbling red-brick wall. There was a good chance Gino would follow her but why should she take the cowardly route and shelter in the relative protection of her friend? Sheena had already helped her out once tonight. Kissing her on the cheek and forcing a smile, she wished Sheena a safe journey home, watching her walk to the night-bus stop fifty metres up the road. She strode, with feigned confidence, in the opposite direction towards the cut-through, which led to her street.

Feeling defiant she decided he had no right to question her past like that. *I'll just have to stand firm*. Her brain tricked her into believing she could win him over. It was all so every day but she was blind to the pattern. *I'll tell him we were talking about last night's TV or something.*

Every step she took further away from Sheena's encouraging smile more doubt crept in. Maybe if she saw less of her friend, Gino would ease off them both. He didn't seem to want her to talk to anyone about anything. All she wanted was for him to love her and make love to her, as sensitively and passionately as when he had first wooed her three months earlier. That Gino was the sweetest gentlest man she had known.

Her barriers had come down after a summer of holding back and she had fallen for him so heavily, she'd felt crushing pain at the thought of losing him. Then it started. When she had given him all of her, and he knew it, the questions tumbled out of his mouth as if a dam had burst. Now, she was trying to shore up the cracks to stem the flow. Her only option to stay rooted to the spot and try to conquer the impossible; use her whole spread-eagled body to stop. Every. Last. Drop. There was no alternative. To step aside and go with the flow would lead to misery. She knew. She'd been here before.

His heavy footsteps echoed in the alleyway. Liza continued forward, her clicking heels reverberating at a much higher pitch. She increased her speed, focusing on the pool of light from the lamppost at the end where the alley opened out onto the street. His pounding seemed louder and more frequent but she couldn't look back in case she tripped. She kicked off her shoes and started to run, the lamppost never seeming to get any nearer. In a thunderous crescendo his footsteps rolled into one and without a word, he closed the gap and kicked her hard in the back of the knee. Buckling to the ground, silent screams bounced around her head as blood, mascara and tears streaked her sad and broken spirit.

Dulcie

Leaving the clinic again, Dulcie had a clear action plan. During the debrief, she had concluded that avoiding Matty was exacerbating her confusion. Of all the possible reasons to stay, in reality, only one mattered.

Lots of events in the past had made her who she was. In her twenties, bold and sassy, she had known her own mind. For every significant decision she had ever made, her intuition had proved worth following. Her gut instinct had been unfailing. She only had one untidy thread. Matty. Now she knew they both deserved to tidy it away. One way or another she had to deal with it; follow the thread into the labyrinth and solve her very own Minotaur's puzzle.

She sauntered through Fitzrovia enjoying the quirky independence of the *Village in a City*. Passing an unassuming café, with a queue of customers snaking around the corner, she joined its tail. If there were that many people in the know, she figured it must be good. She needed a place to stop and plan her next move. This seemed as good a spot as any. Fingers crossed the coffee was up to the standard of the eateries back home. Sure, there were many more outdoor tables in Sydney.

Both the crowded nature of London's streets and the climate meant the couple of pastel-painted bistro tables with matching metal chairs represented the entire al-fresco offering. But they were a perfect complement to the tiny shop front; a sense of the dainty rather than the sprawling of its antipodean cousins.

Quaint though it was, Dulcie felt a pang of nostalgia. For the first time since she had arrived in London, the pull of home yanked at her heart. Nearing the doorway after ten minutes of queuing, she peered through the window at the panini on display. She was momentarily distracted by the allure of a hearty snack. She had skipped breakfast at the hotel. Several days of the same options had finally reached the point of limited appeal. Besides she had been apprehensive prior to her meeting with Dr Kath. Suspecting it might be tough, her appetite had been suppressed by her churning stomach.

By the time she reached the counter, her mouth was watering as she placed her order over the stacks of pre-prepared sandwiches.

"I'll have the ciabatta with mortadella, goat's cheese and black olives please and an Americano with cold milk. Thanks."

"*Certamente bella*. Now, you are a long way from home, no?"

Blushing at the charm of the attractive young waiter, she nodded. "Actually, I was born here. In England, I mean, but I've lived in Sydney all my adult life. So, yes, in a way, I do feel far from home."

"Oh, I love Sydney. I'd go back there in a heart-beat if I could."

"Really? You know it?"

"Oh yes. My uncle and cousins run a coffee shop in Oz. I

toured around in my gap-year, then worked with them for a few months before I came back to uni. Are you here on holiday?"

"Not sure really. Let's call it a reconnaissance. I am thinking about maybe settling back here."

"Are you crazy?"

"Probably. It's not an easy choice. We'll see."

"Hey, good luck with it anyhow. Take a seat, I'll bring it over in a sec."

"No worries, I'm in no rush. Happy to watch the world go by for a bit."

The display on her mobile said 12:20. It would be fine to call him. She imagined he'd be contemplating lunch, if not out already. Fingers crossed he'd be able to talk. Heart pounding in her stomach, she selected Matty's mobile number and listened to the interminable ringing tone. She told herself if he picked up, it would be a sign.

"Hi there gorgeous. Where have you been all my life?" The wink in his expression, sent by digital signal over the 3G network, delivered itself as a vivid picture in her mind's eye.

"Oh Matty! You make me laugh."

"And?"

"Yeah, look I'm sorry it's been a while. I've been doing lots of churning things over. I think we should meet. If you want to that is?" Dulcie said.

"You try and stop me! Hey, I'm free for lunch soon. Where are you? Shall I come and meet you?" This time it was his boundless enthusiasm which came bouncing down the line.

"I'm in a little café, Bianca's, on Charlotte Place, near Goodge Street. I've not eaten yet but I've ordered. Are you sure you can get here?"

"Yep, it's fine. To be honest, even if it wasn't, I couldn't resist." Matty stopped for a moment, weighing up the merits of his next sentence. "I've been desperate to see you. There's only so much waiting a poor boy can do. I respect your need to think things through but enough is enough, you know?"

Beneath his jokiness she could tell he was pleased she had called. Dulcie didn't blame him for wanting to seize the moment. It was time.

"I'm sorry, I'm sorry," Dulcie said, running a hand through her hair. "Get yourself over here pronto! Shall I order for you?"

"Yep, that'd be great. I'll have whatever you're having, with my usual coffee."

"Consider it done. See you soon."

The call over, Dulcie placed her phone under close surveillance. There was a possibility he might call back or change his mind or get lost. She may be left sitting alone, waiting. Though the last was improbable, she found her excitement peppered with pessimism.

Replaying the conversation, she combed through his words for any sign of doubt on his part. Maybe he was just being friendly and upbeat, secretly wishing she would let the past be the past? Maybe he had misinterpreted her meaning? She shivered, touching her temple in place of wood, for luck and redirected her energy towards practicalities. She looked up, instantly catching the waiter's eye. Had he been watching her? She couldn't tell. Questioning herself again, it was as if she had lost all ability to read social cues. Still, he was over to her table in seconds. Had he been keeping an eye on her after all?

"Bella, is there anything I can do for you?"

"How did you know? Can I order another mortadella ciabatta and a cappuccino? If you could hold the sandwiches and the coffee back though? I'm expecting a friend to arrive soon."

"Sure thing. You'd like your Americano now though, right? Whilst you wait?"

"Yes please. You're very kind."

"My pleasure."

He spun on the spot, initiating a brief yet animated exchange with his colleague behind the counter; their fluent Italian colouring the atmosphere with continental tension. Alarmed her request had caused a problem, Dulcie was relieved to witness her coffee pass between them and land before her in a deft manoeuvre. She complimented them on their talents.

"Impressive! Not a single drop spilt!" she said.

"Ah, it's not always been the case. It's taken many years of dedicated practise to achieve a steady hand. When I started. . . hah. . . you might have been unfortunate enough to have most of the drink sitting in the saucer or worse still, deposited in your lap."

Dulcie laughed. "I think it's a skill worthy of mention and you speak Italian too?"

"*Sì!* We always spoke it at home growing up. My mother insisted. Do you speak any?"

"No, no I'd love to though. It's such a lyrical language, occasionally intense too, huh? Often sounds confrontational, don't you think?" Dulcie asked.

The waiter threw both hands out in a dramatic gesture. "Oh that's just the passion people feel. You know, when you are talking about something that matters to you?"

"I get that. I appreciate the openness. Sometimes it's difficult to read people here. It's easier in Oz, people are more straight-forward most of the time. I imagine it's even easier in your culture?"

"Perhaps. Italians can get revved up about all sorts of things, from good coffee to sexy cars. When it comes down to it though, are we really any better at expressing ourselves in affairs of the heart? *Ora mi scusi ma, Signorina*, I'd love to stay and get under your skin, as you have mine, but I fear I must get back to it!" His conspiratorial grin accompanied another burst of Italian rising above the ferocious hiss of the coffee machine's steamer.

Relishing the strong dark taste, she sipped her way through half the cup; the lunchtime regulars providing her with a dynamic view.

"Mind if I join you?" a familiar voice asked.

"Matty! Hi!" Dulcie grinned. "Where did you come from? I've been watching out for you."

"Don't worry. It's packed in here, and I squeezed past the queue. What a super little place!"

Dulcie stood to greet him, waiting patiently whilst he disrobed. After hanging his scarf and jacket on the back of his chair, he leant in, opting to kiss both her cheeks. They had not yet concluded their discussion of etiquette. Both were unsure how to open the conversation.

Now Matty had arrived, Dulcie felt relieved. At the same time, she had become a nervous teenager–scared to say the wrong words, not knowing the right words, electing no words. Avoiding eye contact, she developed a fascination for her fingers, which she twisted together in a cat's cradle. Matty first placed his cool hands over hers, before reaching one out to lift her chin.

"Tell me all about it Dulcie. I'd happily sit and hold your hands forever. I have lots I want to say but I sense you need to talk first. You talk and I will listen, okay?"

Dulcie nodded. "Okay."

Annie

"I just don't get it darling! Why is it difficult to decide? Surely, it's a simple choice? Stay or go. You know I'll back you either way," Colin said.

For several hours following Annie's hypnotherapy session, they had been discussing the prospect of a new life in Gloucester. Caught between his bemusement and her own emotions, her attempt to articulate any kind of cohesive reasoning had disintegrated into defensive anger.

"Don't raise your voice. I know you find me frustrating. It's not simple at all! If you really understood me and cared about how I feel, you'd have worked that one out by now!" Annie's voice was thick. Her eyes brimmed with tears as she turned away.

She did feel sorry for him. Poor Colin. His face had shown all the confusion of someone lost in a foreign country without a translator. Her harsh words raced around in front of her like a breaking news banner on a loop. She wished she could swipe them away.

"I may not understand fully but I do care. I just don't seem to be able to do anything right these days. I try to help but it makes it worse. I feel guilty; I encouraged you to see someone but after all these sessions you are more bewildered and upset now than you were before you started. That can't be right, can it?" Colin asked, rubbing his forehead.

"There you go again!" Annie snapped. "Making assumptions. How do you know whether it's helping? Maybe I have lots of unresolved issues that need sorting first! Unless you have some kind of spy-cam set up going on, how can you know? I think you're scared of things changing. Just because you're self-contained and can't imagine sharing your own private thoughts, doesn't mean that works for me!"

Colin withered, drawing his arms in as if to block her unkind assault. "Fine! I was only trying to help. I can't deal with you when you're like this. You make no sense. I thought you needed my support but since you choose to push me away, I'll leave you to it."

Annie, who had been wishing Colin would leave, missed the implied threat, the vitriol in his words. The red mist had descended, smothering her chances of interpreting, or caring, about his meaning. She bit down hard on her bottom lip and repeatedly jabbed two fingers up behind his disappearing back, as he stormed off to the study. The door slammed shut.

She ached with loneliness as she allowed her tears to fall. Great big sobs shook her whole being. She replayed the conversations with Colin and Kath, her mum and her sisters, rummaging through every sentence, hunting down a way to emerge, sanity intact. How had she arrived at this desperate, wounded place? They were all trying to help in their own way but their suggestions only served to fuel her sense of isolation. *That damn instruction.* Who was this mysterious person to block her from talking to them?

Her mind swung back to craving Colin's understanding; longing for his white charger rescue from the imminent decision, which loomed on the cheerless horizon. She carried the full weight of her family's likely disappointment should she reject the opportunity.

Enduring endless minutes, willing Colin to return, her mind swirled. Every creak of the old house, as it breathed, renewed her hope he would reappear; each time she identified the noise as a draught or a loose floorboard, fresh tears flowed. After some time Annie fell asleep curled up on the sofa.

Waking several hours later, she found herself tucked up with a soft rug, still alone. Colin must have put the blanket on her before heading up to bed. Exhausted, she forced herself to lift her spent body to a sitting position before dragging herself upstairs. Fully clothed she slipped under the covers beside him.

*

The next morning, weak sunlight reached her face through a chink in the curtains, which had been hastily closed the evening before. A few quiet seconds ticked by before reality hit and the argument reared up in front of her again.

She hated going to sleep without a resolution; she hated the feeling of guilt for lashing out at Colin but most of all she hated the realisation he wasn't her knight in shining armour. Maybe he never had been. It wasn't his fault. He tried his best. He hadn't done anything wrong; he just hadn't done anything different. Facing the big decision on her own she could do, facing her demons alone–that was a whole other ball game.

She turned to check on Colin. He was still sleeping. A

lattice of love, remorse and guilt wove itself into her heart compelling her to act. Never mind the ever present greyness; it would have to wait.

Donning her 'provider' hat, Annie left the bedroom with ninja stealth and headed for the warmth of the kitchen. The mission presented little challenge. Sunday family breakfast was a regular occurrence in Clematis Cottage, especially since they had renovated the old AGA.

Annie had fallen for the house as soon as she had seen the dilapidated beast in the corner. It had been a decommissioned, rusting monster, dominating the cramped cottage kitchen. Colin had been ready to replace it with a modern version; she had persuaded him otherwise. By knocking through to the equally cramped dining room, they had created a warm, welcoming space. With a solid farmhouse table, as useful for homework as it was for baking, the room had become the hub of the home.

Annie set to work on the batter for the cinnamon-and-raisin scotch pancakes. Her spirits were lifted by memories of the renovation. Aware the corners of her mouth had followed suit, she celebrated by breaking into a full smile; somewhat of a rarity for her these days.

"Mum? What's made you happy?"

Beth had padded into the room, wrapped warm against the chilly morning, in oversized bed-socks and lilac fluffy dressing gown.

"Oh, nothing darling. I was just remembering the kitchen the way it was before."

"Yuck! It was awful. Dark, cold and greasy! Why would that make you smile?"

"It's more Dad's reaction when he learnt how much the old cooker was worth, even before we got it working again. Not often he admits I'm right. That time I knew better. I'd done my research and his face was a picture!" Annie said.

"Yeah, whatever Mum. When's breakfast ready?"

Her daughter's indifference punctured Annie's delicate joviality. *Sometimes, I wonder why I bother*, she thought.

"About twenty minutes," she said to Beth.

"I'll watch TV then whilst you get it ready."

Beth was gone before Annie could suggest she stay and help. A long sigh emanated from deep in her belly. She retained a sliver of hope that Thomas's innocent presence would soon keep her from falling into complete despair.

She continued on with her preparation, wondering when he might appear. Batter made, table laid, coffee in the machine ready to go. Oranges were freshly squeezed into the wedding present of a jug and still no sign of the boys.

Annie trudged up the stairs to investigate. She found them both in Thomas's room building an elaborate wooden train track covering most of the floor.

"Wow, that's brilliant Thomas. What a great layout!" she said.

"Daddy helped. Mummy come and play too! You can have the red engine, James. I'm blue of course–he's got my name."

His eyes were wide with excitement; hers overflowing with unconditional love. Colin extricated himself from the far corner by the wardrobe, tiptoeing between the tracks to arrive at the small triangle of blue carpet on which she stood.

He leant in close to her ear with a heart-felt whisper, "I'm sorry darling."

"Me too."

Now wasn't the time to mention her mental state. She forced away the tears, which pricked. Again.

"I'll play later Thomas darling," Annie said, holding out her hand for him to take. "Come on, breakfast is ready to go. Time to eat."

Elizabeth

The pianist in the corner of the bar finessed the jazz standards with dedication. To most of the bejewelled guests gathered by the marble counter, he was invisible. They failed to notice him in their eagerness to collect their glasses of Champagne. Elizabeth noticed. She took a moment to inhale the scene: the mirrored columns, the majestic chandeliers, the elegant dresses and tailored dinner suits.

Charged with coordinating this year's event, Elizabeth felt her pride entirely justified. *I've only gone and done it!*

Despite the turbulence in her private life, she had managed to keep it together. Professionalism was such a big part of her personal brand; she could not imagine any situation where she would fail to deliver.

"You look stunning in that red taffeta. Such a befitting outfit for our star partner. Why the frown on such a glorious occasion?" Slimy as ever, Martin made her skin crawl.

Her MD was such an arse. She continued to play her part with elegance, secretly wishing she could kick him in the balls and walk away. He'd caught her unawares by the bar, collecting her thoughts. Air-kissing both cheeks she bought herself some time.

"Martin, what fabulous results the practice has enjoyed this year, guided by your expert hand, of course and thank you. You're such a gentleman for noticing my dress, flatterer!" By way of explanation of the frown she added, "You know me. I'm all about hard work and making money. I'm waiting on news of a big deal so you know how it is. Forgive me if I seem a tad serious." She flashed a smile as she put a little distance between them, hoping he would get the hint and leave her alone.

Dumb, drunk or dangerous, it was not clear which, he ignored her signal and edged closer, his mouth almost touching her diamond-studded earlobe.

"Would you like to find out how expert my hand can be?" He pulled back, searching her face for reciprocation. Instead, he found a medusa stare.

What a prick, she thought to herself suppressing the urge to say it to his face. Instead she replied, "We both know that would be trouble now, don't we. Best we mingle, just in case your *wife* gets the wrong impression."

This time she left nothing to chance, retreating to the relative safety of her team's table. Gliding through the crowds, who had begun gathering in clusters to find their seats, Elizabeth left a bewildered Martin at the bar, wondering whether he had lost his touch.

The last stragglers were peeling themselves away from the bar, consulting the seating plan and searching for their allocated tables, each named after a classic Queen song title. Elizabeth sat patiently at Bohemian Rhapsody.

For the sake of appearances she had avoided Andrew as much as possible. Not long now though. Soon they would be sharing the stage for the charity auction.

Planning for the event had taken place months ago, when things between them had been different. She was thrilled with his U-turn but the situation was still very new. She didn't want to broadcast her relationship status or place it in jeopardy.

Since her arrival for the evening Elizabeth had kept him under skilful surveillance with all the hallmarks of a Bond-girl. She was delighted he was flying solo; this was a good sign.

The smiling egos of her colleagues made even less impact on Elizabeth than usual. Impervious to their pavonine boasting, her inner thespian put on a show of which Dame Helen Mirren would be proud. Appearing to be entirely engaged, in contrast with her true state of utter disinterest, her performance was flawless. Body sparklingly present but mind elsewhere.

Family. There was the issue, right there. Sure, the landmine had always been there, planted beneath the surface long ago, pre-London. Hidden away she'd ignored it, moved forward and built herself a new life. Now though, the years of weathering had worn away the earth, leaving it barely covered by a fine layer of dust.

Her most recent session with Dr Kath had blown the dust away, leaving the hazardous subject in plain view. Once seen Elizabeth couldn't un-see it. Pre-occupied by its enormity, she heard neither the fawning of her subordinates, nor the flattery of her boss.

"Thank you all for coming this evening. I'd like to call upon our stunning Elizabeth Braybrooke to open the proceedings."

An eager nudge from her neighbouring diner brought her to her feet. The room filled with applause. All eyes were on her graceful approach to the stage, where Martin stood waiting, microphone in hand. Of the hundreds in the room only two experienced shared disgust, as he placed his hand on her waist and let it slide below the line of decency to rest on the curve of her right buttock.

"Thank you, Martin, for such a complimentary introduction. You really shouldn't have!" Her gracious smile radiating none of the venom she felt.

She presented an amusing, eloquent run down of the evening's timings, ensuring she gave attention to the V.I.P. guests dotted about the room. Having designed and memorised the seating plan she was able to pick out each one in turn.

She took a distinct delight in thanking Denise Connaught, Martin's long-suffering-wife, whom she had seated strategically on the Fat Bottom Girls table. Her final mention, by way of passing the baton, was to Andrew, who had magnanimously agreed to co-host the event.

"I would like to thank Bonner and Tuce as our sponsors for the Howard Barnard Charity Ball and give a special thanks to their ambassador and our compere for the evening, Andrew Vellacott."

The second round of boisterous applause petered out as Andrew arrived at Elizabeth's side.

"I'd like you all to raise your glasses to Bonner and Tuce. Their generosity has made this event possible and set us well on our way to achieving our fundraising target of one million pounds!"

"Bonner and Tuce!" Everyone cheered.

Elizabeth passed the microphone to Andrew and stepped away, applauding in his direction.

He held her gaze for a micro-moment, sharing his distaste for Martin's slimy nature. Even the keenest observer in the audience would have struggled to read him. Consummate orator, he captivated the guests with his natural charisma.

"... savour the feast, sit back, relax and let the spectacle unfold. Oh, and of course, don't forget to put your hands in your pockets and empty your wallets!"

Elizabeth reached her table just in time to select a miniature granary roll offered by the deferential waiter. Some discussion had bubbled up in her absence, leaving her feeling out of the loop. Tuning in she realised they were speculating about Andrew, the man behind the success.

"I don't get it. How can someone so genuine and charming climb the corporate ladder all the way to the top?"

"I don't know. I mean he could be all show here and an absolute git to his team?"

"True. Although he has got something about him hasn't he? I'd totes prefer to work for him than Martin Connaught any day. He's much more polished, don't you think?"

"Katie! If I didn't know better I'd say you fancy him! Be careful, he's married you know."

"Ah yes Mark, but did you see the empty place beside him on his table and no sign of his wife in tow."

"Didn't think you were the older-man type? I thought you only had eyes for me? You kill me!"

Their peals of laughter caught the attention of those at nearby tables, half of whom looked on disapprovingly, the other with envy. Yes, this was a prestigious event but it would drag without a little light drama here and there.

Elizabeth revelled in the fact she need not join in the speculation. Her intimate knowledge of developments in Andrew's private life gave her more than her usual sense of superiority. Additionally, as the host of her table with responsibility as a senior representative of Howard Barnard, it was her duty to cut in.

"Calm down guys. Remember we are the ones on show here."

Mark and Katie turned away from her, whispering like reprimanded school children. She was out of favour.

No matter. They are of no consequence.

Elizabeth switched to the conversation on her left, led by a studious-looking economist, spouting the gloom of a likely double-dip recession.

"You are preaching to a very tough crowd here. Head-hunters are notoriously egotistical. Most of us believe we are the masters of our own destiny. We aren't about to let a predicted downturn dictate our bonus potential," Elizabeth said.

"Really? Elizabeth, isn't it?"

"Yes and you are?"

"Marcus Hopkins, Economic Researcher, Goldstein and Co."

Elizabeth's provocative interjection netted the attention of the others on the table. She thoroughly enjoyed the spat, goading the Gen-Z analysts who took themselves far too seriously. Sadly for Marcus, she was as skilful at intellectual debate as she was expert in her career.

"Head-hunter. That's a glorified recruitment consultant, right?" he asked.

"Ooh Marcus, how controversial you are." Ever mindful of her extended network, Elizabeth quizzed him with a soupçon of sass, allowing him his self-importance, whilst making it clear she was a worthy adversary. "What makes you ask? Tell me. I'm interested to hear your views."

"If you must know I put recruiters in the same category as estate agents. Often they are ineffective parasites."

"At least you see us higher up the food chain than used-car salesmen. That's the other comparison people sometimes make."

Elizabeth managed to raise a grin on Marcus's serious face. As the meal meandered on, she welcomed their feisty interaction; it amused her. At least he was sharp and a far superior conversationalist to her tedious colleagues. So absorbed by their sparring was she, Andrew's cool hand on her shoulder appeared to materialise from nowhere.

"My apologies," he said. "Please excuse my interruption. I need to borrow Elizabeth if I may? We're about to start the auction whilst coffee is served."

"No problem sir." Marcus assumed the reverence of a person who knows his place in the hierarchy.

"It's a shame. I found you highly engaging. We must catch up for a drink sometime," she said.

"Oh yes, certainly Elizabeth. I would find that most pleasurable. Could I take your card? Here's mine."

With a practised hand she exchanged cards with Marcus, placing his inside her Gucci clutch-bag. She departed with Andrew, sashaying her way to the backstage area, still rippling with delight at her recent catch.

"You're an incredible woman you know. You hooked him without even trying," Andrew said, enthralled.

"He's an annoying upstart. Question is though, who does he know? I've been trying to break into Goldstein and Co. for years. He might just open a door."

"Are you ever off duty?" Andrew asked.

Elizabeth glanced around to check for possible eavesdroppers. With no one in earshot she risked her flirtatious reply. "Only when we're alone my darling. No Valerie tonight? No change of heart?"

"No, don't even think it. You know very well we're going back to yours tonight and I'm going to fuck you senseless. Besides, Valerie isn't even speaking to me. Since she rumbled us, I am out on my ear." With puppy-dog eyes and an immature voice he pleaded, "I can come home with you, can't I?"

Liza

The ringing tone persisted–again!

No point in leaving another message. Who else can I call?

Liza had tried Sheena, texted her too. It had delivered but no answer yet. Her flight from the club had been unencumbered. Gino had no reason to chase her this time. At last she had clarity. After years of indecisiveness Gino's outrageous demands had brought everything into sharp focus. The time had come. She was on the verge of freedom.

Many times she had wondered what it would feel like. Trouble was, as she set about all the necessary actions triggered by his declaration, dread took hold of the pit of her stomach. It crashed through her body in a tsunami of fear. She needed to hear another voice. Her own was filling her head with worst-case scenarios. *Has Gino somehow collected Angelo already? Why isn't Sheena responding? Where is the bus? Kath said to call after the meeting but she's not answering either. Has he got to her too?*

Endlessly staring down at her phone, she willed it to come to life. Then, heralded by the familiar buzz, the little envelope appeared. She pounced on the message. It was from Sheena. A quiver rippled from her heart to her toes.

Sorry Hun. Didn't see your txt or missed calls. Phone on silent. Angelo's fine. Just finished tea. Watching TV. U OK?

Liza dithered. Started a reply. Deleted the text after a few lines. It had been riddled with predictive-text errors and all the wrong words. The bus arrived and she fumbled in her cavernous handbag for her travel card. She swung into her seat as the doors hissed closed and then fumbled again. This time, in a frantic search for her phone; her anxiety paralysing. Logic dictated that it had to be there, yet her blurred brain had no recollection of the moments beyond her aborted text. Struggling to regain her equanimity she breathed deeply.

Start again. It's got to be here.

A further methodical trawl yielded success. There it was, in the very compartment where she always kept it. She peered at her world through the fogged-up expanse of window. A plan. She needed a plan. Sheena would help but she couldn't discuss it in front of Angelo. Maybe a text was best after all, to give her advance warning. In the meantime she could try Kath again. She selected last number redial.

"Hello, is that Kath?"

"Hi Liza. Is there a problem?"

"Yes. . . er. . . no. . . er. . . oh shit I don't know." Liza said willing herself not to cry.

"Where are you?"

"On the bus on the way back to Sheena's. What should I do? I need to see you. I don't know what to do!"

"Something bad has happened? Don't worry. I can help you. Take it one step at a time. Why don't you get to Sheena's first and give me a call when you get there? I'm still in my office. I'll wait, I promise."

"Alright thanks."

Marginally calmer now, Liza fixed her attention on the immediate future. She conjured up joyous images of Angelo's beaming face greeting her in the doorway. It kept her going for the rest of the journey, right to the moment where she stood in the porch and pressed the bell.

She heard his footsteps long before she was rewarded by the sunniest smile and the happiest hug. She held him tight drinking in his love; like Lourdes water it had a miraculously restorative effect. Angelo noticed her lingering longer than usual.

"Mummy! You're squashing me. Let me go!"

"Sorry baby, I'm just happy to see you." Liza said, kissing the top of his head.

"Well, that's no reason to squash me. Anyway you saw me this morning. You are silly," Angelo said.

"Yes, I am, aren't I?"

Thankful for the normality of the conversation with her adorable little man, she wished she could capture the simplicity of his world and convert hers to the same bright, primary-coloured version. Daily reunion done; Angelo opted to return to his favourite cartoon.

Sheena ushered Liza into the kitchen. "What's wrong? You're shaking love. What happened? What did he want?"

"Oh Sheena, I don't know where to start. He's a bastard!"

"Tell me something I don't know. Look, sit down. Give it to me warts and all."

In a clear, concise account Liza relayed the ludicrous events of the last couple of hours. The whole scenario sounded even more ridiculous spoken out loud. It was cathartic. She felt her strength returning.

"What an idiot! Who the fuck does he think he is?" Sheena said, looking angrier than Liza had ever seen her.

"Shhh, look, I have you. I have Kath. I have my new life with Angelo ahead. Everything is going to be fine."

"I'm glad you're sounding confident at least."

"I wouldn't say that," Liza said, tugging on her bottom lip. "I'm still bricking it, but I'm hopeful we can find a way to escape. I can't do it on my own, but you know what? I'm starting to realise the further away from him I am, the stronger I feel. It's like he's Lex Luther trying to cripple me with kryptonite."

"He used to have you just where he wanted you. Not any more though, huh?"

"Nope. It's funny but this time is different. He's broken the last part of me he'll ever break. I should actually thank him. He's made it easier to leave. His biggest mistake was imagining his threats would be more powerful than my love for Angelo." She paused. Glassy-eyed, she stared right through Sheena to a far-off place. She concluded, her voice almost a whisper, "I would die for my angel if I had to."

"Of course you would but it won't come to–"

"Oh shit! I forgot. I'm supposed to call Kath. She's waiting in the office for my call. Shit! Shit! Where's my phone?" For the second time in as many hours Liza scrabbled around in her bag. "Where the fuck is my phone?"

"Look don't worry babe. Here, use mine." Sheena held out her mobile as a solution.

"Don't be a stupid cow. I don't know her number! And anyway what if someone else calls?"

"Someone else. You mean him?" Sheena asked, forgiving Liza's insult.

"Yes, I have to keep him thinking I'm on board with his plan. If he thinks I'm ignoring him, he might start to doubt me! I need to find my fucking phone!" Liza's panic took an exponential path towards aggression, flicking from freaking-out to whirling dervish. She hovered on the edge.

"Darling, we'll find it. Let me have your bag. Let's get everything out and lay it down on the side here."

With a reluctant shove, she passed the bag to her friend, before standing hands on hips, the foreman to Sheena's labourer. Engrossed in their searching, neither noticed Angelo's tousle-haired head poking round the side of the door frame.

"Mummy?" Angelo called out.

"Not now darling. Mummy's a bit busy right now."

Liza attempted to sound as normal as possible. She was mortified. How long had he been standing there? How much had he heard? She never raised her voice with him or swore. However much his father had damaged her, she'd tried hard to shield Angelo from that world.

"But Mummy?"

"I've told you. Wait."

She turned to see his flushed cheeks and fearful eyes, partially obscured by the phone, behind which he was hiding. A mixture of relief and confusion washed over her. The mystery of the how, what, and why of Angelo's possession could be dealt with later.

"Oh, thank you Angel!" Liza said.

"Mum! How many times have I told you, don't call me that!"

"Sorry darling. Can you give it to me now please? Mummy needs to make a call."

"To Dr Kath? Are you sick Mummy?"

That answered that question. He had been listening for a while.

"No, I'm fine. She's just helping me sort things out. She's someone to talk to and get advice," Liza said.

He frowned. "But?" He fidgeted with his ear and stared down at his feet. "But you can talk to me Mummy. I give very good advice."

She crouched down beside him, a whoosh of love zinging through her. "I know baby but I really do need to speak to her first. Is that okay?"

"Okay," he said slowly. "But promise you tell me after?"

"Pinky promise!"

With an affectionate pinch of his cheek, she retrieved the phone and made her way to the patio doors to make the call. She had learnt from experience this was the spot with the strongest reception. She needed to tackle things one by one. One thing at a time and her first task was to get another appointment.

Miraculously, Dr Kath was still waiting. She'd detected Liza's urgency in their earlier call, brief though it had been. It was highly unusual for her to see a client twice in one day, but not unheard of. Her work at the refuge could be intense. The issues Liza was working through, in the main, were not uncommon, and occasionally required unorthodox solutions.

Back in the small consulting room, Liza sat, eyes closed, hands in her lap, under hypnotic trance. In contrast to her jittery gabbling on their way up the stairs, she heard herself answer Dr Kath's questions softly.

"I know what I need to do but how?" Liza asked.

"You know the answer, it's inside you. You know yourself. You know what to do. Any time you begin to question yourself, remember that," Dr Kath said. "Now tell me. What has stopped you leaving in the past?"

"I fell for him." Liza sighed. "I loved him. He saved me."

"In what way?"

"I was alone. I was strong but alone. He came along and swept me off my feet."

"You needed to be saved from being alone?" Dr Kath questioned.

"He was good for me. He was my soulmate. My Mr. Right."

"What does that look like?"

"Strong, handsome, successful, powerful even," Liza said.

Dr Kath took a sip of water. "You could say he was perfect?"

Liza shook her head. "I thought so, but then he was rough and unkind."

"And you forgave him?"

"Yes. Well, no. I mean I put up with it. Kinda goes with the territory."

"Tell me a bit more about it. How exactly?"

"My type. Those men. I can't help it. I always end up with the rough guys."

"Always? It's happened before?"

"Yes. I seem to get it wrong–always," Liza said, her cheeks flushing.

"How do you mean, wrong?"

"I start out assuming everyone is kind. Taking them as I

find them. Trusting my instincts." Liza fell quiet. "Mostly I'm wrong. They turn out to be different. I get taken in, charmed, and bang! Turns out I don't know them at all."

"I see. So, what have you learnt from the pattern?"

"That's just it. I don't learn. I don't want to give up on the idea that people are basically good."

"Even if you get hurt?" Dr Kath asked.

"Yes, even then. I don't want to change. I don't want them to change me. If I do, surely they win?"

"So, what's different now?"

"It's not just me now. I've got to do it for Angelo."

"And you? You've said you need to do it for him but how much do you want things to be different, for yourself?"

"Oh, so, so much." Liza just wanted to stop fighting life and have some normality. She puffed her cheeks full of air, pushing it out with deliberate effort.

"Are you pushing something away?"

"I want to stop running. I've always been running."

Confused, Dr Kath clarified, "But you do want to leave though?"

"More than anything!"

"Remember you can do this. You want it for you. You want it for Angelo. You can make it happen. Let's focus on the positives. Build a picture of your future. An idea of how it might look. Does that sound useful?"

"Yes."

Kath took another sip of her water, and turned the page of her notebook. "Tell me, what do you see?"

"Angelo is running around chasing squirrels through the leaves. He's really smiling and giggling. Wrapped against the cold, his cheeks are rosy, his breath misty in the crisp air." Dr Kath scribbled away as Liza developed her vision. "In the countryside, near the woods. I'm linking arms with someone. My hands are stuffed in my pockets to keep them warm. We're laughing. I might know him already but I'm not sure. He is familiar. I feel safe."

"You want to keep hold of him?"

"Yes, but we're not together. Not in a relationship. He feels more like a friend or brother or something."

"Uh-huh. And Gino? Where does he figure in all this?" Dr Kath asked.

Liza, quiet for a moment, searched for any sign of him in her mind. "Nowhere. Not part of our lives. He's gone."

"Good, let's explore how happy you are there. Give me a number on a scale of one to ten."

"Maybe an eight?"

"What would make it a ten Liza?"

"Hmm dunno."

"What's missing?"

"Er. . . not really missing. . . more. . . lurking."

"What might that be?"

"I really dunno." Liza's brows drew together, the lines on her forehead deepening.

Dr Kath noticed a shift of energy. "Something from before?"

"I think so. It's a bit worrying, like it's threatening to spoil everything."

"Any ideas where it might be coming from?"

"I know the place. The woods we're near. I've been here before. It's something to do with that. I think it's where I grew up. I can't see properly."

"What's stopping you from remembering?" Dr Kath pushed a little. "Is there something that happened there?"

"I don't know. Please. I don't want to be there anymore. It's before. It's family. It's the past. I want to leave now. Please!"

"Don't worry, you're safe. You're back in your safe place. Nothing bad will happen," Dr Kath reassured her.

They were getting somewhere. Dr Kath had underlined the words 'family' and 'past' to focus on next time. Once Liza was out of trance, they set about more pressing discussions for Liza's departure from London. They had their work cut out. Liza was determined. All the uncertainties, all the troubling loose ends from the session, none of it mattered. She was convinced everything would work out the way she wanted.

She left the building with a ridiculously renewed confidence. Armed with a clear set of practical actions, on a long to-do list, she reminded herself to take it one step at a time.

Dulcie

Handbag slipping from shoulder to wrist, hands laden with shopping, Dulcie struggled back into her hotel room. She fumbled with the electronic key card. *Why did these things never work properly?* Always a red light instead of green. No matter how many times she reinserted the card or changed the speed of insertion, as advised by the concierge, it seemed to make little difference. She couldn't take the lift back down to ask him again!

She was hot and worn out and just wanted things to be easy. She needed to dump her appendages. She wanted to jump straight into a cool shower and wash away her confusion. True to form, the meeting with Matty had been both wonderful and confusing in equal measure. At last, green.

She nudged the handle with her elbow, shuffling through the open door in a crab-like manner, to accommodate the spoils of her retail therapy.

Earlier, after an hour of laying her soul bare to Matty over lunch and two cups of coffee, he'd had to rush back to work, leaving Dulcie to head back to Oxford Street souvenir hunting. Primarily in search of something to take her mind off him, she'd spotted Liberty, after accidentally exiting the tube station via the Argyll Street entrance. She may have been born in England but it gave her no advantage when faced with multiple subway exits.

Like a child in a sweetshop, giddy with nostalgia, Dulcie decided to take the lift right to the top of the store and work her way down and round, drinking in the opulence of the place. Browsing the exotic and quirky goods from around the world, she noticed some of the departments had changed location, yet it still had the same lavish atmosphere.

With half an eye on business, she spent a good while exploring the ceramics. Clearly, some lucky artist had made it; their collections spilled over heavily laden tables, cleverly merchandised as stalls from a Moroccan souk. The more exclusive pieces, which fetched exorbitant prices, were showcased to draw the eye and tempt the wallet of many a wealthy customer. None displayed a label. Dulcie had made a mental note to talk pricing with Bruce once she returned home.

After several hours of wandering the wood-panelled halls, squeezing past piles of Persian rugs, peering into cabinets crammed full of proud-to-be-British products, she ended up in the third-floor café for a slice of squidgy spiced apple cake and a cup of tea. Even coffee addict Dulcie couldn't face another cup today.

Her adventure through the store had felt like a tour of the commonwealth, carefully planned to avoid the tourist hotspot of the Scarf Hall. Some things never changed. Despite her love of florals, the prospect of pushing past the throng of sweaty bodies spied from the balcony had been too tedious. To her overloaded senses, the tea and cake option held far more appeal.

Now, standing under the cascade of warm water, Dulcie

experienced a swell of previously suppressed anxiety. Four hours ago, she'd agreed Matty should select the venue and timing of their next rendezvous. Still no text. She was all over the place. Yearning, guilt, love, duty, responsibility all erupted at once. She hated the way she felt.

After years of placid existence, she had no idea how to regain a sense of calm. She'd not been tested this way for such a long time. Tears mingled with the water, trailblazing new tracks down her cheeks for more tears to follow. She hated herself for being so emotional but she let them flow.

Somewhere, from her earliest memories, she heard her father's soothing voice. "Oh petal. Just let it out. You cry as long as you need to. I'm here. Lean on my shoulder. It's okay to be sad."

Dulcie hadn't thought much about him for years. Confident and headstrong in her early adulthood she had emigrated with Peter, with little concern for the life and family she was leaving behind. Early on she had sent postcards, received regular letters. There had been a couple of trips back when the kids were babes, until the cost had become prohibitive for a family of six. Life in Oz felt like a million miles away from Gloucester. All that weight of expectation.

Dulcie had convinced herself her chosen existence, fuelled by the opportunity to explore her creativity, would be the recipe for everlasting contentment. This trip and all its upheaval had sprung a leak through the meticulously papered cracks of her wall. The wall separating past and present was being dismantled by the hypnotherapy sessions. Perhaps they were not a good idea after all? At first it had seemed sensible; it was such a big decision. Reaching out for help, talking things through, surely it would make it easier. Trouble is, she hadn't figured on all the other stuff.

It wasn't just the irresistible pull towards Matty. Her sense of self had smudged. Maybe this was normal? Maybe she needed to re-evaluate her whole life, to understand the feelings and emotions now escaping from their hiding places?

Dulcie stepped out of the shower, shivering as she left the steamy cocoon of the cubicle. She picked up the phone. Still no text. Bundling her hair into a towel turban, she grabbed the large bath sheet she'd left hanging on the heated rail. Stiff and scratchy from repeated washes through the laundry service, it failed to give her the comfort of her fluffy towels back home. The hotel-crested robe fared no better but at least she could tie the belt and leave her hands free to check for notifications. Nothing. Her fingers hovered over Dr Kath's number in the call list.

"Oh, go on you useless Sheila, do something!" Her finger did as instructed. "Sod it. Bloody answerphones!"

The recorded message, spoken in Dr Kath's soothing tones, explained she should leave a brief message and contact details, followed by the promise of a return call.

"This is Dulcie Braybrooke. Please could you call me when you're free. I'd like to talk about what to do next as soon as possible. Thanks."

Her message as vague as her state of mind, she hoped it would prompt a speedy response.

Distracted by the debate in her head, between the tell her 'thanks but this isn't helping' camp and the 'reassure me it's normal and I'll carry on' camp, Dulcie sat in the obligatory reading chair. Waiting.

Hotel rooms always had such a chair, shoehorned in somehow, regardless of the size of the room. This being a small double, its inclusion seemed all the more a logistical contortion, especially since most occupants would only use it as a deposit for coats and bags. Who would bother going to the effort of using the wardrobe, pinned to the corner by the very same chair?

Ping.

Ooh. There it was. A message from Matty. The preview gave her the first few words of his text:

Sorry. I meant to send...

Ping. Before Dulcie could open it fully, a second text arrived:

Hi Mum, Dad said it...

Heart lurching, as if caught in the act of disloyalty, she clicked on the second notification:

Hi Mum. Dad said it was ok to send a short hello. Really missing you. Can we talk soon? Love Libby xxxx

Hitting reply Dulcie began her text, this time interrupted by an incoming call.

"Dulcie? It's Kath O'Hannon. You wanted to talk? How can I help?" Dr Kath asked.

"I'm feeling err–flappy, dithery you know? Is that normal? I mean, do people usually react this way after only a few sessions?"

"That is sometimes the case."

"Oh right. It's just that I don't know what to do," Dulcie admitted.

"In what way? Do you mean about your situation or something else?"

"Erm. . ."

"It's okay. Take your time."

Flipping her focus to the unfinished and unanswered texts, Dulcie said, "Sorry would you mind if I gave you a call back in a couple of minutes? It's just. . . I need to finish something."

"Of course, not a problem. I'm at home now for the foreseeable. You are alright though? I think you were on the verge of discussing something important, maybe?" Dr Kath said.

"Yes, I mean, no. It is important but it can wait for a bit. You're sure it's fine to call back? I don't want to disturb you at home." Dulcie asked.

"Don't be concerned Dulcie. I'm working from here this evening. It's fine. My next appointment's not until later. I'll be here."

"Thank you. I'll call you very soon."

Dulcie sat in silence. Thinking. She planned her next moves with meticulous precision. Get dressed. Answer Libby's text. Call Dr Kath. Matty's text could wait. She did not recognise herself. This frantic flip-flopping was alien to Dulcie. With a plan of action, perhaps there was hope of regaining some calm. Even if it only gave her the next half an hour, it was something.

Out of the scratchy towels into fresh underwear, her favourite jeans, and a soft cotton blouse, she relished their familiarity. Remaining barefoot due to the excessive heat of the hotel room, Dulcie propped herself up on the bed with the abundant cushions.

Loving text to Libby completed. Dulcie exhaled an extended breath. Ready to continue her conversation with Dr Kath, she selected her number from the call history, bypassing the unread message from Matty. As it dialled for the second time that day, she congratulated herself on her restraint.

"Hi Dulcie, I'm glad you called back," Dr Kath said.

Niggled, Dulcie replied, "I said I would."

"Yes. I didn't mean to imply otherwise. Give me a second."

The rustling of papers and scraping of heavy wood on wood transmitted down the line, as Dr Kath arranged herself at her desk in preparation.

"I'm here. I just wanted to get my notes in front of me; not that I can read my writing easily. Typical doctor! You do remember the notes I make are confidential, yes?"

"Sure."

Dr Kath's next words were sprinkled with an infectious giggle. "Goodness. My latest scribbles are so close to illegible they almost guarantee confidentiality!"

"Phew. So glad I'm not the only one with that problem. I could never understand how anyone could be neat and speedy at the same time and I was so relieved to leave essay writing behind." Dulcie smiled at herself in the mirror. "Not much call for it in ceramics."

"Was art always an obvious direction for you?"

"Oh no. My teachers were always trying to persuade me to pursue their academic subjects."

"How did you end up in ceramics then?"

"That's a long story. I'm sure it's not interesting enough to waste any of your time on."

"It's up to you Dulcie. Sometimes, if you are stuck, talking through your personal history can help to unlock a way forward."

Dulcie absorbed the idea. *Maybe it would help.*

Bogged down by indecision, perhaps the answer did lie somewhere in the swamp of the past. She went for it; if Dr Kath had the time (and she had offered) it was worth a try.

"I didn't really have a plan. To become an artist I mean. I kinda just followed my passion. I'd never wanted to opt for something sensible, not from a career perspective anyway."

"From some other perspective?"

"Well I suppose you could describe my choice of partner in that way."

"Peter, your husband?"

"Yes." Dulcie let out a long, slow sigh.

Staring at the elaborate swathes of voile at her hotel window, Dulcie noticed a subtle ripple in the fabric as it was displaced by her out-breath.

"Why the sigh?"

"I guess I feel a little guilty even thinking about it," Dulcie said. "But Peter has always been dependable. Solid. It's his utter reliability that gave me the freedom to be creative. His career was there to support us, me, and I became an adventuress."

"An evocative description."

"Uh-huh. I suppose so."

"Tell me what it meant to you, at that time. What makes you use that word?"

Dulcie shuffled as she settled into a more comfortable position. "With Peter I felt safe. Loved and strong enough to stand on my own two feet and follow where life led us. After he'd graduated in estate planning, I'd already given up on higher education. When he suggested emigrating to Oz with our baby, I thought why not? We were young, optimistic. It just seemed like a huge adventure. He had a solid job offer. He said once we were settled and the babe was a bit older we should be able to afford for me to start my pottery. What did we have to lose? That was that." Dulcie's voice trailed to a mumble. "A perfect match, I thought."

"And now?" Dr Kath asked gently.

"Oh well. Life's different now."

"Life or your view of life?"

"Both really."

"Looking back, is there anything you would change?"

"No. I don't think so." Dulcie's answer surprised them both.

"Oh?"

"I mean, I knew I couldn't stay here, in London, with the baby on my own. He wasn't planned, sure, but it was what it was. James was our little miracle and Peter cared more for me, us, than anyone one else ever could." Dulcie fiddled with the tassels on a velveteen cushion she had been cuddling. She put it to one side in a decisive action as if to reinforce her words. "Going with him was right. At the time, it was right."

"And now?"

"I'm not sure. I don't know. What do you think?"

"You have the answer. I can only guide you to it. Is your confusion to do with Matty?"

"Yes." Dulcie picked up the cushion again and began an absentminded stroking. "We've become very close again. Since I arrived back here. It's unsettling and I really don't know what to do next."

"Ah yes, your message said as much. I understand you're

looking for resolution on this but I do think it might be best if you were to arrange a further appointment with me. I believe you have underlying issues. A session under hypnosis would help you gain some more clarity."

"Do you really think so? I'm finding myself more muddled after each time. I'd never even contemplated any change in domestic circumstances before we started navel-gazing."

"Often clients feel like that. Questioning things at a deeper level does tend to throw things up in the air. If you're honest with yourself and look back, is it possible you may have thought about it before?"

"Maybe," Dulcie said reluctantly.

"Either way, I do think you will be better positioned to make any decision if you continue with the hypnotherapy. Ultimately though, it is up to you." Dr Kath waited.

"Oh, okay. I suppose anything is better than this limbo!" Dulcie said.

"Shall I drop you an email with some slots?"

"Yes please."

"Good. I'll say goodbye for now and look forward to seeing you soon."

"Dr Kath? Sorry if I seemed a bit negative."

"It's no problem," Dr Kath said. "Recognising your inner thoughts can be confronting at times."

Dulcie took a deep breath. "Do you... do *you* think I settled for second best? Is that where my doubts are coming from?"

"I don't know Dulcie. Only you can know. Let's explore that when we meet next time."

Annie

"Thanks for seeing me at such short notice."

"No problem. Remember where to go?" Dr Kath asked. "I've just got to finish something off in the kitchen. I'll be with you in a few ticks."

Annie nodded and made her way to the study. Several sessions in and she was starting to feel at ease with the process, as far as it is possible to feel at ease with hypnotherapy. It was good for her. She knew that, but still, stuff would come up she'd rather not acknowledge, let alone deal with.

She burrowed herself into the comfy chair. Her pulse, loud in her ear, synchronised with the tick of the clock. Every part of her was at odds with another. Her legs wanted to get up and run away; her head determined she should stay to work through her issues; her heart craved empathetic relief and her chaotic emotions demanded attention.

Dr Kath returned, closing the door with a gentle click. "Sorry about the wait. Would you like to bring me up to date on how you are doing?"

"I'm not sure. I keep flitting from angry to sad, to confused and all three at once. You know? I don't know if I've resolved anything yet. I'm not really coping very well, am I?" Annie said.

"You're dealing with lots, all at the same time. It's understandable. Was there something specific you wanted to cover today?"

Annie fidgeted. "Not really, I've been having this discussion with myself, actually, more a battle than a discussion. I know I need to get to the bottom of something, you see, but a big part of me just doesn't want to know. I try and push it away and convince myself I'm fine. Next thing I know, I'm balling my eyes out and the other me is screaming 'get some help!' you know?"

"You feel torn?"

"Yes!" Annie said. "Exactly. Is this normal?"

"As I said you have a lot to deal with at the moment. Never mind the big life change you are facing. You did tell me previously that something wasn't quite right; you were feeling low, panicky–" Dr Kath broke off to refer to her notes. "You said grey. Do you remember?"

"Yes. . ."

"In your situation it is not unusual to feel overwhelmed, especially if you have an underlying low mood."

"You can say that again!" Annie's shoulders slid down, away from her ears, where they had been residing for the past few minutes. "Thanks, I was beginning to feel like I was going crazy."

"Would you like to explore some of this now?"

"Yes please."

"What would you like to focus on? Remember you're in control and I'm here to support you if it gets difficult," Dr Kath said.

Annie took several moments to decide; a few more to answer.

Grimacing, she squeezed out the word "family" through gritted teeth.

Annie was only aware of two voices; the now familiar dull muffled sound of her own answers, and Dr Kath's gentle questions.

"Tell me what first comes into your head when I say the word family?"

"Duty. Doing the right thing. Following the right path."

"Explain, in a little more detail, how that is for you."

"I went into teaching, the family profession. My aunt and my mum are teachers and my dad is a lecturer." Annie sighed. "I did everything in the right order. Went to university, met my husband, qualified, got married, bought a house and had children."

"Where does your idea of the right order come from?"

"No one ever told me, I just knew," Annie said, frowning.

"Maybe think about where you were when you first made a decision by following that path?" Annie didn't answer. Dr Kath leant forward and tried a different angle. "Okay, think about the feeling itself. When I say duty, where do you feel it in your body? What does it look like or sound like?"

Annie groaned. "Urgh. It's a grumbling in my tummy, like a crampy, heavy pain. It's a grey box. . . a dark metal box with roughly welded sides and no way in or out. I don't think I hear the sound. . . it's just. . . oppressive."

"Is there a strong emotion there too?"

"Resentment! It's boiling over. I'm fuming!"

Dr Kath underlined '*Resentment*'.

"What are you angry about?"

"It's the choices. Pretty much all of them in my life. I don't feel like I was in control. They weren't my choices. They were for my family," Annie said.

Dr Kath paused, scribbling *'control'* in her notes and waited for Annie to reflect. "You talked about resentment and the box. Is the box your family?"

"Sort of. Not forgetting flipping–church!"

Dr Kath had touched a nerve. "Okay, that's good. Is that the source of the duty?" she asked.

Annie felt the wooden pew beneath her. She was right back at church, six years old, staring at the tapestry kneeling cushion, wishing she could sit on it and hide from the priest.

"All those catholic sermons! It's the guilt. It's the wanting to be good and not knowing how too. It's the rules–breaking them but not knowing why," she confessed.

"And who are you with? Who was the churchgoer?"

"All of us really."

"But, if you had to pick one?"

"Mum I suppose. She made me."

She could see her mum. Guilt and duty personified. Her face loomed right there in front of Annie with that disapproving look. No words, just the crowded eyebrows.

Dr Kath pushed even harder. "Think back to the time when you first felt the guilt. What can you see?"

"Her face, it's moving closer. It's trapped behind my eyelids when I close them to pray. I'm little. She's big and judgemental. I'm not sure but something has happened. I am being blamed but it doesn't feel fair."

"Is there anyone else there?"

"Oh!" Annie shrank back and shivered. It was as if June's

face hovered next to her mum's in front of her. A mocking grin spread fully from ear to ear.

"What is it?"

"I can see my older sister June. She doesn't like me. She's taking sides with Mum. She's clever. . . done something. . . think the trouble I'm in is because of her. Whatever it is, I know it wasn't me, it was her!"

"Is there anything you want to say to her?"

"Oh plenty! She needs to. . . she needs to back off!"

"Why don't you tell her now?" Dr Kath asked.

"I want to make sure we get things straight once and for all. I need to plan it out first. Think about what I want and stop living in her shadow."

Annie watched both faces fade into the dark, shadowy distance, as if they were icons from a primitive Eighties pop video. Her shoulders dropped once again, the accumulated tension ebbed away, leaving a calmness to settle over her.

"Three, two, one. Now, in your own time, open your eyes."

Dr Kath's count brought Annie back to reality. "How are you feeling?"

Annie took a moment, adjusting to her surroundings, waiting for the wooziness to dissipate. She exhaled a long, deep swoosh. "A little better I think."

Dr Kath closed her notepad and put it to one side. "That's good. You worked hard to identify the source of your disquiet. If you feel strong enough, I think it would be useful to go through the learnings from today. Would you like to take five minutes and reflect on the session?"

"I think so. I have made some progress, haven't I? I guess I kinda need to make sense of it. Don't want to lose the momentum again. I've this terrible habit of thinking too much and messing up all the good work we're doing. Sometimes, even before I've stepped outside!" Annie smiled, sprinkling the air with the nervous laughter of someone suspecting they'd shared a bit too much.

Dr Kath excused herself to fetch another jug of water. Annie sat patiently, keen to analyse the session and find a way to make the most of her newfound knowledge. Perhaps a change of approach in conversations with her family? A bolder way to assert herself.

If nothing else, she was pleased to have reconnected with a piece of the old Annie; back to knowing her own mind, saying no, sometimes and reclaiming some time for herself. The prospect of making progress with her looming decision appeared at least possible now. Better still, some of the greyness had lifted. She looked forward to creating her plan.

Pia

Pia massaged her calves, sweat trickling down her forehead and into her eyes. PJ laughed at her as she collapsed in mock exhaustion on the floor and spread-eagled her limbs in an ungainly snow-angel motion.

"How do you professionals make it look so easy? She whined, grateful of the towel he had thrown over for her to mop her brow.

"No time for chatting now." PJ grabbed both her hands and pulled her up to standing. "We have one more set of *ganchos* to learn before we head to the pub."

Her Tango skills had been developing nicely throughout September and they had taken to rewarding themselves after training with a pint or two at the Yew Trees Inn.

"Do we have to? I just can't get that flicking movement right. It's so difficult!"

"Come on, remember, head held high, spine straight, core strong and chest lifted." PJ said, readjusting her posture, as if she were a mannequin. "Let's do it slowly without the music."

Pia took a deep breath, bracing herself for the exertion. *Still, if something's worth doing, it's worth doing well*, she told herself, regurgitating one of her mum's favourite phrases.

Their practice of the staccato leg hooks for the next ten minutes took on the appearance of a comic slow-motion fight sequence by a pair of crabs. It definitely required some more work.

*

"When are we going to get started with the renovations PJ? I'm getting frustrated with all this waiting!" Pia said.

"I guess we need to be patient. We can't start until we know who will be joining us. The business is for all of us. Finances, decisions on architects, reconfiguration, marketing, pricing, these things all need to be worked on together. At least that's what Dad wanted, no?"

"Dad."

"What about him?" PJ asked.

"It's odd when I hear you call him that. I mean, I know he was your dad but it's just sounds so odd to me. Were you close?"

"He was yours too." PJ said softly. "Look, I understand. It's not sunk in yet and it will, in time. Anyway, aside from his wishes, we've been advised by Samuel to wait until the deadline has passed."

"Yes, yes, I know. I just wanna get started. Maybe be we could do some preparation? Research contractors, check out the competition, dig into the history of the place. I think we should use it as part of the brand."

"The history of the house and bringing it back to life. I like that. I can imagine a glossy editorial in a magazine and if we combine it with Dad's story we've got *el argumento diferenciador*!" PJ said, declaring a 'ta-da' moment with his hands.

"I'm guessing that means the same as USP?" Pia asked.

"In Time Out maybe? Great coverage. Too ambitious?"

"Something no other dance school has. Our story. I like that idea. You read Time Out? Gotta be Cotswold Life, surely?" Pia suggested.

"*Absolutamente!* Whatever you think best."

PJ winked, expecting at least a smile or a giggle from Pia, having slipped into Spanish twice in as many sentences. She'd seemed to like it before. He studied her face as she stared into space. "Would you like another cider?"

"If you like."

"Are you sure? You don't sound keen. I don't want to force you."

He waited, opting to sit down again rather than hover. From Pia's perspective everything was new. He wanted to give her time to catch him up.

Pia turned back towards him. It was difficult to express her feelings. It wasn't PJ. He was great. Full of enthusiasm and confidence; a D'Artagnan of a companion, he was fearless in his defence of their new-found bond. No. She had no issue with PJ. It was more the sudden appearance of a father in her life. Her gratitude towards him for his gift of a new future was emerging. She felt especially grateful for PJ. Their meeting had been as joyful, thrilling and natural as the perfectly choreographed dance she was beginning to master. Yet still, she was angry at Pablo for all her unanswered questions.

"Honestly, I'm fine. I'm sorry, I'm all topsy-turvy. One minute I have boundless energy fizzling through me, the next I can't think straight. There are many gaps, so many things I don't know. My mum has tried her best to fill in the blanks but there's loads she can't tell me and, I think some that she won't," Pia said, staring back out of the window.

"Why don't I get the drinks and you can ask me anything you like? At least I can tell you about Dad."

Pia turned her head towards him again and smiled. "That sounds good."

"Two pints of Somerset cider coming up!"

The pub had started filling up with regulars and lunchtime trade. Pia tried to relax and absorb the scene. It was comfy, if a little worn around the edges; appealingly traditional. Shelves of dusty hardbacks filled much of the wall-space. Faded photographs of local celebrities hung in the gaps in between the bookcases, squeezed in like alpines in the crevices of a dry-stone wall. As she surveyed more of her surroundings, it occurred to her this would be their local, once the school was up and running. Probably a good place to start advertising the launch, although she wondered how many would be Tango enthusiasts. Pia rubbed the back of her neck.

PJ returned to the table with two cold pints, their amber-coloured contents cloaked in condensation. He set them on the beer mats, leaving clear glass in place of warm fingerprints, with trickles like raindrops hurrying to the base. "Are you absolutely sure you're cool?"

Pia nodded. "Just a bit sore. Must have overdone it today. Not getting any younger. I was just wondering who our clients might be. Whether any of them would be the locals? Do you think it might be a bit of a tall order setting up such a specialised business out here?"

"I'm not worried about that. I'm thinking of it as more of a luxury retreat. I'm sure if we get the marketing right, people will come from all over the place, no? From the big cities: London, Manchester, Birmingham," he said with a broad sweep of his arms, almost taking out a stack of empties nearby. "Especially with that Time Out write-up." PJ nudged her playfully.

"But aren't people cutting back? Surely that kind of luxury spending will dry up if the economy doesn't pick up?"

"Look, I'm no expert on finances but we should have plenty of buying power for the renovations. I guess we are lucky we don't have to borrow any money. We should have enough in the bank. The builders will be grateful of the work if things are going to slow down like the papers say. By the time we're ready to open, things will have bounced back, I'm sure," PJ said confidently.

"I hope so."

"Plus you forget the power of dance; it's escapism. A dash of romance to help forget about the mundanities of life. You immerse yourself in a fantasy world for a minute or two, shake off your responsibilities and lose yourself in the music and, of course, remember." PJ paused for effect. "To dance is to live. My motto is true, no?"

"I'm beginning to agree." Pia laughed. "That should be our strapline! Actually it's addictive too. The more you dance the more you want to learn; the more you learn, the more you want to dance. It kinda gets under your skin!"

"Exactly Bella!"

"We can appeal to people's need to find fulfilment. Look at me. Redundant in my forties, facing plenty of uncertainty but somehow more of walking the same treadmill didn't feel right. If the bubble is going to burst maybe something tangible, like learning a new skill, will be just what people are looking for. It's working for me."

PJ chuckled.

"What? What did I say?"

"Nothing Bella. It's just you said tangible. It made me think Tangible Tango that's all!"

"Very funny!" Pia sulked her most melodramatic sulk. She couldn't hold it for long enough to convince PJ, spluttering out a giggle.

They giggled together before they settling back into their chatter.

"What would you be doing if Pablo. . . I mean. . . Dad hadn't bought the house?"

"Nothing much different. Dancing, choreographing for my old troupe. Teaching in Buenos Aires maybe."

"You were happy to move here then? Anyone back home?" Pia asked taking a sip of her drink.

"I've not really stayed in one place. Been on tour most of the time. It's tricky holding onto those special relationships. Either they're a colleague and it's too intense and messy when things don't work out, or the on-the-road absences kill anything off before it can really thrive."

"I'm sorry, I know how you feel. Everything is about career then you wake up one morning and wonder–"

"Told you I needed love lessons. Maybe we should take a class together?" he said.

"It's funny, this is gonna sound strange." Pia traced her finger round the rim of her glass, drawing out the moment, watching the cider bubbles scoot to the surface. "It's just. . . I. . . I feel like. . . like I've known you forever, you know? Like we did grow up brother and sister together." She stopped her tracing. She continued her bubble scrutiny.

"I know," PJ said, grabbing onto her hand and holding it.

"I'm not sure how the genes thing works but I'm convinced there's something to be said for nature over nurture. I mean, how is it possible we feel such a close bond after only a few weeks?" Pia gabbled away.

"You know what is even weirder?"

"What?" Pia asked.

PJ hesitated, as if frightened to pick a delicate bloom for fear of it wilting too soon. He removed his hand from hers. "Don't take this the wrong way."

Pia stopped fidgeting and inched forward. "Go on."

PJ took an unnecessarily large gulp of his drink. Pia waited.

"I think," he continued, after several more gulps, and then in a loud whisper after a further pause. "Secretly I'm a little bit in love with you. It feels like that anyway. Strange huh?" He dipped his head slightly and scrunched up his face, peeking at her through half-closed eyes, wondering if he'd judged it right.

"What a relief! I thought it was just me," she said, clutching her hands to her chest. 'I've lost my appetite, I'm having trouble sleeping, I'm feeling wired all the time and I can't stop thinking about you, us, the future. At first I told myself it was stupid; that it must be the dancing I was drawn to or maybe the adrenaline or the endorphins or whatever."

"It is strange, no? I didn't want to admit it to myself at first. Even though apparently it's quite normal, " he said.

"Really?"

"Dad told me; the adoption advisor had warned him it often

goes this way. It helps us to fill in the gap, make up for the time lost, especially between siblings," PJ explained. "Sometimes it can go the other way though. Sometimes people want to block it out, to go into denial. Choose to ignore it and pretend it's not real. I was just worried because I know how I get carried away sometimes. I didn't want to spoil things."

"A kind of self-preservation,"

"Exactly," PJ said nodding his head. "Because it's too painful to allow the emotions out. Particularly where a half-sister or brother appears from nowhere and their parent is no longer alive to help them understand."

"I'm very glad it went the other way for us." Pia reached out to touch his forearm.

"Me too."

They sipped their drinks in silence. Both reflecting on the impact of their father's actions long-ago. The choices he had made then had kept them apart. The choices he had made recently had brought them together. Neither could know the full facts of his life or his reasons for those choices, but PJ felt he owed Pia as much insight as he could give from the stories he had heard growing up. He guessed from her lack of questions she might be a little scared to ask and decided to make it easier for her by offering anecdotes without any prompting.

"Dad was a handsome young man born to a wealthy Argentinian family. Nouveau riche, they wanted him to have the best, to join the set. For him to follow the path of other wealthy families, so they sent him to Madrid to learn the Tango," he said.

"Ah, that's the connection. Did he stay there? Is that where you were born?"

"It was the done thing in his day–a kind of coming out like debutantes in London society. Except, mostly the boys went to Paris, using their charm to glide through the party season and into nobility."

"But how come Pablo went to Madrid?" Pia still couldn't quite bring herself to call him Dad.

"He was a bit of a rebel. Never really interested in the elite. Actually he met Peron and his wife there in the Fifties. Do you know she used to dance professionally?"

"Evita?"

"No, his third wife. Anyway, she took him under her wing, turned out he was a natural and ended up a professional dancer. He spent a few years building his reputation and focusing on his career, much to his parents' frustration. Apparently Lita, my grandmother, wouldn't stop going on at him. He told me she would say Pablo, *mi precioso uno*, why are you still dancing? You should find yourself a woman. Choose yourself a beautiful wife and get on with making me a happy *abuela*. Dad would laugh it off and tell her he had a plan, not to worry and grandchildren would come when the time was right."

"I suppose he thought he had all the time in the world?"

PJ nodded. "In some ways, he was very determined to make a success of his career; in others, he was an incurable romantic. He often talked with great affection about his performances in London. By then he was a big name in the small world of Tango. It wasn't Beatles mania, but he built up quite a following. He became a dashing idol for a flock of faithful fans."

"Is that how he met my mother?"

"I don't know, I suppose it's possible. Without knowing who

she is, we can't say for sure, eh? All I do know is the search for you became his driving force these last few years. Once he'd opened up to me and told me of the woman he had fallen for and of your existence, I knew I had to help him."

"Didn't that feel like a betrayal of your mother?" Pia asked.

Pj shrugged. "No, not really. I knew my mum and dad weren't getting back together. They'd always had a very tumultuous relationship. My mum had that fiery Latin temperament. Dad was always much more considered, closed even, but I always knew he felt deep and strong emotions. He had this intensity in his eyes; never really spoke much, but almost didn't need to, you know? Plus, when he danced he spoke with his whole body; the liquidity of movement, the rhythm, the chemistry he created was palpable. I wish you could have seen him dance. It was like watching a heart beating; two bodies as one. So vital. So exquisite. . ." His tone flattened. His voice dropped away. PJ sighed.

"You miss him terribly, don't you?"

"Oh, so much."

"Let's call it a day on discussing the past. Why don't we go back to the house? You can teach me some new steps or we could practice the *ganchos* from before. I promise I'll try not to give you any more bruises."

PJ visibly re-inflated at the suggestion. He jumped up, tugging her out from their cosy corner. "What a great idea! Let's get lost in the dance again!"

"To dance is to live, as you would say. Are we ever-so-slightly obsessed?"

"*Absolutamente!* In more ways than one, no?"

Elizabeth

"Here we are again Dr Kath!" Elizabeth said in an overtly upbeat tone.

"Yes indeed. How have the last few days gone?"

"Exceptionally well, thank you. Actually, I'm here to tell you I no longer have need of your services. I'm ready to make my decision."

"Really?" Dr Kath said, trying to hide her surprise.

"I did think about calling to cancel; however I know I hate it when my clients change plans at the last minute. It's very unprofessional, in my honest opinion."

"For sure, sometimes it's unavoidable but thank you for your honesty. Would you still like a session? You're perfectly entitled, since you're here and a cancellation charge would apply anyway."

Secretly Elizabeth wished she could just walk away after a quick chat. The hypnotherapy was redundant now surely? She had Andrew. She had her decision; her acceptance letter already drafted. The process of trawling over old memories and behaviours was pointless.

"Personally I don't think I have much left to work through. Most of my indecision has been resolved."

"You say most?"

"Enough to be able to take it on my own from here. Is there much point in having any more sessions under the circumstances?" Elizabeth asked.

"It's totally your call. Having paid for the session, I'm merely offering you the opportunity to explore some of the underlying issues which were causing you concern last time."

Elizabeth considered the opportunity cost. It was dead money in some ways. Caught up in the headiness of her relationship with Andrew she'd missed that point. Wasting money was against her nature and being reminded of her oversight was irksome.

"I'll defer to your professional opinion Dr Kath. Give me your recommendation."

Dr Kath worded her response carefully. Elizabeth was one of those high-maintenance clients, the ones who assumed they knew best. Often, as in Elizabeth's case, they had the most to gain from spending time understanding themselves, but found it hardest to accept the fact. Plus she was curious to get to the bottom of Elizabeth's U-turn, bearing in mind they had finished the last session on the verge of uncovering some deep-seated issues.

Dr Kath was convinced of the benefit to Elizabeth. On the other hand, her ethical code dictated it was her client's process to control. If she had genuinely made up her mind to stop, they would stop.

"My recommendation would be to take the time and decide whether to continue with another session," Dr Kath said. "Only you can know whether you have sufficiently resolved the issues which brought you to me in the first instance. Having said that, my observation would be that you finished the last session with several open topics." She thumbed through her notepad, skimming the words to find her notes from the previous appointment. "Would you like me to give you an example?"

Had Elizabeth been rumbled? Had she failed to cover her insecurities with her brightness? Most wouldn't spot the subtle shade of blush on her cheeks; the sunny pitch of her voice, one or two degrees warmer than usual. If she had any close friends they might have seen through the act but of course she didn't.

"Yes, I suppose it would be sensible. I was just thinking along those lines myself."

Dr Kath had followed her instinct borne of years of experience and played it just right. She was glad, on Elizabeth's behalf, her façade had come down. "Do you recall we were looking at the possibility of your co-beneficiaries being family members?"

"Ah, yes." Elizabeth acknowledged the issue as she might an undesirable clause in a client's contract. "It is essential we find an answer to that conundrum."

"So that's a yes to your session?" Elizabeth nodded. "You understand it will be slightly shorter than the usual fifty minutes? Quite rightly you've spent some time identifying your position; questioning whether further therapy will be of benefit. Unfortunately though, I do have another appointment directly after your scheduled slot and we are a little time constrained."

"Very well. Let's get started."

The same heavy-lidded and floaty sensation descended on Elizabeth as Dr Kath's rhythmic instructions moved her towards trance. The commands became less obvious, merging with her own subconscious, until a question caught her full attention.

"When we talk about family you tend to block the subject and change direction. Tell me, would you like to share your thoughts on why that might be happening?"

"I don't know. Perhaps because blood ties are not relevant to me."

"Any ideas where that stems from? Perhaps try to think of a time when it was different. Think family and imagine a happy time. Is there a memory there?"

"Hmm maybe."

Dr Kath waited to hear where her question would take them.

"It seems like someone's there to care for me–care about me." Elizbeth faltered. Her memory there but out of focus. " It's good. . . but. . ."

"Yes?"

"I feel very sad too. I don't know. It's a heavy feeling, like a loss or something like my chest is dragging around a ship's anchor."

"Do you see anything?" Dr Kath asked.

"My dad."

"What's happening?"

"I think I'm telling him about a success. . ."

"Go on."

"He's beaming at first, chest swelling with peacock pride. I've just got the results of my professional exams. I'm telling him I have passed."

"Hmm, that would seem like it should be a happy occasion."

"Yes, but I'm sad and now it's fading. I can't see him anymore. I want him back."

"Where do you think he's gone?"

Elizabeth answered in a clear, steady voice. "I don't think he's gone anywhere. It was me."

"You?"

"He wasn't there, when I got my results, I mean."

"Ah I see." Dr Kath jotted down a note. "This was something you would have wanted, yet it didn't happen,"

"Yes, I went away to London. I'm on my own. He doesn't know about my results."

"But you wanted to tell him, you couldn't and it makes you sad." Elizabeth breathed out heavily. "The sadness, if you gave it a number on the scale of one to ten, where is it?"

"Oh ten, definitely ten!"

"What would make it better?"

"I want to tell him. I want to share. I want him to know, to make him proud."

Dr Kath put her pen down watching for Elizabeth's reaction. "What's stopping you?"

"That's simple. We haven't spoken for many years. I can't go back to him. I'm not important to him anyway. He doesn't want me in his life."

"Tell me about it. You seem very certain. How do you know for sure?"

Elizabeth stiffened; her voice much quieter. "It was her. He chose her. I just know."

Leaving the reference to the third person for the moment, Dr Kath steered the conversation back to success and happiness.

"You think he wasn't interested but you must have been proud of your results?"

"Naturally. I'd worked bloody hard. I deserved to celebrate!" Elizabeth declared.

The evening from twenty-odd years before played out in her mind. Salmon-pink paper. Late night outside Charing Cross station. First edition of the *FT* and there it was—her name. Hundreds of others were there too, jostling to snatch their copies, scouring for their names. Lost in the memory, Dr Kath's voice faded in and out. She missed some questions, though the next one came through strongly.

"Did you share your news with anyone else?" Dr Kath asked.

"Oh yes, of course. Not friends. I didn't have many of those. The girls were always jealous of my prowess and quite bitchy; the guys either geeky or arrogant. Anyway, I didn't need them. Andrew was the only friend I needed."

"He was there?" Dr Kath asked, surprised. "You've known him a long time then?"

"He was there for me that night. Someone I could rely on. Someone who cared."

Dr Kath speculated; had Elizabeth ever explored her need for Andrew? "You mean he cared but your father did not?"

Seconds ticked by as Elizabeth deliberated. "He filled the void I guess, didn't he?"

"It sounds like you feel that way. You have made a potential breakthrough here. Something to consider further once we've finished."

Their slot was almost up. It was time to bring Elizabeth back to the room.

"How was that for you today?" Dr Kath asked.

"I don't know. I feel uneasy. I thought I knew what I was going to do before but now this? What now?"

"Without wishing to sound patronising, your need for your father's approval or recognition seems pretty strong. Perhaps we could explore it in another session? I know you had intended to finish today. What do you think?"

"Maybe I need to go away and think about my next move. I thought I could just relocate to Gloucester with Andrew and start our lives together on the new venture. This spectre of my dead family is extremely irritating." Elizabeth folded her arms across her chest.

"Your father is deceased?"

"No, I meant dead to me!" She stood to smooth down her dress and gather her things. "I have to say this therapy seems to confuse things more than it does clarify them."

"That can happen, although at some stage you may find it pivots and issues may become easier to resolve."

"Let's hope so. I'm not paying your fees to become more confused, am I?"

There she was. Elizabeth. Back in the room.

Dulcie

Sitting back against the cushions, Dulcie rested her laptop on her lap. It was a necessary evil apparently, according to Bruce, she ought to stay connected. Yuck. Inboxes. Internet. Everything about it was 'in.' Sometimes all Dulcie wanted was an 'out' away from all that online stuff and to be back in her studio, working clay. Still, she had to book this appointment with Dr Kath and then for today she was free from the thing.

It took forever to fire up. Finally her emails loaded, popping into the list one by one. The counter told her there were twenty pending. She watched the from column, zoning in on the names, intending to ignore all bar the message from Dr Kath.

Thankfully, it loaded as fourth of twenty. After a quick scan of the preview, Dulcie opted for the second of five options, hit reply and sent her confirmation to Dr Kath for four o'clock on Monday. This gave her a few days to work through her thoughts and come up with a clearer plan.

Dr Kath was right, she did have unresolved issues, but she needed a bit of time to process everything. Having decided to continue with the therapy, she realised it was important to leverage as much value from it as possible. Her earlier panic resulted from the realisation her future happiness depended on her handling of the situation. Their discussion of her story, her reasons for choosing Peter, their emigration, brought back much she had ignored for many years. Painful as it was, now was the time to put on her big-girl pants and tackle all sorts of stuff.

She made a bit more of a plan. Tonight, she would order room service. A large glass of wine. Wine always helped. She'd watch some anodyne TV, more for the background noise and to keep her company than anything else. Tomorrow she would get up early and make her way to the V&A. It had been on her list to visit since her arrival and had seemed like an indulgence. All the emotional upheaval had taken over and put the possibility of a museum visit at risk. Now she recognised its importance. She needed to reconnect with the artist inside. An injection of culture would be just the medicine she needed to set her right again. She'd see Matty afterwards.

Ah yes, Matty. What about the text?

Dithering, Dulcie picked up the room-service menu. After a quick scan, she chose the crayfish and rocket sandwich with a large glass of oak-aged Chardonnay. Order placed, she allowed herself to reach for the phone. She sat holding it with the screen in sleep mode. The flashing light on the side indicated the unopened message. Reluctant to undo all her hard work in regaining her balance, she dithered some more. It was no good. Leaving it unopened would only prolong the agony of not knowing his words. Into messages, she clicked on the only bold text, left unread for the previous several hours.

Sorry, I meant to send this at lunch time, but the bid team needed additional competitor analysis for a big pitch at the 11th hr. . .

My Dulcie, my beauty, when we're together I feel ecstatic. When we're apart I hate it. Do you feel that too? I hope so. I've been standing in the fruit aisle staring at the apples for five minutes incapable of choosing between a Pink Lady and a Braeburn, that's how bad I've got it! Save me. I know you said you wanted time but can we meet this weekend? Maybe Saturday? I can take you out somewhere, maybe Hyde Park? I'll meet you anywhere. We can walk and talk or not talk. You choose. Walking, just holding your hand, that's enough for me.
I need to see you. M xx

Cheeks flushing, pulse quickening, groin tingling, Dulcie reread the text at least five times. The words etched onto her retina. She switched off her phone, put it down, picked it up, switched it on and re-read it again. She would respond, her only doubt, to say what exactly? His words had jangled her insides. He was being gentle. He was being honest. He was also, very definitely, letting her choose. Choose the venue, the time, the activity–him.

It would be easier to let go and follow a fatalistic approach. It was much harder to stick to her guns and give herself the breathing space she needed. She would see him, for sure she would, but on Sunday, as she had planned. She composed a considered response, every word checked and checked again.

Hi Matty.
Thanks for your text. Been a long day for me too. I have plans for Saturday already. Hyde Park sounds great, depending on the weather ;-) but can we say Sunday afternoon at 2 instead? Battery low. Turning off the phone now. Catch up tomorrow.
D x

Dulcie finished the text with a white lie. The battery was fine, she just didn't have the emotional reserves to continue the conversation and decided it was safer to pick it up tomorrow. She hoped by then to have developed some resilience. It was a trait she needed, at least until she had made up her mind about her next move.

"Room service."

Suddenly feeling hungry, Dulcie sprang off the bed eager to relieve the waiter of her order. "Thanks, can you just put the tray on the dressing table?"

"No problem ma'am."

He placed it down with precision and was gone as quickly as he arrived. Dulcie took her time rearranging the bedside table to make room for her bounty. She settled herself once more in amongst the cushions and tucked into her food. Her thoughts returned to the conversation with Dr Kath about the past.

Twenty-odd years. Sure lots had changed; lots had happened but she remembered that time vividly. When it came to it, she surprised herself with how much she could recall. Some things she had given little thought to, like her architecture studies. What on earth had possessed her to head off to uni to study that course? She could have gone anywhere; done anything.

With four A-levels behind her, solid Bs across the board, she could have taken up ceramics instead. Admittedly, she'd gone for an eclectic selection of Maths, English, Art and Chemistry. It was almost a protest vote against the system. Why should she have to choose a sensible combination?

Studies aside, what a great time she'd had. Spinning round to the Stock Aitken Waterman beats of 'Dead or Alive' at halls-of-residence discos; all-night bridge sessions leading to bleary-eyed attendance at early-morning lectures; one too many cheap ciders in the bar. Something had happened to her; no longer the avid learner, life and fun times had dominated. Dulcie had escaped her home existence, leaving behind the claustrophobia without a second glance.

Church no longer weighing her down, her mum's heavy expectations no longer weighing her down, she had floated into Peter's arms. There'd been no plan, it all just happened. Events took over and Dulcie had gone with the flow.

Her thoughts, rambling wildly through a landscape of memory mountains, criss-crossed with impassable ravines, kept coming back to family. Her chest ached with guilt. None of it was Peter's fault but the path away from her family started and stopped at him. She had plenty to explore with Dr Kath.

It was the evening in London but it was too early to call home. Peter would be up soon enough though, trying to shepherd their youngest two out of bed. He would struggle. The guilt doubled down. Why couldn't life be easy anymore? Stuff it! She would call him. He might be awake. His ridiculous laughing kookaburra alarm would broadcast soon. She wasn't missing that!

"Pete?"

"Dulcie? You okay?" Mild, disoriented concern wended its way over the thousands of miles, reaching Dulcie as a slurred jumble of sounds.

"Yes it's me. Can you talk?"

"Yeah sure. What's up?"

"Oh, I'm going a bit stir crazy holed up in my room. Wondering what the hell I'm doing here to be honest. Thought it would be good to hear your voice," Dulcie said.

"Oh, I'm not sure I'll be much use. I'm still half asleep."

"Your alarm will go off soon, won't it?"

"Suppose so. What time is it?"

"Nearly six-thirty with you."

The kookaburra cackle rang out. "There you go. You were right! Hold on. Let me stop that awful noise!" Peter gave the bird a sharp tap on its head. "Bloomin' thing. I should get rid of it really. Feel bad though, you know?"

"Because it's from the kids?"

"Yeah."

"How are they?"

"Oh, they're good. Anyway, how are you? What's happening in Pommy-land?" Peter asked.

"Not much really. I've got to get myself sorted. That meeting. It's thrown me, you know?"

"Oh sugar! How do you mean? Tell me about it–oh hold on. I can hear shuffling outside. They're on the move."

Dulcie strained to identify the sounds of the kids as the morning chaos kicked off.

"Sorry love, I've not got enough time to chat just now. Can we talk in the morning, your time? Or can you email me an update? I'm worried about you. Are you sure you're alright?"

Hmm, Peter wasn't really available to help. Email was her only option.

"Sure darling, I'll let you go. Don't worry, I'll send you a long email. I'm sure that will help."

She wasn't convinced it would, but she knew he was doing his best to keep the household running in her absence and didn't want to burden him further.

"Great! Do you want to say a quick hello to the kids?"

"No, I'll let you go. Don't wanna make you late." Dulcie couldn't face being cheery and she didn't want the kids to worry. "Tell them I'll call tomorrow if I can and tell Libby I miss her too. I miss you all." Her voice cracked as the guilt scrambled from deep in her belly to her voice box.

"Bye," he said, failing to notice, distracted by Libby banging on his door.

"Bye—oh and give them a hug and a kiss from me."

"Ha! You'll be lucky. I'll give it a go. Think they've gone past that stage now."

"I guess so. It goes too quickly Pete. Write to you later. Bye."

The line disconnected, his voice gone, Dulcie felt even more lonely. She dropped back into her low, as suddenly as an anti-gravity ride in a theme park. Their brief contact bringing her self-imposed isolation into sharp focus. Bruce was in her head, as if he were a film narrator delivering a melodramatic commentary, "Get a grip woman! What's wrong with you? This mopey Dulcie won't do!"

She was inclined to agree with him. Moping did not suit her. Nor did it serve any useful purpose. When had those big life decisions ever fazed her before? Not when she had dropped out of uni to become an artist; not when she fell pregnant at twenty. Peter had been thrilled. They had barely begun their own young lives before they upped and moved to Australia. Certainly not then. The young Dulcie had taken it all in her stride, followed her instincts and taken risks, gambling her future and only seeing up-sides. Where was she now?

Weary, she drew the curtains, shutting out the driving rain, which had settled in for the evening. She put her tray with the half-finished sandwich outside the door and, still fully dressed, slipped under the covers with the intention of taking a short nap. Decisions could come later.

Annie

"Hi darlings, I'm home!" Annie called out.

She listened for the joyful sound of delighted family members, glad of her return. Cocking her head to one side, she kicked off her wellies, straining for their muffled response, emanating from behind the closed door of the snug. Skidding down the corridor in her soggy-socked feet she experienced a warm bloom of gratitude. The closer she moved, the greater the noise, the more grateful she became.

Tap tap. Her knuckles trilled against the wood. She turned the art-deco blue-glass handle and poked her head around the door before her knocking had been acknowledged.

"Hi! I'm back! Everyone okay?"

"Mummy!" came Thomas's excited shout in reply. At least one member of her family was happy to see her. "Mummy! Mummy!" Thomas bowled over, flinging the door open with enough energy to knock down all ten pins in a strike. "Where have you *been*? I missed you. Up. Up."

"Leave Mum alone you idiot. She's only just got home," Beth said.

Annie marvelled at the difference between her two offspring. Yes, there was a big age gap but surely having both grown up in the same home, you'd have thought Beth's preteen nonchalance and Thomas's preschool enthusiasm would show some evidence of shared family traits. At least Beth's comment had shown some thoughtful consideration.

Annie appreciated the unlikely mellowing in her daughter's mood. Nowadays, her heart skipped a merry polka at the slightest sign of a thaw. No icy stare today. This deserved an Irish jig if not a whole country festival. Careful to keep her fiesta to herself, for fear of triggering the return of *the stare*, Annie announced her acquisition of Eccles cakes from the village store. She took orders for hot drinks and retreated to the kitchen to set about preparing a cosy snack for her brood.

Colin had managed to extricate himself from the sofa, leaving the kids to yet another round of Wii golf, to join Annie in the relative peace of the kitchen. He parked himself on the pine bench.

"How much noise can those two make?"

"I know, I'm surprised you were able to snooze in there with their raging battles."

"Oh, it's not that bad," Colin said. "They were getting along quite nicely today. It's good to see them sharing something for once. Anyway, I don't know what you mean. Snooze? Not me, I was just resting my eyes."

Catching his wink from the corner of her eye, Annie remembered how lovely Colin could be sometimes. She smiled.

"You look happier. How did it go? With Kath, I mean?" he asked.

"Oh, fine. Let me get the kids' hot chocolate sorted first and I'll give you a run down in a bit."

"Wanna hand?"

"I got it. I need to stay by the AGA and dry out. It's lashing it down out there."

Steaming mugs of chocolate delivered to the kids, with marshmallows on the side, Annie joined Colin at the farmhouse table. She chose to sit beside him, facing the window to share his squally view.

"Gosh, the weather really has turned, hasn't it? The forecast did say it would but still, it's pretty yucky this afternoon, eh?"

That was Colin, true to form, picking the safe weather topic whenever he was unsure what to say. Today. Here. That was what she needed. Annie rested her head on his shoulder, content to watch the wind whipping up the swirls of fallen leaves.

"They're dropping early this year, aren't they?"

"What, the leaves? Yeah. Suppose so."

"Seasons are all topsy-turvy these days. Bit like my life really."

Colin slurped his builder's tea. Lifting his free arm over Annie's head he pulled her a little closer. "You'll be fine. You'll sort it out. You always do."

Annie envied Colin his confidence. Life would be infinitely easier if she could be that sure. They sat together for five minutes, each hoping the other would speak first; break the silence. Eventually, Annie took the plunge. "I'm sorry about last night Colin."

"Me too hon."

"It's not just the moving thing, the business with the inheritance."

"I guessed as much. Do you wanna talk about it. . . the other stuff?"

"We probably should." Annie shuffled a few inches away along the bench, displaying some impressive armography whilst disentangling herself from Colin's clutches. "I'm getting to the bottom of my reluctance to move, I think. That emergency session with Dr Kath, it really helped today." Intertwining her fingers with the fraying fringe of her scarf, Annie spoke the words out loud; the ones rattling around her head since leaving Dr Kath's house. "It's June and Mum and kinda Dad and Emma too."

"What is?"

"My worry."

"About what darling? Worry about what?" Colin was confused; sometimes easily so.

"If we move back, I'm in their sphere of influence again."

"But they're not involved are they?"

"I'm not a hundred percent sure but even if they're not, they'll still be around the corner, poking their noses in, trying to make the decisions for me."

"How do you know that? It might be different now."

"I don't think so. You saw June at the barbecue, bossy as ever."

Colin stared ahead, recalling the recent family gathering. Annie had a point.

"It's all the old buried stuff that gets in the way. I've never felt quite as good as my sisters; especially June. I could never live up to them growing up. Why should it be any different now? It's that middle-child thing; not the trail blazer, not the baby, just the one stuck in the corner, trying not to cause trouble and getting the blame for theirs," Annie said.

"I'm still confused though. How does it impact on us now?"

Annie stopped fiddling with the fringe and lifted her head, deciding, for once, to put her own needs first. "Because I need to do this, if I do this, for some reason other than to prove it to everyone else. I have to really want it, for myself."

"And?"

"And I don't know yet, if I do. Not yet anyway."

"Mum! Muummm!" Thomas's yells could not be ignored. That tone, his disaster warning tone, Annie knew better than to try and ignore it.

Letting her guard down and forgetting to follow all the good parenting advice she had read, forgetting to set a good example, she yelled back from her seated position. "What is it?"

"Muummm!"

"Oh damn it!" Annie shook her head.

She shared the knowing look that passes between parents whose lives are the sum of a slew of discarded and unfinished conversations. Pushing herself up from the bench, she succumbed to her summons and shouted back, "Coming darling."

She put her hand on Colin's shoulder, both to steady herself and to stop him from moving. "No. You stay where you are and finish your tea. Once I've got this sorted, we can get back to sorting me out. Why I ever bothered with my degree I'm not sure. All those years at uni, forcing myself to achieve a two-one. Where's the use in that when I have to deal with goodness knows what behind that closed door? Wish me luck!"

Elizabeth

Elizabeth, a voyeur, watched the scene play out from a distance—removed but not remote. There. The couple, rigid, turned away from each other, separated by oppressive silence. She peered in closer at the woman. Her arms forming a straitjacket around her middle, her face muscles contorted, pain emitting from every pore.

Elizabeth recoiled. She knew the couple. She knew that face, the scene and its conclusion. She clenched her fists, digging her fingernails deep into her palms. There was only one way to stop the dread from creeping through her skin. She needed to call out, to break the cycle, to wake.

"No!" Her sleep tried to drag her back. She was still too woozy to shake the memory. "No!" This time so clear and loud, she woke herself and Andrew.

"Hey gorgeous, I'm here. You're safe, I'm here." A semi-awake, Andrew made a half-hearted effort to help her forget. He offered his arm to gather her in towards his chest. "Come here. You wanna talk about it or shall we just snuggle up? Eh?" Andrew slurred his words as if drunk.

"You go back to sleep. I'll go get myself a glass of water. I'll be fine."

Fine she would not be, yet Elizabeth knew he wouldn't be of any use. Padding from the plush carpet of the bedroom through the hallway to the kitchen, her way lit by the LEDs of the alarm system, her feet reached the indulgence of the warm tiles. Thank goodness she'd kept the underfloor heating in the renovation spec. Patting herself on the back for her prowess as a developer, she used her self-congratulation as an antidote to the poisonous thoughts still lingering in her psyche.

That bloody recurring dream. It was all the rumination. Raking through the past to find answers to her inheritance decision. There were high stakes and yet she had spent years suppressing those painful memories. Sitting in the half light of the under-cabinet down lighters, she perched on one of the stools by the central island.

The dream's meaning was clear. Elizabeth had no need to examine it under a hypnotic microscope. It was the moment when her life fell apart. A pivotal moment. Twenty years old, desperately in love and betrayed by one of her own. All her adult life she had carried the contorted pain. How sad for someone so young to have their life change course so dramatically.

Sipping her ice-cold water, feeling it travel down her oesophagus, she concluded the only way to banish the baggage of that dreadful time was to confront it head on. If the sessions had brought it to the surface, and she very much suspected they had, then Dr Kath could bloody well unlock the suitcase and help her shred its contents into tiny insignificant pieces. She did not want to relive that crap ever again!

Resolute, Elizabeth opened the drawer to the dresser, reaching instinctively for her trusty ideas pad and pen. She kept it there, handy for these insomnolent nights when her brain just wouldn't switch off. Her mind was a constant whir of to-dos popping up at the most inconvenient times.

All her energies went on 'splatting the rats' with a mental mallet to keep them at bay. The pad and her 'write it down in a safe place' philosophy enabled her to maintain a swan-like elegance to the outside world. Organisation was the key. Closing the neat and tidy drawer where everything had its place, she slid off the stool and made her way over to her favourite armchair to snuggle up and make a plan.

Not more than five minutes after her legs had curled beneath her on the grey velvet cushion, she felt an undesirable rise of irritation. Her keen hearing detected movement in the bedroom. The grumble of her internal guard dog intensified. Teeth clenched, she waited. Andrew was up, but would he come through to find her, or head back to bed after visiting the en-suite? She hated being disturbed during her thinking time. It pulled her off course.

At work, her staff knew better than to knock if her door was closed; poor Andrew had too little experience of the real Elizabeth. Would he ever be able to match up to the fairy-tale perfect partner? Or would he just begin to get on her nerves? Time would give her the answer and there he was, standing in the doorway, backlit by the subtle wash of light from the kitchen.

Crumpled brow and half-closed puffy eyes, he grunted some kind of greeting. He reminded Elizabeth of a disoriented puppy; unsteady on his feet, seeking reassurance from his owner.

"What's the matter darling?" he asked. "I woke up and you weren't there. I wasn't sure what was going on."

Wide awake and aggravated by his presence, she barked, "Go back to bed! It's early. I'm thinking, it's what I do."

A shoulder shrug and his retreating figure confirmed her message had landed. Immediately guilt and pity mingled in a messy mist. Damn! The clarity on which she had been poised to capitalise had faded back into a confused muddle of thoughts. She sat staring at the virgin page of the notebook, pen hovering ready to stain its pristine surface.

How about a mind-map? Elizabeth used them at work, why not try here? She drew a bubble in the middle of the page. Inside she wrote two names. She circled over the bubble again and again, widening the line, pressing harder each time, circling faster. She did the same to the letters; the ink seeping through the pages below, the paper showing signs of destruction, tearing at points where the ink was now heavy and wet.

She hated them both. It started with them. He had been weak, useless; she had been cruel. Together they had broken her heart. Surely, she'd made the right decision to leave, to walk away. Surely, she had no reason to forgive. It had been her decision, but they hadn't give her much choice. He had been an idiot; she a betrayer.

Elizabeth stared at the page consumed by the memories. When she thought of him she remembered some good times. Intense feelings. He had pursued her; she'd resisted but he had persisted. Not needing a relationship to feel complete, Elizabeth had been confident, self-assured and certain of her direction. It had taken several months before she had relented. He'd made her feel special. Attractive. Mature.

The head-over-heels stuff was for girlie-girls, not for Elizabeth. The falling had been unexpected and hard. Inside she had admitted her need for him. The love, his house, his car, the parties and meals out, all the trappings of a proper boyfriend, had been addictive. Her family had adored him. Sometimes she'd had to pinch herself. Was this really her life?

She had worried about university, about leaving him behind. He had worried about her new life and new experiences taking her away. None of that had mattered to her. She had yearned to be with him and had never doubted he was her soulmate. Then, that summer. Oh that summer. Her world had been destroyed by an incoming meteor; her happiness was extinct.

Elizabeth winced, flinching at the crushing pain of that moment; the moment of discovery; the moment of accusation, of betrayal. The page stared back at her, goading her to write; to brain dump the whole sorry mess. Her pen stayed millimetres from the paper as if repelled by a magnet of the opposite pole. It was as if the act of writing it down would make it real–the dream, no dream at all.

Enough! What was the point of it all? How was this supposed to help? Elizabeth tore off the top few pages of the pad, scrunched them tight and tossed them across the room. She knew better than to keep going on her own. Best to lean on Dr Kath. She convinced herself it wasn't weakness, it was sensible. After all, in business, a leader would surround themselves with experts to counter the challenges they faced. Only a foolish manager would be arrogant enough to assume they could do it all.

Almost ripping the corner of the notebook as she closed it over the spiral, Elizabeth returned the lid to its pen, clipped it through the rings and discarded the paring on the coffee table in disgust.

"Right, time for caffeine, action and relationship building."

Taking herself back through to the kitchen, she set about firing up the Gaggia, ready to make amends with Andrew. Although justifiably feeling provoked, she decided the clever move would be to recapture his heart with a peace offering–two cups of strong black coffee and fresh pastries. She stacked her offering on to the butlers tray, ready to treat her lover to a Saturday morning breakfast in bed.

She parcelled away her dream and its trauma for her next visit to Harley Street. It would do her good to leave the problem alone for another day or two. She would not allow her sister, the betrayer, to steal her happiness today.

Liza

Liza had made her mind up. Gloucester was the way to go. Just under a week had passed since her last session with Kath. She had filled her days with the practical necessities, which would enable her to extricate herself from life in London. Making list upon list of everything she could think of, from utility bills to rental agreements to dental check-ups, you name it, she did it. Staying busy helped keep the panicky sickness at bay.

The chance of discovery was still high. Every evening she turned up to the stinking pit of a club to work, dripping with worry. Had Gino been paying attention? Did he notice how her routines were changing?

She would deserve an Oscar if she could maintain the deception for just another week. It was becoming increasingly difficult to pretend she was okay with his letching and arrogant assumption she would comply with his diktat. What right did he have to believe he would be a better parent to her son? No one could be!

She put the final dab of rouge on her nipples before pulling up the straps of her backless, stretch-lace bodysuit. It clung to her curves in all the right places; black thigh-high zipped boots completed her hostess costume.

The poky dressing room buzzed with activity. The girls were in and out. Some dressing for their sets and some wearing more flesh than clothes having returned from working the room.

Few paid any attention to Liza, standing closest to the doorway, checking out her image in one of the two vanity mirrors. Candy squeezed past, brushing her black satin tassels against Liza's back and caressing her right buttock.

"Ooh, sorry doll. It's a bit tight in here." Candy said. "My you're looking horny tonight!"

Liza knew she was just being playful. She expected nothing less of Candy, one of the few friends she had left at work. Most of the other girls had formed a clique with Rochelle, once they realised she was Gino's new woman. Staying on her right side gave them an easier ride. They weren't stupid. Despite all the stereotypical comments about girls in their profession, most of them understood favouritism would land them much larger pay packets. Staying in with the boss, especially one known for erratic, alcohol-fuelled aggression, was both shrewd business and ingenious self-preservation.

She didn't blame them. Word had got out pretty quickly. Everyone knew Liza was the Ex and she became less important to them than chewing gum stuck to the bottom of their shoes.

"Thanks doll. You're not looking bad yourself. I love your tasselled tits by the way. New?" Liza asked

"Aw thanks hon. Yeah, you like?" Candy said, giving them a shake. "Got 'em from a new indie shop in Soho. We should go one day soon? See if we can't pick you up some new gear?"

"Na, I'm good for a bit." Liza had no intention of ever buying more gear.

She wouldn't need any where she was going, fingers crossed.

Desperate to keep her secret tucked behind her eyes, which usually gave the game away, she made a big fuss of trawling through her make-up bag. She stared into it as if she were Aladdin, searching for the lamp amongst the hoard of his uncle's treasures.

"Watcha lookin' for babe? Need some lippy? Borrow mine if you like. It's called Candy Cool. Bought it for the name but I think it suits me; all sweet and street at the same time!" Candy was distracted, adoring herself in the mirror, preening and posing to her heart's content.

Liza giggled. Camaraderie was key. It would keep her going for her remaining time here. She told herself to join in, act normal and focus on earning as much money as she could in tips between now and escape day.

"I'd better get out there. Lippy's good too, by the way." She caught Candy's eye in the mirror; her wink the final seal of approval for the pink pout, before manoeuvring past and into the corridor.

Wary of being caught alone with Gino, she shimmied through the beaded curtain at the back of the bar area and towards the main foyer, ready to greet punters and position them at the tables, their coats and briefcases already deposited at the cloakroom.

Polite, attentive, seductive, she had all the tricks of a seasoned pro. Not one sweaty-handed virgin nor one arrogant tosser had any idea of the raging plans in her head. With them, she found it easier to conceal her soul. They never looked at her eyes. Whilst flirting, parading, and flashing her flesh to each and every one of them, she took their drinks orders, their attention firmly focused on her neck down.

She recalled a night with a friend in a club years before; a night which had set her down this road. She'd always loved to dance. Performing came naturally to her after years of dance classes and in her drunken teenage years, just after she had arrived in London, they had hit the clubs most nights.

She had been letting herself go on the dance floor, showing off her hip-action in front of a bunch of guys. It was a spectacle. It was INXS. By the time 'Need You Tonight' had ended, her admirers had swelled to a full crowd. Spontaneous applause, shouts of "more" and "show us your tits" prevailed. Uninhibited she may have been, but an exhibitionist? No, not then. Still, as she'd reached for the gin and bitter lemon proffered by her new best mate, Jody, an older guy with a flashy suit and even flashier watch had approached.

"You're a professional dancer right?" he'd asked.

"No! Course not," she'd replied.

What an idiot! If she'd been a professional club dancer what would she be doing putting on a free show? She'd be up in one of the cages thrusting her hips and being paid to do so.

"Why do you ask?"

"Pardon?" He'd scrunched up his face, struggling to hear over the next track booming out of a nearby speaker.

Leaning close to his ear she'd repeated her question, "What makes you ask?"

He'd mirrored her movement, his mouth close to her ear to facilitate the conversation. Together, they'd looked suspiciously like a couple, oblivious to the noise and bodies surrounding them.

"I was just wondering if you wanted to come and work for me," he'd said.

One thing led to another and they had arranged to meet the following week, to give her time to consider his offer. Flushed, nervous and excited she'd searched about for her friend to relay the news. She had found Jody propping up the bar next to some beery blokes.

"Jode! What'd you leave me for?"

"One minute yer with me, the next some geezer monopolises ya and I can't get near ya."

"Yeah. Sorry. Look, he's a club owner and–"

"And what?" Jody cut in.

"And get this, he wants to offer me a job! As a dancer I mean. In his club."

"No way?"

"Yes!"

"Wow! I said you was good. I think you should do it!"

"Reckon I'll give it a try," Liza said. "Why not? What have I got to lose?"

That had been the start of it; her career. Liza hadn't thought of it as a step down, more as a way out of self-destruction. Now, as she barely tolerated the work, using her looks and moves to reel the punters in, she recognised it had been a path but probably not the right path.

The music was booming in the club. Candy was on stage performing her set.

"Oi! You! Come 'ere darlin', I want some of your sweet arse for myself!" some guy shouted at her.

Second set finished, she tried to make her exit off the stage, past the blob of a well-dressed man, who unfortunately happened to be well-oiled too.

Liza looked about for the bouncers and spotted them,

dealing with an incident on the other side of the room by the speaker stack. The club had an edge to the air. It fizzled and cracked with tension. Liza knew times like these were dangerous; testosterone and excessive alcohol an unstable mix. Throw a spark to that tinderbox and it would surely ignite. Tonight, Candy was the spark.

Her show had been steamy; punters crotches and egos engorged. Every man thought she belonged to him. Sometimes you can defuse the situation, spread the lust amongst the girls, satisfy everyone and keep things under control. But not tonight. Everything played out in quadruple time.

The room was turning. Far too many sexually-frustrated men wanted a piece of Candy. No amount of schmoozing would pacify. Fearing for her friend and putting herself last, Liza placed the round black tray with its cargo of three double whiskies on the circular table in the booth to her left. She leant forward to allow her customer to make his payment and with the rolled notes still wedged in her cleavage, she darted towards Candy, placing her body directly between her friend and the blob.

Asserting her authority she said, "I'm the Customer Experience Duty Manager tonight. Can I help you sir?"

"What kind of a bullshit title is that? Customer Experience Manager. Ooh, I'm really scared."

He tried to mimic her, instead sounding like a female impersonator with a poncey accent. Repeating the phrase over and over, he sounded more and more ridiculous with each attempt. Candy had escaped, a fact he seemed to have missed, his aggravation now entirely focused on Liza.

"Sir, if you would just sit down for me, I can take your order."

He squared up to her, eyeball to eyeball, his face as rude and angry as the man himself. She wasn't scared of him. She had known worse. He locked his eyes in hers, trying to force her subservience. Liza stood her ground. Unblinking, she repeated her statement as a clear command.

"Sir, sit down now. If you wish to purchase another drink, I will take your order."

"Bollocks to this. I don't have to take your crap." Noticing Candy's absence, he looked around at his mates, his bluster bolstered by their nods of approval. "Arrange me a private dance with that sissy slut who just ran off, or I'll do you instead."

Taking half a step backwards to be sure he could see her clearly; she raised her voice loud enough for all on the closest four tables to hear. "If you continue to behave like the obnoxious bastard you are, you will leave me with no option but to throw your sorry arse out of here. Now I said. Sit. Down!"

Annie

"Samuel Hampton speaking."

"Hi Samuel, it's Annie Bradley. Sorry Annie Braybrooke here."

"Hey! How can I help?"

"You mentioned when we met I could call if I needed clarification on anything."

"Yes, of course. What is it?"

She didn't want him to hear her rustling through the notes she had made with Colin and tried to cradle the phone in the crook of her neck, away from the sounds of paper confusion.

"It was here. . . just now. . . my list. Sorry, bear with me, I just need to put the phone down for a sec. Do you mind?"

"Not a problem. Get yourself sorted, I'll wait."

Annie put her mobile on the kitchen table before shuffling through the neatly gathered sheets of paper; the product of her brainstorm with Colin over the weekend. It didn't make sense. She knew she had been careful to leave the list of questions at the top of the pile. Forget about the emotional barriers or financial barriers to the inheritance decision, they had figured answers to their legal queries were far weightier in the move/stay debate.

Annie's frantic searching turned the otherwise orderly pile into an abstract scattering, worthy of a Tracey Emin installation at the Tate Gallery. About to give up, she face-palmed in embarrassment. She had taken the envelope with the scribbled questions upstairs the previous evening, just in case more occurred to her in the small hours. She'd been having trouble sleeping and it seemed a sensible idea to capture any late night musings.

"Sorry. I've just remembered it's upstairs. Can you hold a second whilst I fetch it?"

"That's fine. I do have another call to make shortly, but we have time."

"Thank you, you're very kind."

Bounding up the stairs, phone in hand, Annie nimbly avoided the clutter on the bottom two steps. They were never empty; no matter how many times she redistributed her family's possessions to their rightful locations. Arriving a little breathless, she picked up the list from the exact spot she had left it, on the floor by her bed.

Samuel's deft dealing of the first few questions reassured Annie. Certain he knew his stuff, her confidence in him grew with every additional piece of advice. She saved the trickiest to last, reticent to hear the answer to the one question left staring at her in bold, underlined capitals.

"Could you clarify clause eleven, point two point three in the trust document, regarding 'other family members' please?"

"Certainly. It determines that having accepted the gift, you are also agreeing to the division of said gift with the other family members, who should also so decide to accept the gift."

"Sorry, but that's as clear as mud. Could you explain how it might work? In practical terms, I mean."

"I need to be careful here, as there are several clauses explicitly prohibiting me from divulging individual names. Let me speak hypothetically."

"Okay."

"So, for example, hypothetically, there might be, say four other family members nominated as potential beneficiaries. Once I have received decisions from any beneficiaries wishing to accept the gift, say two of them, then, if you say yes, the gift will be distributed equally between the three of you. Your inclusion as a beneficiary is dependent on your agreement to work in collaboration with any or all of the nominated beneficiaries who have accepted the gift. In other words, the assets, the house and cash, the decisions about strategy and the business plan for the Tango school, and all other related business activities must be shared amongst those same beneficiaries. In my hypothetical case there would be three shareholder/directors, with equal rights and responsibilities for the running of the school."

"I see but what happens if we find we are incompatible or differ in opinion? Is there a clause to cover that situation?"

"You mean a termination clause or some such?"

"Something like that. I've been thinking of it as a get-out clause. Not a very legalese term, I'm sorry, but you get my drift."

"There is a minimum commitment of five years. The break clauses cannot be exercised until this period has expired. Subsequently, one or more parties could seek to be bought out of their share of the business. Prior to this, it would be possible to terminate your involvement but without compensation i.e. you would forfeit your share."

"And I would have to sign before meeting the others, right?"

"Yes, that is correct."

She hadn't misread it. She was being asked to decide her own family's future based on little or no information about her potential business partners. At the very best, she would be the sole owner of a risky start-up, the spectre of her meddling family never far away. At the worst, she could be in business with her sisters, something she would never have chosen for herself under normal circumstances. In her silent contemplation of these two extreme scenarios and every combination of the possibilities in between, she left the line open and Samuel wondering how to close without seeming rude.

"Ms Braybrooke? Is there anything else I can help with? It's just the other call I mentioned."

"Sorry Samuel. Of course, you must go. I don't want to hold you up any longer."

"Well, please don't hesitate to let me know if I can be of further assistance between now and the eighth of October."

"Will do thanks." Annie clicked off the phone, absentmindedly flipping it over and over in her hand.

She sat back against the side of the bed; legs stretched out in front of her. *Bugger. Now what?* She had been hoping she had missed something. She'd convinced herself she could accept the gift and find some way of circumnavigating her biggest problem; her bloody family.

After years of trying to shape her own life and family unit on her own terms, far enough away to care a little less about their expectations, here was her chance to prove herself a success under their noses. Yet, their dominance still loomed, threatening to undermine her. Could she risk it? Did she really even want to?

Colin understood her better than anyone and they had decided the deal might be more attractive to Annie if she could at least trial it first; the last few weeks had reminded her just how supportive and patient he could be. She stopped swirling the phone and sent him an update.

A quick note to say I've spoken to solicitor. As we thought looks like all or nothing. Now what? Do you think I need a final session with Kath?
Xxx

Time to crack on. She had the kids' tea to prepare and she couldn't afford another meltdown from Thomas. One unsupervised moment of mayhem in the snug was enough for this week! Adorable though he was, Thomas had a way of ending every crisis with a head injury and a trip to the minor-injuries unit. Annie was convinced she was on a watch list after the latest incident. The last thing she needed right now was bad-mother guilt compressing her torso like a tightly-zipped gilet. The thought of a 'guilt quilt' amused her, particularly as this was the uniform of many a local mum.

She hauled herself up from the floor, her head switching into chef mode, debating the simplest, least stressful meal options, as she made her way downstairs. Pasta with pesto? Why not? Something easy. Sometimes the easy option was the best option.

Dulcie

Peeking out at the swathe of grey across the city, Dulcie could be forgiven for thinking London was never bright anymore. She compared the sky to visions of her youth, when life was vibrant and lived in full technicolour sunshine. Had nostalgia used a filter to enhance the black-and-white memories? Unable to distinguish fantasy from reality, she just wished the dreariness would end. Thankful for feeling better rested after a deep sleep, she hoped she could prevent the return of yesterday's emotional exhaustion with her planned cultural outing.

She showered and selected her outfit from the few remaining options, as yet unworn since her arrival in England. The powder-blue ribbed jumper and dark-blue jeans felt comfy; clean and soft against the skin. Whilst the tan boots were not the best choice for damp weather, she figured they'd be fine for her indoor timetable at the V&A. Plus, most of her route would be undercover, in tube stations and subway tunnels delivering her almost door to door without the need to exit to the outside.

She popped on a bit of lip gloss, swiped a couple of strokes of mascara on her lashes and decided that would do. After all, this was a day to herself. She was going to the museum to see things, not to be seen. Grabbing her rain mac by the collar she slung it over one shoulder, her handbag over the other and headed out to find breakfast. She could have joined the other guests in the morning room but knew she would feel conspicuously solo and today she wanted to blend in not stand out.

The rather beaten up grandfather clock in the lobby chimed nine o'clock as she descended the last stair. As the museum didn't open until ten, she decided to ask the concierge for breakfast recommendations close to the hotel. Whilst she had not been to South Kensington for an age, she did recall the lack of eateries in the area. It was full of imposing Victorian architecture, block after block of museums left little room for buildings of more useful proportions. There was the Lebanese kebab shop, whose shish and kofte had been legendary back in the day, but she had no idea if it still existed. Besides which, kebab wasn't really her breakfast food of choice.

She spotted Carlos, the concierge. "How can I help you?"

"Could you tell me a good place for breakfast nearby? Ideally somewhere with great coffee."

"Certainly madam. There are many places to choose from but I must say my favourite is a little café called Giovani's just around the corner."

He showed her on a map.

"Thank you Carlos, that's very helpful. It's not run by someone you know by any chance, is it?"

"But of course!" He winked and gave her a theatrical flourish of his arms, proclaiming his faith in his uncle's family business to the whole lobby. "He's the best. His coffee is the best."

Leaving the hotel through the old wooden revolving door,

she felt happier with the world. Today was going to be a great day, misty-murky greyness or not.

*

Fuelled full of her favourite poached eggs, with pancetta and porcini mushrooms, she pushed her knife and fork together. The plate was not completely clean. She was trying to be good and had ordered grilled tomatoes to balance the food groups, but, as ever, being one of her least favourite foods she had struggled to eat them. Dulcie didn't know why she made the same mistake repeatedly.

Outside, the streets were full of dedicated fashionistas chasing perfect outfits for their Saturday evenings. Tourists mingled with families, out for the day exploring London.

Dulcie paid little attention to the individual people, focusing on the gaps, to forge her way through the increasing numbers. At one point she nearly toppled a set of teenager dominos when the group decided to stop dead immediately in front of her. Inconsiderate pedestrians really riled Dulcie.

Once down on the platform, staring at the posters for the film of the week, she wondered how Londoners coped with the constant bustle; it appeared not very well from the looks of their faces. She hoped the museum would be less crowded. All these people and not one friendly face. Maybe she should have stayed in the hotel for the day.

The density of sorry souls, as oppressive as the air trapped beneath the city, Dulcie closed her eyes to the scene. She waited patiently for the first breath of warm wind, signalling the rush of the train, as it rattled into the station.

Squeezing through the nearest set of doors behind the same bunch of teenagers she had encountered earlier, her brain puzzled over the crossing of their paths. How had they got ahead of her? What made them stand out from the hundreds of people she had already passed that day? She supposed she had been too absorbed in her own world for them to register, set, as she was, on a mission to find some cultural and creative solace. They made her think again of James and Mikey and wish she could show them London.

At last, the claustrophobic journey ended and Dulcie filed out with the stream of passengers upstairs and through the barriers to the ticket hall. The floor covered in muddy smudges of footsteps, she checked the signs for the right direction and opted for the museum tunnel, the subway running parallel to the road above. Glad to avoid the rain, groups of tourists peeled off at each exit as they reached their chosen destinations, the crowd thinning each time.

Dulcie felt an odd sense of familiarity. She couldn't pinpoint the source. Nothing much had changed about her surroundings since her previous visits, but it wasn't that. It was more a feeling, an atmosphere. Shaking her head and rolling her shoulders several times, she told herself to stop being daft and get on with enjoying her day. She arrived at the entrance to the V&A and reached forward to pull the heavy door open by the solid brass bar running down its full length. Then, an arm appeared in front of her, the fingers on its hand wrapping tightly around the bar.

"Allow me."

The voice belonging to the chivalrous door-opener was unmistakable. Dulcie whipped her head around, meeting Matty's eyes barely twelve inches from her own. She jumped.

Unable to process the situation, she stepped away, speechless and staring, her heart hammering.

"What the?" she began, faltering at the sight of him. "How did you? What are you doing here? I didn't see you. . . I don't get it."

"I'm sorry, I didn't mean to startle you. I wanted to surprise you."

"Think I might need to sit down for a bit."

"Come on, let's go inside. There'll be some seats somewhere."

He yanked the bar with his right hand, holding out his left to Dulcie. If the adrenalin from his surprise had been about to subside, she wouldn't know. Now, it spiked again at the thrill of his touch, as he led her through the doorway. Multiple questions raced through her, yet none surfaced.

She followed him silently as he guided her towards the backless benches, extending several metres along the wall near the cloakrooms. Once settled, he undid the cap and offered her some water from a small plastic bottle. Attentive and considerate as ever, he waited until he thought she was ready and helped answer some of her un-asked questions.

"How about I tell you why I'm here? You must be wondering why, what, when?" Matty said.

Dulcie nodded. Still holding the bottle to her mouth, an excuse not to speak.

"Let me start with the easiest," he said. "How did I know where you'd be? Simple. It's going to sound creepy but I followed you."

"What? From where?"

"I know it's a bit freaky. Please let me explain."

"Perhaps you'd better," she said sternly.

"Look, you know how I feel about you. I respect your need to be alone, if that's what you really want, but I just got the feeling when we spoke, you might need someone to talk to. Other than your therapist, that is."

"Mmm."

"I made a decision. Last night, I was going to come to your hotel and meet you for breakfast. Only when I got there, the desk said you'd gone out." Matty smiled to himself, remembering. "I must have looked really sorry for myself because another guy at the other desk–"

Dulcie interrupted, "The concierge?"

"Yep, must have been. He said he might know where you were. He asked if I was dangerous. I told him no, of course not, unless he thought my being head over heels in love with you was a threat. . ." Matty let his sentence tail off, watching for Dulcie's reaction. Unable to read her face, he continued. "He told me you'd gone to his uncle's café round the corner. He said if I caught you in time I should order Eggs Benedict, 'the best in town.' Anyway, I got there just as you were leaving. I thought, I have not come this far to let you go now. So, I followed you."

"I see."

"I'm really sorry. I didn't mean to startle you. I'll go away again if that's what you want?" He paused. Dulcie remained silent. Quieter now and tentatively he asked, "Is that what you want? Do you want me to go away?"

She squeezed his hand and didn't let go. She couldn't speak but she didn't want to give him the wrong signal. She didn't even know how to give the right signal. She just knew pulling away wouldn't be right.

"I watched you battling the crowds, deep in thought; I watched you down the carriage on the tube, wishing I could read your mind, hoping you were thinking of me. I know I shouldn't have put you through this but all I can tell you is, once I started, I couldn't stop. It wasn't rational."

"No, it wasn't!"

Both had been staring at their knotted fingers. Matty lifted her chin with his free hand, his eyes anchored in hers; deep pools of emotion.

"It wasn't rational," he repeated. "But then love never is."

Elizabeth

"Are you comfortable?" Dr Kath asked, concerned at Elizabeth's inability to sit still.

"Yes thank you. I'm fine." Elizabeth attempted to compose herself, mindful of scrutiny. The last impression she wanted to give was that of being agitated.

"Well, if you're sure, can we begin?"

Dr Kath knew better. This fidgety behaviour in itself was not unusual for her clients, many of whom came to her at times of stress. With Elizabeth though, she had observed it indicated something significant was playing on her mind; something suppressed from the world, probably for some time.

She was the mistress of control. Her obsession with it had become a real problem. Instead of allowing the stresses and strains of life to release when they occurred, she bottled them up inside, desperate to appear self-contained and in charge. For her any outward sign hinted at huge pressures needing an outlet; lava searching for a fissure in the rock. Dr Kath gave her the opportunity to open up before they commenced; Elizabeth chose not to take it.

"I'm ready to start the session," Elizabeth said.

"Okay, just before we do, can I just check dates? You said

it was the eighth of October by which you have to make a decision. Is that correct?"

"Yes, there's a little time left but I'd rather get on with it. I'd prefer this to be my last session."

"Even if you have unresolved issues at the end of it?"

"That's unlikely, but yes, even if I do."

"I must just say, in fact I'm obliged to, it's highly probable you will regress, if you stop midway through a series. To be clear you'd probably need to repeat a similar number of sessions, if at some later date you decided to come back to the therapy. A break usually causes any momentum gained to be lost."

Elizabeth lifted her perfectly groomed left eyebrow. "Really? Well, I guess I'm prepared to take the risk. Thank you Dr Kath. Now, I am eager to get started. Can we?"

Dr Kath chose not to react. Clients often came to her with baggage. She had learnt, early in her training, to leave her personal feelings at the door.

In no time Dr Kath had prepared her for therapy. Once again Elizabeth sat in front of her on the couch, eyes closed and breathing evenly in hypnotic trance.

"Elizabeth, you may recall we were last discussing the subject of family. It was something that caused you anxiety. At that time, you said you wanted to leave it buried. Are you ready to talk about it today?"

"Yes."

"When I say the word family what comes up for you?"

"Sadness, anger, upset and betrayal."

"Which emotion is the strongest right now?" Dr Kath suspected she knew the answer.

"Betrayal."

"Do you know where this comes from?"

"Oh yes! I've never said it out loud before." Elizabeth's voice dropped to an almost-whisper.

"You're safe here. No one else can hear. Tell me."

"I've been thinking about this a lot recently."

Dr Kath remained silent, listening carefully for pieces of the jigsaw. This strand of questions had the potential to get to the heart of Elizabeth's trauma. She allowed her client to dictate the pace.

"A long time ago, before I came to London, something happened. I was stupid. I didn't see it coming. You see I had this boyfriend, Doug. He was amazing. He was older, charming, had a job, a house and a car. At first, I thought he was an arrogant prick, like most good-looking guys. He had all the lines and thought he could pull any girl with a flash of his perfect teeth. I told him I wasn't interested. I was committed to my studies."

"You were still at school?" Dr Kath asked.

"I told him I had ambitious plans. I wanted to go to university. I told him he wasn't in them."

"What happened?"

"He wore me down. He literally charmed the pants off me. We saw each other all the way through that year and the next, my first at university."

"You're saying the relationship was good?"

"For a while, yes. Twenty-three months, two weeks and four days to be precise. I believed he was the one, the love of my life. I had my independence and I had my man. Ours was a bright future. Put it this way, I wasn't thinking babies but I was thinking bells."

"You were certain, you trusted your judgment but something changed?"

"Changed? I'd say imploded." Elizabeth's face and neck reddened significantly.

"Did you talk about it?

"No, I was devastated when I found out. I didn't want to talk. Didn't want to see him ever again!"

"Maybe you could tell him now? Sometimes it helps to have the conversations you should have had," Dr Kath explained.

"I don't want to waste my breath on him. He was a pathetic man. Made decisions with his dick. He's of no consequence now."

"Are you saying he was unfaithful? And you were betrayed?"

"Yes but he didn't betray me. Not really. He was just a weak, pathetic loser."

"Who betrayed you then?"

"My older sister June. It was her. She was doing him whilst I was away at university. She was sneaking around like a tart behind my back."

"How did you react?"

"I told her so. I told her she was a thieving bitch and she should stay away from me for fucking good!"

Dr Kath steered Elizabeth away from her crescendo of emotions, giving her some respite. "Take some time to find your calm place. Breathe deeply. You're safe. She's not here."

Elizabeth followed her instructions, taking just a few minutes to return to an even, rhythmic breath.

"Can you tell me how things are between you both now?"

"We don't talk. We don't see each other. I don't see any of

my family because of her. I'm a bit lonely maybe but really it's their loss."

"Interesting you say a bit. Why's that?"

"I chose long ago to stand up for myself. I don't need them."

Dr Kath considered the possibility Elizabeth may have other reasons for this self-isolation. She checked the clock, They had fifteen minutes left before Elizabeth's fifty minutes were up. She probed a little deeper.

"Was this the first time you needed to rely on yourself? Are there any earlier memories? Times when you can remember having to look after number one, for example?"

"Hmm." Elizabeth lingered over her next answer, an image forming in her mind. "Perhaps."

Dr Kath coaxed her forward gently. "It's okay to tell me. Any snippet might help, even if you feel it's inconsequential."

"Dad is comforting Mum. They're in the kitchen and I'm in the doorway, wearing my pyjamas. I can't see her face but I think she might be crying. He's saying something."

"Can you hear him? Try leaning in," Dr Kath suggested.

"He says something like, we can try again. Mum says something like she can't lose another one. They shift a little and I can see June is with them in the middle of the hug."

"What happens next?"

"June tugs Dad's jumper and points to me. He tells me to go back to bed. That's it. There's no more memory but it feels exactly the same."

"As?"

"As when they took her side every other time in our lives."

"That's a very black-and-white view; a fixed mindset. Would you like to explore this some more?"

"Not really. I know I'm right. They chose her and they always chose her. My only option was to choose me."

Elizabeth saw a collection of playing cards in her mind, fanned out in a spiral, every one depicting another time when she felt discarded. The final card in the centre was the most devastating; the black queen of the pack.

Having been silently analysing her hand, Elizabeth opened up and Dr Kath let it flow uninterrupted.

"Look, they sided with her over Doug, telling me to forgive and forget. Especially Mum. She clearly thought they were better suited. Brushed my feelings under the carpet. Said I'd get over it. Last thing she said was to stop being melodramatic. I looked at Dad. He wasn't saying much. When she said that, I wanted him to defend me, to say something. He didn't care enough to speak. I left and haven't been back since."

"And now you're revisiting it, has your view altered?

"No."

"You don't want to know how he felt? You don't want to talk to him about his perspective? You don't want to know what happened when you were small?"

Elizabeth didn't answer. She couldn't. She was sobbing. She had reached her limit for today.

Dr Kath ended the session.

Fully alert and dabbing her eyes with tissue, Elizabeth felt jaded. Her mask had dropped; she had no reserves of energy to maintain the pretence of keeping it all together. Her voice was small and she stumbled over her words. "I hadn't realised. I mean–I didn't want to. I'm not sure I can."

"Take your time. You're my last appointment today. There is no rush. It was a difficult session but you did well."

"Thanks. I suppose you've seen through my bravado. No one else has seen that."

"I don't judge." Dr Kath said. "I'm here to help you understand yourself and, of course, to help you make your decision about the future and what's right for you."

"What was that about when I was in the kitchen doorway? I know I felt left out. . ."

"I don't know. Sounded like a family crisis. Maybe you were just too little and they were trying to protect you?"

Elizabeth's eyes flitted from side to side, the answer skulking about in the shadows of her brain, playing a sinister game of hide and seek; a little red dwarf behind Venetian archways.

"Take your time. Something might come to you later. Maybe focus on your more immediate needs first."

Following Dr Kath's sound advice, Elizabeth switched her focus to more pressing matters.

"I'd never really considered this stuff relevant before," she said, still searching for a resolution. "I was pretty clear about my plans. What now? Do I or don't I make the move? Do I or don't I take on a new business? Do I risk everything to take a share of something in which I may be compelled to work with my family? I just don't have a clue what's next."

Liza

"Ouch!"

"Stay still will you," Candy ordered, tending to Liza's cuts. "I know it stings but it'll do you good babe."

Liza forced herself to ignore the pain, sucking air through her teeth to prevent more whimpering noises from escaping her lips. She knew Candy was doing her best to help.

"Bloody hell doll. It just hurts so bad!" Liza said.

"You'll have a real shiner in the morning."

"Too right. Still, won't be the first time, and it was worth it seeing that git get dragged away by the cops."

"They asked you for your statement yet?"

"Nope. They're still with Gino I think."

Candy finished dabbing Liza's cheekbone with the antiseptic wipe. "There. Thanks by the way, for looking out for me with that punter. Not sure what would have happened if you hadn't stepped in."

Liza shivered, pulling Tony the bouncer's jacket a bit tighter round her shoulders. "It's all a bit of a blur really. I guessed it was about to kick off and just tried to contain the situation. Didn't quite work eh?"

"You can say that again!" Candy giggled.

Liza tried to laugh, wincing instead. "Ow, that hurts! Don't make me laugh."

Packing away the green canvas first-aid kit, Candy zipped it closed between thumb and forefinger; no mean feat in view of the length of her pink talons. "Sorry. It's just easier to laugh about these things or else you'd cry, right?"

"Right."

"You coming then?" She beckoned Liza with a nod towards the dressing rooms.

"Better wait here. Cop said she'd be back to talk to me soon."

"If you sure? I'll be off yeah?"

Liza nodded.

The office took on a melancholic mood with Candy gone. She reminded Liza of Sheena and their days together in the club, where their friendship had blossomed. Her two friends were completely different, yet remarkably similar. Their humour; that was it, that was their common trait. Life would have been unbearable without humour.

Liza was sad to think of leaving them. Of course she'd stay in touch with Sheena, but it wouldn't be the same, with the distance. She probably wouldn't see Candy again. They'd only become pally in the last few months and Candy was too involved in the chapter Liza was trying to close. She sat on the old splintered desk, head hung and fishnet-clad legs dangling down, her feet a whisper away from the floor.

Still no cops and no call to be interviewed. They were taking a long time with Gino. What were they are asking him? Surely it couldn't still be about the fight? He wasn't even a witness. He'd been off in one of the back rooms, servicing his bitch no doubt. Wherever, at the time it had all gone Pete

Tong, his absence had been conspicuous. When the fists and tables were flying; when Liza was knocked down, where had the King Pin been?

She had lain on the floor of the club, beaten and bruised, stockings ripped, broken glass strewn around her and only then did his face appear. His nose had been inches from hers, upside down like the Child Catcher in Chitty Chitty Bang Bang. First prodding her to make sure she was conscious, he'd spat out the words, "I'll deal with you later." What a nasty man. Oh how she loathed him.

Crunching broken glass announced the arrival of two sets of footsteps towards the office. A rap on the frosted panel followed. Liza saw two figures on the other side of the door, awaiting her response.

"Ms Braybrooke?" one of them called out.

"Yes, come in."

A young police constable with blond hair swept back into a neat bun entered the room with her detective colleague.

"Can you tell me how much longer this is gonna take? I need to get back home to my son."

"Of course Ms Braybrooke. Sorry to keep you waiting. I'm Detective Constable Harmsworth." She extended her hand to offer a handshake before continuing. "And this is my colleague, PC Johnston. We have plenty of witnesses to the incident and PC Johnston's notes from your earlier account. We could leave the formal statement for now if you wish. Are you feeling up to it or would you rather defer until tomorrow morning?"

"Can I do tomorrow? Maybe sometime after the school run?"

"About nine-thirty?"

"Yeah thanks."

Liza inched herself off the desk, stepping down with care. Her muscles tensed as she tested her weight on her bruised left side. PC Johnston placed her hand under Liza's elbow to add support.

"We could drop you home if you'd like," she said. "Unless you want to reconsider and let us take you to hospital. You look like you came off pretty badly. Might be safer to get yourself checked out properly?"

"Nah, I'll be fine. I'm used to it."

"How do you mean exactly?"

"I'd rather not talk about it. Just one of those things. A lift home would be helpful though."

Liza was focused on getting back to Angelo and protecting her plan to leave London. These were her priorities–getting back at Gino or getting justice were not. Still, she was curious to know what happened to him.

Crunching slowly along the corridor she asked, "Where's Gino? Mr Cappelletti, I mean."

"He's been arrested Miss. They've taken him to the station," DC Harmsworth replied.

"Can you say what for?"

"Unfortunately not. We'll need to complete our enquiries before we can be clear on all the charges."

"But can you say where he's being held and for how long? He is my son's father. I want to be sure we're safe."

"I believe he's in custody for tonight at least."

Liza fell silent and stayed quiet for the remainder of her trip home.

With no information about Gino's charges, her mind filled

the vacuum with all sorts of scenarios. When they reached the flat it took her several painful minutes to extricate her shattered body from the back seat. Once on the pavement, she stood for a moment looking up at her windows. Despite the early hour, fingers of pink light were already caressing the top of the building. Time was ticking on towards morning.

She entered the building, reaching for the light switch to the landing. Nothing. As usual the landlord had failed to replace the bulb. Sick and tired of the maintenance battle, she tried to deal with most faults herself. This one required a ladder she didn't possess. The converted property had overly high ceilings. Some would say they contributed to a roomy feel. In practical terms, they were a bloody nuisance.

She reached her door in darkness, noticing a thread of light escaping from beneath it. Odd. Sheena shouldn't be up yet and Angelo certainly shouldn't. She limped towards the door, painkillers wearing off and her body beginning to remember the blows she had suffered a few hours earlier. Listening for sounds of life inside, she opened the door as quietly as she could. The light she had spied was coming from the kitchen.

Delirious with exhaustion, her mind jumped to the scary possibility of finding Gino waiting. The thought, impossible as it was, triggered a spike of fear. She admonished herself. *Don't be daft, you stupid cow. He's locked up at the station. It can't be Gino.*

Motionless, she cupped her ear, straining for clues. Running water glugged into a receptacle; metal snapped on metal; a switch clicked. This, followed by a hiss led her to a conclusion—clearly someone was boiling the kettle and that could only be Sheena.

Bolstered by the deduction, Liza swept into the kitchen with mock nonchalance, her anxiety ebbing away in an instant at the sight of her friend.

"Sheena! What on earth are you doing up? Thank goodness it's you. For a minute I was wondering–"

Sheena replied in a loud whisper. "Quiet babe. Angelo's sleeping."

Turning away from the kettle towards her friend, Sheena was confronted by the unwelcome image of a beaten-up Liza standing before her.

"What the? He's been at it again hasn't he? Come on. Sit down. Poor you!" She ushered Liza into the room, pushing the door to and guiding her to the chipped melamine table. "There. Plonk yourself on that stool and I'll make you a nice mug of strong hot tea."

"Ta. Why are you up doll? It's too early."

"I got a text from Candy. She told me 'bout Gino. Been arrested hasn't he? Said there was a fight. She didn't say he'd had a go at you though."

"Oh, he didn't. This was a punter would you believe. Thing is, how did she know about the arrest? I thought she'd gone already before the cops had finished with him."

"Apparently she saw Rochelle leaving in an ambulance. One of the other girls told Candy. She's accused him of assault. Smashed her nose and goodness knows what else. Police busted open the door of one of the back rooms when they came to sort out the brawl."

The implications of this news trickled through Liza's spent body like honey off a spoon. This could change everything.

Annie

"Do take a seat."

"Thank you Dr Kath." Annie took a couple of long breaths to calm herself before the last session started. The process now a comfort; the prospect of it ending far less so. "Ooh, it's lovely and cosy in here. It's great to get inside out of that bluster. The forecast is possible gales later. Did you hear?"

"Really? I missed the news this morning, and I've been inside all day. It did feel a little chilly earlier. I thought it would be nice to light the fire now the nights are drawing in, any excuse."

On cue, the fire crackled as a gust of wind drew the flames up towards the flue; the latch of a gate rattled in response, answering the call to autumn.

"Are you ready to start? Perhaps you could let me know how you've been since we last met. Give me a bit of an update?"

"Sure." Annie exhaled another long loud breath. "Well, I've made some progress or at least I think I have."

"That sounds encouraging. Go on."

"I've had a good think about what I want, for myself, that is. If I'd had been allowed to discuss the gift–which by the way has felt more like a burden at times –properly with my sisters, I'm sure everyone would think I'm bonkers for not jumping at the chance."

"And it matters to you? It matters what they think?"

"Not necessarily. I'm just saying on the face of it, anyone would think it was like winning the lottery."

"But? I sense a but?"

"Yep, there is a but, a rather large one, actually. So large it might compare to Mr Creosote's backside!"

They both laughed, Annie a little too enthusiastically.

"Sorry, probably shouldn't laugh at my own jokes. My daughter says it's not cool. Sorry."

"No need to apologise. Laughter is an excellent antidote to stress or anxiety. You were saying about the gift?"

"Quite aside from the complexities of my decision and all the factors I need to consider, any sudden windfall, like the lottery, surely must be looked at from all perspectives?"

"That does seem to have been important to you."

"Well, I am the sensible one. . . Don't get me wrong, I can see all the merits of a new start, even with the risks but, I've pretty much concluded it's not really for me, for us."

"Is that because of your family?"

"No. Yes. I mean, if we could explore it again today. I really do feel everything hinges on it. Is that alright?"

"Of course. This session, as with every session, is for you. You came to me for help to unravel your emotional and practical response to an unexpected event. I shall be guided by you."

"Oh, and Mum did say something really cryptic yesterday at the end of our call."

"Do you think it might be relevant?"

"I don't know. She said, whatever it is you choose, make

sure it's right for you. Don't you go repeating my mistakes. Odd, don't you think?"

Swish swoosh. Her heartbeat sloshed in her ears like an underwater metronome. Annie transported to her safe place, felt calm, cosseted by a soft blanket, which floated down, enveloping her with fluffiness. She was ready to start her final session and determine her future.

"Ready?"

"Yes."

"You wanted to look at family. Tell me about family. What does that word mean?"

"Lots of different things; the duty thing we talked about. Guilt, not being good enough, arguments, criticism, holding back, not being me, love, sadness and all sorts really."

"There's quite a bit going on inside, isn't there? Is there one dominant thing preventing your decision? Something perhaps that you feel is stopping you moving forward?"

"Hmm, maybe."

"Which is the strongest?"

"I don't know."

"Let's try this. Imagine each of those feelings as if they had faces. Can you see them in front of you?"

"Yes, I think so."

"How do they look? Tell me what you see."

"They're all jostling, shoulder to shoulder, pushing to get to the front."

"Can you zoom in, see things in more detail?"

Annie frowned. "Guilt is elbowing love out of the way; resentment is standing front and centre, feet firmly planted;

jealousy is jumping up and down at the back trying to get my attention and confidence has been trampled on the floor."

"Good, that's really good," Dr Kath encouraged. "Now, anything about the move and the business in relation to those feelings? Look again. Who's still there standing between you and happiness?"

"Definitely resentment. Still right there slap bang in the middle; a burly security guard with no intention of moving aside."

"So, resentment?"

"Yes."

"Of what?"

"I can't be me. I can't choose for myself. It's stopping me from doing what I want," Annie said.

"And does it have a name?"

"Oh yes! It's bloody June again and Emma."

"Your sisters?"

Annie pressed her palms onto her thighs. "Mostly June."

"Can you remember the first time you felt that way?"

The question took Annie way back into her childhood. "I'm little. I'm not the favourite. No one's favourite. Mum loves the baby. Dad loves June. She excels at everything."

"You feel left out?"

"Uh-huh."

"What else?"

"I must have done something wrong. I don't know why they love me less. I try really hard to be easy, lovable, no trouble. I keep myself occupied. I feel sad. I feel invisible."

Dr Kath kept quiet, letting Annie's thoughts flow, observing without prompting.

"I'm the entertainer. I keep the peace. Boy, those two are demanding and difficult. June is bossy. I'm not the cause of the fights, but somehow I always get the blame. It's so unfair!" Annie broke off, hearing her own voice shouting out the phrase, customary amongst siblings everywhere. It could have been her own daughter speaking.

Dr Kath held back her next question, anticipating there might be more to follow. She waited, patient, the ticking clock making a bid for airwave domination in the absence of an immediate response.

Annie started again. "It's not my sisters at all."

"Can you explain that a bit more?"

"Well, I can see I blamed them, but it's not them is it? It's Mum and Dad."

"You feel they gave more love to your sisters?"

"Not exactly. I mean that's not really true, is it?"

"Tell me how it is," Dr Kath said, flicking back through her notes to check something.

"It feels like that to me but that's just me–my perspective."

"It could be. Is it different now?"

Annie considered the question carefully. "Yes, it is actually, as an adult I can see that."

"That's a great insight. Can we say the resentment belongs to little Annie. What does the little Annie need?"

"To know she is loved. To know she is good enough. . ."

As if she had just swilled out her mouth at the end of a long, drawn-out dentist's appointment, Annie sat with her eyes closed, woozy. She knew she was awake, though part of her still lingered in the past. Fully aware again of the wind battering the cottage, she opened her eyes, catching sight of the flames dancing in the hearth.

"Would you like some water?"

Annie nodded, taking the glass from Dr Kath's outstretched hand.

"Take your time. That was a deep session. You connected with parts of your memory long hidden away. It's normal to feel a little disoriented."

Sipping the water, she nodded again. She didn't want to speak yet. There was a lot to think about, but nothing she wanted to say. All this time, all those years she had been striving to meet expectations. She'd believed these were real. Looking at it now, she understood it was her own perception that had led her to believe she would never be as good as her siblings.

After a little while, some words popped into her head and with no filter, out of her mouth. "Really? I'm this way because *I* made it happen? My lack of self-worth is something *I've* created? Gosh that's a tough one to accept. Are you certain it's not just another thing I'm trying to blame myself for? I'm not sure."

"It's natural to feel a bit angry but Annie, you can choose to view this new understanding as either helpful or unhelpful. It's down to you. Your perception is nine tenths of your reality."

"I was just thinking that, literally, a few seconds ago."

"Having that awareness now can make a big difference. It can change how you see yourself and the choices you make in the future." Dr Kath nodded.

"I guess."

"Shall we conclude the session by summarising your points of discovery and planning your next steps?"

The fire continued to crackle. The carriage clock on the mantle had chimed in again.

"Um, yes, I think I'd like that."

"Let's see looking through my notes here you came to me because you were presented with an inheritance out of the blue. I think it's fair to say it threw you. You were concerned with your lack of business experience, the impact of uprooting your settled life and were uneasy about the prospect of moving closer to extended family. You have since detected a dissatisfaction with your current career and a low mood stemming from a sense of underachievement.

"For many years you attributed this to some kind of comparison your parents have made between you and your siblings–in effect, classic middle-child syndrome. You have been craving approval, especially from your father, but have now realised your self-esteem is something over which you have control. Does that sound about right?"

"Phew! There is a lot there, isn't there?"

"You covered a lot of ground in relatively few sessions."

"Would you say I'm ready to make a call on the big question?"

"More importantly, do *you* think you are ready?"

"Well, I still have the deadline to contend with. Either I decide or time decides for me, I guess." Annie stood, pulled her shoulders back and smoothed down her jumper. "Colin has been an absolute star. I'm sure we'll work out what's best and I've made one decision at least–I'm going to ask Mum and Dad what they think."

"Now that sounds like a plan," Dr Kath said.

Elizabeth

"Today's the day?" Andrew asked.

He had taken a five-minute window between meetings to give Elizabeth a quick call, on the off-chance he might catch her; something which was proving more and more difficult these last weeks. Was his allure fading?

"Yes, I'll be speaking with Samuel Hampton at three. I've arranged it between my team meeting and a disciplinary for Katie. Lovely girl, but totally ineffective."

"Hmm."

"Are you listening Andrew?" Elizabeth snapped. "You're doing that absent-minded thing again. You know how I hate having to repeat myself. Where are you anyway? I've not got long. Just nipped out for a mid-morning caffeine fix."

"Sorry, I just got an email from my solicitor. More crap about the financial settlement or something. God I sometimes wish I'd never married. You're lucky in that regard Elizabeth. No ties!"

"What?"

"I mean—you know."

"Yes, well, perhaps we should have a chat about all that later. Clearly it's not my priority at the moment. As you said, today's the day for more important decisions, isn't it?"

"Of course gorgeous. Sorry, I didn't mean to be distracted. You were saying?"

"The call with Mr Hampton later, do you think I should have a chat with Dr Kath first? Or see her even? I'm not convinced I've concluded all the work I need to do with her."

"Whatever you think darling. You know best."

"Probably. I'll consider it. I shall love you and leave you. Speak later."

About to click off the call, Elizabeth heard Andrew's after-thought wafting towards her. Returning the phone to her ear she just caught his last sentence.

"You'll be late again anyway. I thought that would be okay," he said.

"What? I missed that. I thought we were finished."

"I was just saying I might go see the kids this evening, assuming you'll be late home, as ever."

"Whatever suits you. I have to go."

Unbelievable! How could Andrew be so insensitive? So selfish? Here she was about to make the biggest decision of her life, second only to cutting ties with her family in the first place and there he was putting himself and other people first!

Snatching the cup holder from the sugar station, she shoved the coffee inside the cardboard sleeve and headed back to the office, anger percolating in her stomach. Far from being the stress reliever she had planned, ten minutes out of the office and her mood, re-entering the revolving door of the foyer, was as dark as the hot liquid she had just purchased.

Elizabeth barely acknowledged the security guards at the reception desk, as she headed for the lifts.

"I wouldn't want to be her next meeting. Got a face like thunder," the lanky one whispered.

"Yeah, it's not like Ms Braybrooke. I always enjoy our little chats. Usually she is totally charming," his rotund colleague replied.

"You what? Not to me. Very hoity-toity with me she is. Reckon she fancies you. Her bit of rough, eh?"

Ping.

The lift arrived and a bunch of slick-haired, shiny-suited youngsters piled out–trainees heading for an early lunch. To Elizabeth they seemed cocky and carefree. Oh, to be young and optimistic again.

Stepping in, the doors closed behind her, muffling their banter to nothing. Alone in the lift, her only company the panpipes, she examined herself in the mirrored wall. Ascending to her floor, she straightened her jacket and smoothed a few wisps of hair back into position. It was important to arrive back at her desk wearing her corporate persona.

Letting Andrew in may have been an error, but she had no intention of allowing her colleagues any insight into her introspection whatsoever. Floor nineteen.

Ping.

The doors opened. Elizabeth made her presence felt.

"Right team. You've got five minutes. Meeting room six. No stragglers please. Time is money and mine is far more valuable than yours, so don't waste it!"

She strode with purpose to her office, her authority withering colleagues in her wake. Nothing new there. No one liked her. Everyone feared her. To them it was just another day in the office. Elizabeth watched the worker bees buzzing, gathering their projections, assignment briefs and longlists. She revelled in the power she held over them.

Returning to her own number-one task, she dialled Dr Kath, hoping she wouldn't reach the dippy receptionist who always insisted she take a message for a call-back. Clearly, she was unaware of Elizabeth's importance.

"Dr Kath's office, Trudy speaking. Can I help you?"

"Yes Trudy. Put me through to Dr Kath please. It is urgent I speak to her and I only have two minutes. I'll wait."

"I'm terribly sorry, she is in with a client at the moment. Who's calling? Can I ask her to call you back?"

"Really?" Elizabeth sighed. "Must you always filter her calls? I only need a brief conversation. It's Ms Braybrooke."

"Yes Ms Braybrooke. It's my job to manage Dr Kath's communications. She is genuinely occupied, often, I'm sorry if that causes you an inconvenience. Can I help?"

"Can she call me back at twelve-thirty?"

"That should be fine. I'll pop it into the calendar. Thanks for your patience. Dr Kath will call you then."

Elizabeth tucked the leather folder under her arm, phone in one hand, remains of the coffee in her other, and swished her way from her desk to the head of the table in meeting room six.

For once the team were on form. Elizabeth chaired the meeting as expertly as ever, but this time hardly needed to intervene. At last, they had got the message. There was less waffle, and more identification of suitable candidates for key campaigns. Job done.

A rare smile spread across her face. "Thanks guys. That was great. Looks like the research strategies are paying off."

Most of the team filed out, chatting like kids at break time. Only Katie held back for fear of being trampled by the hoards.

"Ah yes, Katie, could we move our meeting forward a little?"

"No problem." She hesitated. "Should I call Janata in HR and let her know?"

"Don't worry. I've already asked her and she's free. Best get it done sooner if we can."

Elizabeth watched Katie's dejected figure hover. Honestly, where was her resilience?

Bang on twelve-thirty her phone buzzed. She shooed Katie away, with further hand signals requesting she close the door on her way out.

"Elizabeth, it's Dr Kath. You called and said it was urgent?"

"Yes, it's D-day today. You may remember?"

"Of course. I have a few minutes to speak. How can I help you?"

"I'm having trouble making the final decision."

"Have you had any insights since we last met? Anything to give you a clue about the source of your indecision?"

"Not really. Aside from the obvious mother, father, sister stuff."

"Could you expand on that a little?"

"You know. The side taking and the rejection. I mean, really, they pushed me away. Understandably I'm doubting the wisdom of returning to the den of vipers."

"You're not compelled to visit them are you?" Dr Kath asked

"No but they'll be round the corner even if they aren't part of the deal. I'm really not happy with the prospect of seeing them, especially my father."

"You feel he let you down?"

"Without question!" Elizabeth thrust her chin forward and pursed her lips. "He was meant to be on my side!"

"You need to sit down and think about how that impacts you now. Which is more important? Starting your new life? Starting your new venture? Or maintaining the separation of the last twenty-odd years."

"You think?" She spat the words out like an angry teenager.

"Elizabeth."

"Yes?"

"You have some strong emotion there. It's understandable. Today is a big day for you. Are you alright?"

"No, I'm bloody irritated with everyone to be honest."

"Including me, my assistant and I'm guessing your colleagues too," Dr Kath said.

'Oh, everyone. All ordinary people appear to be idiotic to me in some way or other. Today it's amplified ten-fold."

"Is it?"

"Yes. It. Is!"

"Or is it your way of coping with your emotions, maybe? Taking it out on others." Dr Kath let the idea sink in before continuing. "I'm sorry Elizabeth. I need to finish now. I have another appointment. Do you have room to squeeze in one more session? I do think it would be beneficial. I have a slot later at three."

Elizabeth took a deep breath. "Let me have a think. I'd need to rearrange a couple of things. You're probably right. I'll call back to confirm later. Look I'm sorry if I came across as uncompromising. It was not intentional."

"No problem."

"Later then."

Dulcie

"Here we are."

"Indeed."

"I can't believe this is it. Dr Kath I'll always be grateful to you for helping me out. Being here with this thing hanging over me, I'm not sure how I would have coped without your support."

"You're welcome Dulcie. Don't forget you're the one who has been doing all the work. Really, I'm just a facilitator."

"I think you perform far more than just that role. You are too modest."

"Thank you again. Now, is there anything you'd like to discuss before we get started?"

"Nope, I kinda wanna get on with it, you know? I've been doing lots of thinking, but it's still quite muddled in here." Dulcie tapped her temple with her forefinger to emphasise the point.

"That's fine. Can I just say though, you may not get everything clear in the next fifty minutes. Don't put yourself under too much pressure or set unrealistic expectations, okay?"

"Yeah sure."

"What would you like to work on?"

"It really is the take it or don't take it decision. Crunch time."

"Great. Make yourself comfortable and when you are ready, close your eyes."

Focused on her breathing, Dulcie enjoyed the relaxed sensation of her hypnotic trance. As instructed, she let her mind wander back to a happy time.

"Where has that happy memory taken you?" Dr Kath asked.

"I'm with Peter. It's a time when I'm carefree. I am literally glowing with happiness. It's like a sunrise spreading slowly through me, bathing me in warmth."

"What do you see?"

"We're outside in a park. I sense lots of people are around us but I can only see Peter. His face is really close to mine. He's been chewing a mint. I can smell its sweetness on his breath. The baby's in the buggy beside us. We're lying on his Pete's coat for a rug, propped up on our elbows side by side. He is my mirror image, our postures perfectly matched."

"Are you talking or silent?"

"Hmm I think we're discussing the future."

"Focus on his face, can you see him talking?"

"Yes, he suddenly looks very serious. His forehead is wrinkled like ripples imprinted in the sand at low tide."

"What's he saying?"

"Something about leaving."

"Leaving where? The park?"

"No, it's more important than that. Bigger, more crucial."

"How are you responding?"

"I'm fine. I'm not upset. Actually, I'm quite excited, butterflies in my tummy excited."

"Anything else?"

"Yes I remember. He's talking about leaving the country, moving to Australia. . . it's the moment we decide. I want to be with him. I don't care about anyone else."

"Are you certain in your decision? Any doubts?"

"Right back there, I can feel it at the back of my mind."

"What is it?"

"A niggle. A grumble. It's pulling me like a belt caught on a door handle. I have to shuffle about to get unstuck and break free."

"Put some more words to it for me. Tell me."

"It feels like. . . it feels like sod you then!"

"Who do you want to say that to?"

"It's them. They're going to miss out. If they can't be happy for me, if they can't see my baby is a blessing. Sod them. We'll bugger off halfway round the world and I won't care if we never see them again!"

Dr Kath gave Dulcie another gentle nudge. "Who are they?"

"Mum, Dad, the rest of the family. Everyone pretends to be nice to Peter, but they blame him."

"For what?"

"Everything. He's not good enough for them. They are disappointed in me."

"And yet you're happy, on the grass, making plans?" Dr Kath asked gently.

"Yep. That's why I said sod them. That's it. Defiance! That's what I feel. We'll make a good life without them. It's their loss."

"Now come back to the present. How about working with them? How does the prospect make you feel?"

"I don't know. I guess it would be a bit awkward. But I

reckon I'd be okay. Not sure about them though!" Dulcie said.

"Would you say your pregnancy was the trigger for all those feelings, or is there something else?"

Dulcie frowned. "I'm not sure. How do you mean?"

"Perhaps you've always been a little bit separate, self-reliant even?"

"Maybe."

"Let's go back a little further. Can you think of a happy time when you're still at home with them? Anything come to mind?"

Dulcie paused, letting an earlier memory rise to the surface. "Ooh yes. I'm quite little. I'm twirling in a pretty white dress. My father has picked me up and I'm spinning through the air. I'm loving it."

"Is he saying anything to you?"

"He's smiling. He's telling me I'll always be his special little girl. Even when the baby comes."

"Whose baby? Yours?" Dr Kath asked.

"No, no, this is before. It's odd. I've no idea what it means... now it's murky and I'm sad."

This could be significant. Dr Kath waited. Was Dulcie on the verge of a breakthrough? She seemed unruffled but quiet and still, as if this was a missing memory. Something didn't quite fit. "Shall we explore this further?"

"There's nothing else there... I really don't remember..."

They'd reached a dead end. Dr Kath changed direction.

"Okay, don't worry," she said. "Can you think about the next few days? What else is there you'd like to resolve before your decision on the inheritance, if anything?"

"I don't think there's anything else."

"Nothing to do with Matty?"

"Nope. That's a separate decision I have to deal with at some point," Dulcie said firmly.

"You're sure?"

"I'm not trying to unravel that one yet. Best to put it to one side."

"That's fine, let's begin now to become aware of our surroundings. Begin to notice light in the room. Gradually become aware of the sounds of traffic outside the building and voices in the corridor. Pay attention to your body and how it feels in contact with the couch. Perhaps wriggle your fingers and toes. Notice my voice, louder and clearer, and when you are ready, open your eyes."

Dulcie sat for a moment, blinking in the light. In the short time since she'd met Dr Kath she had begun to enjoy the process in a perverse way. Coming back to full consciousness always left her serene, but a bit out of it too. As if she were still only half awake. Whilst the self-discovery sometimes sat awkwardly, the overall feeling of calm and wellbeing at the end of each session had become addictive.

"How was that today?" Dr Kath asked.

"Good, good. Just getting used to being back in the room." Dulcie smiled.

"You look happier."

"I am. I'm reflecting on some of that stuff. It's good. I'm clearer now. Thank you so much."

"My pleasure."

"Do you know what's made me smile most?"

"Tell me," Dr Kath said leaning forward.

"I've realised what's most important to me. I know I've not got it all worked out yet, but that doesn't matter, you know?"

"I understand."

"It feels like I can put all the tricky stuff to one side and in some ways I can go back to being me," Dulcie explained. "I know it sounds clichéd but it really does seem that way. Focus on the good and be grateful."

"That's not a bad philosophy to have. Now take your time and when you're ready I'll see you out in reception."

Dr Kath left Dulcie alone in the consulting room to gather her thoughts.

Taking a few deep breaths, Dulcie filled her lungs with the scents of the expertly blended essential oils emanating from the diffuser nearby. She swung her legs off the couch, pulled on her boots with the tabs at the back and wallowed in the satisfaction she had come to her decision. Now all she had to do was put her plans into action.

She glanced around to check she'd not forgotten any possessions, and headed out through the same door Dr Kath had used a few moments earlier. Dulcie was on a mission and the sooner she got back in touch with Samuel, the sooner she could make it a reality.

Liza

Liza sat on the same shabby chair, in the same draughty corridor, fretting again and eager to be invited up the stairs. Truth be told, she had thought a move to Gloucestershire was a foregone conclusion. Until a few days ago, it had seemed her only means of escape from Gino and his threatening ways.

One of the residents shook off the rain from her umbrella, as she backed into the porch, retreating from the deluge falling from the charcoal skies. Liza counted her blessings, knowing she too would have been caught in the downpour had she not accepted Sheena's kind offer of a lift. It had saved her valuable minutes, not to mention metres she would otherwise have had to walk to the bus stop from home.

She had kept the refuge's exact location safe by asking her friend to drop her close by in the Waitrose carpark. She'd be buying Sheena a great big bunch of flowers there on her way back.

"You don't have to be a weather forecaster to know those clouds are full and ready to burst, eh?" Sheena had said.

Leaning back down to reply through the open window, Liza said, "What am I thinking? The showers in Gloucestershire are meant to be even worse. Anyway thanks for the lift again doll."

"No worries. Need collecting?"

"Nah, you're alright. I'll get the bus back to Angelo's school. Pick him up on the way home."

Liza had waved as Sheena had slotted herself back into the traffic, with a nifty move that would make even a stunt driver envious.

At the memory, gratitude for her wonderful friend welled up again and propelled Liza to rush to help the poor woman at the door, who was still struggling to haul her shopping bags inside.

"There you go. Is that everything?"

"Yeah thanks. Got myself all tangled up with that bloody umbrella and stuff. Are you new here?" the woman asked.

"I'm just visiting upstairs," Liza said.

"Dr Kath? She's great."

"Yeah she is. Been seeing her a bit recently. Think this'll be my last time. At one point it looked like I'd be moving in, but not now."

"How come?"

"Things have changed. It's complicated," Liza said.

"Isn't it always? Anyways, better get in and get my stuff away. Thanks again." The woman smiled before walking off.

Liza returned to her uncomfortable position for no more than a couple of minutes, before she heard her name called. She felt odd, making her way up the stairs towards Dr Kath, who waited for her on the landing. She wondered if this really would be her last visit.

She had become so accustomed to the monotonous drumbeat of her life. For as long as she could remember, some man or other had been in control of her movements. Liza couldn't really comprehend the likely changes ahead.

"Afternoon Liza, good to see you again. Please do come in and take a seat. How are you doing? You seem calmer since our last meeting. How are the plans for the move going?"

Liza sat down and bit her lip. She wanted Dr Kath's approval and didn't want to say the wrong thing.

"I'm fine. Really good actually."

"You seem a little unsure."

"No, honestly, I am much, much happier. Calmer I think you said. Yes, much calmer."

"There's something else?"

"Yes but I'm just not sure what you'll think," Liza said.

"It doesn't matter what I think. I'm not here to judge you." Nodding by way of reassurance, Dr Kath deliberately kept her voice soft. "Why don't you tell me about it?"

"You see, the thing is now Gino's out of the way, kinda out of the picture, I'm looking at the situation a little differently."

"He's out of the way? How do you mean?" Dr Kath frowned.

"He's been arrested. Some kinda fraud charges I think. I don't know all the details. Anyway, the point is, I don't have to run away any more. Not if I don't want to. So, now my decision is all about whether I should stay or go for all the other reasons."

"Are you worried I would think badly of you if you stayed?"

"Maybe. Actually, it's more about me wasting your time," Liza confessed. "I mean you've been incredibly helpful and if I stay, what was the point of seeing you? If nothing changes, you know?"

Dr Kath moved her hands together from their resting place in her lap, matching the pads of each finger like the trusses of a roof.

"You have not wasted my time at all. Please put that out of your mind. My role here is to support you through your decision in an objective manner. If you feel the threat has now passed, that's great news. We can still work together through anything else you need to consider. Perhaps you could look at it this way: if Gino was a push factor, we could try and find out if you have a pull factor, something pulling you towards Gloucester?"

"Sounds like a good idea. Thank you for being understanding. I just thought, since I no longer have the extreme emotions, I don't need to keep going with you." Liza had a lingering concern. She wavered, unable to voice it. What if they strayed too far into the past, or uncovered something else to upset her equilibrium? She had only just got herself feeling level again.

"As ever Liza, I'm here to help you," Dr Kath said. "My aim, as far as possible, is for you to reach a clear understanding of the pros and cons. Life will be full of change if you decide to leave London. If I can help you take the next step, either way, with your eyes open, I'll have done a good job."

Liza took a deep breath. "Thanks."

"Ready?"

"Yes."

"You are safe. Everything feels tranquil. Now, we're going to take a walk and explore the past. You're walking up the path to your home, back from school, what do you expect to find when you go inside?"

"Mum will be there and maybe my sisters too. It'll probably be busy. They might ignore me. They usually do."

"How do you feel about that?"

"Okay, I suppose. I'm used to it. Never been the special one," Liza said.

"Let's open the door. What do you see?"

Liza frowned. "Mountains of school kit on the floor. Muddy shoes left where they parted company with their feet. Mum coming through from the kitchen. She's telling me to make sure I've put my shoes away properly and take my clobber upstairs. Typical. She's having a go at me, but not them."

"What do you do?"

"I do as I'm told. I try not to be any trouble. Anyway, I can look after myself. I don't mind. I have my friends."

"Let's move forward now. When do things change?"

"In what way?" Liza asked.

Dr Kath referred to her notes. "You mentioned a falling out." She flicked through the pages. "Yes, here it is. You moved in with Jody at sixteen."

"Yeah, my best friend."

"What made you leave home though? What changed? Lots of people fall out with their siblings but not many move out at sixteen."

Liza shrugged. "Plenty do. Most of my friends did. Who needs parents and sisters anyway?"

"You just wanted independence? Or was there something else?"

"Both. I stuck it to 'em. If they didn't want to be there for me, fuck the lot of 'em."

"You felt rejected?"

"Too bloody right!" Liza snapped. "First time I'd been in trouble. I knew Mum would be angry, but thought she'd come round but oh no! She hit the roof. I remember the moment clearly. Fuck you, I thought, I'll leave then. I can look after myself."

"Interesting, you said that before."

"I did? What?"

"You used the phrase 'look after myself.'"

"Story of my life that is."

"Interesting. The whole of your life?" Dr Kath asked, suspecting there was more. "Is there a time, further back say, when you did feel looked after?"

"Maybe."

"Would you like to take a look?"

"I dunno. What will happen?" Liza's body tensed.

Dr Kath repeated her reassurance. "You are safe. No one will hurt you here. You are in control."

"I'm safe," Liza repeated.

"Good. Now imagine you are that little girl. Bring any happy times to the front of your mind. Really feel them, experience them as if you are there, this very moment. Tell me what you see."

Liza breathed easily. "I see my dad with a camera. He's smiling and I'm smiling back. I'm in a soft white dress with a silky bow. He's taking a picture and I pose. I like posing, I love the attention."

"Are you alone, the two of you?"

"No June is there and Mum. We're all smiling. I feel gooey-happy and loved."

"Where are you?" Dr Kath asked.

"Outside our front door and it's sunny and warm. My tummy is skipping. . . someone goes round the side of the house, down the alleyway to fetch the pram. I think it's Mum.

She asks me if I want to help but I don't like the alleyway. It's dark and smelly. I don't like the dark. She tells me to wait with Dad. I'm holding Dad's hand, really tight." Liza's tone shifted.

"Still happy?"

"Not any more. Mum comes out with the pram. Everyone else is cooing but I feel tears coming. I feel odd. Right and wrong, hot and cold, happy and sad."

"Are you still with your dad?"

"Yes but he's let go of my hand. He's leaning over the pram. Now he's cooing and saying come on princess. Now I'm crying. I'm your Princess, Daddy, I tell him but his princess was baby Emma."

Liza's imagined tears, now real tears, trickled down her face, plopping in ever increasing wet patches on her top. "Can I leave now please? I want to leave."

"I understand. Take a moment. Imagine your safe place. You're no longer that little girl." Dr Kath gave her some space to settle again, a break from her abreaction. "Shall we go on? Or shall we finish?"

"I'll go on."

"Let's go back to when you left home, the trouble you experienced at that time. How does it affect you now?"

"Don't think about it much." Liza frowned.

"Could it have an impact if you move back?"

"Nah, I don't think so".

"But it was a big deal?"

"Yes, but I'm older and wiser. I'm not bothered by it anymore."

Dr Kath observed carefully. Liza's body language gave

no indication of internal conflict. She pushed a bit harder, suspecting there was something else there. "Let's presume you bump into them. You've moved back and you bump into them. What might happen?"

"Nothing."

"You see them in the supermarket, picking up some potatoes."

"Yes, that might happen."

"And you have no reaction?"

"No."

"You've not seen them in–" She looked down at her notes. "Twenty-odd years and you have no reaction at all?"

"Nope."

"What does that tell you?"

"I walked away for a reason. It was horrid at the time. It changed my life because they wouldn't help. But do you know what? It's their loss. They weren't there for me when they should have been. I've moved on." Liza's speech quickened; her shoulders raised.

"As I said, imagine they are there, standing in front of you at the potatoes. What would you say to them?"

Liza's expression turned into a snarl. "Hello Mum. Have you got over it yet?"

"What does she say?"

"She'd probably say over what dear?'"

"And you say?"

Liza couldn't get her words out fast enough. "The dreadful thing you couldn't cope with. The thing which made you drive me away. It just wasn't the done thing, was it? You and your perfect family up on the hill. You couldn't have your perfect life ruined by my scummy boyfriend, could you? That was bad enough, but when I confided in you, it got worse. You put your foot down. You said I couldn't break your precious Catholic rules. That was it. You didn't want to know. You didn't want to help. You wanted no part of it. I had to go through that fucking abortion all on my own! I wasn't surprised. Tell you why? Ever since your precious Emma was born, I've been invisible to you!"

"Liza, when you are ready you can open your eyes."

Liza breathed out deeply. She crossed her arms and hugged herself tight. "I feel drained. That was tough,"

"Yes, you covered a lot there. You did really well." Dr Kath offered Liza a tissue. "You want to wipe your face?"

Liza's fingers touched her wet cheek. "Was I crying?" She dabbed her eyes with the tissue. "I mean, I knew I'd been through it, but I'd no idea how much pain I still carry. I thought I'd accepted it. Obviously not."

"How does this affect your view of the gift, if at all?"

"Good question. I'm not sure if it does really."

"In trance, you did display a strong sense of independence. Typically a trait this deep-seated will tend to prevail. It's just that–"

"What happened was a big thing, with my family, I mean. Getting pregnant and not keeping it is massive anyway." Liza shifted in her chair, crossing and uncrossing her legs. Her words reverberated around the room.

"Is this the first time you've spoken about it?"

"No but it's been a long time. I try to focus all my energies on Angelo instead. Trying to look forward, you know?"

"I understand. Do you know why they forced you out? Why it went bad?"

"I don't think it actually happened like that. It was just I'd felt left out for a long time. My sisters had always had all the support, I was just stuck in the middle."

"Sometimes the recollection in trance becomes an exaggerated version of reality. Think of it a bit like gravy where the flavours intensify, as it's reduced on the heat."

"Hmm, that makes a bit more sense. I remember it took a few months to reach breaking point."

"Interestingly, you seem reasonably certain you will cope if your paths cross but of course, you can't predict their reaction."

"They probably wouldn't recognise me."

"But if you end up in business with them?"

Liza stared ahead, her stomach tightening. "If I decide to take it on, I will make it work. I'll have to for Angelo." A smile spread from her lips to her eyes, dewy and brimming with love; any family conflict would be no match for its power. "Talking of which, I'd better get going. Need to get back in time for the school run. Thanks again for everything."

Dr Kath stood to close the meeting with a handshake. "Best of luck Liza. I hope you find happiness in whichever direction you take."

Pia

"You alright up there? Fancy a cuppa?" Helena called from the kitchen.

"Love one Mum. Don't worry I'll come down."

Pia removed her reading glasses from the perch on the end of her nose, rubbed her temples, stood and stretched. Gosh eleven-thirty already. No wonder she needed a break.

She had been up with the sunrise, woken up by the neighbour's cockerel. Once awake, she couldn't get back to sleep. Only a few days now until D-day. She was too excited. She had crept downstairs, to avoid waking Helena and made herself a tea before heading back up to her room, thankful for the constant supply of hot water from the AGA kettle; none of this modern, fast-boil, noisy beverage preparation and much more considerate for the early-morning riser.

Popping the mug on her bedside table, she had grabbed her laptop and snuggled up in the duvet for some serious research. Why not make the most of a few hours of peace and quiet?

Deciding to delve into the house history first, she'd wondered how much she might find online. The recent history was sketchy to say the least. Helena had talked a little about Sir James and his reclusiveness. Pia presumed there might be some more information from even further back, before the property had fallen into disrepair. It was such an impressive place and must have been stunning in its heyday.

As is often the way, once she had got started, she had lost herself in the quest for answers. After trawling through hundreds of entries relating to Lord Hyett, the founder, she found she had developed an affection for him, as if he were still alive and able to articulate his aspirations. The similarity with stories of her father struck a chord; he too had been a man full of determination and grand vision.

The successful merchant had enjoyed a reputation for sound business savvy, but unfortunately, his poor health posed a perpetual threat to his high-society ambitions. After much world travel, as his health deteriorated he had needed to find a site to lay down his roots and invest in a semi-retired convalescence.

Excerpts from books, historical-society web pages, and county-library archives led her down burrows. Some of the records were missing; minutes of parish-council papers were referenced but yet to be digitised. A trip to the library looked on the cards.

Then, she had unearthed a fact that made her heart skip. Something she couldn't wait to share with PJ. If she had been a superstitious person, she would have seen it as a sign. It was certainly serendipitous. She wasn't due to see PJ for a couple of days, and decided it was best to reveal it to him face to face. She could watch his reaction. In the meantime she could tell her mum. It was too good to keep it to herself.

Flinging back the duvet, she shoved her feet into fluffy slippers, pulled a chunky fleece over her head and shuffled downstairs, beckoned by the aroma of freshly baked bread. Pia was not the only member of the household to have had a productive morning. She skipped into the kitchen, as much as a pair of slippers allows.

"You're full of the joys this morning darling!" Helena said.

"Full of the joys of autumn," Pia replied.

"And what's wrong with that? We both love autumn, don't we? Cereal or toast?"

"It's fine, I'm almost too late for breakfast. Happy to wait for your delicious bread if that's alright? It is for lunch, isn't it? Please tell me you are not torturing me with that smell and I have to wait more than half an hour for it?"

"You're in luck. It'll be out in about ten minutes. Here's your tea." She handed Pia an earthenware mug in speckled greys and blues from the local artisan pottery, steaming with strong tea.

"Thanks Mum."

"So, what's your excitement all about? What's got you so chipper this morning?"

"Chipper! Not heard that for ages."

"Oi cheeky, you know what I mean. I'm not that old fashioned."

"No, of course not, but you are adorably traditional."

"I wouldn't say that. There's lots of, how you would say—edginess to me. You just don't know all about it. I got up to all sorts before you blessed my life. Now go on, tell me what's got you like a kid in a sweetshop?"

"That's a bit of a build-up Mum, it's not that exciting." Pia downplayed her discovery, realising Helena might not share her delight. "It's just some research I've been doing on the house and the guy who had it built, Lord Hyett."

"I vaguely remember some of his story. Some merchant or other?"

"Yes, that's right. Well, I was digging around this morning and you'll never guess what."

"What?"

"He was suffering with ill health, asthma or something, and needed to live somewhere away from city pollution. He chose the site of the Big House for its elevated position and fresh country breezes."

"Right and. . . ?"

"Yes and guess what he named it? Drum roll please–Buenos Aires!"

"No! Really?"

"Yep. Spooky huh?"

"That'll be great for your marketing, won't it?"

"Exactly."

"Does PJ know?"

"Not yet, or at least I don't think so. I'm gonna pull everything together and share it with him on Tuesday before we see Samuel. I'm going to have a go at drafting the about the house section of the website. Nobody can object to that surely?"

"Whatever you think's best darling." The kitchen timer buzzed, baking time over. "I want to hear all about what else you found. Let me get this bread out and you can fill me in and I'll tell you a little about Sir James, the one who owned it before you."

"Technically, it was Pablo who owned it Mum. I've inherited it, or part of it to be accurate, from him."

"Oh! That's a shame."

"It was his investment, so, whatever feelings I have about him, I do think it was up to him, who to pass it on to."

"Don't be silly darling, not the inheritance–the bread! Look, it's overdone at one end."

Pia looked. "It's fine Mum. I like it crusty. You're just a perfectionist."

Loaf now resting on the cooling rack, Helena grabbed a stool and sat opposite her daughter, ready to download her knowledge. "Now, you may not realise it, but after Lord Hyett, the house eventually came down into Braybrooke ownership until Sir James died a few years ago."

"Really?" Incredulous, Pia rattled off a machine-gun-magazine's worth of questions. "What? Your relatives? How did I not know this? For all my searching this morning, I never made the connection. How bizarre is that? Is it a coincidence? Do you think Pablo knew?"

"He did. During his search for you, he found out Sir James, your grandfather, had passed on. When the house came up for sale through a sealed auction he bought it. He wanted it to return to the family and for it to be your legacy."

"Sir James, the recluse, was my grandfather? Mum! Honestly, how come you never told me? Here's me researching away in the murky light of dawn and you already know all about the house!"

"Not all about it. I've not been there since I was a young woman."

Helena turned away, pretending she had spotted something of great interest in the garden. She moved over to the window, her back to Pia, closing the conversation.

Remorseful, Pia let her off the hook. They had always been

so close; she could tell it was best not to push any further for now. Her mum would open up when she was ready. Still, it was strange. One minute Helena had volunteered her help, the next she had revealed a connection and then clammed up. It was totally at odds with her usual candour.

"I'll head upstairs for a shower, shall I Mum?"

Helena replied with an absent-minded, "Yes."

What on earth needed that much contemplation? Pia wondered if she would ever find out, as she returned to her room to prepare for the day.

*

By the following Tuesday, the whole exchange still dominating her thoughts, she needed to talk to someone other than her mum. She couldn't shake the feeling of being shut out.

"But PJ, I don't understand. She's never kept anything back before it's just not like her–pass that screwdriver would you?"

"I don't know. I don't know her that well. Which one by the way?"

"The medium-sized Phillips one please. I *do* know her, so if I think it's odd, it must be, right?"

They continued their discussion with PJ at the base of the stepladder and Pia at the top, until she secured the final bracket for the pelmet above the drawing-room bay window.

"What are you doing up there anyway? I thought we were meant to be dancing again. You did say you want to be as good as me, which, by the way, will never happen."

"Oi cheeky! I'm finished now." Pia descended with confidence. "I'll have you know I can turn my hand to most things once I've set my mind to it–DIY, Tango, you name it. I was just fixing the curtains. Someone must have yanked them too hard at some point and left them drooping unsupported. Last time we visited it bugged me. I thought I'd do something about it."

"Hmm, but we did say we'd leave it until everyone was on board."

"Or not?"

"True. Remind me, when's the meeting planned?"

"Next week. The fifteenth of October. Look, I know we said we'd leave it, but it's just a quick repair and I feel responsible for giving the house its best chance to make a great first impression. Don't ask me why, I just do," she said.

"Alright then. Now come on. Let's get on with our practice and work on perfecting those *sacadas*. If we can get them a fraction as excited with our demonstration, as you were when you first started dancing, we'll have half a hope of making this crazy idea of Dad's happen."

Pia collapsed the ladder as PJ gathered up the tool kit and together they stored them neatly against the long wall opposite the window.

Their journey through the corridors from the front to the back of the house took a good five minutes. They ended up in another oak-panelled room with large doors opening onto a raised terrace. It was a smaller version of the room where they had first danced. In its most recent incarnation it had been used as a bedroom for the ailing Sir James. Now empty of furniture, parquet floor exposed by the removal of the rugs, it felt like a delightful space to practice the intimacies of their steps.

"It needs a lot of work, but I do love this room," Pia said, looking around.

"Me too. I can see it being used for my one-to-one tuition. The light here is fabulous."

"Yes and the air, with those doors open in spring. Mind you that's not surprising bearing in mind the name of the house. What did you think when I told you? You didn't say."

"Oh, I think it's a wonderful way to tie the house into our story but there are missing pieces still, with your mum closing up about the family connection."

"She did hint at something just as I was leaving to come here. She said there's something else she needed to talk about, something to do with old man James and her sister."

PJ pulled away to examine her face. "Sister?"

"Yep. I know. I didn't even know she had a sister. I'm beginning to think I don't know my mum at all."

part four

the decision

October 2007

Annie

Mr S Hampton
Currie, Hampton and Stephens LLP
Hampton House
32 Clarence Street
Gloucester

5 October 2007

The Tango Trust

Dear Mr Hampton,

I am writing to inform you of my decision regarding the potential inheritance first explained to me at our meeting of 25th August 2007.

As you can imagine it's been a difficult process. If the decision had been mine alone, perhaps I would have found my deliberations more straightforward. As it is, the prescriptive nature of the trust's conditional clauses, the uncertainty around my potential co-directors/unknown beneficiaries and the real value of the gift in practical terms, have led me to conclude, a return to Gloucester would not be in the best interests of either myself or my family.

As you will remember from our last discussion, my research found most of the funds would be tied up in the renovation of the building and grounds and the remainder needed to cover the business start-up and running costs.

With two children settled in their schools and an established career elsewhere, I feel it would be foolish to take on such a venture, especially as I have been offered a new post as acting Deputy Head, following the sudden departure of a colleague. Despite the generosity of the gift on paper, I am unable to see enough positives to compensate for the upheaval, or financial insecurity of the move.

To a lesser extent I am wary of the secrecy surrounding the unknown benefactor and the connection she or he may have to my family. As you know, the Braybrookes are an interesting bunch but I, for one, do not like surprises. Clearly, since the individual is no longer alive, it is difficult to know who to thank. I will therefore leave it to you to communicate my gratitude to the necessary parties.

Thank you very much for your patience and support over the past weeks. I'm sure I'll bump into you next time I'm back visiting my parents and look forward to doing so.

Yours sincerely,
Annie Bradley (née Braybrooke)

Elizabeth

Mr S Hampton
Currie, Hampton and Stephens LLP
Hampton House
32 Clarence Street
Gloucester

8 October 2007

The Tango Trust

Dear Mr Hampton,

I have decided, on balance, I shall not be accepting "the windfall with strings attached." Recent changes in my personal circumstances have led me to believe I am better off choosing the life I have already established for myself. Being financially independent, it was never about acquiring assets or wealth, more the business opportunity, which initially attracted me.

I feel there are certain conditions which prevent the viability of the proposition. My primary concern being the location of the house and its proximity to my estranged family.

Having done my due diligence, I believe such a venture to be foolish in these times of economic uncertainty. Further, should my sister, June, have been involved, I would not have been able to participate. To be clear, this is one risk I am unwilling to take.

There are many twists and turns in life and, whilst I could see the venture's appeal, this is a path along which I am disinclined to travel.

I close by thanking you for your time.

Yours Sincerely,
Elizabeth Braybrooke.

Dulcie

From: hello@dulcie.com
To: Matt841@gmail.com
Subject: Us

Hi Matty,

Please forgive the late night email. I've been struggling with jet lag for most of my trip and somehow now it's getting worse as I prepare to fly home. Maybe it's my body clock trying to adjust ahead of time. Anyway I doubt you're awake and if I'm honest I hope you're not. It is easier if you're fast asleep—easier for me, anyway.

I've been trying to pluck up the courage to phone you all day but I'm afraid I've taken the coward's way out. I'm not sure I'm strong enough to stick to my guns if I hear your voice and I don't want you to argue with me, in person or by email.

No doubt you've worked out by now I've decided to decline the inheritance. You probably think I'm mad and would tell me it is a chance of a lifetime. Thing is, it's not as simple as that.

Knowing how you (we) feel, made it even harder to work it through and I'm truly sorry for stirring up the past. Please don't think badly of me. I've loved every minute we've spent together, but now it's time for me to go home. You deserve to hear my reasons and if I could articulate them clearly I would. All I can say is, in the end, the reality hit me. My life is not here anymore. This is not my home. I chose to leave all those years ago. I know some people thought I was running away. Actually I was running towards my future, to a fresh start. I still have everything waiting back there for me, and more. It's taken me the last few weeks to realise that.

In the end, that's what matters and no crazy, madcap, Tango dancing thing can ever hope to compete. You and I know you were my first true love. Nothing will ever take that away but we just can't be together now. Too much has changed. I'm so sorry to hurt you this way and I do hope you'll understand it's for the best.

T.T.F.N. Dulcie x

The cursor hovered over the send icon. Seconds multiplied to minutes before Dulcie's brain sent the impulse to her finger, delivering the desired click of the mouse. It was done.

Pia

Pia picked up the tatty back-copy of a celebrity magazine. Thumbed by many a previous client, it could no longer be described as glossy. Once again she waited for her sister. This time, instead of skulking outside, hiding in her car, she sat in the outer office of Currie, Hampton and Stephens, eager for their first meeting. A childish excitement fluttered inside. Would they hit it off? Would there be a genetic resemblance? Would she know more about the family history and be able to fill in the missing pieces?

She and PJ had decided it might be too much for him to be there too. He'd suggested he would wait in a coffee shop and join them when the coast was clear.

"Call me when you're done," he'd said.

Pia exhaled. The sound reminiscent of a hot-air-balloon burner: forceful, steady, loud.

Mrs Rathbone couldn't miss the long out-breath. Peering over the top of her glasses in Pia's direction, she asked, "Are you all right dear?"

"Fine thanks just a little nervous."

"That's understandable. Are you sure you wouldn't like a cup of tea? It's no trouble, honestly."

"No, no. I'm good." She glanced at her watch. "It's only a few more minutes to wait, hopefully."

She went back to studying her magazine, flicking through the pages, pretending not to be interested in the gossip. She never bought these things but they were a guilty pleasure. She always surprised herself when she got caught up in the soap-star romances and double-page photo shoots in glamorous locations. Nothing wrong with a little bit of escapism now and again.

The door to Samuel's office opened just enough for him to poke his head round. "Ms Braybrooke? We're ready for you now, if you'd like to join us."

She discarded the mag on the coffee table, fumbling around to collect her paraphernalia.

Observing her fluster, Samuel said, "No rush, we've plenty of time, when you're ready."

"It's just this weather. You end up covering all options just in case. Coats, scarves, gloves, layers, umbrellas, then you end up losing half of them, because the sun's come out and you forget you brought them with you."

Samuel laughed. "I'm the same."

Grateful for his patience and efforts to put her at ease, doubting he was ever this flustered, Pia followed him into his office.

"Hello." Liza stood and offered her hand.

After dumping her stuff on the nearest chair, and completing an awkward handshake and hug manoeuvre, Pia stood back with a quizzical smile. After a brief pause she broke the ice with her second attempt at a hug, which was much more successful.

"Oh, it's great to finally meet you. I'm sure it's all a bit overwhelming for you. I should know. I was in your shoes just a short while ago, trying to get my head around my Dad's reappearance in my life. Even though he's not with us anymore, he sure knows how to make an entrance, don't you think?"

"Blimey, do you always talk this much?" Liza asked.

"I'm sorry." Pia smiled apologetically. "It's all this build up."

"I usually witter on myself when I'm nervous." Liza winked at her.

Samuel suggested they all sit and take a few moments to get settled. "Tea?" he asked.

Liza nodded. Pia gave in and nodded too. He buzzed the intercom and requested tea for three.

Chirpy as ever, Mrs Rathbone responded, "Okey dokey Mr Hampton, three teas coming up."

"What a lovely lady she is," Liza said

"I don't know what we'd do without her. Keeps us on our toes and looks after us all wonderfully at the same time."

"Mother hen?" Pia suggested.

"Oh totally. That's it. That's definitely it!" he said, grinning.

Samuel had a good feeling about this meeting. He let them chat away without interfering. This was a big moment for them. He had suggested a neutral, less formal venue, thinking it might have been easier for their first encounter, but they had both been happy to meet in his offices.

He had been wary of proceeding in PJ's absence but they had compromised and agreed he would join them, once introductions were done. The three of them could review the contracts for the Tango school, decide if they could work together and sign the documents all in one session.

Mrs Rathbone announced the tea with a tap on the door. Samuel jumped up to let her through and relieved her of the tray. She lingered in the doorway to throw in her own contribution to the occasion.

"My! Seeing you together, you two do look alike, don't you?"

Looks passed between Pia and Samuel.

"Thank you Mrs Rathbone, I'll take it from here," he said.

Liza remained quiet until the door closed, leaving the three of them together. "What was that?" she asked.

"How do you mean?" Pia asked, scrutinising the pattern on the tea set as closely as if she were an auctioneer evaluating its worth.

"That look between the two of you and what did she mean by lookalike?"

Samuel stepped in with a suggestion. "Would you like me to explain on your behalf? Would that be helpful?"

"Yes please." Pia sat back, relieved he had taken up the baton.

"Explain what? Look, I'm getting kinda annoyed here, you know. What is this all about? I feel like I'm the only person who's in the dark here," Liza snapped.

"Liza, we've reached the point where I can reveal a little more information regarding your inheritance. If you'll bear with me, everything will become clearer very soon. It is my job of course, to make sure you are comfortable with the legalities. More than that though, I want to help this whole transition feel as smooth as possible. Finances and contracts and beneficiaries aside, understandably, all of this has had a huge impact on you. I think it's important we give you time to take it all in."

"I'm all ears Mr Hampton." Liza said

"I've told you before, call me Samuel."

There it was, that flash of a flirty smile. Liza recalled their first meeting when he had been just as lovely. "Alright, go on. Tell me."

"Let me start with this: your benefactor was a gentleman called Pablo Alverez. He is Pia's father. She was unaware of his identity until recently, when, like you, she was notified of her inheritance. He, and we, believe he is your father too. Pia is your older sister."

Liza shook her head. "I don't understand. How can we be sisters?"

"Well, that's the complication. Pia's birth mother, Elizabeth, was only nineteen when she fell pregnant. Her family decided, as she was unmarried, it was best to have Pia adopted when she was born, against her wishes I might add."

Liza looked at Pia, then back at Samuel.

"Hold on a minute you said sister? We have to share the same parents to be sisters. I was born in nineteen sixty-six. My parents married in nineteen sixty-four."

"Yes, that is true. Elizabeth, known as Betty Braybrooke, your mother, married Michael Cummins in nineteen sixty-four, but Betty had fallen for Pablo before even meeting Michael."

"You're saying that my mum had Pia before she even met my dad?"

"Before she met Michael Cummins, yes."

"And Pia has only just found out her birth mum is my mum too? That means we're half-sisters?" When Samuel didn't respond straight away Liza asked again, "That's right, isn't it?"

"Well, that's the part of the story we need to clarify. Pablo was searching for you. He believed he was your father too."

"How do you mean? I really don't get it! How is that possible? And you said clarify. You mean you're not sure? This is ridiculous! I've changed my life for this crazy, albeit wonderful, handout and now that I have said yes, now I've pulled my son out of school and yanked him halfway across the country, away from everything he knows and now." Lisa paused. "Now you're telling me I don't know who my parents are and you're not sure? What the fuck?"

Liza sprang to her feet, just missing her porcelain cup, and its lukewarm contents, balanced on the edge of Samuel's desk, and paced up and down in the narrow space behind the chairs.

"I know, I know. It's crazy isn't it?" Pia tried to offer support, twisting in her chair in an attempt to keep eye contact with Liza.

Liza stopped directly behind her, voice steady and cold, "Crazy doesn't even cover it."

"Please, take a seat Liza," Samuel said softly. "Let me give you as much information as I have. I understand it makes no sense yet. I do believe though with all the facts in front of you, and with time to absorb everything, lots of things will fall into place."

Liza returned to her seat, arms crossed. "Go on, I'm listening!"

Samuel shuffled his notes as a newsreader would before a broadcast. "I have a letter from Pablo. My instructions were to give this to you, if and only if, you agreed to the terms of the trust. Namely, that you were prepared to accept the gift on face value, and commit to working with Pia and PJ, your joint aim being to bring the Tango school to life."

"PJ, Pablo Junior, our half-brother," Pia added.

Liza dug her nails into her palms. Without lifting her head, she spoke, slowly and deliberately. "Right, I've done that. I'm here aren't I? I never questioned who was behind this. I never spoke to my family. Why would I? I have no desire to rekindle those dysfunctional relationships and then it turns out, whoop-di-do, I have another bonkers family I didn't even know about! How many more rabbits do you have up your sleeve Samuel? Go on, let me have it."

Samuel cleared his throat. "The story goes that recently Pablo discovered that his sweetheart Betty, and he, had conceived a second child after she had married. He had left England and cut ties with her before you were born. After much research he tracked you down. He believed you were that child. He believed you were his daughter."

"Fuck! So Mum had a thing with him after she got married? You can't be serious? You're telling me that my fucking father, Michael, is not my father at all? That's not what my birth certificate says. Does he even know?" Liza slumped forward with her elbows on her knees and face in her hands. "This is just too much."

Pia wanted to hug her but kept her distance. She wanted to say something but couldn't find the right words. If anyone knew how this felt, she did. Revelations had also been laid at her door, but she'd had all her life living with the mystery of unknown parentage. She understood this was much bigger for Liza. What a shock, believing your dad was one person and being told it was probably not true.

Pia felt useless. The silence expanded like an activated airbag, filling all the space in the room and pinning them to their seats.

Samuel knew better than to intervene. Something would give when they were ready. The minutes ticked by.

Unexpectedly, Liza's indestructibility turned up like the fire brigade and released them from their silence. She straightened her body, turning her head towards Pia, then Samuel.

"Do you know what? None of this relationship shit matters. I came here to do this, to make a go of it for me, for Angelo. There was always a chance I'd come up against the Braybrookes. I mean, I grew up here and they stayed when I left. They disowned me; I disowned them. All of them: Mum, Dad, June, Emma. I've no real interest in delving into the past." She paused, focused her attention on Pia and continued. "Honestly, none of this is your doing, and I won't bore you with the details. I hope we can make this work and I look forward to trying."

The sisters smiled at each other.

Liza turned once more to Samuel. "Can you please take us through the remaining legalities? I'm in!"

Reaching over to squeeze Liza's hand, Pia said, "I'll do everything in my power to make the venture a success. We have much to discuss and I can't wait to show you the house and introduce you to PJ. I'm so sorry about all that paternity malarkey. I know it's a shock. Please let me help, if there's anything I can do to make it easier."

"Thank you."

Samuel passed Liza an envelope with her name neatly written in blue ink. "For you, the aforementioned communication from Pablo. Please feel free to take it away and read it at your leisure."

"Thank you Samuel. I will."

"Ready to fetch PJ you two?"

The sisters replied in unison, "Yes please."

Dr Kath O'Hannon

Working her way through the week's diary, Kath was pleased to see a number of new clients interspersed with the recurring appointments. Preparation for these often took a while longer than her regulars. She liked to make sure there was plenty of time built in both before and after the initial session; to familiarise herself with the case, allow for the briefing and debriefing.

She had two such sessions scheduled for today, followed by a meeting with her agent at five o'clock to kick around the proposal for her next book, the idea for which had occurred to her following the final session with one of her clients.

The case had been different. Interesting yes but different. The therapy had revealed many pivotal moments. It got her thinking how things could have been if those pivots had led to alternative outcomes.

What if Liza had chosen to stay part of the family, like Annie and never quite broken free of Gloucester and her mother? What if she'd had one less sibling and like Dulcie, had found the confidence to tap into her adventurous side? What if her first toxic relationship had pushed her to become hardened, self-assured and self-reliant, like Elizabeth? If Liza's family had supported her when she'd fallen pregnant at sixteen and her mother had shared her own pivotal heartaches and decisions, what choices would Liza have made then and who would she have become? Would she still be Liza? Or would she have followed the paths of Annie, Dulcie or Elizabeth?

When someone came to her stuck and asking endless what-if questions, identifying the multiple pathways their life could have taken based on those choices, might just help them get unstuck.

Often, she would expect her client's newfound knowledge, through therapy, to help steer their future life choices. The power of self-discovery via hypnosis never ceased to amaze her and its usefulness as a planning tool for life's big decisions would make a great concept for a self-help guide. She could record a couple of self-hypnosis CDs and include those with the book too.

Dr Kath closed Liza's case file; not a dusty manila folder of the pre-digital era, but the password-protected folder on her desktop. She dragged and dropped the icon into a shortcut titled Past Clients A–D. It would stay there until her end-of-year clean-up, in case, in the short term, she needed to resurrect her notes. Thereafter, she would move it to her archive folder.

Such an ordinary life and yet altered to be potentially extraordinary. She wondered if she would ever hear any more about the mysterious benefactor and his part in the pivoting. Ah well, that was for her client, Ms Braybrooke, to discover. Usually she was able to predict whether a client would return for any follow-up sessions. Often, she couldn't be sure whether her clients had truly finished their work and with Liza she couldn't call it.

Before she shut down her laptop to prepare for today's first client, she double checked the report's file-path, just to make sure it had saved correctly:

C:documents/pastclients/a-d/Braybrooke-Dulcie.Elizabeth.Anne

Liza

Liza held on to the car door handle with her left hand, the letter squashed tight against her thumping chest with her right.

"I'm not sure I can," she said, her eyelids shut, rapid shallow breaths misting the windscreen ahead.

"I'll be waiting here. I'm not going anywhere, not until I know you're safe." Pia tried to reassure her; glad Liza couldn't see how white her knuckles were, as she gripped the steering wheel.

"You must be feeling it too though. How can you be so calm? This is the woman who gave up on me. That's bad enough, but she actually gave you up!" Liza opened her eyes, searching Pia's face for any change of heart.

"Look, we talked about this didn't we? I'd love to come with you. To meet her could be a wonderous thing or it could be a disaster. Believe me, I've always had a tiny piece of me reserved for the day I might meet her and how that might go." Head tilted down; Pia pushed her glasses back up the bridge of her nose before looking back at Liza. "It's alright, honestly. Today is not my day. She's not expecting me."

"Hmm, maybe we should be getting back to Angelo? It's

not fair to leave him with PJ for too long. Not yet. It's too soon maybe?"

"But she's expecting you. Both of us together would be too much." Pia said trying to convince Liza, to do the right thing, as any sensible older sister would.

"I wish I had your confidence," Liza said. "I can feel my heartbeat everywhere. What if she won't open the door? What if she looks at me with that disappointed look I remember? What if I puke over her feet?"

"Angelo's fine. You'll be fine. Come on." Pia lent across and opened the passenger door. "Out you get. Don't want to be late."

Liza made her way up the slight incline of the path, still clutching the letter to her body. With each step she felt like she was Alice shrinking from the drink-me potion, so by the time she arrived at the front porch she had reverted to her sixteen-year-old self. She turned back to see Pia nodding her encouragement from the car, the Gloucestershire hills behind her, falling away from the road. Before she pressed the bell, Liza lifted up the letter and read it through one more time.

Betty stood in the open doorway, smaller than Liza remembered, her fingers knotted around the latch.

"Hi Mum."

"Dulcie, darling you're here," her mum replied in her brightest BBC voice, after what seemed a five-minute pause.

"Mum, I told you last week I don't use that name anymore. Not since I left home, remember?"

"Elizabeth then. That was your grandmother's choice, not mine, like most things."

"Actually, it's Liza now. Can I come in?"

"Of course, of course. Come through. I wish you'd have let

me invite the others. June and Emma will be very disappointed to have missed you."

"I doubt that."

"And Dad, of course. . ." She tailed off, her eyes darting towards a closed door across the hallway. "To be completely honest–and let's face it, we probably ought to be–your father is in his study, but he's promised not to interrupt. You did say it was important. You wanted it to be just me. Tea?"

The obligatory cup of tea.

"Thanks, just a quick one though. I'll have to get back soon," Liza said, setting herself up with an excuse for a get-away should she need it.

To be fair, things weren't as awkward as she had expected they might be. Her mum was on her best behaviour. Liza guessed the phone call they'd had the previous week had delivered the initial shock, which the intervening days had now dampened down.

Whilst Betty scurried off to the kitchen to make the tea, Liza scanned the sitting room for memories of her childhood. Almost nothing had changed. Even the air was perfumed with the same potpourri freshener. Except, no longer on trend, the décor and furnishings now looked out of place, stuck in an Eighties time-warp, as if the room had been waiting patiently for her return.

Bright red spots stained her cheekbones. She felt tempted to run away, again, from the guilt, from the past which had crowded back in and the message she had come here to deliver.

"What are you doing still standing there? Sit down you silly thing," Betty said, just about placing the tea on a nested table beside the sofa without a spillage and seating herself in the matching armchair opposite, smoothing down her skirt. "Now, tell me everything. Again, I can't tell you how sorry I am we left things as we did but I'm determined we should make up for lost time. I want to know all about my grandson for starters."

Liza took a deep breath then sat on the edge of the sofa, expelling all the remaining air in her lungs. "I'm sorry too." *It's now or never.* "I have so much to say Mum but first I have to show you this." She handed the letter to Betty, before she could change her mind.

My darling daughter Liza,

If you are reading this letter it means, by now, you will know a little about me. It means you will have decided to take a leap of faith and accept my gift. It means you will have discovered you have a half-brother and a sister with whom I hope your shared decision to choose this path finally brings you happiness and you can all enjoy a new and exciting future.

You have much to learn from each other. PJ can teach you both to dance. He is a fabulous dancer, better perhaps than even me in my time. Help him learn to love England in return. It may be a tough transition for him from Buenos Aires. He reassured me not, but he thrives in the pulse of city life. If he finds things too quiet send him off to London now and again for his urban fix.

My original intention was to buy the house and build the school with PJ. I had planned to contact you and Pia, once it was ready and let you decide whether you wanted to be involved, whether you wanted me in your lives. Sadly, life, or should I say death, got in the way. After my diagnosis, I had to think again. My dream was to still bring us all together, but how? On the one hand, I knew Pia had Helena to support her, to explain, but I had made my solemn promise to your mother to stay away all those years ago, to help her keep you secret. I tried to find a way to honour that promise.

I'm sorry if the mystery of the inheritance caused you upset. Tracking you down was harder than I'd hoped it would be, especially since you'd moved away and changed your name. In the end I thought it best to propose the venture and allow you to decide on its own merit, rather than be encumbered by relationships, past and present. It is my dying wish that you will all grow to love each other and the Tango as much as I love you.

It is my biggest regret that we will never meet and that I can never sit with you, hold your hands and explain why I stayed away. If I was with you now, you would see it in my eyes, you would feel it in your heart, you would know the truth of it. I absolutely chose to leave, to say goodbye and not look back. I chose that path. Blame no-one else for that. But never, ever, believe it was what I wanted.

Betty is the love of my life. My failing heart aches now but this means nothing compared to the pain I felt when I walked away from her that last time. For her, to protect her from her family, the scandal and the judgement, the hurt and the tears, I had to let her go for good, back to the family life she had started to build. When you love someone so completely, it is the only gift you can give.

I must apologise for leaving you once more, especially with the burden of this knowledge. It is entirely for you to share or not share, as much or as little as you wish.

Your ever-loving Papa
Pablo x

epilogue

Betty

January 1966

She ought not to be there, in the cobbled lane behind the club. The grime, the sooty film, coated every vertical surface of every building, making it impossible to tell where one ended and its neighbour began.

Her mother might have disapproved; if she had lived long enough to provide that moral compass. Instead, here she stood, a young woman, feeling the full weight of her grandmother's disapproval, even in the knowledge she had made the journey to London without telling a soul. Who could she have told anyway? Her only confidante, her sister Helena, two years out of her life, would have cautioned her not to make the same mistake, again.

Part of her, the obedient part, wished she had never boarded the train at Gloucester; the other, the rebellious part, relished the thought of breaking the rules. Who was she kidding? Once she had known he would be there performing, she had to go. Married or no; baby June or no. Nothing else mattered. It was as if he had special powers of mind control, or had deployed some device heralded as the next innovation on that new television show her father was always talking about.

Never mind 'Tomorrow's World,' it was tonight's world that dominated her thoughts.

Had he spotted her at the back, mesmerised, following his sinuous fluidity? Breathless, she had watched him cradle each of his partners in the smalls of their backs, fancying she would take their place and it would be her body he would pivot, his shoulder on which her head would rest.

Of course, she had seen him dance the Tango many times before, each occasion as thrilling as the last but tonight. Tonight had blown her mind.

She probably cut a peculiar figure in her prim tweed suit, pillbox hat and matching gloves, still waiting outside the stage door. She had no care. She was here for him and here she would stay. No strange looks brought about by her incongruity would move her along; not from the dancers as they said their goodnights on the threshold. Nor from the policeman doing his rounds.

"You alright there?" he asked, clearly of the opinion she should head home.

"I'm fine thank you," she said, her reply altogether more steadfast than her wobbly legs. "I'm waiting for someone."

"Are you now? A beau is it? Make sure he treats you right young lady. It's not safe loitering round here in these back streets, not at the best of times, let alone at nearly midnight."

"Thank you officer. He'll be out soon."

She hoped he would be out soon. Whilst it was exceptionally mild for a winter's evening, she shivered at the possibility he might not emerge alone. The longer she waited, the more foolish she felt. Heart thrumming in her throat, she steadied herself against the wall once the policeman had passed.

Oblivious to the black smudges on her, now soiled, white gloves, eyes fixed on the door, she practiced her planned greeting over and over, polishing her words like lines in a play. When it came to it though, when the door swung open and he stopped there, alone, right in front of her, all the sophisticated phrases vanished. Rendered speechless by his living, breathing proximity, she stayed rooted to the spot, as if in a frame, frozen on a screen, waiting for the projectionist to wind on the reel and move the action forward.

This moment. This pivotal moment, when he whispered her name, when he opened his arms wide and she ran into his embrace, when she knew she would never truly love anyone else, this was the moment when her world shifted its axis.

She allowed him to remove her gloves and kiss each finger in turn. Taking her by the hand, skin on skin, he led her into a night of temptation, which was both the beginning of Dulcie Elizabeth Anne and the end of Betty and Pablo.

book club questions

For more questions please visit www.nikkivallance.com

Pivotal explores the multiple paths a life may take at the crossroads of each significant decision. From who you meet to where you live, from your career choice to your relationships, the decisions you make impact the person you become.

1. Can you identify the significant pivotal moments in the lives of Dulcie, Elizabeth, Annie and Liza? At what points do the four paths converge?

2. Are these turning points governed by destiny or self-will?

3. Is it nature or nurture which determines the way the characters react to events and make their choices?

4. Discuss the similarities and differences of the four main characters and their personalities.

5. How did you feel when the mystery of the connection between Dulcie, Elizabeth, Annie and Liza was revealed in the final twist? What, if any are your unanswered questions?

6. Betty was a young mother in the Sixties. How different were the choices available to women like her compared to her daughters?

7. Dulcie, Elizabeth, Annie and Liza seek support from Dr Kath to aid their big decision. How useful was the hypnotherapy in that aim?

8. How have the pivotal decisions you've made in your own life been shaped by your personality?

9. Where do you believe your own personality comes from?

10. The main characters are women in their forties facing a life changing decision. How many books have you read with protagonists at this stage of their lives and do you think this demographic is under-represented in fiction?

about the author

Nikki is a writer and coach who works with others to unlock their writing talents. She runs coaching programs and one to one sessions to help aspiring writers achieve their goals.

She began writing her debut book Pivotal nine years ago, whilst still working in her recruitment career, following a flash of inspiration in a session with her own coach. She has given talks and presentations on her writing process and career.

Nikki is married with a blended family of five children across two hemispheres. Although a beginner, she's a big fan of Argentine Tango, which she hopes to dance in Buenos Aires one day.

www.nikkivallance.com
www.facebook.com/NikkiVallanceAuthor
www.twitter.com/Nikki_Vallance
www.instagram.com/nikki_vallance